DEATH AT THE EDGE OF THE DIAMOND

PAUL H. RAYMER

Salty Air Publishing
www.PaulHRaymer.com

Publisher's Note: This is a work of fiction. Names, characters, places, and incidents are a product of the author's imagination. Locales and public names are sometimes used for atmospheric purposes. Any resemblance to actual people, living or dead, or to businesses, companies, events, institutions, or locales is completely coincidental.

Death at the Edge of the Diamond/ Paul H. Raymer. -- 1st ed.

ISBN 978-0-996781-5-1 (Print edition)

ISBN 978-0-996781-6-8 (Ebook edition)

Dedicated to the People of Williams Harbor/Rexon's Cove, Labrador, Canada

Warning

This book is a work of fiction but Carbon Monoxide (CO) poisoning is real. According to the CDC, every year, at least 430 people die in the U.S. from accidental CO poisoning. Approximately 50,000 people in the U.S. visit the emergency department each year due to accidental CO poisoning.

CO is particularly dangerous because it is a colorless, odorless, neutrally buoyant deadly gas. Unlike smoke, you can't see it or smell it. Most CO detectors are alarms and not monitors. They are manufactured to alarm only when the level of CO reaches a deadly level and remains there for an extended period of time. If your CO detector alarms, leave the building. Never silence the alarm by removing the batteries. Replace your CO alarm every 3 to 4 years whether it is battery operated or hard wired.

Sometimes we have troubling dreams, meetings with ourselves in dark hours, and then we have to face the fugitive life we are perpetuating. Something within us always knows and always registers its opinion. Naturally, we avoid this subpoena from the soul as long as we can, until it knocks so forcibly that we have to answer the door. The moment we say, "I am responsible, I am accountable, I have to deal with this," is the day we grow up, at least until the next time, the next regression, the next evasion.

— LIVING AN EXAMINED LIFE: WISDOM FOR THE SECOND HALF OF THE JOURNEY, *BY JAMES HOLLIS, PHD*

I
CAPE - JUNE 8, 1979

Jon Megquire's mother was the first dead person he associated with Cape Cod. It wouldn't be the last. On this particular, sunny June day in 1979 his mother's death was just one of the colors in the tapestry of his thoughts as he drove his MG Midget, Maybelline, to the Cape to play baseball.

In fact, the Cape was meant to be a postcard of pleasure - a happy, beautiful, joyful summer place, a place to make life-lasting, fond memories not a place to contemplate death and dying. But memories are not always predictable.

Two years before this particular day, his parents told him about their friends' wedding plans at the historic resort on the south side of the Cape; Jon had been away at school and hadn't paid much attention. His parents' friends had arranged a ceremony on the beach and invited everyone to share their precious moments. Jon obliquely blamed the couple for his mother's death. Should it have occurred to them that even the most beautiful of settings can be deadly? Should they have recognized that the membrane between happiness and pain is shockingly thin?

As the miles of highway unrolled in front of Maybelline, Jon thought about his parents, Margy and Andy, driving up from their home outside New York City and checking into a motel tucked among a collection of neon touristy American strips of establishments promoting family fun: French fries, clam rolls, miniature golf, and cheap rooms, color television, and heated pools.

Jon could hear them laughing at the tackiness and his mother saying with a soft smile, "It's only one night." She would have excused the tackiness if the sheets were clean and the room didn't stink of air fresheners. They would have dressed in their stiff but beautiful wedding attire. Margy would have put on makeup and fixed her hair. Andy would have told her she looked beautiful. They might have laughed about this return to their youth - no kids and a night in a motel on Cape Cod. Then they drove to the resort.

It pleased Jon to think they would have had a happy night. They were together, laughing and joking with their friends and the family members of the couple. They were drinking and might have been singing snippets of songs they grew up with. The weather had been perfect. His father had told him later the ceremony on the beach was interrupted only once by a happy Irish Setter carrying a Frisbee in its dripping jaw. The dog shook the water off its sodden fur in front of the minister and then dashed back to its master who waved an apologetic hand and disappeared quickly over a dune. "There's nothing friendlier than a wet dog!" his father told him. At the reception, one brief flare-up occurred between two brothers who apparently never got along, couldn't hold their alcohol, and raised their voices above the refrain of the "Chicken Dance" and had to be asked to leave the room by their embarrassed mother.

Finally, in the early hours of the morning, Andy and Margy had gotten in their car and driven the short distance to their motel where they had climbed to their second-floor room and dropped onto the creaky bed. Each time Jon imagined the scene, he wanted them to turn around, go back down the stairs, and never go in that room.

Apparently, the maid found them the next morning. He imagined the woman screaming, freaking out, dropping her cleaning tools, then calling the front desk in a panic. When the EMTs got to them, Andy Megquire was still alive, but barely. Margy had died in her sleep. At least death was probably painless so the authorities told him. But how would they know? They'd never experienced dying. The coroner's office blamed the incident on a faulty pool heater from the indoor pool just below his parents' room. Turned out other people had complained about that room. The owner, under legal pressure, claimed he had been told the problem had been addressed and fixed.

The local press was all over the story. It had even made the national news.

Jon found out when his sister, Cornelia, called him at his dorm in North Carolina. "Jon," she said.

"What's up, Corny?" he replied. The unfamiliar tone in her voice made him wary.

"There's no good way to tell you this." She paused, and he heard her swallow. He held his breath. "So I'm just going to say it: Mom died." The final word was almost a whisper. "Dad's going to be okay, but Mom is dead."

"What? No. What do you mean, 'Mom is dead'? They're on the Cape for the weekend."

"Yes. They did go to the Cape for that wedding. Mom died in the motel. During the night. She didn't wake up. Mom's dead." Without being able to see her face, Jon struggled to assimilate the message. More than the words, more than the sound of her voice was required. He faced the shock of unannounced death.

Jon remembered pulling the phone away from his ear and looking at it as though he were dreaming. The news was inconceivable. Life just didn't move that way, that suddenly, without warning. Even dropping a glass on a tile floor offers a split second for a gasp before impact.

But Cornelia insisted she wasn't making it up. And then the questions came flooding out. How? Why? When? His sister was an engineer, and she treated her grief with analytical precision, talking about building pressures and stack effects and the molecular weight of carbon monoxide. Those were not the answers Jon needed. The only fact that registered was that his mother was gone.

In the days that followed he moved through the gathering of family and the wake and the funeral and the burial like an automaton, smiling when he had to, accepting and returning hugs as required. He was grateful his father, pale and drained, had chosen to have a closed casket. Jon hadn't wanted to see his mother's body. He wanted to see her as he remembered her. Even now, two years later, he could see her curly hair that he'd inherited and her sparkling, blue eyes. Even now he could hear her laugh.

When it happened, he had been in the trouble-free groove of his junior year in college far away in North Carolina. Devoid of responsibility. And life was good. Just twenty-two, he was aware of burgers, sports cars, baseball, and girls. The order of importance among those elements was situational. He found scary movies cool, girls mysterious, and future responsibility annoying but to be accepted as inevitable.

Until his mom died, life had been as simple as walking. The abrupt news eliminated the comfort of inevitability and made each step forward a question where a decision had to be made. He was forced to face growing up.

As he was reaching the end of his senior year, he'd been offered the opportunity to play baseball in the Cape Cod Baseball League, and he accepted it as a challenge to the past. So, he packed up Maybellene and hit the road. Just a year before this moment, when Jon had turned twenty-one, his father encouraged him to use inherited money to buy the convertible MG. His father balanced fatherly fears about safety on the road with the hole the loss of his mother had made in his son's life.

When he first met Maybellene, Jon didn't know if there was a word to describe the transition from admiring an object to the soul-fulfilling understanding of owning that object. Maybe it's love fulfilled. Maybe it's lust, but magic happens in reaching down for the door handle, opening the door, and slipping into the driver's seat.

The MG was a combination of delicacy, grace, and muscle instantly responding to his will. The car was just a pile of parts, craftily assembled, adding up to something that gave him an irrational charge. There was an indefinable, emotional transition from utilitarian device to passionate possession.

His father had agreed that a first car no matter what it looks like is the key to the castle, the opening of the doors to freedom, the outer manifestation of adulthood and maturity. A first car is a step up onto the stage of recognition . . . especially when the car has a zing of its own. It's akin to being the friend of a star.

The Midget was a head-turner because she was different. She was dubbed "cute" at times by people who did not respect her classic lines, her regal heritage. Her pert, round headlights peered eagerly forward. The leading lips of her black bumper pouted for satisfaction, licking up the road ahead. Her dual, chrome side mirrors sprouted on both doors, offering a view of the past. Black bands at the bottom of the doors proudly, but quietly, displayed the Midget brand. The twin, sloped, two-color taillights procaciously blended into the small tail fins on either side of the curving top of the tiny trunk, barely large enough to hold the spare tire.

Jon liked the subtle curve of her hood, to run his hands over the surface of her leather seats, to stroke the polished wood of her steering wheel, and wrap his hand around the smooth black top of the shift lever.

She was boxy. He admitted that. She wasn't particularly powerful. And reliability was not the first word that was used to describe British cars. But that gave her a dash of spice, a spark of adventure. Unreliability was flinging rationality into the face of the future.

So, life had gone on, but 'normal' had changed. Jon graduated from college without his mother and without purposeful plans for the future. He had climbed the logical ladder of his education - elementary school, high school, college - and arrived at the top. Bob Dylan insisted that twenty years of school gets you on the day shift. Jon didn't have time to stand there at the top of the ladder of youth and look around; there were social pressures to move on, to use the investment in learning, to start contributing to society. Spending the summer on Cape Cod playing baseball was a simple choice.

Finally, the road had unraveled to the final traffic circle, and he was confronted by the towers of the Bourne bridge and the Cape Cod Canal. Listening to "The Logical Song" on Maybellene's radio, Jon felt an unexpected queasiness: "My mother went this way and never came back."

He crossed the bridge onto the Cape and reveled in the opening miles of the mid-Cape Highway. The sky was clear and the sunlight was warm. On a day like this, driving with the top up would have been sinful. His mother had told him that.

The highway wound around over the undulations of the Cape. The landscape glowed green with the warmth of early summer. The distant scent of the unseen sea filled the air. Jon wondered what the town of Tilley would be like. He pictured the town in Jaws with people running around screaming. He wondered about the Wentzells - the people he would be living with. He wondered about the Tilley person the town was named for. Some dead Pilgrim, no doubt. He pictured the baseball fields and wondered if they would have lights for night games. He thought about great players he heard had come out of this summer league, like Thurmon Munson and Bobby Valentine, and how much money good players could earn in the majors. He thought about his mother and sleazy motels.

The highway seemed to go on forever. He hadn't realized the Cape was so long. He had imagined that he would have arrived when he crossed the bridge, but mile after mile rolled by until he reached the Tilley exit. And then he was expecting a quaint little, picturesque village but it was just a normal neighborhood - houses and lawns and weathered shingled siding. And finally, there was downtown Tilley. Jon thought he was there to play baseball and enjoy a fun-filled Cape Cod summer, but the future doesn't always dance to the tune you expect.

2

JOLO

Garrett Scoles was already in Tilley, and he didn't give a shit about baseball or Jon Megquire or wouldn't have if he'd been aware of his existence. Honestly, for such an analytical mind as his, he hadn't planned his summer, and he didn't have murder on his agenda. He wasn't born to be a murderer any more than he was born to be rich. He might even have been cute as a baby. Being cute and being a killer are not mutually exclusive. Life forced him into it. And he hadn't killed anyone yet. And when he did kill it wasn't to be a political act or hatred of humanity or seething revenge or some other waste of time. It would be practical and purposeful. Just business. In fact, not taking advantage of the opportunity, the motive, and the means that presented themselves to Garrett would have been an impractical waste. It would have been like wasting a stock split or a bankruptcy. And besides, Faith Salsberg was a pain to live with. Not to put too fine a point on it: she was a bitch.

And the scenario would have worked to plan for Garrett if Jon Megquire had not chosen that summer of 1979 to fart around in the Cape Cod Baseball League in the uncertain pursuit of a career as a major league player.

Tilley just happened to be the convergence point for these

events, a place where Garrett didn't even want to be. The town was tucked into a curving corner on the south side of the Cape. The heart of the town was the Green and the surrounding buildings. Sticking out at one end of town was a point arched around the outer edge of the harbor. The land on the point had been considered useless in colonial days because it was so exposed to the weather—only good for what the fishermen call *stages*, warehouses, places to clean fish and store nets and have a smoke and get away from family chores.

The land remained nameless until some wealthy people came along and realized the point could be an exclusive spot cosseted by beaches on both sides - so isolated it could be a gated community that didn't need a gate. They built what they considered to be summer *cottages* - cottages in name only - and they named the place Jolo Point. They liked to give the 'J' a Spanish pronunciation, making it sound like Holo Point. If you didn't know how to pronounce the name, you didn't deserve to be there.

No community association was needed to keep the eight houses on Jolo in harmony, with their sweeping lawns and dry-laid stone lace walls and brilliantly white shell driveways curving up to front doors flanked by columned porticos. Their occupants just knew. But about every ten years some new family would sweep in and tear down one of the existing houses and build something grander. To keep up, the other homeowners had to remodel and add on and over and up.

The Salsberg family owned the *cottage* inside the elbow of the point, giving them a landing and a mooring. Christopher Salsberg, founder of Salsberg Homes, had bought the place when his company reached its stride in 1959. He hung onto the house through some lean years, retreating to it in the summers with his daughter, Bryce, from his first marriage. In 1965 he married Faith Reese, and when Christopher Salsberg finally died in 1976, he left her the house, the Salsberg name, and his company.

Real estate agents might have gushed that it was an "elegant and architecturally significant oceanfront estate in a setting of unsurpassed beauty." The house's seventy-five hundred square feet had eight bedrooms and twelve bathrooms, and stretched out to embrace the lawn with no pretense of subtlety. Garrett got there by marrying Bryce which he considered the culmination of an excellent plan. He reveled in the value of every tangible detail of the house and the community on Jolo Point.

The floor plan wrapped around a central courtyard dominated by the pool and the separate pool house affectionately called the "Lanai" by the family, which also served as a guesthouse, encompassing its own living room, kitchen, two bedrooms, and two bathrooms.

Although the substantial master bedroom in the big house had a view across the lawns to Vineyard Sound, Faith Salsberg had decided it was too confining. So now, in the spring of 1979, she was expanding the space by having a wall pushed out and adding a hot tub under skylights where she proposed to sit and soak and stare up at the stars, which was about as likely to happen as a duck on stage at the Metropolitan Opera singing *Aida*.

The project was supposed to be finished before Memorial Day, but it wasn't. Much of the work on the house (including the construction of the Lanai) had been done by Ace Wentzell, a reliable local builder, and he had been contracted for this renovation as well. It might have been completed on time if Faith and the architects hadn't constantly tweaked and adjusted the design throughout the renovations. Wentzell labored over details only to be told to rip them out the next day because they were too narrow or the wrong material or the grain of the wood didn't match.

The project had dragged on through the spring and was now colliding with arrival of FAMILY for summer vacations. Bryce and Garrett as well as Faith's biological son from her first marriage, Brian Reese, and his wife, Audrey, and their two children, Brian Jr. and Peter, known as Pee Wee, had all arrived and settled in. To Garrett it seemed he couldn't turn a corner without running into an adult or screaming child only vaguely related to him.

Garrett knew that his wife had not been happy to see her father remarry and was definitely not happy about renovations to *her* house. She was as possessive of the house as she was of her father and didn't like change. She even objected to other people being in *her* house. She tolerated Faith for her father's sake. But she didn't have to like Faith hacking the house apart.

It was clear to Garrett from the start of their marriage that Bryce was not pleased with many things. She had never forgiven her mother for her stupid name. What was the point of giving a girl what sounded like a boy's name? Her displeasure showed on the sharp features of her face. Her mordant blonde hair was sharp. Her eyebrows were sharp. Her carefully manicured nails were sharp. She even had a pointed chin. Garrett considered Bryce's displeasure with her life a small price to pay for his connection to the family wealth.

Now, she stood beside Garrett in the disarray of her step-mother's master bedroom and shook her head. The outer wall had been removed and the structure was supported by posts. The beautiful view of the Sound was hidden by blue tarps that ballooned in the breeze. In the master bathroom Ace Wentzell's crew created a shattering racket as they attacked the tile.

"Jesus!" Bryce muttered. "Why did she have to start this now? Why did she have to start this at all? The noise and the mess! It just drags on and on!"

"Thoughtless. She's thoughtless. She doesn't think of anyone but herself," Garrett replied. "And what the hell are we going to do trapped in this house with Brian and his bratty kids and whiny wife?"

Bryce blew out an exasperated sigh.

"We didn't have to come, you know," Garrett said. If he *had* been cute as a baby, the cuteness was long gone. He did not look as he thought he looked. He pictured himself as a handsome devil, but he was, in fact, a ratty man: slightly below average in height, a bit chunky, and despite the fact he was not yet thirty, he sported a dyed blond crew cut to keep himself looking young, avoiding a gray that didn't exist.

"It's expected," Bryce replied. "It's what we do every summer. It's what this house is supposed to be for."

"I know," Garrett said. He turned away from his wife and the construction turmoil and went out to the pool to read the papers and annoy his brother-in-law.

Garrett had little patience for anything, but he was particularly averse to doing things he thought were a waste of time. He tolerated being on the Cape because a lot of wealthy, well-connected people spent time on the Cape in the summer . . . relaxing. As the Chief Operating Officer of Salsberg Homes, he needed to stay in touch with development opportunities, not just on the Cape but in other parts of the country like Florida and Arizona and closer to home, Pennsylvania. Ideas were thrown out on the golf course or tennis court, gently pursued, and assembled before returning to the offices and the lawyers. The *New York Times* and *Wall Street Journal* were delivered daily. Garrett pored over every word.

Not that he liked every word. The country was going to hell in a bucket with Jimmy Carter leading the charge. The Europeans were messing around with this common market thing, but at least the British had Margaret Thatcher. Oil prices were climbing through the roof. The big Ixtoc I oil spill in the Gulf of Mexico was making the oil markets nervous, and the Three Mile Island thing was still bringing out the crazies. Even the president said the country would be running out of oil in less than a decade so nuclear energy seemed a logical alternative, something that Americans could control.

Although Garrett had differences of opinion and little respect for his brother-in-law, he and Brian agreed on one thing: Democrats in the White House were not good for the housing industry. Garrett had a laser-like vision of an ideal, Garrettcentric world, a world devoid of anyone or anything that stood in his way. That vision was not biased. It universally applied to anyone of any race or religion or political persuasion that could not be imminently useful to Garrett, and it irked him to think that he was compelled to allow anyone to impact his future. It also irked him to admit that his brother-in-law had similar thoughts.

Sitting beside Brian at the pool and holding the *Wall Street Journal* in front of him, Garrett mumbled, "What the hell is happening to oil?"

"It's the Arabs," Brian replied. "I've been watching. In '73 they had us and they want control again. They have been paying off Carter, controlling him. I'm sure. He dances to their tune as long as he can get himself free of the Jews. I can say that here, can't I? Between us? . . . Particularly the New York Jews. Oh, yes. He does what they want him to do. We get them in Florida too, you know. Jews. They think they own everything. You can't even find a decent place to park. They don't have class. Just new money."

Garrett set the paper on his lap and studied Brian. Brian was a result of Faith Salsberg's first marriage and only because she was his mother, had she put him in charge of her Florida development company, Buckingham Palms Properties, which had been merged with Salsberg Homes. Garrett was sure Christopher Salsberg had married Faith Reese to bolster his *own* company and give him Florida development control. Garrett regarded that as a smart business move. Unfortunately, Brian came along as part of the package.

"I know what you mean," Garrett replied, burying himself in the paper again. "They do own everything . . . the Jews."

"Oh, yes," Brian continued. "Have you been to Florida recently? No, you haven't. You should visit. It's getting really bad. Of course that's good for the housing market, isn't it . . .? It's just not the way it used to be at all. It's damn near impossible to find new development land.

"Pee Wee! Be nice to your brother!"

Brian Jr. and Pee Wee were attempting to drown each other in the pool, which suited Garrett just fine. Brian and Audrey were of the liberal parenting point of view: give your children freedom to make their own choices. Garrett had been brought up to believe in the biblical mantra of "spare the rod and spoil the child." His parents hadn't seen anything useful in the word 'liberal'.

"When does Faith get here?" Garrett asked.

"Next Wednesday," Brian said. Garrett watched Brian's eyes narrow. "But you knew that, didn't you? You should give her some respect, you know? She's my mother – your mother-in-law – the stepmother of your wife." He glared at Garrett. "And . . . and she's our boss. You work for her! So you need to show her some respect . . . on some level anyway."

Garrett grunted as he thought, Respect? Sure. I respect her for being a greedy old bitch. I respect her for . . . No, it's not respect, is it? Respect requires caring. And I sure as hell don't care what goes on inside that twisted brain. Out loud he said, "Yeah sure, Brian, whatever you say. She's getting old and slowing down. I'm sure you haven't noticed. You're down there in your glitzy air-conditioned Florida office. I have to put up with her every fucking day."

Brian's mouth started blubbering. He reminded Garrett of a blowfish with a perpetually surprised look. Garrett watched him stumble through the silence.

"Maybe you two should think about getting out of the pool now!" Brian suggested to his sons.

Garrett snorted in exasperation and stared through his dark glasses at the shimmering water of the pool. He pulled a cigarette out of his pack of Pall Malls, tapped it on his thumbnail, flicked his Zippo lighter, and lit up. He inhaled deeply and then blew a stream of smoke out into the breeze. He liked Pall Malls because he had been told they were the cigarettes convicts preferred.

"The renovations to her room won't be complete," he said.

"Obviously not," Brian retorted.

"So where is she going to sleep?"

"That would be up to her, wouldn't it? I would suspect in a bed!"

Garrett thought, That was typically stupid. "Ha. Ha. Very good, Brian. Don't give up your day job. If you actually have a day job."

"Boys! You need sunscreen!" Brian shouted. They continued to ignore him.

"No empty room in the big house," Garrett said, mostly to himself. "I suppose she'll sleep in the stable with the donkey and the sheep!"

"I suppose," Brian replied, ignoring Garrett's biblical slur.

Garrett ground his cigarette out in a "Dubonnet" labelled ashtray, pried himself out of his lounge chair, and crushed the paper, dropping it in Brian's lap. "Here," he said, "you might learn something if you read the news once in a while."

Brian cleared his throat and stopped Garrett from leaving, shocking him by laying a hand on his arm. "Listen, there's something I've been meaning to talk with you about."

Garrett pulled his arm away. And then he started to smile. Something potentially useful was about to be . . . oh-so reluctantly revealed. "Yeah?"

"Um. . . we've had a bit of kerfuffle at Buckingham Palms, and I don't want to talk to Mother about it yet. I'm sure I can get it sorted out, but you know how she is . . . how she can get. I'm not even sure it *is* a kerfuffle."

"What the hell is a *kerfuffle*? A *financial* kerfuffle? What's this all about, Brian? I see the books."

"I know you do . . . normally, but this hasn't made the books yet. I mean not that there are 'other' books or anything. Nothing like that."

Watching his porcine brother-in-law squirm in his own fat,

Garrett crossed his arms across his chest, waiting, stretching out the silence.

"Well, it's not all that bad, really. I mean it may not be bad at all. Really. In the long run. It shouldn't be. It might turn out to be quite good. I mean, these things happen all the time in the real estate business, right? Wrong place? Wrong time? Opposite of right place or right location, location, location. Right? Guess wrong about where things are going to go? Right? Or maybe guess right. Guess right after all. It's just awkward, you know?"

"Jesus! Get on with it, Brian."

"It's the boatyard."

"Faith's boatyard? Her father's boatyard?" Garrett knew The Boatyard was sacred. Faith's father, Emeryk Smoljanovic, had been a real estate developer when Florida was nothing but a swamp. He lost his shirt when the land boom collapsed in 1926 and tried his hand at smuggling, but he was able to hang onto some property and recover when the navy moved in to set up training facilities. The boatyard was one of the last pieces left, a piece of Faith's father. Besides that, it was prime real estate.

"Uh, yeah, the boatyard. I sort of made . . . you know . . . a deal, an arrangement." He sheepishly grinned.

"You what?"

"This opportunity came up; you know how that sort of thing just happens. And you've got to take advantage of those things, right? I mean strike while the iron is hot. I thought she'd be proud if I seized the day. Well, I mean it's not finished yet. It's not cast in stone, but I sort of agreed. You know. Said I *would* sell. I mean they're talking about a new baseball stadium! A new team."

Garrett took a moment to process this, mentally fondling the permutations and combinations and complexities and opportunities. Good side. Bad side. Upside. Downside. Which way to go? What was the best way to leave Brian on the cutting board? Oh, my!

"You can't do that! Not without consulting Faith. Did you sell it or not?"

"Well, I sort of. . . gave them an option. But think about it! It could be a new major league franchise! And the offer was really good and the time seemed right and these guys seem to really know what they are doing. You know, you have to jump on these things. It's just a boatyard. You're always saying we have to get the sentimentality out of these things. Get unattached from . . . *things*."

"Oh, Brian, you've really screwed the pooch this time! You're going to have to tell her."

Brian looked like he was on the verge of tears. "I thought it made sense. But . . . how can you tell about these things?"

"Oh my god! You made a bad deal for Emeryk's boatyard! You are in trouble, my man. You are definitely in trouble," Garrett said with his best sympathetic smile.

"No! No, I didn't think it was a bad deal. It didn't sound like a bad deal. It sounded like a fantastic opportunity. And you know how I feel about baseball. And besides I didn't know there were boats in the sheds."

If Garrett had been chewing gum, that revelation would have made him swallow it. Brian had made a blind deal? Really? Garrett's brain nearly self-destructed. "What? You sold the whole thing including everything inside the buildings?"

"It was just sitting there. Nobody goes in there. I mean, the deal hasn't closed yet. I mean, things happened so quickly, you know. It seemed like the thing to do to seize the opportunity. But it's nothing to worry about. It's not, you know, cast in stone yet."

Giving away waterfront, developable property in Fort Lauderdale was one thing, but considering Faith's unstable, emotional attachment to the place put it over the top. She was going to explode. So much to think about. So many guns on the poker table. Timing would be important. "Even if you don't tell her, Faith's going to find out."

"I know," Brian said. "I'm just not ready to tell her yet. Maybe . . . we can think of a way out. Maybe I won't have to tell her. Maybe you can help me think of . . . something?" He looked up at Garrett hopefully, like a puppy looking for a treat.

Brian had done some stupid things, but this took the cake. Garrett virtually drooled at the smorgasbord of opportunities. "Maybe," he replied.

He spun away and returned to the cool shade of the house and poured himself another cup of coffee. He went to the living room to stand in front of the big glass sliding doors that looked out to Vineyard Sound and watched a sailboat work its way across the wind.

Salsberg Homes was developing into a power player. Construction was slowing, the perfect time to consolidate resources, thin out dead wood, and prepare for when demand returned. It was time to look in new directions, spread out from the base.

Faith was a survivor, growing up in the Depression and watching her father struggle with the boom and bust of Florida land development. Garrett knew the survival mentality was no good now. A down market was not the time to hide, to keep your head down and wait. Now was the time to grab with gusto, to seize what sniveling wimps like Brian dropped as they fell by the side of the road.

The boat fought its way across the channel, but Garrett didn't see it or the beauty of the blue sky, blue water, and green grass. He saw rolling hills of houses, paved streets, and rapid, assembly line construction involving minimum costs and maximum profit. He saw what he considered Faith Salsberg's plodding hammer and nails process standing in the way of the speed of nail guns and spray paint, and decided she would have to be removed. She was getting old and he couldn't allow her to ruin the company by choosing the gasping blowfish to replace her. And would Brian even be in the ascendency picture after this latest move? Perhaps this revelation would kill her. Garrett really didn't want to wait and leave it to chance.

He assessed the remaining coffee in his cup. Faith would have to be dealt with. Brian was clearly incompetent. He professed to know everything about everything, blustering his way through every situation. Garrett smiled to himself. No. The road ahead was clear. Except for Faith. She was like the deer in the headlights that simply couldn't be avoided. Splat! Whoops! Sorry about that. If Garrett couldn't persuade Faith to see what was in front of her nose, he would have to kill her. It was sensible. It was good for the business.

3
TILLEY

Jon Megquire was more responsible than typified a youth's shrugged 'Whatever!' because he had purpose thrust upon him due to his athletic talents. His *long term* vision ahead included a couple of months of sports, girls, and goofs with the guys. And then he could consider seeking an answer to the age-old question, "So what are you going to do now?"

He was solid – six foot one and one hundred and ninety-eight pounds. His hazel eyes twinkled when he smiled and blazed when he was angry. He had funny hair. People said he had funny hair - out of control much of the time – curly and reddish – like his mother's. He had gained the moniker JC from Jonathan Creesy Megquire. He didn't think of himself as holy.

Jon pulled Maybellene in beside the station wagon in the Wentzell's driveway, shut off the music, and turned off the car. As he approached the front porch, the door swung open and a small, round woman stepped out, wiping her hands on her apron and pushing a stray strand of hair off her forehead.

"Can I help you?" she called out to him.

"I'm Jonathan . . . Jon . . . Megquire!" he shouted. "They told me . . .."

"Jon!" she said, striding down the front steps with her hands outstretched. "We've been expecting you! Welcome. Welcome. I'm Babs Wentzell."

It was the kind of greeting an old friend who hadn't seen you in years would give – welcoming, natural, effusive, full. Her greeting couldn't help but make him smile.

"Did you have any trouble finding the place? How was your drive? Beautiful day for a little car like yours. Sporty little thing isn't it? But it is a long way, isn't it? How far is it? How long did it take you? Can I help you with anything? Are you hungry?" The questions flowed easily, not waiting for answers.

Jon mumbled about five hours and, no, he didn't need anything to eat. He had stopped along the way.

"Well, bring in your bags and let's get you situated," Babs replied.

He hefted his duffle out of the back of the car, slammed down the trunk, and followed her up the steps and into the house. It was cool and dim and smelled of home. She swayed ahead of him up the stairs and showed him into a cheerful bedroom on the second floor facing the street.

"Bathroom's down the hall. You probably want to wash your hands after that long ride. I'll be downstairs in the kitchen when you're ready. Ace'll be back soon. He knows you're coming. We're glad to have you with us."

Jon mumbled something about "Glad to be here," although he was a bit muddled and overwhelmed. He wanted to sit on the bed for a minute and acclimatize himself to his surroundings.

He walked over to the window and looked down on the street and his car. Away from home again; but not like college. New place. New people. New beginning. Accompanied by an odd feeling of maturity. Living in someone else's house. Sharing their world. Sharing their food. Sharing their time. They might be horrible. The whole experience might be a disaster. Immature fears in a maturing world, and he pushed them aside. Maybellene was there. She was his, his link to his life. He had to keep that in mind. Simple. He could always just grab his bag and go. He wasn't going to be locked up in this room, chained to the bed, thrown scraps of food through the door! It seemed more like milk and homemade cookies! Quaint, cozy, New Englandy stuff. Boring, maybe, but not ghoulies and ghosties and long-legged beasties and things that go bump in the night!

Back in the kitchen, Babs urged him to take a seat at the table and thrust a glass of water at him with a smile. The kitchen was a cheery yellow with frilly curtains surrounding windows looking out on the back yard. There was an old gas stove and vintage refrigerator, a sink, counters, cabinets. Everything was clean and well maintained. Hanging over the stove was a large, black exhaust hood almost like something you would see in a commercial kitchen.

"How long have you lived here?" he asked.

"Oh, we've been in this house a long time, now. Seems like a long time anyway. Let's see. We moved here in 1962 when Ace brought the business up here. You're the college student. How many years is that?"

Jon smiled. "About seventeen."

"So, tell me about you. How long have you wanted to play baseball?"

Jon wasn't sure how to answer that question. "Most of my life, I guess," he replied finally. "You know it's something you hear on the radio and see on TV. Baseball stars are like . . . stars . . . like other impressive people. I don't know if I'll ever get there, but it's a fun game."

She wiped her hands on her apron and looked at him apprais-ingly. "Do you want to get there?"

Jon swallowed a gulp of water and looked away, and after a moment he replied, "Ye ah. Sure! Why not?"

"Here's Ace," Babs said, although Jon hadn't heard a thing. He looked out the window and saw a black pickup pulling into the driveway. The door slammed and a large man appeared at the back door. Jon jumped up from the table.

"Honey, Jon has arrived!"

"I can see that," Ace replied. "We need to find a better place for that car. Pleased to meet you." He thrust out a large hand.

Jon took it and felt the pressure and strength and roughness of a contractor's grip. "Pleased to meet you as well, Mr. Wentzell. Thanks for everything."

Asaph Wentzell was taller than Jon and much heavier with his weight settling down toward his middle. His suspenders clung to his pants, stretching out over his belly. He had the stub of a pencil perched behind his right ear, almost hidden in gray hair. There were a thousand stories in his face and around his eyes.

"So, you're here for the summer," he stated.

"Yes, sir," Jon replied.

"For the baseball. What position?"

"First base."

Ace grunted. "Are you any good?"

"I guess," Jon said.

"Must be or you wouldn't be here," Ace answered himself.

"Don't grill the boy," Babs interjected. "He's barely had time to shake the dust off."

"Need anything? Want something to eat? I'm sure Babs has offered you something. Cookies? A sandwich? Where do you think this belly came from?" He slapped his stomach. "I used to be skinny like you."

Jon didn't think of himself as skinny, but he smiled. "No. Thank you. She did. I'm good."

"Well, if you're all settled in, we should meet the coach before supper," Ace said. "Let's go."

They piled into Ace's pickup. "Been to the Cape before?" Ace asked. "Vacation, summer home, family visit?"

"No, sir," Jon replied, as he watched the town slide past.

"Old town. Lots of history. The British shot cannon balls at it during the war of 1812. You probably didn't know that. They don't get into those little details in school. There isn't enough time. Have to cover the major points. The big wars, depressions, slavery. The big points. Kids don't spend enough time learning all the details. Especially nowadays. Time goes by too fast. So, what do you know about carpentry?"

"Not much, really. I built a treehouse, once. More like a board on a branch."

Ace laughed. "Board on a branch. I like that. The real question then is, do you want to know more about carpentry? Do you want to learn? Are you interested?"

"Sure."

"Houses have lots of stories to tell, you know," Ace said. "People think they own their house, but they don't. If the house has any substance, any real character, it's been there and will be there a long time. Understand? People built it, lived in it, moved out and other people moved in. They live in it for a while, move out and other people move in. It's like life. We're just passing through."

Ace pulled the truck into a gravel parking lot and up to the tall wire backstop behind home plate. Jon looked out at the field and watched players tossing the balls around.

"'Salsberg Field," Ace said. "Your home away from home. The Longliners, the Tilley Longliners, your team, they're one of the newest teams in the league and this is one of the newest fields. Team's only been around since 1974. You'll get to meet some of that family. We're working on their house."

"Nice," Jon replied.

"No lights. Christopher Salsberg put a lot of money in this before he died but they only went as far as they needed to to get the name on the door, if you know what I mean. Wife isn't fond of baseball. To be honest, I don't think she's too fond of Tilley either. Just a summer stop."

A chunky man with a crew cut and Tilley baseball cap rolled up to Ace's open window. "How ya doin', Ace?" he asked.

"Hey, Graham. Guess it's starting again."

"Yup. Another season. Never know. Maybe this will be the one."

"Graham, this is Jon Megquire. Your first baseman. Jon, this is Graham Russell, the coach."

Jon reached over Ace to shake the man's hand. "Pleased to meet you, sir," Jon said.

"Heard good things about you," the coach said. "Want to look around? Not much to see. Not exactly Fenway or Yankee Stadium. Some of the other players are here, but you're earlier than most. Been to the Cape before?"

"No, sir," Jon replied after climbing out of the truck.

"You'll get used to it." Graham showed him the field house and his locker and introduced him to a couple of the other players. He handed him a Xeroxed list of the league and team rules and the practice schedule.

"Any questions," the coach asked.

"Don't think so. Not yet. Just got here, actually. I guess it's just baseball."

Graham stopped walking and turned to look at him. "What?"

Jon turned toward him.

"It's just baseball? Are you saying it's *just* baseball? It's a lot more than just baseball, kid. It's Baseball with a capital 'B'. This is life. This is your chance for a ticket to the *bigs*. Don't shrug it off as just baseball. Don't blow it before you start it."

Jon was taken aback. "I didn't mean . . ."

"This is . . . this is a rare opportunity. I hope you appreciate that. You're not going to win unless you take it seriously. Seriously! And we don't win as a team unless everyone feels that way. I hope you understand that. It's so fucking easy to miss chances. Understand?"

Jon looked at him. Wow! he thought. This is going to be interesting. This guy has issues. He'd had passionate coaches before, but this guy was way out there. "Yes, sir," he said out loud.

~

When they got back to the Wentzell's kitchen it was filled with the smells of supper. Babs bustled about setting the table, pulling a peach cobbler from the oven, wiping her hands on her apron, and pushing a stray hair back from her forehead.

After Ace finished eating, he pushed away from the table and fussed with his pipe until the smoke began to curl around his head. Babs poured herself a cup of coffee and sat down at the table across from Jon.

"So, tell us about yourself," she said.

Jon looked up from the remnants of his cobbler and wiped his mouth with his napkin. "Not much to tell," he replied with a smile.

"The league told us that you're from New York State and go to school in North Carolina. Graduated? What did you study?"

Jon replied, "Liberal arts. You know, general stuff. I took some religion courses. History, art, writing. General stuff."

"That's nice," Babs said. She sipped her coffee and looked at her husband.

Jon recognized his response was barely adequate. "I don't know what I want to do yet. You know? Haven't made up my mind, haven't found that . . . thing."

"What thing is that?" Ace asked.

Jon had known before he said it that his answer had been far from satisfactory. It was certainly not the first time he had been asked about his future intentions. For a moment he mentally toyed with the hole that was the future. He felt he needed to offer these people something deeper and wiser than the usual prepackaged prognostication he handed adults. But it was only a twinge and it passed quickly and Jon only pulled out, "I haven't found what I want to do with my life yet." He looked at Ace and changed the subject. "How did you decide to build stuff?"

"Just happened," Ace replied. "Got out of the army after the war and I needed a job. Got hired to work in Levittown. On Long Island."

"Oh," Jon said. The conversation lapsed. Jon connected Long

Island to Carvel ice cream and new strip malls and an overcrowded Jones Beach. War? What war? How old was Ace anyway? Too old for Vietnam. Korea? World War II? Jon wondered if it would be polite to pry into the Wentzells' past.

Finally Babs asked, "And what about your family? Brothers? Sisters?"

"I have a sister. Cornelia. She's an engineer. Graduated from Rensselaer last year."

"Cornelia's a nice name. Engineer, well! Is she married?"

"No. I don't think she really cares about getting married. She's always been driven by her academics. Kind of a brain." Jon smiled.

"What kind of engineer?" Ace asked, puffing smoke from his pipe.

"Not sure. She knows a lot about a lot. We don't talk much."

Ace got up and walked across the kitchen to the sink, reached into a cabinet, pulled out a glass, and filled it with water. Then he turned and leaned against the sink and watched Jon.

"So why baseball? Is that the 'thing'?" Ace contemplated the water. "I like baseball. This league is competitive. There are scouts here for the major leagues. I adopted the Red Sox when the Dodgers snuck off to Los Angeles in '57."

"Year before I was born."

"So obviously you don't remember, but that was traumatic. Those rivalries don't go away easily. Giants left too. Same time. Both to California. Wasn't much left to root for except the Yankees!"

"I know what you mean," Jon said politely. Although conceptually he knew that one of the major differences between college and professional baseball was team loyalty, he couldn't completely understand how Babe Ruth could play for the Yankees after playing for the Red Sox.

"Do you?" Ace replied. "A guy I knew killed himself when the Dodgers moved. Jumped off a building. Could not root for a team in California. Couldn't start liking the Yankees!" He paused. "There are certain things you think are constants in life. You think they're going to stay there. You think they'll always be there. Baseball is one of those constants. Maybe your team will win. Maybe they'll lose. But there's always next year. With all the other crappy things that hit you in life, at least there's always hope next season will be better."

Jon didn't know how to respond. He looked down at his plate and scraped his fork through the remnants of cobbler but there was no answer there. He wondered if cobbler could reveal the future in the little fragments of the orange fruit like tea leaves at the bottom of the cup. It wasn't working. He looked up at Ace.

Jon felt Ace tighten his focus on his eyes, like he was looking into his brain. "So, what's baseball to you? Just something fun to pass the time or is it *it*? Passion?"

Jon laughed nervously. "Don't know," he mumbled.

"The thing is, kid, you must have some talent, talent a million others would give their left nut for. You're taking up one of their spots. If you don't really care, you're disrespecting them. All of them." Ace paused. "So, what do you expect to find here?" Ace punctuated his thoughts by emptying the glass into the sink.

Babs pushed herself up from the table. "Enough, Ace. The boy just got here. Not everyone is as crazy about baseball as you are. He'll find his way. Give him time." She took the glass from Ace's hand and rinsed it in the sink.

Ace pulled a dishtowel out and dried the glass and put it back in the cabinet. He grunted acquiescence. "Six," he said. "We're outahere at six a.m. Okay?"

"I'll be ready," Jon replied.

Up in his room, Jon lay on the creaky twin bed and studied the ceiling. The old plaster was smooth. The light fixture had a pull string to turn on the one bulb covered by a yellowing lampshade. Jon listened to the night outside the open windows, the occasional bark of a dog and whisper of the leaves, and thought about what Ace had been talking about. Fans were passionate about their sports teams. Jon thought baseball was fun. It was an interesting game. But it was a game. His was not a passionate family. Passion was not . . . proper. Like sex and bodily functions, you didn't talk about that sort of thing at the dinner table. Passion? Hell, you didn't express or show emotion of any kind. Killing yourself because your team moved to another city? That was passion.

No, that was insanity.

Jon wondered what he would die for. His family, of course. And his car. No, that was stupid. He wouldn't jump out of a building because something happened to Maybelline.

He flashed back to when he was little and some bullies on the beach had given him the choice between kissing a girl he liked or eating sand. He intuitively knew that kissing the girl had uncertain consequences: the bullies would laugh, the girl might cry or slap him, and the witnessing adults? Their reaction was completely unpredictable. He had chosen the sand. True, sand wasn't exactly death, but it had seemed close at the time.

He couldn't remember the girl's name. Did names increase the passion? He'd named his car. Did the Brooklyn Dodgers become something different when they became the Los Angeles Dodgers? Maybe if you called baseball something other than a game it would be different, more formal, less of a child's activity.

Had he been raised, conditioned to avoid passion? His parents had lived their lives, had their friends, did their jobs, drank their cocktails, and . . . kept a stiff upper lip. They kept their emotions properly to themselves.

Was Cornelia passionate about engineering? Was Ace passionate about houses? Was it possible to learn to be passionate about baseball? Could you learn to be passionate about anything? He shrugged, got off the bed, and went off to brush his teeth.

The five AM dawn sunlight blasted through Jon's window as the alarm beside the bed began its infernal buzzing. He reached out and began fumbling for a rapid means to silence it without destroying it. A daily dawn awakening had not been on his list of giggles and goofs for summering on Cape Cod. Ace, however, had not delivered the morning schedule as a suggestion so Jon extracted himself from the bed, dragged his fingers through his hair, rubbed his eyes, and stood. He pulled on clothes he pulled out of his duffle, splashed water on his face in the bathroom, and considered shaving as he peered at his face in the mirror, weighing the effort against the available time. Later.

Farmers and contractors greeted the dawn every day so Jon was not surprised that the Wentzells were moving calmly through their morning harmony. Babs bustled about the kitchen making breakfast, frying eggs, buttering toast, pouring coffee, clearing the table. The room smelt comfortable to Jon. Ace sat back in this chair, holding up the *New York Times*. After his comments about the Yankees the night before, Jon wondered why New York? He thought Ace had given up on the city when the Dodgers left. The morning talk show from a Boston radio station quietly babbled the news and the sports in the background.

"Sit," Babs smiled at Jon. "Did you sleep well? Move your elbows, Ace. Give the boy room. Coffee?" She held out a steaming mug and her finger danced around the handle and the rim until Jon got a secure grip.

Ace grunted, shifted his bulk in his chair, and rattled the extended pages of the paper.

"Was the bed comfortable?" Babs asked as Jon devoured the food. "It's an old bed. We've been meaning to replace it. Did you have enough hot water? Ace keeps promising to get someone to look at the system. But you know . . .."

"I'll get to it," Ace harrumphed. "Ready to go?" he asked Jon as he rough folded the paper and dropped it on the table. "Meet you in the truck."

Ace was silent as they drove through the early-June morning and Jon didn't want to interrupt the older man's thoughts. Ace flipped on the truck's wipers to clear the windshield of dew. The streets looked damp and Jon wondered if it had rained. He stumbled through morning thoughts of etiquette. Was there something polite and companionable to say? He turned his head and watched the light from the low sun blaze off the windows of the houses. The town Green was deserted. Sensible people were still in bed. Jon chastised himself for not getting up early more often.

They drove through the middle of Tilley and past the stone pylons that marked Jolo Point's entrance. Private Road – No Outlet.

Beyond the breakers the waters of Nantucket Sound sparkled. Small waves lapped against the stony beach. Gulls swayed overhead, hunting for breakfast.

Jon turned away from the water and looked up across the sweeping lawns to the columned houses with their commanding views. "Like something from the movies," he said.

"Yup," Ace replied.

"Must get kind of windy out here in the winter."

"They don't care. They're not here in the winter. Just use these things for a few weeks a year. They think of them as summer *cottages*."

Jon wondered at what point a house became a mansion. The grandeur of the houses spread out to encompass the world, proudly thrusting out their front porches to greet the morning sun. Not a thing out of place – no cars, no lawn furniture, no swing sets, no laundry. Just manicured emerald grass and shrubs, as if nature would not dare to put a leaf awry.

"Seems like everything's perfect."

"Yup," Ace replied. "But they always want change. They get bored. They think they can make it better. It gives them something to do. Law of impermanence. Nothing is permanent. Everything changes as the Buddhists say. But they don't know that."

"But these houses look like they've never been changed and never will change."

Ace snorted. "That's the point." He looked at Jon. "And it gives *me* something to do. A remodeler is an Agent of Change."

Jon envisioned a team of masked remodelers with capes billowing out behind, peering into the future.

Ace pulled his truck into a driveway, and it crunched over the white shells. "This is *Casa Grande*. They like to name these things. I don't know why. I don't understand these people. British tradition, maybe, but they like to use Spanish names. Maybe because Spanish sounds more romantic or mysterious. Or maybe it was so they could find the house when there weren't street names. Back in England, I mean. Of course, that wouldn't explain the Spanish. We got street names here."

"Maybe it's like naming a boat," Jon suggested.

"Nah. Boats are different. Boats always have names. They have character. It's different. You can talk to a boat. They are one thing. Understand? Singular." He looked at Jon. "Houses have character too, but houses are many things. Lots of different things. Rooms and light and color and textures and angles and shadows. Hard to explain. You can talk to a house too, but it's more specific, like a particular room. And when you don't understand all that and you just stick an arbitrary, hoity-toity name on it . . . it's just silly."

"Oh," Jon replied. And he wondered again why he had named his car? Where had that come from? Was it the same thing as naming a house? No. It was more like naming a boat. Ace was right: his mind could grasp the entirety of the car. It had a lot of parts but one, singular character. A house, he thought, is a house. Period.

Ace was still talking. "Rebuilt the pool house here last year."

He pulled the truck around to the back. "Don't really like us coming in the front way. They would have liked a service drive, but there isn't room out here on Jolo."

He stopped the truck but made no move to get out. Jon put

his hand on the door handle but didn't move it. He looked out at the house as Ace talked.

"The Salsberg family," Ace said. "Actually, been here longer than most. The old man bought the place back in 1959, about twenty years ago. Brought the family up every summer. Just the one daughter, but they added on to the house anyway. The core of the house was built in 1918. Even before my time!" He snorted.

Jon thought of history books. Black and white pictures. Guns and mud and trenches with guys in funny helmets.

"It has good bones," Ace continued. "But of course the owners had to add electricity and improve the plumbing and add central heating over the years. Then they had to wire them up for telephones even though some of these people didn't want phones out here. Big fight over that, I'm told. Wanted to get away from the office.

"The worst part came when they put in air conditioning. These houses weren't built for central air. Walls weren't built for the moisture issues." He looked at Jon.

Jon didn't know what Ace was talking about. "How do you know so much about these places? You haven't lived here that long, really."

"Nope," Ace replied. "Only a handful of years. Moved up in '62. I'm still considered a *washashore* because I wasn't born with sand between my toes.

"I know about this house because I've touched her bones, opened up walls, seen the old wood and the new wood. Craftsmen worked in these places. Back then people cared about the details, how things fit together. It wasn't because they had more time. Christ, they built the clipper ship *Flying Cloud* in just over three months! Three months! Fastest ship of her day. They used hand tools, of course—on the ship and the houses. No, I think they . . . cared. Attitude. You'll see."

As he followed Ace out of the truck, Jon realized that he had never heard anyone talk about a house like it was more than an object. It was that passion thing again. He looked at the porches and porticos and gewgaws. It was a big house, but it was a house.

They reached the blue tarp that covered the wall where the house had been cut open, where the symmetry of the façade had been disturbed. Jon turned away and looked across the lawns to the water and couldn't help but appreciate the beauty. Nature had been carefully tamed.

There were beautiful houses back in New York along the river, mansions where the Rockefellers and the Roosevelts lived. And they had spectacular views, but something about the ocean satisfied the soul, felt eternal. A house like this had a permanent view of the natural wonder of the ocean in all her moods. You could sit here and stare at the water as long as you liked. You could stare at it in the wind, rain, snow, or sun. But only if you were one of the privileged few who could own a house like this. Or knew someone who owned a house like this. Or you could momentarily enjoy the view when you worked on a house like this – as an employee . . . the help.

Jon pushed aside the tarp and followed Ace inside.

Ace pulled the pencil from behind his ear and pointed as he explained how the owner wanted a larger bedroom so Ace had opened up the outside wall to push out into the yard. That meant adding to the foundation. Ace explained that they would be raising the roof with some scissor trusses and gusseting the walls like ribs of a ship, adding some big glass surrounded by the jack studs and well supported on setting blocks, headed by the cripple studs, changing the ceiling to a tray, and reconnecting to the existing HVAC ducting and electrical connections. "Understand?" he asked.

Jon nodded. *The toe bone's connected to the foot bone, the foot bone's connected to the ankle bone.* What's the ankle bone connected to? he thought to himself. Now that's going to be stuck in my head.

Back outside Ace handed him a shovel. "We need to cut in the new footing along these string lines. Need a trench three feet wide and three feet deep. Clear the sod off first. Do what you can to save it."

Jon wondered as he contemplated the grass before him, is the ankle bone connected to the shin bone? Is there a shin bone?

His father took care of the lawn at home – mowing it in summer, feeding it in the fall. Poisoning the dandelions, cutting the edges around walks. When he was around, Jon raked the leaves and hauled the grass clippings to the mulch pile. But this lawn was maintained by professionals who manicured the bejesus out of it. Seemed a shame to mess it up, but Jon put his foot on the shovel and dug down, cutting out the sod like peeling a toupee off a banker. He worked steadily, feeling the shovel sliding against the skin on his hands and the heat of the sun warm his face and neck.

A man lugging a toolbox came lumbering around the side of the house. He stopped and nodded at Jon. He had startlingly blue eyes.

"Hi," Jon said.

"You working with Ace?"

"Uh, yes."

"You play ball?" The man put down the toolbox and pulled a cigarette from his shirt pocket.

"Yes," Jon replied. "With the Longliners."

"Uh huh. Ace does that. Every year. What position?"

"First base."

"Got your eye on the pros?" The man dragged down the smoke.

"Yeah. I guess."

"Hmph. Big dreams. Maybe someday you can own a house like this."

Ace stepped into the yard. "Hey, Frank," he said. "This is Jon. Jon Megquire. Jon, this is Frank Shalala. He does heating and cooling."

Jon reached out and shook the man's rough hand.

"Yah. We were just talking," Shalala replied, picking up his toolbox and grinding out the cigarette in the dirt. Jon watched Ace and Shalala push back the tarp and slip into the house. and then returned to cutting back the sod, humming the seven dwarfs' song to himself.

"HEY! Is that necessary?"

Jon looked up to see a stocky man with a blond crew cut. He was wearing a green polo shirt with a little alligator over his left breast and carrying a mug of coffee. "What the hell?" the man demanded.

Although it seemed obvious to Jon, he looked down at the dirt and said, "I'm digging the foundation?"

"Don't be stupid! Of course, you're digging. The question is who told you to dig up my lawn?"

Although Jon was just twenty-two, he had lived long enough to know that some people in life are just consummate assholes. It oozes out of every pore of their bodies. They don't have to work at it. It just comes naturally. This person was one of those. It blossomed his cheeks, bugged out his eyes, wrinkled his forehead, and caused the thinning blond hair on the top of his head to sprout like crab grass.

"Mr. Wentzell's inside." Jon pointed to the house.

"This . . . this . . . " the man waved his hand. "This construction is a blasted inconvenience! You're new," he stated. "I don't forget faces and I haven't seen yours. I'm Scoles. You can call me Mr. Scoles. I'm the owner."

"Pleased to meet you, Mr. Scoles," Jon replied. He wasn't sure if he should pull on his forelock or bow or click his heels together so he kept his hands on the shovel.

Scoles glared up at Jon over the top of his mug. "Shit! This is not making me happy. Contractors always say things will take 'two weeks'. Two months is more likely. We don't have two months, do we? Don't answer that. Don't try to answer that because you're incapable of such difficult questions." Scoles' eyes challenged Jon to disagree. He continued, "Stop hanging around leaning on the shovel and get this done. Understand? This work is a disruption. I don't like disruptions. Mrs. Salsberg is arriving next week. This is her room! She doesn't like disruptions either! Not at all!"

"Ah," was Jon's neutral response because there was no point in feeding the man's assholian nature.

Scoles spun on his heel and with a final "Harrumph!" stomped back around the corner of the house.

"Have a nice day," Jon muttered under his breath.

A BIT BEFORE NOON JON HEARD ACE SAY, "LUNCH". THEY climbed into Ace's truck, and he drove them into town to a strip mall along Route 28 where they pulled up in front of *Clegg's Lunch* at the end of a building that included a Cumberland Farms convenience store and a smoke shop and was right next door to a mini golf course.

The waitress greeted Ace with a smile and pointed to an empty table by the window. "New helper?" she asked.

"Summer helper. Some are not," Ace replied, returning her smile. "You know how they are."

"Oh yeah. Burst onto the beach like a tourist then they're off. Coffee?"

"Worst coffee on the Cape," Ace said to Jon under his breath.

"I heard that," the waitress retorted. "And proud of it."

"And the grease! They tell me it's not good for my heart, but I can't resist Amanda's smile. She leads me on! One of these days Babs is going to come down here and tell her off!"

"Jury's still out whether or not you have a heart," Amanda added. "Know what you want, hon?" she asked Jon. "Need a menu? Burger? Fries? Only the best. Or pick your own poison. I'll be back." She tossed a menu on the table and turned back to the kitchen.

Jon picked up the food stained menu and then looked around the room, taking in Clegg's functional décor. It was fifties, modern diner design like a dozen other slip-in-the-pocket mall restaurants he had been in – half a dozen pink Formica topped tables, a short counter with a handful of stools, walls a pale lemon-yellow graced by a mixture of black-and-white photographs of Tilley Longliner teams and prints of watercolors of lighthouses and Adirondack chairs on the beach. The windows looked out on the parking lot in front and a big shade tree on the side which made the room dark enough to require suspended fluorescent lights during the day. The air was saturated with the aromas of grease and fried onions, coffee and bacon, and the wooden floor squeaked as people walked across it.

"Yup," Ace said, "this is the little piece of heaven where the Longliners hang out. Attracts the groupies. People want to get close to the soon-to-be-famous athletes. They can say, 'I knew him!' when they see players in the majors. But you're used to the fame, right?"

Jon looked at Ace as he stirred his coffee, to see if he was kidding. He hadn't yet learned to read that passive New England face. "Some," he replied. "I guess. Groupies hang around the fields sometimes."

"How big a crowd do you get at your games back at school?"

"Big games, maybe a couple hundred."

"Pfffft! You're going to see ten times that this summer! A lot of people go to these games. This is summer paradise. Young girls whose parents dragged them here for vacation, with nothing to do? Hanging out with you guys is a dream for them. Closest thing they can get to a star. Better be careful not to rob the cradle. Sort of like being in the army. Not the local girls, they're okay. But you never know what the tourist girls bring from home. Know what I mean?" He leaned across the table and looked Jon in the eye: "Chlamydia!" he murmured and then he sat back and nodded his head. "Got a girlfriend back home?"

For a moment Jon was at a loss for words. "Girlfriend? Not really. Don't know. Friends, you know. Nothing serious really."

"Yeah, yeah," Ace commented. "I know. Too soon to commit to anyone. And you're still looking for that 'thing'! Youth is wasted on the young.

"When I was in the army there was a kid who had the biggest ears I've ever seen. Red hair. Freckles and a goofy smile. We called him Wanky. Can't remember why now, but Wanky drove the girls crazy. They couldn't figure him out. Girls like guys they can't figure out. He wasn't smooth or cool or hip. Or whatever word you're using now. He was goofy. We had fought our way to Paris and one day he tripped over a curb in the city and just fell into the arms of this gorgeous French girl. Wanky turned seven shades of red and practically wet his pants. I mean the guy had been through the beaches at Normandy, slogged through the mud with bullets flying, been shot at a million times, and here he was blushing because he tripped and fell into the arms of a beautiful girl." Ace laughed quietly to himself at the memory. "Jesus, we were young. . .. We were also very old. War does that."

Jon looked at Ace. "What happened to him after that?"

Ace looked out the window at the tree. "Not sure. Kind of lost track. War does that too. I heard he didn't make it. Maybe he did. Maybe he married the girl. War kind of scrambles things up. Changes all the rules."

Jon's father never talked about the military. Had he thought about enlisting? Too young for WW II but did he have friends that went to Korea? What if he had gone in and something had happened to him?

One thing about baseball, Jon thought, was that the rules were clear. It was life that got scrambled.

JON'S SENSE OF THE PURPOSE OF HIS SUMMER ON CAPE COD grew as other players gathered as their seasons ended. Each day little groups formed and grudgingly accepted the new arrivals. Leadership shifted. Egos rubbed up against other egos. Players evaluated other players for their individual skills, their ability to make the team successful, and the competition they posed each other to entering the major leagues. There was a serious, adult quality that was different from his college experience.

Jon fought against the group anxiety that rattled in his gut no matter how often he told himself that it was stupid and he shouldn't care. But his sense of duty kept sucking him in. "I should care," he told himself. "I should care. That's why I'm here, right? But it's not cool to care. These other guys care."

Coach Russell was the leader, the person the players looked to to familiarize them with the fundamental local rules -- curfew, practice schedules, where the bathrooms were, town rules and regulations, drinking. All the basic team related, day to day blah, blah, blah stuff. What his father might refer to as boilerplate when he talked about work. How were you supposed to remember all this stuff? Of course, there were those who needed to know what the rules were so they could break them.

The atmosphere felt more intense than in college. In college, players developed relationships over years on the field, in the classrooms, and in town bars along with allegiance to their school. Bonds like that are tough to break. Team and school loyalty were fostered by the coaches, the parents, the boosters, the cheerleaders, and the marching bands.

Now they had to play together as some other kind of team. Switching off the yay, rah, rah, school forever state of mind or transferring it . . . to what? Money? That was a skill he was going to have to learn if he moved into the professional ranks where he might easily be playing for the team he had grown up demonizing. It wasn't easy for a player from Clemson to watch the back of one from South Carolina State or a Rice outfielder to ignore the sideway slurs of a second baseman from Texas A&M.

Jon wondered if playing the game professionally would still be fun. Money is a serious purpose.

~

NO MATTER HOW MUCH JON WOULD HAVE LIKED TO THINK otherwise, not all of life was under his control. Saturday evening when the phone rang, he just sensed that something was wrong. Phone calls were unusual at the Wentzells.

Babs answered the phone in the kitchen with a guarded, "Hello?" that softened and led into a, "Yes. He's here. I'll get him." She turned to look at Jon as though she were gauging his telepathic understanding of the conversation. And then she said, "I think it's one of your neighbors," and held the phone out for him.

Jon tried to envision his parents' neighbors – what they looked like and why they would be calling him.

"Who?" he asked even though he knew Babs wouldn't have that answer. And then there was a sudden drop in his stomach. He gasped for air. Not again. "Hello?" he mumbled into the phone.

"Sorry to bother you, Jon," the voice said. "It's Neil Watson. Your father's neighbor? It's your father. But he'll be okay, Jon. It was just a stupid accident. He didn't want me to call you."

"What? Who? Why? What happened?"

"Your father had to go to the hospital." The man's voice explained that his father had been working in the attic, moving some old boxes around looking for god-only-knew-what, when he slipped coming down the steep steps and bumped his head. "I guess he managed to get to the phone. Not sure. Of course, he did 'cause he called me. I called the ambulance, you know. Couldn't go with him of course."

Jon pulled the phone away from his ear and looked at it as though it wasn't real. "Are you kidding me?" he asked.

"'Fraid not, Jon. No, but it's nothing to worry about. That's why Andy didn't want me to call you. He knew it would worry you, and he didn't want you to worry."

"You called the ambulance, Mr. Watson?"

"I did, yes."

"Why did he need an ambulance?"

The voice on the phone paused. "Well, you know. He fell down the stairs. I didn't know what else to do. I'm not a doctor, you know. I'm an accountant," he said with a dry laugh.

"I need to come home," Jon said. "I guess I need to come home. Do I need to come home?"

"Um. Well. Of course, that's up to you. I know you just got up there for the baseball. Your father's proud of you, you know. But as far as his injuries go . . .."

"Injuries!" Jon said. "I thought you said he just bumped his head? Were there other injuries?"

"No. No. No. Just his head. Just a little bump on his head. It's nothing. At least that's what the EMTs said. I think that's what they said. Maybe I shouldn't have even called the ambulance. Maybe I shouldn't have. Maybe I overreacted. I can do that, you know. But I didn't know what else to do. But they seemed to just want to check him out at the hospital. Can't be too careful these days, can they? All the legal issues, you know. Can't be too careful. No. He'll probably be home soon and you can call him . . . talk to him yourself. I'm sure he'll tell you to stay with your game."

Jon wanted to get off the phone so he could call his sister. "Thank you, Mr. Watson. Thanks for taking care of him."

"Oh, it was nothing," Watson replied. "That's what neighbors are for, don't you know? We take care of each other. Glad to do it. You take care of yourself, now. If you do come home, not that I'm saying you should, but be sure you stop by and say hello."

"I'll do that," Jon replied. "Thanks again." He hung up the phone and realized that he didn't have the phone number for Cornelia's new apartment. He heard his mother's voice warning him that he should always be prepared and have a way of getting in touch . . . just in case. His head was swimming and he sat back down at the kitchen table, Ace asked, "Okay?"

Jon nodded. "Don't know. I guess. Dad slipped on the attic stairs and bumped his head. That was our neighbor. He said it's nothing to worry about."

Ace grunted. "Hmmf. Heads are funny things. They're like a piece of tempered glass: you can bang 'em with a hammer . . . bang 'em on the surface and nothing happens. But just touch the edge the wrong way, they shatter into a million pieces."

Jon looked at him but wasn't able to connect his father's head to a glass door.

"Ace! That's not helping!" Babs said.

"I bumped my head once . . . at least once . . . well, more than once," Ace continued. "Didn't I, Babs? More like smacked with a two by four! Load wasn't tied down on the truck. Whole stack of two-bys came tumbling down on top of me. Thought I was done for. Really did. Took me to the hospital for sure. Construction can get you real friendly with the emergency room personnel. Good people."

"Ace!"

"Weren't nothing, really. See. I still have my brain! Lived to tell another tale."

Jon smiled weakly. "I guess."

"Don't worry about your dad. I'm sure he's tough as nails. I'm sure he'll be fine."

"I need to talk to my sister."

"Sure, you do. Go ahead. Use the phone," Ace said.

"I don't know her number. New apartment. Recently moved. She moved in a few weeks ago."

"Call information. They should have her number if she has a phone. They can even connect her. They do that these days. As long as you can remember the town."

Jon looked at Ace as though he was proposing something magical. He should have thought of that. Problem solving could be just that simple. Of *course* he knew about calling Information to get a phone number. He'd done it before to get pizza. His mind must have been severely scrambled.

"Right. Thanks," he said and went back to the phone, called Information, waited while they looked it up in the new listings, found her number, and let them connect the call to Cornelia.

Worst case scenario, he thought, worst case: his father was in a coma! A vegetable. Couldn't take care of himself. Drooled down his shirt. Oh my god! Why didn't she answer? Was she at the hospital? Why was he always the last to know these things? Is this going to ring forever? What should I do if she doesn't answer?

When he finally heard his sister's quiet, familiar voice after a quick gasp he asked, "What happened? Why didn't you call me? Should I drive home?"

"Don't swallow your gum, Jon. It's nothing. Dad's okay. I would have called you if it was anything serious. Mr. Watson overreacted. He does that. Remember the thing with the cat on the roof? He probably would have called the National Guard."

"Why didn't Dad call me? Or you? Why did he have to go to the hospital? In an ambulance?"

"Don't really know. It's good they checked him out."

"You sure I shouldn't go home?"

"No. I mean no you don't need to drive home. I think dad overreacts too, these days," Cornelia said. "You could probably just call him . . . but maybe not now. Call him in the morning."

After he hung up Jon was partially reassured as he evaluated the 'right' thing to do. Go home? Call? Ignore the whole thing? Corny should know. Mom would have known. He went back to the Wentzells' kitchen.

"Corny, my sister, said I didn't need to go home. That I should call him in the morning. That our neighbor overreacted."

Babs nodded. Ace said, "Sounds right."

Jon stood still for a moment.

Babs asked, "What would your father want you to do?"

Jon looked at her and envisioned his father's face and he knew that Corny was right. "I'll call in the morning."

4

FAITH - JUNE 13, 1979

On Wednesday afternoon the thirteenth of June, Faith Salsberg swept into her house on Jolo Point, her driver depositing her suitcases in the front hall behind her. Dark brown eyes, dyed blond hair, and at five foot four, she was the same height as Queen Elizabeth. At just sixty, the family felt she was eternal. Amongst her well maintained wrinkles and her expensive makeup, her South Florida tan survived despite the fact that for the past eleven years she had lived in the posh pocket of Caerwys in Pennsylvania. The 'locals' pronounced it with a soft '*care*' up front, a rolled burr of an '*r*' in the middle, and ending with a '*wiz*'. Although she never could quite handle the rolling of the 'r', she put up with such wealthy idiosyncrasies because they were good for business. Social standing was important for banking and political connections.

Her family politely greeted her at the door to Casa Grande. Her son's wife, Audrey, gave her a tentative hug, doing her best to avoid Faith's carefully crafted hair and makeup. Audrey had a Soup Kids look to her amplified by a rounded face, jolly cheeks, and hair coifed to curve around the lower part of her jaw.

Brian was more nervous than a whore in church. He stood back, waved, and said, "Hi, mom."

Her grandchildren noticed and then ignored her and ran back out of the house to the pool.

"Did you have a good trip?" Brian asked.

"I'm fine," Faith replied. "Get these things to my room."

Brian looked at Audrey. "You know your room is under construction? We thought you might use the pool house . . . the Lanai."

"That's awkward," Faith replied, pulling off her patterned, silk scarf with a matador flick. She looked at Brian as though he could somehow solve this problem, filling the room with a moment of shuffling silence.

He felt compelled to apologize and excuse himself. "I'm sorry. But it was your plan . . . I mean your project, your summer project."

She let him squirm a moment longer. "Yes," she said finally. "I know." After another awkward pause, "Well, it has to be the Lanai then." A trace of a smile graced the corners of her mouth. "I'll have to slum it for a time."

Garrett came into the room folding the paper under his arm. "Ah," he said. "You've arrived."

"I suppose I have," Faith replied.

"I suppose that Brian has told you he put you in the Lanai?"

Brian looked at Garrett. "That wasn't my decision."

"Stop sniveling, Brian," Faith said. "Just take these bags out there and let me get off my feet."

"Drink?" Garrett asked.

Faith waved her hand in acquiescence and Garrett wandered off to the bar.

Faith and Audrey headed for the living room, Audrey making small talk about her sons and their stay here in Tilley and the weather and a smattering of local events, none of which Faith reacted to.

"What have you done to your hair?" she asked.

Audrey involuntarily put her hand up to her recently coifed head. "Oh," she said, "do you like it?"

"It looks a bit tawdry," Faith replied. "Was it a local person?"

"I tried a new salon in town, yes. Thought it was easier than . . ."

"And it looks like you've put on a few pounds. Have you been eating well? Summer foods will do that to you. I have a theory that all this fuss about cholesterol is just a fad. I think it is important to just keep a steady diet in moderation."

Audrey dropped her gaze to the floor.

"Moderation," Faith emphasized. "You'll feel better. You don't look well."

Garrett handed her a vodka tonic. "You're looking well, mother-Salsberg," he said.

She had settled herself into the armchair looking out over the lawn toward the harbor. She looked up at him. "Where's the lime?" she asked.

"Ah!" he exclaimed and slithered off to the kitchen and returned moments later with a slice of lime tweezered between his thumb and forefinger.

"Fingers!" his mother-in-law said. "I don't know where those fingers have been. You should use a plate. It's polite. Are you just going to deposit that well-handled piece of fruit in my glass? Really, Garrett!"

He looked at her still tentatively clutching the slice of lime although he wanted to squeeze it over her head or grind it into her face like James Cagney did with the grapefruit to Mae Clark in *The Public Enemy*. He stomped back to the kitchen, glanced around, licked the lime slice, and put it on a Crown Derby plate and returned to the living room with a beatific smile.

"Better," she said as he offered it to her. She plucked it off the plate and dropped it in her drink.

"I'll just go check on how Brian is getting along with your bags," he said and headed to the pool house.

He met Brian beside the pool. "Settled?" he asked.

"I don't know what she puts in those bags," Brian said, breathing heavily.

"Her witch's cauldron no doubt," Garrett replied.

"Oh, come on, Garrett. She's not that bad. She's just getting a bit old."

"There's no doubt about that. Senile maybe. It's time she retired."

"When she's ready."

"She can't see what's on the horizon for the housing industry," Garrett added. "She's mired in the past."

Brian looked at him blankly.

"Well, she is. She wants to recreate her father's piratical activities. Flailing about randomly."

"I don't see that," Brian replied.

"She's your mother. She has a theory for everything and most of them are grounded in her la-la land. What meds is she on?"

"I don't know."

"We should know, you know. We really should know. She could run us all off a cliff. Did you unpack for her?"

"I don't do that," Brian replied.

"Wouldn't it be polite and thoughtful if we did?" Garrett said with a watery smile.

"She'll lose it if we touch her things!"

"We're just trying to be gentlemen," Garrett persuaded and grinned. He put his arm around Brian's shoulders and guided him back toward the pool house - two, stocky, oleaginous men, brothers in name only, slinking through the evening light. In the bedroom, Garrett heaved one of Faith's suitcases onto the bed. It was beautiful, light tan leather, burnished to gentle gloss with a pair of broad straps running around it. "Jesus," he said. "You were right. This weighs a ton. Maybe she's carrying her gold around with her. Someday maybe they'll put wheels on suitcases." He reached down, unbuckled the straps and clicked the latches.

To Brian it sounded like gunshots. "We shouldn't be doing this!"

Garrett flipped the top of the suitcase back on the bed and

stood back spreading his arms wide. "There," he said. "No cats or other live creatures inside. Looks like just clothes."

"What did you expect to find?" Brian asked, looking at his brother-in-law.

"Maybe we should hang stuff up for her. It will get all wrinkled stuffed into this . . ."

"No! We should close it back up and get out of here."

"We need to know what drugs she is on," Garrett insisted. "We'll just look and then close it up and she'll never know the difference. You're right we shouldn't hang anything up because we won't do it right!"

"She probably keeps her medications in her handbag which she has with her."

Garrett ran his hand around the outside edge of the top and bottom of the open suitcase, allowing his fingers to seek out anything that might resemble medication bottles. Without success.

"What's in that little thing?" Garrett asked pointing to a carriage bag on the floor.

Brian shrugged. "Close the other one!"

Garrett waved his hand toward the bag on the bed indicating that Brian should deal with that while he reached down and lifted the smaller, carriage bag up onto the bed. He undid the strap and pulled back on the latches and pulled it open.

Faith was an organized and fastidious woman. Garrett peered down into the bag while he held it open by pulling back both sides of the top. The contents had been positioned there – segregated, organized, packaged, and maybe cataloged. Were he to move something and not put it back in exactly the same place, Faith would notice. She was one of those annoying people. He could hear her yelling, 'Who touched my bags? Who moved my personal paints and pills and drugs? Was it you, Garrett?' She didn't even have to speak. He could hear her in his head, hear her scrape across the tones in her strident voice. He could feel her presence, invisibly looking over his shoulder. Over the years of his marriage to Bryce, Faith had made it politely but abundantly clear that she didn't approve of his lineage. Bryce had reached across the tracks to marry him.

"We should get out of here," Brian whispered.

Garrett reached down into the bag and pulled out what looked to him like a medicine case. He placed it on the bed, carefully unzipped it, and flipped the cover open. A small bottle popped out of the top sleeve, rolled across the bed and dropped onto the floor.

"Shit!" Brian said. "What was that?"

"No idea," Garrett replied. "Just find it."

"We need to get out of here," Brian whispered again.

Brian slid around the side of the bed. The pool house was not just some little out-building in which to change into a bathing suit. It would have served as a comfortable average home with two bedrooms, two bathrooms, a casual walk-in kitchen and a wide-open, cathedral ceilinged living room with a cast and colored concrete floor that was as smooth as glass. The Lanai was as lovely as an oleander flower: beautiful but potentially deadly in the right hands.

The bedrooms were small and the queen-sized beds filled them so that there was barely room on either side for the ornate nightstands. Brian was worried the bottle of pills would open and the pills would lodge themselves in cracks so he scrambled down to his knees on the side of the bed and peered underneath into the darkness.

"It's dark!" he said.

Garrett didn't reply he was looking through the array of drugs remaining in the bag. "This woman is a veritable pharmacy!" he said. "Elavil, Mellaril, Miltowns! What the hell is all this stuff? Did you know your mother was an addict?"

"She's not! Help me find that bottle. Do you have a flashlight?"

"Must have left it in my other suit! Do I have a flashlight?

The bottle just rolled across the bed. It can't have gone far. Just find it!"

Garrett joined Brian on the floor on the opposite side of the bed and peered underneath at his brother-in-law's face. He pulled his Zippo lighter from his pocket and flicked the cover open.

"No!" Brian yelled. "Jesus, you'll set the bed on fire."

Garrett peered under the bed at his brother-in-law's shadowed face, shrugged and spun the wheel on the lighter, and the stubby flamed licked out. And for a moment, the darkness retreated.

Brian gasped. But no bottle appeared. "We shouldn't have opened the bag. Shit. Shit. Shit!"

"Look under the nightstand!"

"I did!"

"Maybe it rolled into the closet behind you."

"How could it? The door was closed. Wait! There!"

Brian stood up, proudly holding the very small bottle between his thumb and forefinger. "There. Now put it back and let's get out of here."

Garrett took the bottle from Brian and held it up to the light. "What the hell is it?" he asked rhetorically. "I don't know anything about these drugs. 'Proternol'. Looks potent. I mean I don't know how it could look potent but they're really small pills. Can we ask her about them?"

"Shit, no!" Brian replied. "Then she'd know we'd been in here."

"We should know. Maybe this is something we should know about. Maybe she's got a condition that would impair her judgment. Know what I mean? Hurt the company. Hurt our jobs. We should know about stuff like that."

Garrett looked at the small brown bottle in his hand and then tried to estimate where it had come from in the top of Faith's case. There was no obvious spot. If he put it back in the wrong location or even in the wrong orientation she would notice. Maybe she would think that it got jostled around in transit. Maybe. . . maybe not. He shrugged. Not much he could do about it now so he shoved it in and closed up the small bag and replaced it in the carriage bag and carefully closed that up as well.

The two men skulked out of the Lanai and back to the big house.

~

MEALS, ESPECIALLY DINNERS, WERE TURMOIL AT CASA Grande. Should they be grand or casual? Should they plan for the family to all be together once a week, twice a week, every night? Should they try only speaking French so everyone would have a chance to practice their language skills? Who should cook? Who should plan? How should they dress?

The number of decisions and opinions drove the tension to a snapping point where everyone suffered in some way or another through the hour or so that they gathered in the formal dining room in the big house. It was Garrett's opinion that they should simply hire a cook to plan, cook, and serve the meal. But there was an underlying need in the group that required 'slumming' it and independence. The intention was to be more casual and more suitable to the mode of the vacation environment - to do vacation right. Garrett thought it was foolish and unnecessary and a pain in the ass.

Audrey had seized control for this particular evening's festivities and marshaled the troops and bought the food and pulled out the cookbooks with the not-so-subtle goal of impressing Faith. Everything Audrey knew about cooking she had learned from watching Julia Child on TV, which had emphasized the need for lots of wine. Although Audrey recognized that she didn't know a lot about cooking, she knew she knew more and had better taste than anyone else in the group. She planned to cook what Julia called *Poulet au Porto*, risotto, asparagus tips and a fresh strawberry pie for dessert. It hadn't sounded all that difficult – basically just a roast chicken with some other stuff added. Everybody likes chicken and there were lots of local strawberries. She could send . . . or at least ask Garrett to find the wines and Bryce could get some fresh flowers for the table at the florist and some bread from the bakery in Chatham.

She had planned all this the week before, copied out the recipes from Julia Child's cookbook. The process of copying them helped her to remember them or at least the basics of them. Her major project back home in Fort Lauderdale was creating a cookbook for her Junior League. It had been her idea, and it consumed her and plagued her as she sought recipes from other members and bought dozens of cookbooks and tried the recipes out on her family. She harassed other Junior League members for family dishes having some connection to Florida because they insisted the cookbook have a theme. "You don't want just another cookbook!" they said. "It won't sell. It just won't, don't you know? There are a million of them out there. Well you know! You must have bought at least half of them!"

Brian had tolerated the strange concoctions that she sometimes chose and their Cuban cook, Consuelo, misread. Each morning at home Audrey would take out one of her cookbooks and leaf through it looking for a recipe fitting the section of her project's cookbook like beef or chicken entrees or soups or desserts and carefully copy out the recipe for Consuelo. She would take it to the kitchen and proudly hand it to the cook who would take it from her, shrug, and 'harrumph!' Rarely would Audrey get a smile or a sound indicating pleasure on Consuelo's part since Consuelo knew what Consuelo knew about cooking and recipes were not necessary! And certainly not these random comestibles from random places by random people. And so, recipes like *Poulet au Porto* would come into the dining room of the Reese house covered with sofrito sauce – a mixture of onions, green peppers, garlic, oregano, and bay leaves. In

Consuelo's opinion everything up to dessert was better when it was doused with sofrito!

This was not good for Brian's stomach, but the boys seemed to tolerate it well, and they had developed a strong relationship with Consuelo who had become a house mother to them, hugging them to her ample form when they came home from school with their puerile problems. Any time Audrey talked with Brian about maybe replacing Consuelo, the relationship with the boys got in the way. She was unarguably a permanent fixture.

Audrey had been looking forward to breaking away from Consuelo's cuisine, cooking for herself and her family at the Cape house and seeing how these recipes really should taste. Audrey had been laboring over the League cookbook for several years and the other Junior League members were growing impatient wondering if it would ever be finished.

Faith had grown up in Ft. Lauderdale and she was probably used to Cuban cuisine. Most likely she would not have been put off by a modicum of sofrito, but Audrey felt that Faith might be insulted – an insinuation of lower-class taste. French cuisine, on the other hand, had coined all the regal terms in cooking like *cuisine* itself and *gourmet* and *epicure* and *connoisseur*.

She was taking a risk making a chicken dish. Chicken was not regal. Making it fancy, elevating it was akin to putting lipstick on a pig. But there was inverse class in slumming it - in cooking the food of the people, like Marie Antoinette and her cake. Audrey felt she could pull it off as long as she got the right chicken and the right accoutrements like the bread and the wine. If the chicken failed, the blame could fall on Garrett or Brian or Bryce.

To Garrett, wine was fancy grape juice. Cheaper and more was the best answer. Delicate issues like the flavor of food or the aroma of wine did not crease his consciousness. Audrey had to prod him a half hour before dinner to buy the wine. He shrugged, jumped in the car, and drove to the local liquor store.

He was thinking about other things, more practical things, like how he could just help Faith fall asleep and stay that way.

She had the drugs. For a moment it puzzled him that any doctor would prescribe all that medication. In a way it seemed irresponsible, but he was grateful for the tools.

Once Faith was gone and he was in control, he could start advancing the company forward. Thoughts of running the company on his own titillated him. People wanted bigger houses. The average price of a house had soared in the last couple of years exceeding seventy thousand dollars and there was no reason to expect it not to keep going. He had heard his parents whining about the risks of investing in real estate, but they had been through the Depression which Garrett was sure had been an aberration.

Salsberg Homes was in an ideal condition to lead the charge with new production building techniques and Garrett wanted to be in control. He wanted it so badly he could taste it. He was annoyed he had to sit around wasting time. He was annoyed that socializing was necessary, but he was practical enough to know it had to be done.

That was one thing he had learned at Princeton. He had been surrounded by people who had grown up socializing, having wine and wit and winning at the center of their souls. He had abandoned his plebeian roots, retaining his accountant father's affection for numbers he let dance through his own analysis of everything he did. Like buying wine. What was the long-term value of a liquid that you would consume and then piss into a toilet an hour later?

That evening when the family sat down to Audrey's cooking, the fantasized harmony was not there but the chicken hadn't burned and the risotto wasn't too soggy and Audrey was pleased. She waited for the compliments or the gratitude, but the best she got was a minimum of complaints.

"What's this?" her son Pee Wee asked pointing at the gooey blob of what appeared to him to be similar in structure to snot on his plate.

"Risotto," his mother replied with a smile. "Try it. You'll like it."

"I won't," he said.

"It's Italian," Brian explained.

"I won't like it," Pee Wee reiterated.

"We should get a cook," Garrett said. "It's foolish to stress about meals . . . about cooking."

"I like cooking," Audrey said. "I'm working on a cookbook."

"We know," Bryce said. "You've told us."

"I think it's important to try recipes before I put them in the book, don't you think?" Audrey replied.

Faith looked at her plate, "Well, I'm not very hungry in any case. The flowers are nice. I think it's important to have fresh flowers. They give sparkle to a room."

Garrett refrained from saying, "We know. You've told us before." Instead he asked, "Are we going to be able to get that property in Newtown Square?"

Faith twisted her face and said, "You know we don't talk about business at a family dinner. We don't get a chance to get together like this very often."

More often than I would like, Garrett thought. "But wasn't that what delayed you getting here? Negotiating with the owners?" he said.

"We'll see," Faith replied. "We'll talk about it later. This isn't the time or the place. As the Bible says, 'a time for every purpose under heaven.'"

The Bible and the Byrds Garrett thought. He watched Faith's face as she manipulated the family gathering. The conversation bounced from one meaningless topic to another, all of which would be forgotten in minutes. Audrey was wagging her tail, looking for praise, perhaps a little respect which Faith would dangle in front of her nose like a carrot in front of a donkey.

Bryce was doing her best to ignore her stepmother. She had received a pat on the head for the flowers, but she was staring at her plate, stirring the risotto around with disdain. She turned to her husband. "This wine is really bad," she said in a stage whisper.

Garrett shrugged. "The guy in the store said it was great," he replied shifting the blame.

"Which store?" Brian asked. "You know the people at Hannigan's will say anything, but they really don't know anything. They're just salespeople, you know? If you want to get a half decent bottle of wine you have to go to The Wine Seller in Cotuit. Those people have actually been to France. One of them, I forget which, has actually been a part of Challenge International du Vin." Brian rolled it off his tongue. "Now that's extraordinary for someone from a small place like Cotuit!"

Who gives a shit, thought Garrett. It's just fancy grape juice.

"I talked with him about it last summer," Brian continued. "It takes a lot of training and practice. They have to be able to identify which part of a particular vineyard a wine comes from! One thing he told me was that winemakers are often overcome by carbon monoxide fumes when they are treading on the grapes!"

Garrett looked at him. "Really?" he asked.

"Absolutely. Apparently it happens all the time. You know those farm buildings are not well ventilated. You see it in the news."

"Really?" Garrett asked again. "Carbon monoxide? How do you get carbon monoxide from . . . grapes?"

Brian back peddled. "That's what he said."

"That's extraordinary," Faith said.

"Were they burning the grapes? I didn't know you burned grapes to make wine?" Garrett asked. "I thought you just . . . squished them. Grape juice. Fermented grape juice." He held up his glass to the light as if he were looking for pollutants. "I mean, usually you only get carbon monoxide when you burn stuff. That's what they told me in my physics classes at Princeton. Were they wrong?"

Brian looked at him . . . his story crushed.

"Did you mean carbon dioxide, Brian? DIoxide. Two oxygen molecules. DI, Brian. Not MON. Not monoxide. Carbon dioxide. I'd believe that. I mean it takes a lot of carbon dioxide to hurt anyone. Way over two thousand parts per million. But it only takes a little carbon monoxide to rob the oxygen from your brain. Carbon dioxide is sometimes used to create a hypoxic environment for carbonic maceration. But you probably knew that!" He sat back and crossed his arms.

Brian glared at him. For a moment or two the only sounds in the room were the occasional clicking of a silver fork or knife on good china.

"I have strawberry pie for dessert," Audrey said with a grin.

"Any carbon MONoxide in that?" Brian asked with a grumble.

"No," Audrey laughed. "Of course not."

"I have a theory," Faith said, "that there are elements in all foods that are bad for you . . . perhaps just small traces of this or that chemical. The fact is that when they test these things, they provide massive doses to the rats in the laboratory . . . far more than we would ever see in reality. The tests are just not real. If you listen to the scientists, they would tell you that the world is melting. They do it, you know, so that the drug companies can sell more drugs and the chemical companies can sell more chemicals. It's simple economics."

There were blank looks around the table. Finally Bryce said, "Are you saying that science is a conspiracy?"

Faith dabbed her mouth with her napkin. "Politicians use science to support new laws and make new rules. They twist the results to their own purpose. Do you see people dropping dead on the street when they smoke a cigarette? No. My father smoked a pack of cigarettes a day for forty years. He didn't die from the cigarettes! He died playing poker! Probably would have gone on living for another twenty years anyway if he'd been a better card player."

Garrett tried to dig out the nugget of logic from this

monolog. He took a deep swig of his wine, pushed back his chair, stood up and said, "How about that pie, Audrey?"

After the strawberry pie, Faith let everyone know that she was headed for the Lanai to unpack and settle in. Bryce helped Audrey clear away the dishes and clean up the kitchen, and despite the cool evening, Brian and Garrett headed out to the patio where Garrett pulled out some cigars.

Brian coughed. "Was it really necessary to do that . . . you know . . . monoxide thing? Lot of people make that mistake!"

"Oh, just suck it up, Brian! That's a childish mistake. A misquote of a folk tale." He sucked on the cigar. "When are you going to tell her about the boatyard?"

"Jesus, I don't know. She's going to be pissed."

Garrett looked up at the stars and blew out a cloud of pungent smoke between his pursed lips. There was no breeze and the temperature was in the low sixties. The lights of other houses sparkled across the water. And for just a brief moment, Garrett speculated on the beauty of his surroundings. "What if you didn't have to tell her?"

Brian coughed again, snapping his head around to his brother-in-law. "What do you mean? She's going to find out. If she hasn't already. She knows everything about everything."

Garrett let another moment of silence grow. "Maybe not." He puffed. "Maybe she's getting senile. She has all those drugs."

Brian shivered. "I don't know."

"What if she . . . I'm just speculating here . . . what if she . . . you know . . . stepped down . . . or something? She wouldn't have to know. She would never have to know."

Brian said, "She wouldn't do that. She'll never do that."

Garrett puffed again. "I don't know. We could . . . you know . . . encourage her. Wouldn't it be a relief that she would never find out what an idiot you are?" Garrett looked at him. "Or I could tell her for you?"

"Oh, no. No. No. No. That wouldn't be right. That wouldn't

work at all. You can't tell her. I'll do it. I will. I just have to find the right time."

Another sinkhole of silence grew. "All right," Garrett said finally. "But think about it. Wouldn't it be a relief if you never had to tell her?" His tone changed to a fraternal softness. "No, seriously, Brian, I don't really think you're an idiot. We have to work together, don't we? I can help you with this if you'll let me."

In the pale illumination of the lights from the house, Brian could see the glow of Garrett's teeth when he smiled at him. "I appreciate that, Garrett. We should probably go in. This isn't Florida weather." He laughed drily.

"Think about it," Garrett replied.

5

POOL HEATER

Jon's sister, Cornelia, had made a good call on the status of their father. He was just clumsy. That's all. Of course, Jon still had a twinge of guilt for not dropping everything and dashing back home, which looked great in the movie in his mind, but then what? His father had gone back to work the next day with a little bit of a headache. "Stay on the Cape," his father said. "Play ball. I'm okay."

So, he did, and after two weeks on the Cape, Jon was settling into a routine and working regularly at Casa Grande. The first part of the day was always the best. Before he started cutting boards and hammering nails, he could stand still and look across the lawns to watch the early morning mists float off the warming wetlands. The days were long and the sun had pushed away the darkness of the night several hours before they got to the house. If he could have gotten there early enough, Jon would have liked to watch the sun rise, splitting the horizon in the east, driving the stars away.

Jon associated dawn awakening with camping trips with his father and his Boy Scout troop, after a night in sleeping bags, staring up at the stars and imagining just how far infinity might be.

That was personal. This was work where they were intruders where they couldn't disturb the family. "How do we do this? How can we hammer quietly?" Jon asked.

"Nope," Ace replied. "Just ignore them. You do what you gotta do and they do what they gotta do. Simple. Just don't cross the line."

"What line is that?"

Ace sighed. "You're not them and they certainly don't want to be you. See what I mean? Their world is different from your world . . . my world. You're the help. You don't matter. There's a line. They're from 'away' . . . off Cape . . . money. See?"

"I'm from off Cape."

"Yeah, but you're with me and besides that, you're a Longliner . . . a baseball player. That makes you doubly strange! I'm sure you've got the picture."

Jon wasn't sure he did have the picture. Although he was just beginning to understand that if you weren't born on Cape Cod it didn't matter how many years you lived here, you were still from "away." But the players from the Cape Cod Baseball league were special. They were summer entertainment, like an athletic summer theater. They were separated from ordinary mortals by the star barrier, elevated by stepping up on the stage in front of the audience. They were stars whose ascendancy was just beginning. Some of them would be famous someday, and young boys and girls hung around the diamonds to gape and touch and dream.

Jon went from "help" to potential star on a daily basis, and it was a challenge to keep it straight and not step over someone's invisible and mysterious line somewhere along the way. His primary role for Wentzell Construction was as a gofer: "Hey, Megquire, time to go for coffee! Hey, Megquire, get that shoreline out of the truck – ha, ha, ha! Hey, Megquire, we need another five pounds of tenpenny nails. And don't get the brights this time! Galvy, or they'll rust!"

Jon would drop his tools, pull off his canvas nailing apron, jump into Ace's truck and head off to the lumberyard or coffee shop. He was learning his way around town.

The lumberyard had a hardware store that sold tools and nails and bolts and paints. The place had been around for a million years and the wide board, wooden floors squeaked as he walked across them. It smelled of varnish and dust, old rope and turpentine. Builders and staff chatted as old friends, catching up on families and projects and politics. They turned when Jon walked in . . . recognizing him as an outsider and then as special when their smiles returned.

"Hey, you're a Longliner, right? How's the team shaping up? How's Graham doing? Treating you well? You're working with Ace, right?"

Jon would grin and fumble with Ace's list until someone stepped up with a smile to find the right finish nails or lag bolts or trim boards without a twist.

That Thursday morning back in Casa Grande, Jon was restacking the latest load of lumber when he was interrupted by a member of the household he didn't recognize, a short, stocky guy with wire-rimmed glasses. The man stood in the doorway surveying the disarray. The project was at the stage when things had been ripped down, walls and ceiling opened up, wiring and pipes exposed, and contractor tools set up. "You gotta tear it apart before you can build it back up," Ace had told Jon.

The man at the door didn't speak. Finally, Jon asked, "Can I help you?"

"No," the man replied. "I'm just looking."

"Okay," Jon said and went back to work.

The man asked, "When do you think it will be finished?"

"Not sure, sir," Jon replied. ""You should ask Mr. Wentzell. He should be here soon."

"Oh, you're the baseball player," the man said, his face lighting up. He stepped into the room. "You know, I love baseball. I live in Florida, but I root for the Dodgers . . . at least when they played in Brooklyn. I don't know why. Maybe because they weren't the Yankees. Pee Wee Reese used to play for them. No relation. My name's Reese. Brian Reese. Do you remember Pee Wee Reese?"

"No, sir," Jon said. "I think that was before I was born."

"Probably was. Dodgers left Brooklyn in 1957. I still root for them, but they're not the same. Pee Wee was quite the athlete. Don't think my son will be at that level. What position do you play?"

"First. First base."

"Are you any good? Don't answer that. Must be. I hear the Cape Cod League is just one step before the major leagues. Pretty exciting. Are you going to play in the majors?" He pushed his glasses up his nose.

"I . . ."

"I'll have to come watch you. Not much else to do around here in the summer. I always wondered if I could play in the major leagues. I guess every young boy does. Admires those guys. Makes them into heroes. The girls go after the movie stars. That's where girls get their ambition. I guess they also go after the musicians. You don't play music too, do you? That would be a double whammy. The Beatles don't still play do they? Who are the stars now?"

Jon looked from the man to the lumber pile, hoping the former would go away. "No, sir. The Beatles are not together as a group. I like Supertramp."

"Who? Isn't there a group known as The Who? Weird names. Where do they come up with these things?" Brian looked over his shoulder and back at Jon. "This is my mother's house. I live here. I mean, I don't live here. It's the summer. I live in Florida."

"Ah."

"When do you think this will be finished? It's noisy and messy and disruptive. I don't know why my mother chose to do this now."

"You would have to ask Mr. Wentzell," Jon replied.

"Yes. I'll do that." said Brian and turned and left.

"Yes, sirree!" Jon said under his breath.

AT BATTING PRACTICE THAT AFTERNOON, JON FELT THE "TING" as each ball collided with the aluminum bat and soared over the fence, one right after the other. There was rhythm to the drill as the pitcher picked a practice ball out of the basket, set up, threw it, Jon whacked it into the sky, and the pitcher picked up the next ball and repeated the routine. Swish, TING, pause. Swish, TING, pause. One right after another. A handful of his teammates leaned against the fence and cheered him on.

As a team, the Longliners were just stirring the pot, barely beginning to gel, coalescing from a group of random individuals to an effective system. They'd only played one game together and each of them struggled to refocus their individual egos. The world was changing and the pressure for personal and professional success was enormous. This wasn't just a friendly game anymore. Professional athletes' salaries were rising into the land of fairytales and magic kingdoms. Only the year before in 1978, Mike Schmidt had raked in five hundred sixty thousand dollars and Rod Carew had jumped that up to eight hundred thousand this year. Sports commentators were predicting players would soon be paid a million dollars a year. Pirates and kings had fought and died for less.

And it wasn't just the scouts or all that money. Jon also appreciated the attention of the girls who gathered around the field to watch and gape and giggle. Jon was surprised but pleased they didn't seem to notice the early summer chill and dressed to expose and flaunt their charms.

He sauntered away from the batting cage, pulling off his gloves, holding his bat in the middle like a rifle, and smiling. One girl hung back behind the others, her straight brown hair tumbling over her left eye. For some random reason she reminded him of one of those cute animated squirrels in a Disney movie. She wore glasses and had a nice smile and a dimple in the middle of her left cheek. He smiled at her and then dropped his bat into the rack and sat on the bench with the other players trying to focus on the game.

Coach Russell had told them the Falmouth Commodores had good players and were forecast to take the league, which was not the most inspiring pep talk. But this early in the season, none of the teams were working smoothly as teams, and the Commodores came into the Tilley field that day, feeling cocky, but the Longliners managed to pull together and beat them.

After the game, the team headed down to Clegg's to talk things over and celebrate, and the girls followed along. Jon spotted the brown-haired one with the dimple, and he slid over to sit at her table.

"Hi. I'm Jon."

"Okay," she replied, pulling off her glasses and brushing back her hair.

"I noticed you hanging out at the field."

"We all do. I don't really know why."

Jon considered her face and decided he kind of liked it.

"Do you like baseball?" he asked.

"Not really," she said. "But it's something to do in the summer. It's good for the town, I guess. But baseball players have a lot of entitled attitudes." She looked him in the eyes as she said this. "In fact, I don't think I really like baseball players."

He did not register the insinuation to move on. He did notice her eyes were a remarkably warm shade of brown and her gaze was unwavering. Her face was smooth and tan. Her shoulders were covered by a white T-shirt stroked with thin red horizontal lines that highlighted the rising of her chest.

He quickly raised his line of sight before she noticed. "No," he said. "Not entitled. It's a matter of focus. When you get to the top level of anything you have to focus all your energies to succeed"

She smiled. He really liked that smile. "Sure. Focus. Top level! Really? Sounds like a rationalization to me."

"Oh," Jon said. "Yeah. A rationalization. I guess. Maybe. Something like that. Can you share your name?" He wondered why he'd said it that way. Awkward or what?

"Lisa," she replied. "Lisa Prence."

"You live here?"

"All my life. A native of Tilley."

"I didn't think anyone was actually from here." Another winner line.

"Listen, Jon–that's your name, right? Why don't you just go hang out with your entitled—excuse me—*focused* teammates and stop trying to hit on me. I'm just a townie."

Jon sat back in his chair. "Sorry," he said. "I didn't mean anything bad."

"The fact is," she said, "when you tell someone you're from Cape Cod, they think you're rich. They think of the beach. They think we're all on vacation all the time. Not true. Cape Cod is like any other place. We have our poor. People struggle to buy groceries for their kids. We have our working people who take care of the rich people – scrubbing their toilets and washing their floors. We even have homeless people. Drinking is a big problem here. We have crime too. Sometimes violent crime."

Jon watched the corners of her mouth curl. Watched her eyes dance. "I'm sorry." But he experienced a small jolt of anger at being forced to apologize, mingled in the soup of his confusion and embarrassment as she mentally slapped him for his lack of understanding. He objected to being glommed in with the unfeeling attitudes of rest of the world. He knew he was more worldly and sophisticated than that.

He glanced out the window as a police cruiser pulled into the parking lot. "What do you suppose this is all about?" he asked. "Are we being raided? Local headlines read, 'Evil activities at Clegg's'?"

Lisa followed his gaze out the window. "Guilty conscience,

Jon? Don't worry about it. It's my father. He's a cop." She put her glasses back on and pushed her hair back again.

Jon looked at her. Her father's a cop, he thought. Oh, shit. Hope he can't read minds. "Well?" he said out loud, starting to stand up to disappear. "Your father? Great. Um. It's been good to meet you, Lisa."

A large man in a police uniform stepped into the room and scanned the occupants. He held his hat in his hands. His face lit up when he saw Lisa, and he ambled over to her table as Jon was rising from his chair.

"No, no, sit, Son," he said to Jon. "I don't want to interrupt. Just here to say hello."

He seemed friendly enough. He had a badge, a round face, a small black mustache, and arched his eyebrows when he smiled. Didn't look much like Lisa.

"Hello, Dad." Lisa said with a sigh.

"Aren't you going to introduce us?" the badge asked.

"This is one of the Longliners. I think he said his name is Jon. My father. Officer Mark Prence."

Jon shook the man's hand. "Sir," he said. "Jon Megquire. Lisa and I just met. She was just telling me about your town."

"Nice to meet you, Jon. It's quiet here," the badge said. "We like it that way. Summer gets crazy. We know that. The baseball is . . . uh . . . good. Good for the town."

"That's great," Jon said. "Well, I need to talk to the coach." He backed away from the table, smiling. "Good to meet you both."

The glasses made her look older but maybe she was twelve or something! He should just concentrate on what he was there for, and he resolved that was what he would do. Baseball. Yes. Baseball and . . . other stuff. Focus. Lose the distractions.

~

GARRETT WAS BROODING WHILE HE STARED AT WHAT WAS LEFT of another family dinner. It may have been beautiful outside Casa Grande that evening as the sun set over the water, but the natural environment was just another piece in a scattered system that he had to connect in the right order so the result would be the most advantageous outcome. Each action or event leads to another action or event. He had to deal with timing and opportunity and personalities and means and so much more. The mélange almost overwhelmed him with pleasure. He smiled. No one noticed.

Faith said she was feeling a chill and wanted the heat turned up.

"But it's a beautiful evening," Audrey said. "We should open more windows. Look at that light!"

"Lovely," Faith said. "I'm still chilly."

"The boys want to go for a swim," Audrey said. "The pool is lovely in this light. I think that should be all right. Don't you, Brian?"

"They'll catch cold," Faith advised.

"The pool heater works, doesn't it?" Brian asked.

"It's not the water," Faith said. "It's the air that causes colds. Exposing the skin. People cool down too quickly and their bodies can't cope with the change. I am not alone in this thinking. It's an historical fact. My grandmother told me the same thing."

Garrett grunted. "Another theory is not much of a surprise," he mumbled. Nor was it a surprise that he did not feel the warmth in this forced family gathering.

"Did you know one of our construction people plays for the Longliners?" Brian asked.

"Who? What are the Longliners?" Faith asked.

"The Longliners. You know, the local baseball team. Part of the Cape Cod League," Garrett said.

"Yes," Brian added. "I was talking to him. Seems like a nice enough boy. It's pretty exciting, you know. We could be seeing him on TV someday! I've never actually known a professional baseball player. We should go to a game. See how our guy does."

"What does that have to do with turning on the heat?" Faith asked.

"Anyone interested?" Brian asked. "I think it's a good idea to support the local community while we're here. The team is relatively new to the league, you know."

"Of course, I know," Faith replied. "Your stepfather was instrumental in getting it started. Installing this coach was one of the last things he did before he died. I've never been particularly interested in sports and neither was he, but he thought baseball would be good for the town, for the summer visitors to have something to amuse them."

"He knew the coach?" Brian asked.

"I don't think he knew the man," Faith continued, "but he was involved in the selection process in some way. A local man but with some experience. It was never clear to me why Christopher cared. I suppose he enjoyed controlling the situation. And he had the money to do it. When you have money, there's always interest."

"Why does it always have to involve money?" Bryce said. "People are always whining about not having enough money. Baseball is a waste of time. It's a game, for god's sake! Men should grow up."

"It's the national pastime," Brian said. "The American game."

"We should be thinking more serious thoughts," Bryce said. "We need to end this energy crisis. I hate waiting in line to buy gas. Some of us just don't have time for that sort of thing. Why doesn't the president do something about it?"

"He's a Democrat," Brian said. "I'm sure he won't get a second term. He's destroyed the economy. He's got no guts. He can't even get our people back from those Iranian idiots. He's letting them make fools of us."

"What's happening with my boatyard?" Faith asked.

Brian looked as though he had been slapped. Garrett shrugged.

"Boatyard?"

"Yes, you heard me. What's going on?"

"What do you mean? What makes you think anything is going on? Isn't this business? Are we . . .? I mean, we aren't supposed to talk about business at the table."

Faith looked at him.

Garrett watched the cat stalk the rabbit, a rabbit that sensed danger but didn't know where it was coming from.

"Um. There's some interest in developing it, of course. Always is," Brian mumbled.

"You know what that property means to me . . . what it meant to my father," Faith said. "You'd tell me if you were considering doing anything with it?"

Garrett was disappointed she let the rabbit go. Where was the fun in that?

"Of course, I know what it means to you." Brian paused. "But we might start thinking about it sooner rather than later. I mean, the market looks pretty promising right now and . . ."

Rabbits are dumber than shit, Garrett reveled.

"I'm not selling it to any foreigners! Ever! Do you hear me! It's American land and it will always be American land. Don't even talk about selling that property without talking to me first. Is that clear?" She glared at her son.

Oh joy, Garrett thought. Go ahead. Poke her with a stick, Brian. Tell her you sold it. Tell her you didn't look inside the boat sheds. Now's the time. Go ahead.

But Brian backed away. "Absolutely clear, Mother," he said and looked down at his plate.

The fun was over so Garrett sought a new path of local gossip. A juicy scandal would liven things up. "What's happening in Caerwys?" he asked. "Any new debutantes we should know about? Does it look like it will be an eventful season?"

"When is my project going to be finished here?" demanded

Faith, not to be deflected from the family issues. "Has anyone asked? Wentzell did a good job last year, but I don't want this to drag on through the summer. Cape Cod contractors have a magic 'two weeks' answer to everything. Have you asked, Garrett?"

"I haven't seen him."

"You need to ask him directly. You won't get a straight answer unless you confront him directly. You have to be direct. Sometimes confrontation is required . . . as I think it may be in this case. I don't want to be sleeping in the Lanai all summer."

"How long will you be with us?" Bryce asked.

"Trying to get rid of me?" Faith asked.

"No! Of course not!" Bryce pasted on a smile.

"I don't know. Don't know how long I'll be able to be here. I have things to do. Have to keep up appearances. There are things we need to talk about. Don't know how long I'll be here."

Bryce looked at her husband and then back at her stepmother. She put on the mask of concern. "Is everything all right . . . Mother?"

Garrett wondered if another puzzle piece would be revealed. Faith let them wait. "Audrey," she said finally, "be a good girl and clear these plates away. What sort of dessert do you have for us tonight?" she asked with a watery smile.

There was a pause as the family looked at each other, and then Audrey said, "Of course. I think we have some fruit."

"Oh," Faith said, "if you have oranges make sure you cut mine up in slices without the little skin things. There is an art to doing that right. With a little sugar, if you don't mind."

"I don't know if we have oranges, but I'll see." She paused and then added, "I'm going to tell the boys it's okay to swim."

"I'll check the heater," Garrett said.

Brian followed him out of the room after throwing his napkin on the table. Out on the patio he hissed, "Did you tell her about the boatyard?"

"Of course not," Garrett said. "Why would I do that? She

knows what an idiot you are. I certainly didn't tell her anything. I'm shocked you would ask."

Brian shoved his hands in his pockets and slouched along beside the edge of the pool. "She's my mother, but god, there are times when she is a pain in the ass! Picking on Audrey like that! Treating her like a maid! Jesus!"

"I know," Garrett said, patting him on the shoulder. "I know." Then he stopped walking. "What do you suppose she meant by 'I don't know how long I'll be here'?"

Brian shrugged. "Nothing. I'm sure she's just being overly dramatic." Garrett couldn't clearly see Brian's plump face in the twilight, but the house lights flared off his glasses. His brother-in-law was slightly taller than he was, which annoyed Garrett. Why couldn't he have had ancestors who cleared six feet? But you can't choose your parents, can you? If he had been able to, he would not have chosen the ones he had. He deserved parents with money and power and success. Brian just abused the gifts of his lineage. He didn't take advantage of his assets. He didn't build on them. In fact, Garrett thought, the man wasn't worth spit, and when Garrett ruled the world, Brian would find life was very different.

"What?" Brian asked.

"Just thinking," Garrett said. "What do you think she meant?"

"No idea. I never have known what she's thinking."

"She's dangerous, you know," Garrett said, moving toward the Lanai.

Brian's son Pee Wee ran out of the main house and cannonballed into the pool. "Wait!" Brian said. "We haven't got the lights on yet!"

"I think they know that," Garrett said and disappeared into the Lanai where he flipped on the pool lights. His footsteps echoed as he walked across the glassy concrete floor through the kitchen, and pulled open the door to the utility room where the gas-fired pool heater lived, its indicator lights glowing in the dark. Powerful thing. Takes a lot of heat to heat all the water in a pool. Burns a lot of gas.

Garrett flipped on the room lights, peered at the thermostat, and raised the setting until the machine clicked its relays. He heard the *whump* as the system fired. He shook the flue. Not such a secure connection, he thought.

He noted the clothes washer and dryer were in the utility room. But the pool towels have to be clean and dry and fluffy. He grabbed a couple off the stack and left, closing the utility room door behind him. Back outside, he handed the towels to Brian. "Have the boys throw these in the dryer when they're done," he said. "The dryer's in the utility room in case you didn't know."

"Of course, I know." Brian looked at the towels. "Oh," he said, "don't they need to be washed first? What's this black on them?"

Garrett looked at his hands. "Must have been something the cleaning people missed."

"Audrey says drying will make stains set."

"How the fuck does she know that?" Garrett asked. "Does she ever do laundry? Tell them to put them in the dryer when they get out of the pool. Seriously! I don't want damp towels lying around. They'll get moldy. All right?"

"All right. Geez. If it means that much to you."

And now, Garrett thought. It's just that simple.

6

FAITH DIES - JUNE 15, 1979

When Jon came into the Wentzell's kitchen on Friday morning, Babs greeted him with a cheery "Good morning! Coffee?"

He grunted his thanks and dropped into a chair.

"Rough night?" she asked as she broke eggs into a pan. The smell of bacon began caressing his senses. The kitchen radio was tuned to a Boston radio station crooning Frank Sinatra.

"Not bad," he said. "Just don't seem to be able to get enough . . . sleep." He ran his hand through his uncombed hair, yawned, and swallowed a mouthful of coffee. "Ace leave already?"

"Uh huh," Babs confirmed. "Not the Salsberg project. But you might see him there later." She set the breakfast laden plate down in front of him.

"Thanks," he said. "I really appreciate it. Not much good first thing in the morning."

She smiled at him. "I understand. Your body is still growing. It takes a lot of energy to keep all those parts of you getting bigger and stronger. Being a part of those changes is one of the reasons we like having players stay with us in the summer. Reminds me of my son, Dwight." She returned the pan to the stove.

"Didn't know you had a son?" Jon asked with a mouthful.

"He died," she said. "Vietnam."

"Oh!" he exclaimed. "I'm sorry."

Babs busied herself with the pots and pans. "While ago. But you never get over losing a child." She smiled quietly. "And Father's Day is this Sunday, remember. Hope you'll talk to your dad."

"Sure," Jon mumbled, wondering for a moment how his father was recovering. "Sure." Jon watched Babs, waiting to see if she would elaborate on her son or Vietnam, but her body language made it clear she didn't want to talk about it anymore so Jon plowed through his breakfast and headed out to his car.

Maybellene's windshield was covered with dew. Jon watched the stubby wipers swishing back and forth in front of him, waiting to be able to see, clearing his head. His thoughts flicked to Babs and Ace's son. He tried to picture Ace as a father and imagined the home movies. The war in Vietnam had ended when Jon was eighteen. He had missed all the student turmoil and political purpose. For Jon the draft was a remote, twisted, unfair lottery of death. The war had become almost fictional: a televised event that people watched on the news every night. Body count reports daily, like sport scores. What did it accomplish? What did it prove? Whom did it save? The old men start the wars that the young men fight and die in. And yet it just kept happening. Young men had mustered on this green full of patriotic spirit to change the world. Was that why a couple of hundred years after that Jon was able to drive through this peaceful early morning light of a Cape Cod day, surrounded by wealth and security?

Tilley was stirring to life. People were retrieving their newspapers from their lawns, climbing in their cars to head off to work, walking their dogs. Located out of the main touristy stream of miniature golf parks and motels and fast food restaurants, it clung to its New England charm of white clapboard and shingled homes with big front porches and stone chimneys. The imposing mass of the Episcopal church faced the green surrounded by a white, split rail fence and centered around a flagpole.

A smattering of newer homes faced the streets that led out to Jolo Point. Stone pylons flanked the entrance to the point, standing in mute warning that beyond that spot the road was privately maintained, there was no exit . . . no outlet. It was a dead end. Although he had been down this road a number of times before, Jon did not feel welcome. There was an ominous threat in the massive mansions.

He pulled up the drive to Casa Grande. None of the other crew had arrived. He thought about sitting in the car and waiting. Instead, he walked around to the back of the house. The blue tarp covered the opening. He pushed it aside and walked in.

Ace never left a messy construction site at the end of the day. "I hate looking for things," Ace had told him. "It is a waste of time. And time is what I'm selling as a contractor. I don't have to figure things out. I know how houses work and how the pieces go together. But if I can't find the pieces or the tools to put them together, I'm wasting my client's time . . . and money."

The house was quiet. Jon stood still, holding his breath, surveying the room and the materials, trying to decide what to do. He poked at a pile of boards with his foot. Waiting.

The silence was suddenly punctuated by a distant shout, a shout of alarm, that he couldn't make out. Then he heard running feet. His curiosity was restrained by Ace's privacy mandate not to intrude on the life of the house: their house, their problems. Whatever was going on was abrupt and unusual, but had nothing to do with him so Jon just listened.

He stepped outside. He moved toward his car and looked across the water. The view was ageless and immovable. The land and water dominated, pushed around by the forces of nature. Man's little scratching would be gone. The houses could be wiped out by a hurricane or some human failing like a nuclear war. But the rocks and hills and water would still be there.

All right, Jon thought, good philosophical thinking, but who gives a shit? What am I supposed to do if no one shows up? Is it like when the professor doesn't show up in twenty minutes, the class is cancelled?

Jon noticed a spot on Maybellene's hood, opened the trunk, pulled out the chamois his father had given him, and wiped the remaining dew off the car. With the cloth softened and damp, Jon gently rubbed the small spot on Maybellene's hood and surveyed the shiny surface.

And then a siren ripped the morning. At the entrance to the enclave was a police car, lights flashing, dust flying, hurtling into the Jolo Point sanctuary. That'll wake the neighbors, Jon thought. He wondered if it would be Officer Prence, Lisa's father. Probably. Were there more officers than Prence on the Tilley police force?

Jon folded the chamois, put it back in Maybellene's trunk, and started moving toward the front of the house. Had something happened to Ace? Is that why he hadn't shown up yet? Had to be someone in the house.

The police cruiser pulled to a crunching stop on the white shell surface and Officer Prence jumped out, spotted Jon, and said, "Hey. What are you doing here?"

"I'm working here with Mr. Wentzell. What's going on?"

"Don't know yet. Don't leave. What was your name?"

"Jon. Jon Megquire."

"Right. Don't leave."

Jon kept moving toward the front of the house, following Prence's route to the front door. He turned as he heard another siren coming up the Point and saw it was an ambulance.

Prence had disappeared into the house. The ambulance slid to a stop behind the police cruiser. The EMTs jumped out, grabbed their bags, and scrambled to the front door. "What's going on?" Jon threw the question at them but they didn't notice.

As the EMTs disappeared, Jon wondered what he was

supposed to do. He had no role in this family crisis. He didn't know why Prence was there, but he didn't know anything about police or emergency procedures. Maybe the medicos and the police always came when the operator was told it was an emergency. But maybe it was some sort of criminal behavior. Maybe it was nothing. He started walking back toward his car when the HVAC contractor, Frank, pulled into the driveway.

Frank climbed out of his truck. "What the hell is going on now?"

"Don't know," Jon said. "They haven't told me anything. A lot of shouting and running around. The police are here."

"I guessed that," Frank said. "Where's Ace?"

"Don't know. Haven't seen him." He looked at the older man. "Should we just ignore all this?"

"Yup," Frank said. "Their business until they make it our business."

"Anything I should do?"

"Nope. What would Ace have you do? Do that."

Frank shuffled off toward the back of the house.

Jon shoved his hands in his pockets, and his mother popped into his mind. She had always advised him to have a book handy for moments like this because life was full of moments of waiting, and reading was a good way to engage your mind while you're waiting for something to happen, no matter what it was. But it would have been weird to sit down here and start reading a book and, unlike his mother, he didn't carry a massive handbag where he could have stashed a book. And besides that, guys on construction sites or baseball fields thought that guys who carried books around with them all the time were strange.

If he'd had a cup of coffee, he could have stood there looking wise, sipping the coffee. But he didn't have a cup of coffee. He didn't smoke, so he couldn't puff on a cigarette or a pipe and look like he was considering the meaning of life. He didn't have a camera to capture early-morning pictures. He didn't have a newspaper or a notebook. He didn't have any . . . props to provide a purpose for that moment in his life.

He pushed the shells around in the driveway with his foot. This was Limbo, uncertainty, waiting, an unfilled and undefined block of time that seemingly couldn't be moved or replaced with something meaningful. Unlike waiting for a bus or the results of a medical procedure, there didn't appear to be a specific event that would end this void. It was like standing at a fork in the road and waiting for a wizard to tell him which path to take and knowing that wizards are not real. Finally, he said to himself, "This is crazy. I've got to do something."

He stood at the front door for a moment with his hand on the knob, turned it, and walked into the entry of the house. He closed the door quietly. It was the first time he had been in the front part of the house, and he stood for a moment, getting his bearings, meeting the building. The space was grand, solid and secure. A place of substance. The large black-and-white tiles of the entry centered an array of doorways. The stairs spiraled up to the light from the windows on the landing sparkling off the crystal chandelier.

He listened. A clock ticked. In the distance he heard voices. "Hello!" he called out just because it seemed like the thing to do. If he were a burglar, he wouldn't be hailing the household! He followed the sounds through a doorway and down a hall past a library and into a dining room where the French doors opened out onto the patio by the pool. He turned in surprise at the sound of feet running up behind him. A boy glared up at him.

"Who are you?" the boy demanded.

"Uhm. My name's Jon. I'm working on your house."

"Oh," the boy replied and pushed past him and out onto the patio. "I want breakfast and no one's around."

"Sounds like they might be outside." The boy ran toward the doors to the patio with Jon following.

The boy had stopped in front of the pool house by a woman who was insisting that someone, "Do something!" The man who had identified himself as Mr. Scoles when Jon had been digging the foundation was standing with his arms crossed.

"Auntie Bryce, I'm hungry," the boy insisted. "Where's Mommy?"

There was no sign of Prence or the EMTs.

Scoles ignored the boy and turned toward Jon and demanded, "What are you doing here?"

"I'm working with Mr. Wentzell," Jon replied.

"Here? Now?" Scoles looked around as though searching for Ace or construction activity. "Well, he's certainly not here, is he?"

"No. I didn't mean here. I didn't mean I was working with him in this part of the house."

"Well, go find him then!"

"I don't believe he's in the house, sir," Jon replied. "I wanted to see if there was anything I could do."

"No, there is nothing you can do!" Scoles blasted.

Jon thought Scoles seemed unnecessarily annoyed or nervous. Maybe that was just the way Scoles was – the evil wizard sending Jon back to Limbo. But Jon didn't want to be considered *help*, an object to be swept aside. He had a right to know what was going on and internally he heard himself asking before he actually heard the words coming out of his mouth: "Can you tell me what is going on?"

"No!"

Another man whom Jon recognized as Brian Reese came out of the pool house holding his head. "She's dead!" he puffed. "She's really dead. I didn't believe it. I still don't believe it. I mean we were just talking to her, having dinner with her. And now she's dead."

"Shht!" Scoles hissed. "Your son needs his mother, Brian. He shouldn't see this."

Reese looked around in confusion. "What?"

"Here. Your son needs attention. Wants you. Wants breakfast. Wants something. Take your son, Brian. Get Audrey to mind her children! Don't do this in front of outsiders." He looked back at Jon.

"I'll go find Mr. Wentzell," Jon said turning back to the house.

"You do that," Scoles replied.

Dead? Jon thought. Who's dead? Seemed logical that it wasn't either man's wife so it had to be Mrs. Salsberg! Jesus! As Jon walked back through the house, oddly he wondered who would inherit all of this. He imagined that the lawyers would have a field day sorting through all the family layers of possession and greed. That was the trouble with owning a lot of stuff!

When he emerged into daylight, he saw Ace's truck pull up. Ace jumped out, saw Jon, and asked, "What's going on? What were you doing in there?"

"Somebody died," Jon said.

"What? What do you mean, 'Somebody died'? Who died?"

"Don't know," Jon answered. "They wouldn't tell me."

"How? Was it Mrs. Salsberg?"

"Don't know. They wouldn't tell me. Officer Prence is here and so are the EMTs. But no one told me anything."

Ace looked at him and then at the front door of the house. "You probably shouldn't have been in there. Whatever is going on is not our business. You better get out of here. You're going to be in the way and we won't get anything done here today anyway. Family won't want us making noise. Shalala here?"

"He is."

"I'll tell him to wrap it up too."

"Officer Prence asked me to stick around."

"Why?"

"I don't know," Jon said. "But that's what he said."

"All right, but get your car out of the way."

"Right," Jon said.

He weaved his way between the vehicles in the driveway and got into Maybellene. The inside of the car was his space, sovereign territory. He jockeyed her around and into an out-of-the-way spot, kept the car running, and turned on the radio – waiting for the time wizard again.

He hadn't found a good station on the Cape yet. WCIB in Falmouth played some easy listening stuff like "Muskrat Love" by the Captain and Tennille, which drove him crazy. WQRC in Barnstable didn't appeal to him either, but it gave him some of the local news and weather. There were a lot of old people living on the Cape. Maybe what his mother called schmaltz was their kind of music.

Someone slapped the top of the car. Officer Prence was peering in the window.

Jon extracted himself and stood in front of the policeman. "All right. What are you doing here?" Prence asked.

"Um, working on the house. With Mr. Wentzell," Jon replied.

"Okay. When did you get here?"

"About seven-thirty or so, I guess. The usual time."

Prence was writing this down in a little notebook. He looked skeptical. "What were you doing outside when I arrived?"

"Waiting for Mr. Wentzell. I didn't know what he wanted me to do next."

"Uh huh. Did you see anyone?"

Jon looked at him. "Like who? Is this a crime? Who died? No, I didn't see anyone until you arrived."

Jon felt Prence scan him, from his sneakers to his T-shirt to his messy, reddish hair and back to his eyes. He found it unnerving, like the man was trying to pull out his soul. They stood facing each other, eye to eye. Prence had almost thirty pounds on Jon but Jon was an athlete—solid and in shape. His shoulders stretched his shirt. Prence's uniform showed his gut. Jon wondered how much crime there ever was in a small, exclusive town like Tilley.

"Can't say," Prence said finally. "Let me ask you again: did you see anyone?"

"No," Jon replied. "I was just waiting."

"Jon, right?"

"Yes. Without the 'h'."

"What?"

"Jon Megquire. Without the 'h'. And Megquire with a 'q'."

"Maybe you better write it down. And put your home address on there too. You guys float in and out of here. You're in Tilley for the baseball, right?"

Jon wrote his contact information into Prence's little notebook.

"You like my daughter?"

Jon was surprised. "No," he said. "Just met her."

"You don't like her?"

"No, that's not what I meant. I mean yes . . . no. I mean we just met. Talked for a couple of minutes. Don't know her."

Jon felt like Prence was doing the policeman's mind probe thing again.

"Okay," Prence said, closing his notebook and turning away.

"So, what did happen?" Jon asked.

"Woman died. Mrs. Salsberg."

"Mrs. Salsberg? Wow! Was she sick? Oh, wow."

Ace came back out of the house. He nodded to Officer Prence as they passed each other. "Prence through with you?" he asked Jon.

"I guess."

"We'll just have to get out of here when they get . . . the body out. Life does go on, but we have to show some respect," Ace said.

"What happened?" Jon asked.

"She died. Don't know why yet. During the night." Ace shrugged. "She wasn't all that young. From what I understand she led a pretty hard life."

"This life doesn't look all that hard to me."

"No. But you can't always tell a book by the cover or a person by the house they live in or the car they drive." He looked over at Maybellene. "They obviously don't want us banging and sawing at this point. We'll have to wait. When this dust settles here, head over to the Thompson's. That's where I was this morning."

Ace gave Jon the address and some basic directions. Eventually the EMTs brought Faith Salsberg's body out on a stretcher and efficiently inserted it into the ambulance, slammed the doors, got into the cab, and backed down the driveway, lights flashing.

Members of the family stood around the front door, watching. Jon noticed that Scoles stood off to one side with his hands thrust deeply into his pockets. Reese wiped his eyes, and a woman, Jon assumed to be his wife, had her arm around his waist.

Prence got back into his police car and followed the ambulance down the driveway.

Ace walked over and shook Scoles' hand. "Sorry for your loss," he said.

"We'll contact you," Scoles replied. "We need to get this wrapped up."

"Ah. Certainly." Ace looked puzzled.

"We need Faith's project . . . Mrs. Salsberg's project wrapped up. How soon can you be finished?"

Ace was surprised. "I thought you would like us to stop. At least for now."

"Be back on Monday. Get it done."

"Certainly, Mr. Scoles."

Ace waved to Jon to be on his way.

Jon left Casa Grande, trying to keep the directions Ace had given him straight. It was a small town. How lost could he get?

Most of the morning had slipped by when Jon got to the Thompson's job site. The house was a world apart from Casa Grande. It was not on an exclusive street, and it didn't have massive neighbors or fancy landscaping. Ace had called it a ranch, although Jon didn't know how the term fit the design. It was probably a label that some salesman had come up with to sell blocks of houses in a development, houses that were crammed next to each other with their living room windows looking into their neighbor's kitchen. The term "ranch" gave it a wide-open-spaces brand like those streets named "Waterview Lane" that had no water anywhere near them. It was just a one-story rectangular box. The house did have a limited water view of a communal pond and was larger than it appeared to be from the front, which included just the entrance to the garage and the long porch, shielding the front door. In the back of the house, the living room had wide windows that looked down into a dell by a pond, and the house dropped down to a walk-out basement and an old swimming pool surrounded by a flagstone patio.

Ace had told Jon that the house had been an uninsulated summer cottage. The interior walls were open to the framing. Ace had been hired to winterize the house so it could be lived in year-round when the Thompsons retired. Jon wandered through the empty rooms smelling the damp chill of the spaces, imagining the sounds of family birthdays and summer vacations. Working with Ace had begun to sensitize him to the "bones" of the building. The exposed framing allowed Jon to better understand the skeleton, the pieces that held it up, kept it from blowing down in the wind.

In the basement, he looked up at the ceiling and saw the underside of the floor boards and the big joists that ran from one side to the other. Wires and copper pipes ran between them. In a corner rested a small plastic truck some child had left behind. Up on the top of the concrete block foundation wall was a gallon can of pink wall paint. The old hot air heating system and rusting ductwork ran under the basement ceiling. There was a squat metal box that sparked Jon's curiosity. He bent down and read the label on the control panel. Pool heater. Why did people need pool heaters in this climate?

Jon felt as though he was intruding on private memories,

trespassing, expecting someone to yell at him to get the fuck out of there! And yet, in a sense, he felt deputized.

Coming back out of the dim chill of the basement, shielding his eyes from the glare, Jon saw a couple of Ace's crew stripping the shingles and shoveling them down the roof. It was a messy job but not particularly strenuous because of the low slope of the single-story house. Jon watched the crew move around with ease.

"Hey!" he called.

The roofers stopped and looked down at him.

"Yeah? Can we help you?"

"I'm Jon." That didn't seem to register with the men standing on the roof. "Ace sent me over."

"Oh, yeah. The summer help. The baseball player."

"What do you want me to do?"

"Grab that shovel and get your ass up here."

It was awkward climbing the ladder carrying the square blade shovel. At the edge of the roof, Jon paused and threw the shovel up on to the roof decking where it skidded back down toward the edge. He eyed the roof surface with suspicion, assuming the loose shingle fragments and layer of light gravel dust would make it slippery. Leaning forward, he climbed to the top of the ladder and eased himself onto the roof on his hands and knees, feeling the heat of the sun-warmed surface and the fine gravel cutting into his skin. Pausing occasionally to drag the shovel, he scuttled up to the ridge of the roof on his hands and knees and sat there surveying the neighborhood.

Standing casually and holding his shovel like a rifle, the man who had called out to him when he was on the ground grinned and said, "I'm Billy, Billy Badavas and this is Ryan James."

Jon considered standing and shaking hands but it seemed more than a bit awkward at that particular moment.

Badavas grinned. "First roof?"

Jon grinned back holding the roughness of the ridge in one hand and the smooth, bat-like handle of the shovel in the other.

"You'll get used to it. But you can't get anything done sitting on your ass!"

Jon swung himself around until he had one foot on either side of the ridge, worked himself onto his hands and knees, and then gradually eased himself up until he was standing. He leaned down and picked up the shovel.

"Sometime today would be nice," Badavas said.

Jon waddled across the ridge of the roof and then stepped onto the slope, feeling for his footing. Where the men had been working, he saw the bare wood of the roof decking, blackened in places from the tar paper that had formed the first layer of protection for the house.

Badavas showed him how to stand with his back toward the edge of the roof and thrust the blade of the shovel under the shingles and rip them off, pushing them to the sides so they wouldn't slide down and hit his feet. The process made a satisfactory, crunching feel as the shingles pulled up and broke apart, nails squealing as they pulled out of the decking. He developed a swinging rhythm as he worked, the asphalt pieces sliding down behind him to slap the ground below. He began to forget he was standing on a roof until he had worked down to the last couple of shingle courses at the edge of the roof with not enough room to thrust the shovel.

Badavas sent him over to the next section of the roof. Jon walked up to the ridge and stepped onto the steeper section overhanging the back of the house. For a moment his stomach registered the drop, but the roof was wide enough that the height wasn't imminent. He started pushing his shovel under the shingles, prying them off and sliding them down. Step, step, swing, crunch, hiss. Step, step, swing, crunch, hiss. There was a dance step to it, a productive, non-thinking motion that caused him to forget about the events earlier in the day, where he was standing, and the increasing heat of the roof surface. Until his stomach told him it was time to eat.

"I gotta go. Practice!" he called to the other men who

nodded at him. He walked down toward the ladder at the edge where he sat down. He tossed the shovel onto the lawn, turned around, and felt for the rungs tentatively with his left foot. For a moment he wondered if the ladder was still there, finally found a solid purchase with his foot, and stepped down until he could get both hands on the tops of the side rails. He looked across the roof at the two men, expecting them to be watching him, but they couldn't have cared less.

He backed Maybellene down the driveway, turned on the radio, and turned up "*My Sharona*," accompanying the rhythm of the drums with both hands. He wove through the neighborhoods and the summer cottages and back onto the bustle of Route 28.

Stark's Homemade Ice Cream was close enough to the Tilley ball field that it essentially served as a concession stand for the games. It was a local landmark — a single-story white shingled building with overhanging porch roofs, open only in the summer. It had two windows in front — one for ordering and one for pickup — covered by sliding insect screens. The kitchen was populated by a man who was probably the owner and three college age girls, one at the "Place Order Here" window, one at the pickup window, and one that shuttled between them. There was a massive menu on the front of the building listing all the various combinations of burgers, fries, chicken, drinks, and ice cream flavors.

Jon peered through the insect screening at the "Place Order Here" girl and smiled.

"Yup?" she asked, ruminating her gum and looking down at the pad in front of her.

Jon order two burgers and fries and a milkshake.

"Two patties!" she yelled. "That it?" she asked Jon.

"I got a game this afternoon," Jon explained.

"Good for you. Two thirty-five." She snapped her gum and slid up the screen to accept his money.

He slid a five-dollar bill under the screen. She pushed his change back to him the same way. "Next," she said.

He noticed Coach Russell at the pickup window. "Hey, Coach."

"Hello, Jon. Ready for the game?"

"I was born ready," Jon said with a smile.

"I hope you don't eat like this every day."

"Hey, it's food," Jon replied. "That's what counts."

"You have to take care of your body if you're going to play in the bigs."

"You went that route, didn't you?"

"I had my shot. Got to play in the minors with Juan Marichal and Philipe Alou for the Springfield Giants. Good times. But life caught up to me." He looked at Jon, seemed to remember how young he was, and looked back to the "Pickup" window. "You got to take advantage of opportunities. People always think, 'If I don't get it this time, I'll get it next time.' But life doesn't work that way. You find yourself wallowing in a hole, surrounded by bills, and the bus has gonc on without you."

Jon didn't know what to say. He just wanted to eat his lunch without some sort of confessional conversation with the coach.

"You want to remember that, Jon. The Cape Cod League is an important opportunity for you. It can open up a world to play in the major leagues, and not too many people get that opportunity."

"Number forty-three!"

"That's me," the coach said, looking down at his receipt. "You're working with Ace Wentzell, aren't you?" he asked, as he gathered his food.

Jon nodded and emitted the briefest "Yes" that sounded more like a hiss.

"Did you hear about Mrs. Salsberg?"

"I was there. This morning," Jon replied.

"What did they tell you?"

"Not much."

"Did they tell you how she died?"

"No. I don't think they know, do they? How did you hear about it?"

"Number forty-four!" the girl yelled.

Jon stepped up to the window and pulled his tray out. He walked with the coach to a table. A car pulled into the parking lot and a family piled out. A little girl with a bow in her hair shouted, "I want peppermint stick!"

"Food before ice cream," her mother advised.

Jon and the coach dropped their trays on a table in a distant corner. "It's a small town and the Salsbergs are a thing here. Mr. Salsberg, Christopher, supported the Longliners. The field's named after him. Their money is important to all of us."

Jon swallowed his first burger and took a pull on his shake.

The coach looked at him and then shrugged. "She seemed in pretty good health when I saw her. I guess that's how it happens, right? You're fine and then you're dead."

Jon was distracted by the boy from the *peppermint stick* family who had his hands thrust in his pockets. "I don't want to eat here again," he said. "We ate here yesterday."

"It's quick," his mother explained.

Family vacation, Jon thought. Lovely.

"You have a girl?"

"Not really," Jon replied. "There is a girl I grew up with. Back home. But we're mainly friends."

"I don't want to pry," the coach said. "Just want to make sure you can focus on the team and the game, you know? Not get distracted. Things like girls. And Mrs. Salsberg . . . dying. Stuff like that can make you lose focus."

He leaned toward Jon. "And you seem unfocused." He waved his hands around, indicating a cloud or a void. "Like you don't really know what you want. Like you don't have passion! You know: the Passion! For the game. You have to find it, Jon. You have to find it. If you don't . . . " he leaned back in his seat, "if you don't, you'll just be playing a game. Huh? It's not a game. Not something to play with. I want to see you focus!"

Jon slurped the last of his milkshake. "Okay, Coach." Everybody's a shrink, Jon thought. Filled to the brim with how to live your life.

~

JON GUESSED THAT FOR SOME PEOPLE BASEBALL WAS THEIR LIFE. It's what they did every day. It's what they worked at. It was their vocation. For someone like Coach Russell, it was a job. Jon knew he managed a supermarket. He had had a serious dream of becoming a professional baseball player. Professional. Maybe that was the defining word. Was he a professional supermarket manager? Did he have a dream of becoming a vice president or maybe even president of the supermarket chain? Jon laughed at the thought. He couldn't see Coach Russell sitting in an office pushing papers around, ordering his secretary to get him coffee. Nope. Wouldn't happen.

So where was the line between life and games? And who drew the line? Who was the authority? Mrs. Salsberg had been leading her life, living her routine. And now she was dead. The plug was pulled. Her lights were out. He didn't know anything about her life, about what she had done, about where she had come from, and certainly not about her dreams for the future. Her husband, Christopher Salsberg, was dead too, and his money had brought this baseball team to life. Maybe the line was money. If you got paid, you became a professional. Requirement number one for getting serious about life: you got paid to do whatever it was you were doing.

And if you got enough money to do what you were doing, it became really serious and inscribed the line between life and a game or a hobby. You don't get paid for a hobby. You don't get paid to have fun. Jon had that ingrained into the genetics of his life. The line was drawn by money and being serious. "Get serious about your homework." "This isn't a game, you know. Be serious. Grow up!" If that was what life was all about, then they weren't selling it well!

Other players—even the word implied a lack of seriousness —took playing in the Cape Cod Baseball League very seriously. They worked out in the weight room, ran for miles, ate well, stressed about their batting averages and their field skills. They wanted to win personally and as a team to impress the scouts so they could get drafted and get paid money, enough money to draw the line. Jon had read Somerset Maugham's novel *The Razor's Edge* and understood the balance. Either side was failure. Success was staying on the edge.

But now it was time to play ball. Now was not the time for deep thoughts about death and money. Life and baseball didn't wait until you were ready for it. The field announcer slapped Jon back to reality by asking the crowd for a moment of silence for Faith Salsberg whose family had been so important for the team and the field.

As the game evolved, Harry Dupin, the Longliner's pitcher was getting behind on the batters. He didn't seem to have control of his curve ball, which usually danced in front of the batter's eyes, which was why he had acquired the nickname Hoppin Dupin. Dupin's lack of control this afternoon was reflected by the score. The Longliners got behind Orleans by three runs in the sixth inning with the bases loaded.

The coach finally jumped up and strode out to the mound. As the first baseman, Jon joined him and the catcher, trying to calm Dupin down. "Focus!" the coach demanded in a hoarse whisper. "What are you trying to do? Focus! Get your mind in the game. What's the problem?"

"Don't know," Dupin replied, kicking the dirt.

"It's time to be serious. Time to bear down. Take 'em out one at a time. One at a time. That's all. How hard can it be?"

Dupin couldn't hide the "You've got to be fucking kidding"

look on his face as he watched the coach walk back to the dugout.

Jon slapped Dupin on the butt and jogged backward to first base. "Make it hop, Dupin! Make it hop. Let's get this done!"

The Orleans runner on first led off the bag by six feet. He was the Orleans catcher, a big, awkward guy with blond hair and freckles. He glanced toward second base to check the runner ahead of him and back at the first base coach.

"How's your summer been?" Jon asked without looking at the runner.

"What?"

"It's been pretty cool down here. The Cape's great in the summer. The girls? Man! You get connected yet?"

"What?"

SLAP! Dupin zinged a fast ball past the batter into the catcher's mitt.

"When you get a chance, you might want to check that knot in your left shoe."

The runner looked down.

SLAP! Dupin zinged in another fast ball. When the ball came back to him, he spun and powered the ball to Jon who smoothly fielded it and flowed down to catch the leg of the off-balance runner.

"You're out!" yelled the first base umpire.

"No way!" the runner shouted, glaring at the umpire.

"Not even close!" the Orleans coach argued.

The umpire turned away. The runner looked like he was going to debate the issue, but the coach pulled him away. Dupin grinned at Jon. SLAP! Third strike. Two outs and no harm done. The Tilley crowd cheered.

Dupin got the next batter to pop up to the short stop, and the Longliners jogged back toward the bench, slapping the pitcher as they came up beside him. "Yah! That's the way it's done, Hoppin! Let's get it back now!"

The Orleans players tossed the ball around the infield while the pitcher warmed up. Jon stood in the on-deck circle swinging a couple of bats, getting used to the weight, feeling the cold smoothness of the metal. He scanned the field, taking in the early summer green, the colors of the crowd, the blue of the sky. It was a great place to play. There was a summer joy in the atmosphere.

Jon noticed Lisa Prence hanging out with some friends. Probably not good to get involved with a cop's daughter, he thought, and he also reminded himself of his thoughts about focusing. But she was intriguing. He looked up behind her toward the parking lot, wondering if her father followed her around. She seemed independent, and he challenged himself to not let her father bother him.

The Tilley batter dropped a single into short center field, and Jon was up. The catcher said, "That your girl? The one you were talking about?"

Jon peered through the slats in the catcher's mask trying to see the eyes. He glanced over to where Lisa was standing. "Nice, isn't she?"

Jon scuffed up the dirt beside home plate, checked the runner's lead off first, then concentrated on the pitcher. The caliber of the pitching in the Cape League was close to major league speed and control. The Orleans pitcher was known as one of their best. Jon watched his arm, watched him exchange signals with the catcher. Jon settled into his stance - legs spread, weight on his back foot, bat high in the air waving, in motion ready to slice through the strike zone, contact the ball and instantly reverse its direction. A snap of the fingers. A blink of an eye. A split second of time. An almost incomparable change in the fabric of history, similar to pulling the trigger of a gun.

The pitcher's arm cocked back. There was no time for a conscious decision between whether to swing or not to swing. It had to be an unconscious twitch. The mechanics in Jon's mind had to put together what he knew about the pitcher, the weather, the time of day, the presence of the scouts and the girls in the audience, his family, and his hopes for the future. The players on the field and on the benches watched and waited. So did the coaches. In less time than it took to take a breath and have the air reach his lungs, it was over. A spot zipped by him and into the catcher's mitt. "SSttrrike!"

Jon lowered his bat and stepped back. He kicked the dirt off his shoes. Have to stop thinking, Jon thought. Have to stop thinking about Lisa, dead bodies, major league scouts, sunset on Cape Cod, Maybellene. He shook his head as if he could shake out the fairy dust of his monkey mind, and he stepped back into the batter's box, raised his bat, and stared at the pitcher.

Once again, the challenge developed as the pitcher responded to the catcher's signals. The pitcher made eye contact with Jon. Suddenly the pitcher swung his head toward first base, spun his body to his left, and fired a shot to the first baseman. The runner safely scampered back.

Jon dropped his bat off his shoulder again and stepped one foot out of the box. The pitcher caught the throwback from the first baseman and stepped to the back of the pitching mound. He rubbed the ball with both hands and moved back into position.

Jon reset, lifting and waving the bat in the air. He tried to let go of everything in his mind . . . to be one with the ball. As long as the ball was in the pitcher's hand, it belonged to him. When it left his hand, it was free. For the split-second it hit Jon's bat, it belonged to Jon. He could change its direction and send it anywhere in the universe. All of life was reflected and repeated in that simple and instantaneous exchange that was over in a moment. Here it had little substance or meaning. No one was likely to remember this particular game in the town of Tilley on Cape Cod on June 15, 1979. The statistics would make it into some record book. Somebody might look back through the roster of players for that season, but the substance of this particular game on this particular afternoon with this particular pitcher and batter would be gone as fast as the second pitch that flew by Jon as he started thinking about Lisa.

Out of the corner of his eye he detected her staring at him. At least he thought she was. And he shouldn't have been thinking at all and certainly not about a girl in the stands, a girl that he barely knew. Again, he told himself to focus. The challenge was to focus without thinking. And then, as if a magic cloak had been thrown over him, he did stop thinking. The pitcher cocked back and threw the ball. Jon swung the bat, interrupted the ball's trajectory, and sent it over the left field fence — a home run to run home. To run around all the bases. The solid feel of the ball striking the bat was unlike any other feeling. That feeling was the reason he kept playing baseball. It was right without knowing.

He dropped the bat and, grinning, jogged toward first base. As he ran, he became aware of the noise of the crowd. He resisted the urge to wave. He saw the other Longliner runner jogging ahead of him. He touched first base with a dance step, rounded second, touched third, and jogged toward home trying to look serious. He looked into the stands, found Lisa, and touched his cap as if to say, "There! What do you think of that?"

"All right, now!" the coach shouted. "Keep her going!"

But they didn't. They lost to Orleans six to two as the sun set and the fog started rolling in. At the end of the game, the players gathered by first base and threw out cheers and jeers about the day, keeping themselves going, bringing the team together despite the loss, trying to focus on games that hadn't yet happened.

Jon broke away from the team and walked toward the stands, half hoping Lisa would be waiting for him in the gaggle of girls hanging out like groupies. There was no rational reason why she would be. They had barely talked. And he really didn't have a girl back home. Just long-term friends. He was free. Time to play the field . . . to start fresh. Lisa had that freshness. Jesus! His brain was treating people like laundry!

She wasn't waiting for him. Disappointing, perhaps, but not surprising. He saw Dupin in the squash of girls and called out to him, "Hey, Hoppin! Clegg's?"

Dupin nodded and climbed into Maybellene. Jon cranked up "*Y.M.C.A.*" on the radio and spun out of the parking lot. Dupin's knees were crushed into his chest. He worked his big, black eyebrows up and down - Groucho Marx style. "This is not a car for big people," he said. "How do you carry anything in this?"

"Admittedly it's not a truck!" Jon said with a grin. "But it gets me where I want to go."

"What about girls?" Dupin asked. "I mean there's no back seat! There's barely a front seat! Has to be a bench in the front, you know, so the girl can slide over next to you. I mean, this four on the floor stuff is cool, but it's not exactly a lover's car, if you know what I'm saying. You can lure 'em in, but where do you go from there?"

Jon grinned at him. "Hey. It's summer. There's more room outside the car anyway!"

They laughed a knowing, team spirit, boys-together laugh.

CLEGG'S WAS CRAMMED WITH THE AFTER-GAME CROWD. THERE were celebratory shouts of greeting as Jon and Dupin walked in. Dupin was dragged off to settle an argument, leaving Jon alone to contemplate the mysteries of baseball, death, and houses.

And then Lisa stepped up to his table while he was immersed in these thoughts. "Nice hit," she said.

"Oh," he replied. "Thanks." He noticed she was wearing a 'Clegg's Lunch' tee shirt. "Hey, you work here?"

"I do," she said. "Summer job. I'm off shift now, though. Join you?"

"Sure."

"I don't have to. I can leave you to your thoughts."

"No," he stumbled. "No. That's okay. Please." He indicated the other chair. "Want something?"

"You mean to eat?"

"Yuh. Sure. Something like that."

"No. Thanks, though. Nice thought." She looked at him for a few moments. "So, what are you going to do now?"

"What do you mean?" There was something about this girl that kept him off balance in a way he wasn't used to. He wasn't sure where she was leading him.

"Where are you from?" she asked.

"New York. New York State."

"I knew that much from the license plate on your car. Cute car, by the way."

"Thanks."

"Where in New York ? It's a big place."

"Yeah. I know. It is big. About halfway between the city and Albany."

"Small town like this?"

He looked around as though she were referring to their immediate surroundings. "Sort of. No, not really. Different. More trees."

She smiled and he realized that he liked her smile. "You come from a place in New York State with more trees. Interesting. Anything more you care to add? What about your parents?"

So, he told her about Millbrook, New York. He told her about his father working for a hospital group. He told her about going to boarding school. He told her about his sister, the engineer, graduate of Rensselaer.

"Sounds like you're jealous," she said.

"No," he replied. "She's always been the smart one. Getting the great grades. I don't know. Jealous? No. Envious, maybe."

"What about your mother? You told me about your father, but what does your mother do?"

"She died," he said.

"Oh. Oh, I'm sorry."

"No. No, it's all right. Couple of years ago. Here, as a matter of fact. She died here on Cape Cod."

"How?" Lisa asked.

"My parents came up for a wedding and there was some bad stuff in the air at the motel, and it killed her. Made my father pretty sick too."

"Really?" Lisa asked. "Couple of years ago? It wasn't the A1 Motel, was it?"

"I don't remember the name."

"If it was the A1, my father was involved in the investigation. It was carbon monoxide. I remember. Took 'em awhile to figure it out what it was."

"Yah! It seemed to take them forever to find out what it was. I would have thought it would be pretty obvious. But what do I know? She was there and then she was dead. Not supposed to happen that way. Aren't these hotels tested . . . licensed? Somebody screwed up. If they ever found out, they didn't tell us."

"There was a lot of excitement around here. That was your mother, huh? Wow. I'm so sorry, Jon." She reached out and covered his hand with hers.

He was surprised by the understanding in her eyes. It was a connection he hadn't expected to make.

"Wow," she said again and pulled her hand away.

John suddenly felt as though he had sprinted a mile. The overwhelming memories of those days after his mother's death piled on him. The unanswered questions. The face of his father twisted in anguish. He hadn't intended to think about those moments, those hours, those days. Was it the touch of Lisa's hand or the look in her eyes that had pulled them back to the surface? And so he changed the subject and asked her about herself.

"No," she said, not allowing him to dump the melancholy. "I didn't mean to cause you such pain. I didn't know that was your mother. I didn't know."

"It's all right," he replied, ready to move on. "Tell me about yourself."

"Not much to tell," she replied. "Born here. Grew up here. Daughter of a cop."

"But that must be interesting. Does he talk about his work?"

"It's usually pretty quiet around here," she replied looking down at the table.

"But what about murder, like Mrs. Salsberg?"

She looked at him. "Murder? What makes you think it was a murder? Who said anything about murder?"

"No one," he replied. "I'm just saying. The coach was talking about it. Seems kind of suspicious, doesn't it? Does your father talk about his work?"

"No. I haven't seen much of him today. I didn't even know about it. But it is a small town and they–the Salsbergs–are a pretty big deal even though they're summer people. Kids don't go to school here. They just infest us for a few weeks, leave some money behind - like for the remodeling stuff you're working on - and then leave their mess behind for us to clean up.

"Don't get me wrong," she continued, "we like their money . . . and yours. They say it's a big part of the economy. I don't know."

"Man, does that sound stuffy!" Jon said. "'Leave us your money and leave us alone.' Is that it? Where are the Salsbergs from?'

"Some little ritzy place in Pennsylvania," she replied.

"How do you know?"

"Town chatter."

"On the Main Line?"

"What the hell is that?"

"Near Philly. Some of the kids in my boarding school came from there." That sounded pretentious, Jon thought. It was hard to think of Cape Cod as being junky, small town, backwoods, like a country town in New Jersey or Nebraska or Mississippi. Strange the way people paint parts of the country with an economic or sophistication brush. There are class levels within levels—the locals that attended his boarding school were looked upon as 'townies' but they were socially ranked higher than the students at the high-end academies on Cape Cod who were socially ranked higher than the public high school students. Anyone who said the U.S. was a classless society was full of shit. "I suppose they'll take Mrs. Salsberg's body back there."

"I suppose," she said.

"What happens next?"

"About what?" she asked.

"About . . . her? I mean what will your father do next?"

"I haven't got a clue," she replied. "Nothing to do with me."

"I guess," he replied. "How about you? What are you doing tonight? Boyfriend?"

She looked at him. "What are you suggesting? A date?"

"You make it sound so freakin' formal! No, I was just wondering . . . You know, what you are doing. Tonight."

She smiled at him. "Nothin'," she said finally. "No plans."

"What is there to do around here?" he asked, and then realized that put him in the category of not being local. Why did he want to be accepted into her world? It was Friday night and she didn't have any plans? Maybe he was missing something. Maybe he was lonely? He was never going to admit that to himself.

"The usual," she replied. "We are on the same planet as you off-Cape people! We have all the modern conveniences. Food. Electricity. Telephones. Movies."

"Have you seen *Alien* yet? Is it playing around here? I haven't seen it. Some of the guys said it was good."

"No. I haven't seen it. Hey, I think it's playing at the drive-in."

"That would be weird!" he said. "Space movie at the drive-in. Let's do it!"

"We're back to this date thing, right?"

"What have you got against dates? You're not . . . weird or

something, are you?" He wasn't confident that he could ask questions like that.

"What are you implying?"

"Nothing!" he replied.

"Are you saying that since I don't have a boyfriend or a date on a Friday night that I'm maybe an alien myself?" She looked at him with a frown that made him lean back in his seat. Then she gave him a reprieve by smiling. "I'm just pulling your chain."

"You do it well," he replied. "*Alien* at the drive-in it is, then. Want to get something to eat first?"

"This does sound like a date!"

"You're starting to worry me about your classifying everything: on-Cape, off-Cape, dates, not-dates. Do you always have to have categories for stuff?"

"It keeps life organized," she replied. "Helps to know where you stand."

"You'll have to show me how to get to the drive-in. What time are the shows?"

"They have to wait until it gets dark, don't they?"

"That makes sense," he said. "Do you have to call home or anything to let them know what you're doing? I wouldn't want to get stopped by the cops or anything." He felt like everything he said was like stumbling over rocks running down a dark tunnel.

She laughed. "Funny. Very funny. Maybe that's why I don't have a date on a Friday night! Never thought of that! Pick me up at Stark's at seven?"

"You know the movie schedule off the top of your head?"

She shrugged and grinned. "I live here," she replied as she got up and walked away.

A CROWD OF KIDS JOSTLED EACH OTHER UNDER THE LIGHTS AT Stark's when Jon pulled Maybellene into the lot a little before seven o'clock. He didn't see Lisa, so he parked the car and sauntered to the 'order here' window to get a burger.

A young man in a black "No-Nukes" T-shirt slid up beside him

"You baseball?" he challenged.

Jon looked at him. "What?"

"You that baseball player?"

"Which baseball player? I play for the Longliners."

"Thought so," the boy replied. "You have that fancy car."

Jon didn't reply. The boy was a couple of inches shorter than Jon. Besides the T-shirt, he wore shorts and Keds with no socks. His unkempt hair hung down around his shoulders. He pushed it away from his empty, grey-green eyes.

"You going out with Lisa? Going to take her to the movies?"

"Who *are* you?" Jon asked.

"I am who I am," No-Nukes replied.

Jon scanned the people in the parking lot.

"Hey!" the boy said. "Watch yourself. Know what I mean? You do know her father's a cop. Right?" And he winked lasciviously and disappeared into the surrounding darkness.

Jon shook his head. "Great," he muttered. He scanned the parking lot again. Maybe she got the time wrong. Maybe her father wouldn't let her out. Maybe he had the wrong Stark's. The kid in the Keds was probably right. This was a mistake.

"Number thirty-seven!" the girl called from the pickup window. Jon looked at his ticket. He walked up to the window, picked up his food, turned, and there was Lisa as though she had popped in from another dimension. He impulsively grinned as he noticed that she had changed from what she had been wearing earlier. Her loose fitting, silky shirt was untucked at the waist of her cut-off jeans. He couldn't help but think about her body as the air flowed up inside the fabric. Her lustrous straight, brown hair flowed down over one eye, and she casually pushed it back behind her ear. He liked the shape of her body, the intensity of her eyes, and the curl of her lips, and he thought, "Wow!"

"You can get food at the drive-in, you know," she said.

"I was hungry," he replied. Why did it seem as though he always needed to defend himself to her? "Want something?"

"I'll wait."

They slid into a picnic table, opposite each other.

The table was painted red and had initials and hearts carved into the surface. There was a partially filled ashtray at the end. The table wobbled as she dropped on the bench seat. "So," she said, "where are the ducks?"

He looked at her. "What?"

"Where are the ducks?"

"What ducks?"

"Just trying to make conversation," she said. "I like saying stuff like that. Keeps people awake. Not what they expect. What kind of music do you listen to?"

He swallowed a bite of burger.

"All sorts. I have a cassette player in the car."

"I'm sure you do. No eight-track for you. Did you ever have one of those? Probably would take up too much room in that car."

"Nope," he replied. "Maybellene's my first car."

"Why Maybellene?"

"Oh, I just like the name, you know. Chuck Berry. 'Can't you be true?' Ooh, ooh, ooh."

She smiled. "Nice! Better stick with baseball!"

"Where's the drive-in?"

"I'll show you," she said, getting up from the table. "Coming?"

"You bet," he replied, crumpling the burger paper and throwing it in the trash.

They walked side by side to the car, she around the back to the passenger side, he reaching down to the driver's door looking across at her and then dropping into the seat. He reveled in the instant purr as he turned the key. The gravel crunched under the tires as he pulled through the lot and up to the asphalt surface of the road.

"Left," she said. Jon could smell her perfume when she pointed.

Small talk seemed to stick in his throat. "What do you know about the Salsbergs?" he blurted out.

"Why?" she asked.

"Oh, I don't know. All that money."

"I guess. Take the next right."

They didn't say anything for a couple of minutes. "You probably don't get a lot of crime around here, do you? Just can't imagine a lot of bad things happening in a place like this."

"We like it that way."

"I don't know. What's your father doing about Mrs. Salsberg? Investigating? Is it like what happens on TV?"

"Listen, Jon," she said, "you have to get my father out of your head."

He glanced over at her. "No. He's not in my head. No. I was just thinking, you know."

She put her left hand on his right hand as it rested on the shift lever. "You have to get him out of your head."

Startled by her touch, he jounced the car slightly off line and back and attempted to recover his cool. "He's not in my head! But if it was a murder . . . if someone really did kill her, it would be weird . . . working in a murdered woman's house! That's all. End of story."

He felt her looking at him again and it confused him. "All right," he said, "enough about that. Where are we going?"

"Follow those cars," she pointed to the cars ahead of them turning into a driveway. Another whiff of perfume.

The line of cars slowly snaked down the dirt road to the ticket booth. The giant screen loomed ahead.

"Two," Jon said to the woman in the booth.

"Yeah?" she replied looking down at the little car. "Nobody in the trunk?"

Jon looked back as though to refresh his memory about the size of Maybellene's trunk. "Not since the last time I looked."

"No alcohol. Yellow tickets park next to the yellow poles. You gotta wear shoes at all times. No grills, fireworks, or sparklers. Is that understood? Read the rest of the rules yourself. Here are your tickets." She snapped her gum. "Park near the front. That car's *small*."

"Yes, ma'am," Jon replied as he pulled into the parking lot. There were cars and pickup trucks scattered by the posts that held the speakers. "Yellow ticket - yellow pole," he said. He turned the car into a spot with no one on either side and eased up beside the speaker post. The lot was graded so headlights angled toward the screen.

Lisa lifted the speaker out of its cradle and hooked it on her window. He wanted to tell her to be careful and not scratch the car, but he held his tongue.

"Did you want something to eat?" he asked. "We should probably have done that first."

"I can still get out," she replied opening her door.

He held his breath while he watched her climb out around the pole, leaving the speaker attached to the window.

"Shit," he muttered to himself, worrying about Maybellene again. He pushed the thoughts away as Lisa stood waiting for him. He took her hand and they walked over to the bright lights that surrounded the *Snack Bar!* Red and blue neon strips ran around the overhanging edge of the roof of the white-shingled building. Large posters hailing coming features were illuminated in their frames. Animated drawings of grinning and dancing popcorn boxes, drink cups, and hot dogs ornamented the walls. Jon held the glass door open for Lisa.

Jon was leery about having food in his car. He envisioned popcorn kernels under the seats and Coke stuck to the carpet. Had to be cool. Had to be loose. Those were old-person thoughts, thoughts his father might think, and he had to get his father . . . and Lisa's . . . out of his head.

Standing in front of the candy counter he asked, "Popcorn?"

The yellow light from behind the glass seemed to make her glow while she was grinning at the goodies and his thoughts seemed to explode like the corn kernels in heated air. She was young but oh, so mature. Innocent but with a salty, buttery topping. Independent but under his protection. And then she looked up at him with a simple smile and said, "Yes," and he almost wet his pants.

He bought a large container of popcorn for them to share. And grabbed a handful of napkins. He wondered how they were going to deal with cups of Coke.

Walking back to Maybellene through the fading light he held her hand. More cars had pulled into the lot. A buzz of background movie music rattled through the speakers on the posts. The air was perfumed by popcorn and car exhaust and a salty breeze. And Lisa's perfume.

Lisa was just shutting her door when a black Chevy Nova pulled into the slot beside them. The long-haired kid in the No-Nukes T-shirt leaned out the front window and yelled, "Hey, Baseball!"

"Hey, Baseball!" the kid yelled again. "You're Mr. Baseball!"

Jon smiled acknowledgement, said nothing, and dropped into the driver's seat.

The kid in the Nova turned to his friends and they all started laughing. Jon asked Lisa if she knew them. "Wise-ass kids from High School," she replied, sucking on the straw from her Coke.

"Hey, Lisa, slumming it tonight? Didn't know you hung out with summer people. You know she's underage right, Baseball?"

"Knock it off, Jimmy," Lisa shouted back. "Grow up!"

Jimmy said something to his friends in the Nova, and they all laughed.

The lot lights dimmed and trailers for coming attractions flickered across the big screen. "Rocky 2," "The In-laws," and "The Prophecy."

"Why don't they just leave things alone?" Lisa asked. "Why

do they have to make sequels? Rocky was okay. Suppose they'll make sequels to this movie too."

"I guess," Jon replied through a mouthful of popcorn. But his thoughts were not on movie sequels. His thoughts were on the warm body beside him. He settled back in his seat and thought about some of the things his friends had said about the awkwardness of the Midget as a dating car. It was designed to be driven, not for lounging. The dashboard offered little space to rest drink cups on, and if he wanted to put his arm around Lisa the shift lever and the handbrake were in the way. The steering wheel was large and confined his legs to their driving positions. And it was great to have the top down to enjoy the night air and see the stars, but it didn't afford privacy. In his peripheral vision, he could sense the boys in the Nova watching them. Probably should have put the top up, but it wouldn't be cool to do that now. Maybe it would start to rain. He should just do whatever he wanted. He was a rising star, a college graduate, older than they were. But there was still the problem of what to do with the drinks and the popcorn.

The opening frames of *Alien* began blossoming in front of them. The camera panned across the starlit universe as the credits rolled and the five letters of the title gradually formed across the top. Dark, eerie space music rattled through the little speaker. Images of the inside of the sleeping spaceship flickered on the screen in breath-holding silence. Jon felt Lisa inadvertently jerk when the computers came to life and equipment began to click and whirr when no one was moving on this vast space ship.

Lisa leaned her head against his shoulder. Her touch made him wish for a moment that he was on the front seat of the family station wagon. He had the urge to toss the containers out of the car. He needed to put his arm around Lisa. In his attempt to chug down the Coke he managed to dribble some of it down his shirt. Lisa noticed and laughed at an inopportune moment of the movie. The boys in the Nova "Shshshsh'd!" She used a napkin to dab the front of his shirt.

"Don't worry about it," he whispered. He took the opportunity to put his Coke cup into the virtually empty popcorn bucket, nodded at her cup questioningly, took it from her, and put it in the bucket as well. He quietly opened his door and placed the bucket on the ground. The light on the dashboard obediently illuminated the interior.

"Will you two settle down?" Jimmy hissed. "Jesus Christ! We're trying to watch a movie!"

Jon dropped the bucket and thumped the door closed, the dashboard light went out, and now his hands were clear, but buttery and he thought of the silky fabric of Lisa's shirt. He noticed a napkin lying on Lisa's lap where the edge of her shorts met the tan skin of her legs. He reached for it.

She slapped down on his hand. "No," she hissed.

"Just the napkin," he protested. "Butter on my hands!"

"Oh," she said, handing him the napkin.

As the menace of the narrative spread out before them grew, building up with the spider web of the music, they settled into their seats, and Jon was carried away by the story, losing himself in the plot. Almost without thinking he managed to get his right arm around her shoulders. The tension in the tale increased, and Lisa gripped his left hand and pulled it toward her belly, twisting his body. He felt the warmth of her head on his shoulder. Paying attention to the images on the screen was increasingly difficult. And when the Alien's head erupted from the spaceman's chest, he felt the whole car rock.

"Hey!" he exploded and pulled away from Lisa. "What the hell?"

"Giving birth, love birds?" Jimmy asked. "The Midget was about to start rockin' and rollin'! Thought we'd help it along."

Someone yelled from another car, "Hey! Shut up!"

The boys from the Nova chuckled, slapped each other on the back, then scuttled off in the direction of the snack bar.

Jon turned to Lisa and asked, "You okay?" He struggled to read the expression on her face. Anger? Frustration? Women are so hard to read, he thought. What did she want?

"You can't take the ducks out of the pond at the farm," she said with a grin.

"What?"

"Forget about them. Where were we?" and she pulled his arm back around her shoulders. Jon tried to turn his attention back to the actions on the screen. He fought to suspend the reality of the present and Lisa's touch and wondered when the jokers might return and what else they might do.

Alien is not the kind of movie that anyone could sit motionless in the confined space of the little car and coldly observe the violence on the screen. Jon was sucked back into the unreality on the screen as he empathized with the terror of the handful of crew members as they sought to eliminate the threat to their lives, to deal with the traitorous mindset of the people who had coldly subjected them to death and the eternal isolation of boundless space. Reflecting those emotions, Jon felt Lisa grabbing his arm, squeezing his hand, seeking comfort and protection, turning her eyes away at times of exceptional stress, burying her head in Jon's shoulder. The explosive size and grotesque ugliness of the alien queen's oozing mouth and eyeless head, had Jon turning away from the screen as well, and the real, physical contact of Lisa broke through the fiction displayed in front of him and in his head. Their lips met. And like the prince kissing Sleeping Beauty, the illusions surrounding him became mere noise. Lisa's lips became reality, breaking him away from the fictional horror. He felt her pulse through his lips. His mind lost its analytical control for a moment, and suddenly it was over and they pulled back and looked at each other breathing heavily.

A bubble of pregnant silence dropped into the car. Emotions raging all around. "Wow!" Lisa whispered, leaning back toward him with a smile.

"Yeah," Jon grinned. "Guess we got carried away." He found it very hard to reestablish his empathy for the struggling characters on the screen. Their words seemed to just be, "Blah, blah, blah . . ." The music was just annoying now.

And when the movie ended, they sat for a moment while the credits rolled up the screen, car headlights flashed on, and Lisa lifted the speaker off the door and returned it to its cradle. Jon started Maybellene and began backing up.

The blare of a car horn snapped him out of his abstraction, and he slammed on the brakes. The black Nova blocked Jon's way out.

"Hey! Asshole! Look where you're going!"

All the jokers jumped out of the Nova, surrounding Maybellene. Jimmy stood in front of Jon's door staring down at him. Jon pulled on the handbrake. He pushed the kid back with the car door and climbed out.

Jon was a good five inches taller than Jimmy, big enough to pick up the scrawny kid with his black T-shirt with the rolled-up sleeves. "What's your problem?" Jon asked. Jon could feel the heat rising up the back of his head. Numb nuts like this were always causing pointless problems. "Did I touch your car?"

"You should look where you're going! You blind?" the kid shouted.

"Didn't see you," Jon huffed. "Why did you stop?"

"And you should pick up your trash! We don't like litter in Tilley. It's not your town! Don't treat it like a dump."

Jon realized that he had left the popcorn bucket on the ground. He leaned over and picked it up. "You're right," he said. "I should have thrown it away."

Jimmy stepped back. "Yeah!" he said.

Horns honked. "Hey, asshole!" someone yelled. "That piece of shit Nova is in the way."

Jimmy waved his hand over his head. He glared at Jon and kicked dirt against the side of Maybellene. Jon wanted to grab the kid and throw him across the parking lot.

Lisa inserted herself between the two combatants. "Go home, Jimmy. Nothing happened. Go home."

"Why? You going to call Daddy?"

She kicked him in the shin. "Don't be such an ass!"

He hopped backward in mock distress, flicked his head up at his buddies, his battle apparently won, and they all climbed back into the Nova, and drove away, radio blaring.

"He's a jerk," Lisa said.

"You have something going with him?" Jon asked.

"He only wishes!"

Back in the driver's seat, Jon grabbed Maybellene's steering wheel. He struggled to focus and hide the unresolved violence and interrupted passion bubbling in his brain, and carefully drive his car out of the parking lot without further incident.

7

FATHER'S DAY

When Jon Megquire woke in Tilley, Massachusetts, on Cape Cod on June 17, 1979, and realized it was Father's Day, he thought of how little he knew about his father's life. His thoughts twisted back through the long string of history that wanders through the generations, through the line of fathers, grandfathers, great-grandfathers, some known and some unknown, spreading out and expanding into the past, miraculously connected by fate always hoping that the line will continue into the future, spreading out again as the years flow by. Lying in bed in the small room that had once been occupied by Ace and Babs Wentzell's son, Jon stared at the ceiling wondering what thoughts Dwight Wentzell might have had before he went to Vietnam. What hopes had he had for his future? What kind of son had he been? Did he wonder if he would ever return to this room and to this town?

Dwight never came back to this room. He died in a swamp halfway around the world—his hopes and dreams snuffed out. His parents' hopes and dreams for him, imagining their son's future, imagining grandchildren, also ended. Although Jon was only twenty-two, he could sense the layers of pain and longing for a lost child that were painted across the Wentzells' lives.

They say parents live vicariously through their children. Jon wondered if they also die vicariously.

Jon shook off the depressing thoughts, showered, dressed and clomped down the stairs to the kitchen to find Ace reading the Sunday *New York Times* while Babs conjured a massive breakfast. Peaches and Herb crooned, "Reunited" on the radio.

Jon said, "Happy Father's Day!" to Ace. Ace looked up from the paper and Babs turned.

The moment Jon said it he wanted to recall the words. He opened his mouth to try to suck them back, but realized any apology would only widen the wound to allow the father and son memories to flood in.

"Thanks," Ace replied.

"Breakfast will be ready in a moment," Babs said. She pushed the sizzling bacon around the frying pan. "You're going to call your father today aren't you, Jon? Coffee?"

Babs held out a steaming mug.

"Gonna be a hot one," Ace said from behind the paper.

Jon sipped the coffee. He looked at Babs' broad back bent over the stove. The light curtains in the window facing the yard billowed in the gentle morning breeze. The aromas of bacon and coffee and toast blended into a homey perfume. This, Jon decided, was the simple meaning of life. Why did the devil and all have to get so complicated?

"I'm sure your father misses you," Babs said without turning around.

"I guess. I think he's used to it. I've been away at school."

"That doesn't mean he doesn't miss you. What does he do again?"

Jon didn't know how to explain what his father did. Dad's work life had always seemed kind of vague. "Health care," he replied. "He manages a health care group."

"Is he a doctor?" Babs asked, placing a loaded plate in front of Ace, who pulled back his paper to give Babs access to the table.

"Uh, no. He's an administrator. A manager of some sort."

"He must be important. Did he go to school for that? Oh, I'm sorry. I don't mean to pry," she said placing a full plate in front of Jon.

"Thanks. This looks wonderful!"

Babs smiled.

Jon wasn't sure what his father had studied in college. He knew he'd graduated from Cornell in the mid-nineteen fifties. He was a private man who didn't talk much about his youth except for snippets about his dog independently riding the bus in Ithaca and knowing when to get off. Or when he sang in a barbershop quartet or when he met Jon's mother at a dance. His parents had different versions of that meeting. Jon made a mental note to ask his father about his past.

"Leave the boy alone," Ace murmured into his paper.

"No. No, it's okay," Jon said with a mouthful. "He went to Cornell."

"Ace went to Rutgers. Studied psychology. Can you imagine?"

"He doesn't want to know about that."

"Then he joined the army after Pearl Harbor."

Jon put down his fork. "Psychology? Did you want to be a psychiatrist?"

"Hmph."

"That's quite a jump — from psychology to construction."

Ace lowered his paper. "You know how often people go into the line of work they've studied in college? Want to guess? Hardly ever. I don't know why I studied psychology. Maybe I was led astray by a good-looking girl. Girls do that to college students, you know."

"Asaph!" Babs reprimanded, using his full name.

"They lead you on. Take you on paths where you probably shouldn't go. I'm not saying there was a girl, but maybe I studied psychology so I could figure out what women think! I could have made my fortune if I'd figured that one out."

Babs joined them at the table, setting down her mug of coffee.

Ace started to lift his paper again, but suddenly lowered it. "Rutgers is a good engineering school. I should have studied engineering. That would have been useful. But no. I stood in line in the gym where you register for your courses, and I didn't have a clue what I wanted to do. The lines for the engineering courses had all these guys with glasses and slide rules hanging on their belts like swords. I remember clearly when I turned toward the other side of the room, there were the girls, all registering for psychology classes. One girl in particular." He looked at Babs.

Babs smiled.

"Mind you," he said to Jon, "this was long before I met my sweetheart. I don't even remember that other girl's name. She was young and pretty and had gold curls, and I couldn't help but notice how she filled out her sweater! She was wearing those brown and white shoes. What did they call them?"

"Saddle shoes," Babs said. "I had a pair of those."

"Yeah, well she was like one of those models they use to sell a college education. You know, clutching her books to her chest. Hm, hm, hm." Ace said, remembering the scene from more than forty years earlier. "I had to know. I had to know what she was studying. I had to know what the fascination was with studying the human mind."

Ace lifted his newspaper again. Jon used his last bite of toast to wipe up the last bit of egg on his plate.

"Did you?" Jon asked finally.

"Hmm?"

"Did you find out?"

"Find out what?"

"Find out her fascination with the human mind?"

"Nope."

Jon looked at Babs, who shrugged. "More coffee?" she asked, as she picked up Jon's plate and carried it over to the sink.

"Thanks," Jon replied. "What happened . . . with the girl?"

"The war happened," Ace said. "The Japs dropped bombs on Pearl Harbor. That's what happened. And that changed everything. When I enlisted, the government thought I was a doctor so they put me in the medical corps. Gave me some training, but no training would ever prepare you for the blood and guts that you see on a battlefield. I would have felt better carrying a gun than a little bag with a red cross on it, that the Japs had very little respect for, I might add."

"Ace. You can't say 'Japs' anymore."

"Why not?" Ace replied. "They're not our friends. They're not nice. I'll call them Japs until the day I die."

This was a side of Ace that Jon hadn't seen. He was too young to understand the bitterness of the enemies of World War II or the Korean War, and he had no personal, face to face animosity for the Viet Cong. They were not his enemies, but he didn't doubt the hatred that eternally festered in other people's hearts.

"When would you like to call home today, Jon?" Babs asked. "You can certainly use our phone."

"Thank you, Mrs. Wentzell. Probably a bit later." Then he looked at Ace. "Can I ask you something, Mr. Wentzell?"

Ace lowered his paper.

"Why do you read the *New York Times*? I would have guessed you read the *Boston Globe*."

"Because the news of the world is in the *New York Times*. A remnant I never surrendered leaving New York. Babs and I lived on Long Island after the war. I worked on Levittown where the returning veterans could find houses. I've lived here a lot of years now, but I still consider New York home. Football Giants, Rangers, Knicks, they get under your skin. I'm not one of those crazy fans. I couldn't care less, but people get pissed off thinking I would dare to root for the Knicks. Good god! What an idiot, they think." Ace shrugged. "Changing papers would be . . . I don't know . . . sort of like being a traitor. So, when I want to know what's going on in the world, I read the *New York*

Times. When I want to read the comics, I read the *Boston Globe*."

Ace folded the paper. "What do you think of your car?" he asked, news of the world resolved.

"She's fantastic!"

"She? Yeah? What's so fantastic about a car?"

"Oh. She's . . . you know . . . cool." That was lame, Jon thought. There's got to be a better explanation than that. "The Midget's a sports car. Sports cars are easy to drive. Easy to park."

Ace grunted.

"You could get killed in a little box like that. Your father's in health care! Didn't he think it was dangerous?" Ace said.

Jon realized he didn't have a clue what his father had been thinking. From Jon's point of view, it seemed like such a simple decision. He knew he could handle Maybellene. "I guess I'm lucky," he said.

"I hope you realize that."

"Hey, want to drive her?"

Ace leaned back in his chair. "That dinky thing? I wouldn't fit."

"You know how to drive a standard, right?"

"Since I was in diapers."

"All right, so let's go for a ride. Ever driven a sports car? They can be touchy."

Ace looked at Jon and then at Babs as if to ask, "Should I tell him?"

"Kid, you don't know the half of it. After the war, a bunch of companies were manufacturing cars to compete with the vehicles GIs had seen and driven on the continent. Those flighty Italian jobs— Alfas and Ferraris. And the British bugs made by companies like yours. All the American cars were big and bulky and a combination between the family touring car and something aerodynamic - rounded boxes. Don't get me wrong. They got the job done, but they weren't flashy like those foreign jobs.

"So, a few small American companies started making fiberglass body copies of some of the Italian cars. They stuck the body on a variety of chassis and dropped different engines into them. They were sort of like flashy, aerodynamic Frankensteins." Ace chuckled.

"The guy I was working for on Long Island had one of those. The kid came from money. His family collected houses and managed to hang onto a bunch of property on the Island. During the Depression, builders would drop the deeds for their houses on this kid's father's desk and walk away. Couldn't afford the mortgages. Not all of the houses were finished. Some of them, he told me, Murder Incorporated used for body dumps! But somehow his father hung onto the houses and after the war with the soldiers all returning and people trying to rebuild their lives, he ended up with half of Long Island!"

Babs smiled at her husband. "So?"

"So, the point is that this kid didn't know a hammer from a toothpick, but he did know something about cars. His father bought him this kit for a car called . . . I forget. Some kind of bird. Anyway, he got this kit and an MG chassis and engine and the kid put it together in a garage. I think it had parts of an American car . . . like a Pontiac . . . taillights."

"There was a connection to the war . . . in the name," Babs added. "Line or Allies or . . ."

"Right!" Ace said. "The Allied Swallow. Weird name. Weird car. Plastic car. Who ever heard of a plastic car? And the kid did a good job, which surprised me." Ace shook his head. "Allied Swallow. Hadn't thought about that in years. Gun-metal gray. Looked pretty nice. He would tool that car out to the jobsite and sort of pose. You know, leaning on the car waiting for someone to take his picture. Guys on the sites thought he was a spoiled brat; which I guess he was."

"An MG chassis and engine?" Jon asked. "Really? Where did he find that? Couldn't have been too many of them floating around then."

"Don't know. When you have money, it's amazing what you

can find. People needed a little fun in their lives. Times had been tough." Ace paused, his mind drifting back to cars and job sites and the war.

"Get to the point, Ace," Babs prodded.

"The point is," Ace replied, "the point is that he let me drive it! Yeah. He let me drive it. He came out to the site where I was working and posed himself, and I approached him and told him he had a great car. Don't know why. I didn't give a damn about the car."

"You were brownnosing!" Babs laughed. "Trying to get into the good graces of the boss!"

Ace shot her a look — then smiled. "I suppose."

"It was that psychology stuff. You knew what buttons to push. You still do."

"Anyway, he asked me if I wanted to take the car for a spin. I was pretty big even then and I didn't know if I would fit in the car. He was a scrawny kid. But I wasn't much older than you are now. Thought I could do anything."

"You were a lot older!" Babs replied. "You were over thirty! Dwight was a toddler."

Jon felt a chill in the room as the words touched the nerve of the Wentzells' memories of their son – their boy grown to be a man only to die all alone in some dirty, sodden foreign place. Jon couldn't share that memory. He looked from one to the other. "So how did the car drive?" he asked.

Ace replied, "Uhm. It was okay. Kind of wimpy, if you ask me. I like bigger, stronger, more powerful cars. You know it's been a lot of years . . ."

"Sounds amazing," Jon smiled. "Wish I'd seen it. Never heard of an Allied Swallow. I thought the only fiberglass car was the Corvette."

"As I say, people experimented with a lot of stuff in those days. Gas had been tight during the war. People couldn't drive simply for fun. Fuel was rationed. Sort of like what they're threatening to do in some places now, except now we're not at war. Now the problem is nothing but those damned A-rabs!"

Ace walked to the sink and rinsed his coffee cup. "Now that I'm remembering," he said, "the car was awful! Wallowed like a whale. Probably bad suspension."

"Didn't you have a bit of an accident?" Babs asked.

"What? It wasn't me. The car didn't corner well."

"Oh."

"And there wasn't an accident. Nothing happened. I was just showing the kid how . . . you know . . . how cars should be driven."

"What about the ice cream truck?"

"What about it? I didn't hit anything or the kids. They were on the sidewalk. And that stupid 'ding, ding, ding.' The bells, the music on those trucks drive me crazy. Didn't hit anything. And . . ." he paused for effect, "the kids got quite a thrill seeing that car spinning around, tires squealing, smoke coming off them. I knew what I was doing."

"I remember your boss not being too pleased with you. Seems to me . . . I could be wrong . . . but we left Long Island pretty soon after that," she said.

"Ahh. The kid was a spoiled brat. He was, wasn't he?" Ace looked at his wife for confirmation.

Babs looked at Jon with a conspiratorial smile. "Ace was pretty wild in those days."

Jon had a hard time thinking of Ace as wild. Or young. He couldn't think of his father as young either. Dad was so controlled, so organized, so disciplined, with his life planned out like the paperclips in the little magnetic holder on his desk. Wild, messy, random were not words he associated with his father. Or with Ace. Jon smiled thinking about either of them as boys. "Well, want to drive mine? See the difference in a production car? I think you'd like it. She's not powerful, but she's a kick to drive."

"I don't think so, Jon," Ace replied. "But thanks for the offer. I'm not the same now."

"That's good." Babs laughed. "I wouldn't want you to go spinning around on Main Street here!"

"Come on, Ace. Let me see how a pro does it. Shift on the floor."

Ace's mouth started to curl into a smile.

"Oh, go on," Babs urged.

"I don't think so," Ace replied, fussing with the water.

Babs walked over and laid her hand on her husband's. "Go on. The boy wants to show you."

"I'll get the keys from my room. Meet you outside." Jon ran upstairs. He hoped Ace wouldn't strip Maybelline's gears or lose control. He wondered if Ace would have trouble fitting into the car or if his feet were too big to fit between the pedals and work the clutch.

Standing next to the car, Ace looked enormous as he scanned the Midget from hood to trunk. "I don't know," he said. "You sure about this?"

"Yeah. Let's go. Give me a hand taking the top down."

Ace followed Jon's moves to put down the visors, move the latches, unsnap the snaps, fold in the rear windows, unclip the back edge, and fold the fabric top into the space behind the seats.

"I can see why you might be tempted to leave the top down," Ace said struggling with a piece of the tonneau cover.

"Yeah, and you gotta see the sky," Jon replied with a smile.

Jon tossed Ace the keys and jumped into the passenger seat. This was the first time he had been a spectator, the first time anyone else had driven Maybellene. Why hadn't he let his father drive her? Finally, Ace opened the door. Jon felt the car take up the man's weight as he squeezed his body into the driver's seat. Ace put his hands on the wheel and then looked at his feet, locating the pedals. "This is no truck!"

"Feels okay, right?"

"Yeah. Sure. Like riding a bike!"

Ace flipped the shift lever back and forth to make sure it was in neutral, pushed in the clutch, and started the car. Maybellene coughed once and then started to purr.

Ace strained to twist and look over his shoulder at the driveway. He punched in the clutch and pushed the shift lever into reverse. The car lurched as he pulled his foot off the clutch. "Touchy!" he said. Ace smiled, shifting Maybellene into first gear, and the car leapt into motion.

Father's Day morning, and Bartlett Street was silent. A few cars were parked at the curb. Sprinklers ticked on lawns - a neat, tidy, well-groomed, well-ordered neighborhood on a Sunday in June on Cape Cod.

Ace turned at the Green and passed the Episcopal church. He worked the car through its gears. On a straight stretch of road, he juked the steering wheel, making Jon lean one way and then the other.

"Tight." Ace grinned, straightened the wheel, and punched the accelerator. Jon felt his body pinned to his seat, and he grabbed the arm rest. The car felt different responding to someone else's touch, and Jon wasn't feeling the joy in Ace's pleasure. It made him nervous.

Ace took them up to Route 6A, the Old King's Highway, which wound along the north shore of Cape Cod. The two-lane road passes through neighborhoods of old houses protected by historical societies ensuring their appearance is maintained no matter who owns them. The road twisted around corners, up low hills, under narrow railroad bridges and under the branches of old trees, past an occasional ice cream stand, art gallery, or quaint shopping center. The old road was unlike the glitz and flash of the miniature golf courses, touristy "water view" motels, and fast food restaurants that abound on the south side of the Cape along Route 28.

And on this Father's Day morning, the Old King's Highway was quiet and Ace urged Maybellene along, downshifting and braking and diving into the corners, accelerating and upshifting out of them. Jon could feel the rear of the car slipping slightly. "Whoa!" Ace said with a grin as he pulled his foot away from the accelerator.

"Yeah!" Jon laughed. "You have to be careful powering off in the turns! Back end can get a bit loose."

"I noticed," Ace laughed. "That's what she said!"

Ace came out of a turn and had to rapidly down shift and apply the brakes as they converged on a Buick poking along. The driver appeared to be an old man wearing a hat. Jon felt it was okay to poke along in a bulky Buick, but a sports car is not meant to be poking along on a beautiful morning with the top down, the light twinkling through the leaves. Maybellene grumbled. Ace rested his left elbow on his door in a sign of forced relaxation that made Jon feel Ace's impatience.

"Maybe he'll turn soon," Jon suggested with a dramatized sigh.

"Maybe."

"It's a narrow road."

"Old road. Twisty road. Fun road. What do you think?"

Was Ace asking advice? Permission? "What do I think about what?"

Ace looked at the rearview mirror. "You know," he said, "the second car in line has an obligation to pass on a two-lane road. Unwritten rule, I know, but how else are the cars behind going to get by? Only makes sense. One car at a time."

The old man in the Buick didn't change speed, applying his brakes in every corner. "Oh, god," Jon muttered to himself.

"Yeah, well . . . what the hell?" Ace said. He punched in the clutch, downshifted into second gear, slid the car to the left into the oncoming lane, kicked in the accelerator, upshifted to third. But suddenly Maybellene started to shudder and slow.

Jon saw another car appearing around a turn ahead, coming straight at them. Beside him, he could see the old man driving the Buick. A dozen thoughts crowded Jon's brain, thoughts about his future or lack of one, thoughts about his family, thoughts about his car, thoughts about the man he was sitting beside. "Shit!" he yelled. "What are you doing, Mr. Wentzell?"

The car was staggering, stuttering, and had lost the ability to accelerate. There was no way he was going to be able to pass the Buick in time. The woman behind the wheel of the oncoming car swerved onto the verge of the road and blared her horn. Ace tapped the brakes and ducked the little car behind the Buick while Maybellene continued to buck and shudder as though she had had too much to drink the night before and was going to be very sick. Ace pulled her over to the side of the road. She gave a couple final coughs and then stopped.

"What the hell!" Jon said. "What happened?"

"I don't know," Ace replied scanning the gauges. "The car just lost power. Like . . .? Uhm. Did you buy gas recently?"

"Oh, shit. I didn't mean to let it get so low. I meant to get gas when it was my day. Maybellene's license ends in zero. Is that odd or even?"

"So, were you going to wait until you ran out? We don't have that kind of rationing yet in Massachusetts."

"Well, we do in New York."

"You're not in New York anymore, Jon. Good intentions won't fill the gas tank, and we're not going to get anywhere this way," Ace said. He heaved himself out of the car and looked up and down the road. "Not much along here. They like it that way. Historical Societies to protect us from ourselves."

"I'll go," Jon said. "Which way?"

Ace considered their surroundings and pointed ahead toward the way they had been going. "Find a phone and call Babs. Ask her to bring us some gas. Tell her there's a can in the garage."

Jon felt incredibly stupid for letting this happen, and he was glad to be able to sprint down the road, to take out the frustration with himself in the sweat and the exercise. He felt badly leaving Ace to just stand there. And then he wondered if he had a dime for the call.

8
ELKS

Saturday afternoon, the thirtieth of June, the Longliners played the Cotuit Kettleers. You can't make up names like that, Jon thought. At least the Longliner name had something to do with fishing. Kettles were apparently linked to a trade with the Indians for the land. With that logic, the Yankees should have been the Trinketeers according to the exchange with the Indians for Manhattan Island.

It was fun to feel the Longliners coming together. Jon embraced the cohesive movements and reactions to events throughout the game, like a band playing together without thinking. That afternoon they played well, beat the Kettleers, and celebrated in the basement of the Elks Hall.

Jon wound his way out of the celebratory crowd at the end of the evening. He noticed a face that seemed out of place, a face from a different context. A children's song popped into his head about one thing not belonging with a bunch of other things and he stopped. One of the Salsbergs. The other one. Mr. Reese. The son. Why was he hanging out here? Jon didn't know anything about being an Elks member – was it a local thing or if you were an Elk somewhere you could be an Elk anywhere? For no justifiable reason, he had a negative social consciousness about fraternal organizations, that it wasn't what upper-class people from the Pennsylvania Main Line did. Mr. Reese was out of place because he was from out of town. He was also out of place because these *weren't his people*. What would his family say?

Jon thought the Salsberg family had gone back to Pennsylvania to bury Mrs. Salsberg. Not that the movements of the Salsbergs meant anything to him, but he didn't know they'd come back. He would have preferred they stay away. He didn't like them, and they just caused conflicts.

Jon realized Reese had seen him and was sliding through the crowd in Jon's direction. Jon ducked, turned, and started to move toward the door when he felt a hand on his shoulder.

"Jon? Thought that was you."

Jon turned to find snorts of alcohol breath wafting up at him. "Mr. Reese," Jon acknowledged. "I'm surprised to see you here."

"Ah," said Reese as he waved his hand over the crowd. "Yes. Here. Among friends. Real people. People to drink with and talk to."

Reese removed his wire rim glasses and wiped them with his handkerchief. He was sweating. His round face was furiously flushed. The knot of his tie hung loosely on his chest. He had a rich five-o'clock shadow and his eyes were watery and bloodshot.

"What can I do for you, Mr. Reese?" Jon asked.

Reese lowered his voice. "Actually, actually, you know, I don't really like these people very much. They're not . . . my people. I know you know what I mean because I can tell. You're not from . . . here."

Jon didn't accept that he had such personal biases.

"No, no, no," Reese babbled on. "I just buried my mother, you know. Burying is such a barbaric custom. I'm sure you agree. Why do we bury the dead? So, we can dig them up again and reuse them? It's permanent. Permanent! They don't come back. But people keep doing it. Done it for thousands . . . millions of years, you know. They used to smear red ochre on the body, you know. Keep doing it because . . . because God tells them to.

What the hell does God know? What the hell does God care? They're dead!"

Jon didn't know how to respond. He muttered, "I'm sorry for your loss." The people around them were scowling.

Reese returned his hand to Jon's shoulder and guided him to a corner of the room.

"Uhm, it's good to see you, Mr. Reese, but I've gotta go meet someone."

"You're young," Reese stated. "You're young. You have your whole life in front of you." He attempted a smile, but it emerged on his face as a grimace. "You could be a star! A pro ballplayer. I always wanted to be a pro. And I could have been. I had the talent for it." He nodded his head and his chin hit his chest. "I had the talent. I had the desire. But that wasn't what Mother wanted. It wasn't right. Not the right class. You know? Does your mother tell you things like that? You have a mother, right?"

"She died," Jon said.

Reese leaned back as though he'd been slapped. "Died. Oh. I'm so sorry. But I know how you feel. I *do* know how you feel. I can say that because my mother just died too. You know? We often say things like 'Sorry for your loss' without really meaning it. Because it's the right thing to say, you know? But I can really say it this time. And mean it. I really am sorry for your loss. It's hard to lose your mother."

Reese's eyes were welling up with tears. Jon thought, The man is wiped! Over the hill. Down the block. Under the bridge with the trolls. How do I get out of here?

Reese stood still, trying to breathe. "Did I kill her?"

"What?" Jon asked.

"I don't know. Maybe she found out. She knew everything. Couldn't hide anything from her. Maybe she just knew. I was always disappointing her."

"Found out what, Mr. Reese? Maybe you should sit. Can I get you something?"

Reese dropped into a chair. Jon looked around without

knowing what he was looking for. A doctor? A psychiatrist? Help? He found himself towering over the man who appeared to be melting in front of him. He didn't want to prolong his involvement in Reese's meltdown, but it didn't seem right to walk away and leave the blob sliding the rest of the way into la-la land.

"How about some coffee?" Jon asked. "I'll get you some coffee."

Reese waved his hand over his head again and sniffed.

God, Jon thought. In a moment the man is going to start balling or sobbing hysterically! But what if he did kill his mother?

Jon pushed through the crowd toward the bar, waited for the bartender's attention, and then asked, "Can I get a cup of coffee? Black? Big?"

The bartender grinned at him, flipped a cup into a saucer and filled it with steaming coffee. "Problem, big guy?" the bartender asked.

"That man over there," Jon nodded his head in Reese's direction, "is having a meltdown. Thought this might help. Thinks he killed his mother."

"Oh, that guy! Reese. Faith Salsberg's boy. Acts like a boy anyway. Tourist really. But he is an Elk. Otherwise . . . well, you know."

Jon didn't fully understand the bartender's implication. "I'm not an Elk."

"You're a Longliner," the bartender smiled.

Jon didn't feel up to unraveling the logic of the bias. "I mean, should we report what he said to the police? He did say he thinks he killed his mother."

"Ah! It's just alcohol talking, kid. People always have guilty feelings about their mothers. People say shit like that all the time after someone dies. Jesus, if you arrested him for that, he'd probably wet his pants." The bartender laughed. "We'll take care of him."

"Why me? Why did he come to me?"

"You're his hero, kid. One of them, at least. You're his dream that never came true. His star that never rose. He's nuts about baseball. Comes in here to get away from his family, and all he talks about is baseball. Thinks he knows everything about the game. Keeps challenging people to take his bets on winners and losers. You're his hero."

"No shit?" Jon asked.

"No shit," the bartender replied. "Whether you like it or not. Comes with the territory. They want to be you."

Jon looked at Reese slumped over the table against the wall, a pile of convoluted hopes and dreams that would never come true.

The bartender repeated, "We'll take care of him. Leave him to us. You can carry on with whatever you were doing."

Jon shook his head in wonder of the follies of the adult world and gratefully seized the opportunity to leave.

9

THE FOURTH - JULY 4, 1979

Jon had not expected Tilley to take the Fourth of July seriously. People in his hometown in New York didn't take holiday frivolity seriously. New England was where all the hubbub with King George started, and besides that, the tourists were entertained by the festivities and that was always profitable! The lawns were mowed and the hedges were trimmed. The weather was perfect if a bit cool for a July day, with a slight breeze from the north.

The town was decked out in red, white, and blue bunting from the fences around the green to the balconies overlooking Main Street. American flags hung from every house and fluttered from the tall pole in front of the Elks hall. Tilley was wound up to celebrate the country's birthday with fireworks and a parade. Businesses were closed, and in garages and empty lots, Boy Scouts decorated contractors' trucks and trailers.

Ace had loaned his construction trailer to the local Veterans of Foreign Wars chapter to decorate and carry the Longliners. With the help of VFW members, Ace had built a platform on the trailer for the players to stand on. They constructed a wide bench in the middle and skirted bunting around the edges of the trailer, hiding the wheels.

The parade route originated in the supermarket parking lot, wound down Main Street, ending at the Elks hall. The Longliners' trailer was near the end of dozens of floats.

The players gathered before the parade at nine, hanging around telling stories and making jokes, waiting. Some sat on the edge of the trailer, swinging their legs. First-year players believed this was going to be a hokey small-town event, but returning players recounted legends of past parades. Like the time all the players piled on top of the coach's pickup truck, hanging off the back, clinging to the top of the cab, perching on the hood. When the coach needed to see, he turned on the wipers to get players to move out of the way. The truck took a beating with a handful of dents and broken windshield wiper motors; it was never quite the same.

Apparently, one year a local engineer created a couple of mechanical players that twisted their torsos and swung regulation bats. The robotic figures lasted a few blocks until one of the real players stumbled when the trailer hit a pot hole, falling into the mechanical counterparts so that they appeared to be hitting each other, like a full-size Guignol or Punch and Judy.

Another year, team marketers gave the players schwag items to toss out into the crowd. "Pens were a disaster!" one of the players laughed. Someone might have been killed. They tried foam baseballs, but they were difficult to get any distance on. This year they had bags of past-season baseballs. The players wrote messages on them like, "Show us your tits!" along with their names and phone numbers.

"Underhand," the coach insisted. "Toss them gently underhand. We don't want to kill anyone!"

Icky Bartholomew, the Longliner shortstop, showed up late on his bicycle, overheated from the effort. "How was she?" one of the players joshed. They all laughed. Jon doubted Icky had gone all the way. But it was possible.

Icky grinned and said, "If you ate pasta and antipasto, would you still be hungry? Parades like this are all a waste of time. Small town. Small time."

"You have been the star of a parade then, Ick?" one of the returning players asked.

"Nope. I'm no movie star!" He pulled his uniform into shape and wiped the sweat off his forehead.

"I think you're going to be surprised by this one," one of the veteran players said. "This parade is a big deal here. A shitload of people come out to line the streets. They pull out their lounge chairs to get settled long before we ever get there. You'll be surprised. Look at all the wackos in this parking lot!"

"I saw them getting here," Icky replied. "I thought they were a bunch of crazies."

The parking lot was full of people in costumes complete with hats that looked like lobsters and shoes that looked like bloated bare feet. There were a couple of local marching bands squawking out sounds, drummers drumming, lords-a-leaping! Members of the local National Guard held flags while their streamers fluttered. The Boy Scouts were trying to keep the Cub Scouts in line. Town dogs had scarves tied around their necks and sunglasses perched on their noses. Members of a local dance school stood around looking awkward in their tutus. A group of girls in bikinis from a modeling agency in Hyannis preened their hair and grinned. "Let's follow that one!" a player yelled. A woman brandishing a clipboard drove around in a golf cart shouting instructions. She had flaming yellow hair and wore large, very dark sunglasses. She reminded Jon of one of the cafeteria madams from college.

"Didn't know there were this many people in this town," Jon said.

He watched clowns dressed like clowns and someone dressed like an onion and another in a codfish costume and yet another in waders and foul-weather gear. "Jesus. He's going to be hot!" Dupin said.

Gradually the line of parade participants started snaking out of the parking lot. The players jumped up on the truck. Ace drove his truck into line, creeping across all the parking spaces, following the float in front of them - a local religious group starring Mary and Joseph with some angels behind them.

"Wrong holiday!" someone muttered.

"Maybe that's the only costumes they had."

"They could have thrown a red, white, and blue blanket on the kid!"

Sinking into the vortex of the festivities, Jon didn't notice the bravado of his teammates as they talked over each other and vied for attention—much like they did on the field. The camaraderie and exuberance were just there.

Someone yelled, "Why couldn't we have followed those models in the bikinis?"

"You would have been distracted!"

"You bet!"

The truck bumped out of the parking lot. The players who were standing grabbed something or someone to hang on to. When the parade line emerged from the last building in the shopping plaza and onto Main Street, the players gasped.

"Holy shit!" Jon said. "Is this everyone on Cape Cod?" The crowd packed the street, cheering, waving American flags, and clapping their hands.

"Wow!" Icky exclaimed. "Where the hell did all these people come from? Do they get trucked in from other parts of the country? Why the hell are they here in this little burg?"

The players grinned and waved back and started tossing out the balls, picking out smiling girls and little kids. "Hey!" they yelled. "See you at the field!"

"Go 'Liners!" the crowd yelled back at them. "Go 'Liners!"

The band marching behind them got through "*America the Beautiful*" and "*This Land Is Your Land*," attempted "*The Stars and Stripes Forever,*" and then lurched into their own version of "*Bad Girls*," the Donna Summer song. They had the whistles down and the rhythmic "beep, beep," but they tried to fill in for the lead with a couple of trumpets that were a brash stand-in for Donna Summer's silky voice.

But the rhythm and the noise of the crowd and the surge of energy were infectious. Some of the players pranced on the flat bed, making it rock. They waved their arms over their heads, bending occasionally to grab another baseball to toss into the crowd. Jon felt the whole world was out to party.

Jon grinned and waved and danced, too, but as the truck reached the green, he noticed Garrett Scoles standing in the reviewing stand with other town notables, his arms folded across his chest and a grim look on his face. He wore dark aviator glasses, a white Lacoste shirt, and salmon Nantucket shorts capped by a blue-and-white whale belt. Jon felt an irrational anger sweep over him. He simply didn't like the man, and obviously he wasn't having fun.

"Think that guy can catch?" Jon asked, as he reached into the bag of balls.

"Which guy?" Dupin asked through an ear-to-ear grin.

"Go 'Liners!"

"Yeah!" Dupin replied and tossed a ball to a kid in the front row wearing a red, white, and blue top hat.

"That guy. In the stand," Jon replied. "Here. I'll show you."

Jon leaned back, gripped the ball, and zinged it at Scoles—not as hard as he would have thrown a ball to home plate to cut off a runner, but hard enough. Jon was not a pitcher, but his throw was accurate, passing between the two people standing in front of his target. Scoles noticed the missile at the last second and put his hands up to protect his head, knocking his aviator glasses askew.

"Hey!" Scoles yelled. "What the hell?"

"Oh, that guy!" Dupin yelled. "We're supposed to throw underhand!" Dupin threw a ball, underhanded, to a girl dressed as Lady Liberty.

Scoles scrambled to regain his composure, pushed his hair back into place, and reseated his glasses. "Whoops! My bad." Jon said. Then he waved and grinned. General turmoil erupted among the official reviewers, pushing each other around as Scoles stumbled and the others tried to maintain their balance and not fall off the stand. Jon watch Scoles hurry to get down.

"I don't know if that was such a good idea," Dupin said. "What've you got against that guy?"

"He irks me," Jon replied. "I was just pointing him out to you. He couldn't catch after all! I hope that wasn't one of the balls that requested he expose his tits!" He laughed and resumed prancing about on their float while the band behind them resumed their squeaky rendition of "*The Stars and Stripes Forever.*"

The Longliners' truck followed the parade past the green, back to the Elks parking lot where the players jumped off and milled around with other participants still wearing their costumes and funny hats.

Ace climbed out of the truck and came around to the players. "So that's the parade, boys" he said and shrugged.

"Thanks, Mr. Wentzell!" Dupin yelled.

"Yeah, thanks!" other team members shouted.

"Play well today," Ace replied.

Jon heard a car horn beeping repeatedly. The players turned in the direction of the noise and watched Scoles forcing his Mercedes through the crowd. People yelled, "Hey!" as they jumped out of the way. He pulled to a stop in front of the team

"What the hell do you think you're doing?" he yelled at Jon.

Jon adopted his best innocent look and asked, "What?"

"What do you think you're doing throwing a baseball at me like that?"

Jon widened his eyes. "Souvenir for the crowd, you know, to promote the team."

Scoles closed the space between them. Jon looked down at the older man and noticed his own face reflected in the aviator glasses. Scoles' face was red and a rim of sweat beaded his forehead.

"You threw that ball at me intentionally!"

"Nah," said Jon. "Just thanking you for your support of the team."

"You threw that ball at me intentionally, you bastard!" Scoles said.

Jon shrugged. "What's your problem? This is a celebration! Have fun!"

"I should have you arrested!" the man fumed, standing inches away from Jon.

"Yeah? For what? You could have caught it!"

"I should have you arrested!"

Jon wiped the man's spit from his face. The crowd of players and onlookers had drawn tighter around the two men and the laughter and music died.

Ace pushed his way through the players. Ace's bulk made Scoles seem even smaller than he actually was. A lot of Ace's weight had gone to his gut, but when he lifted himself up and pulled his shoulders back, he was intimidating.

"Back off," Ace said quietly. "This is a celebration. Back off now, both of you."

Scoles ripped his glasses off and glared at Ace. "You'll regret this!" he yelled.

Jon stepped back into the line of players who shifted their positions to line up beside and behind Ace, leaving Scoles standing by himself, chest heaving, like a stray dog.

"You should get back in your car now, Mr. Scoles. Why don't you get back in your car and on your way? No more trouble. We'll take care of this."

"I want that kid off the team and out of this town!"

"I don't think that's going to happen, Mr. Scoles. We'll take care of this," Ace repeated.

For a moment no one moved. Holding on to one bow of his aviator glasses, Scoles tried to flick them open with a flourish and succeeded in poking himself in the eye. "You haven't heard the last of this!" he spat. Scoles spun around and stalked back to his car. Honking his horn, he forced the car back through the crowd.

The players started dancing around slapping each other on the back and laughing. Ace didn't look happy. "What happened?"

Jon shrugged his shoulders. "Nothing, really. Just tossing balls out to the crowd, you know. Like the coach told us to. Thought Mr. Scoles might like a souvenir."

"That wasn't very smart, Jon. You didn't think."

"Sorry, Mr. Wentzell." He looked to the other players for support.

"It was a good throw, Mr. Wentzell," Dupin added. "It was pretty funny seeing the guy try to swat the ball away like it was a bee or something!"

"Not too smart," Ace said. "You need to grow up."

Jon felt a mantel of remorse settle on him as he watched Ace walk away. It wasn't Scoles he was sorry about. It was letting Ace down.

10

TROUBLE

The news story of Faith Salsberg's death faded off the front page of the *Cape Cod Times* and the town settled back to the placid rhythms of Cape Cod summer. The early scents of the high season floated on the air in the first days of July. Jon witnessed the blossoming of the crowds of tourists and the damper that the death of a local dignitary sometimes has on the free-flowing fun of vacations in the sun. Death makes exciting news but is a definite downer to a carefree vacation. It didn't fit into the lyrics of *Old Cape Cod*! Vacation was beaches, quaint old New England, the smell of newly cut grass, and the American flag flapping at the post office in the warm summer sunlight. Gentle breezes and baseball.

Jon's life had settled into a routine. Babs made him breakfast of bacon and eggs and coffee and toast and orange juice. He drove to the Thompson project where he was tearing out interior walls and piling the rubble from the horsehair plaster and lathe in the middle of the rooms. There was joy in swinging a sledge hammer against the wall, punching a hole in it, and then ripping the plaster off. It hung together like thick, hairy slabs of dry, dusty fondant icing. Jon wondered about the workers who originally created the stuff and spread it smoothly over the walls, horizontally tacking up the hundreds of sections of rough wood, about three eighths of an inch apart, enough spacing for the wet plaster to squeeze between the rows of lathe. The plaster, permeated with black horse hair, had been drying and hardening and clinging to the walls for almost a hundred years.

The removal of the wall surfaces exposed the homes of the uninvited biology that had been living there: old, paper thin wasps' nests, pathways mice had made, the little pile of leaves or acorns that had been their nests and food supplies. The builders had signed the wall, "Palmer boys! April 1926."

It must have been a messy job going up. It was certainly a messy job coming down. The lathe split and cracked as Jon ripped it off the old studs. His face was white with the dust, his nose was full even behind the paper mask, and he had to turn away periodically to step outside and breathe fresh air.

Some days Babs would make him lunch. Jon would sit on the back lawn with Badavas and James to eat the white bread sandwiches, munch on the carrots while they watched the birds around the pond and talked about their lives, their families, working for Ace, and construction in general. They painted a picture for him of living year 'round on the Cape and the idiosyncrasies of the local politics of Tilley. Whatever the issue was, it was "all politics" they assured him nodding their heads in harmony.

They had a lot of questions for Jon about baseball — what players he liked, what teams would do well, who Jon hoped he would play for. "Realistically. What are your chances?" Jon would shrug. They wanted to know somebody famous, wanted to say they worked with a big shot, wanted to be sure he didn't forget them when he was a headliner.

Baseball was the constant that tied all his days together. The Longliners travelled to the fields of the other Cape League teams. They were all different, with different surfaces and different accommodations for the fans and the players. The surface of the Wareham Gatemen field was hard and caused the ball to bounce through the infield at a weird rate. Rumor was they kept it that way to provide a home field advantage.

Longliner team rhythm was still out of sync. The players hadn't shrugged off the change from home team hero to incipient professional. They were unsettled. They hadn't developed the instinctive understanding of each other's movement and reaction — move to the left, move to the right, the speed of the motion, how to fill the space they weren't in a moment ago. But Jon did enjoy the dance.

~

WHEN JON RETURNED TO THE WENTZELLS AFTER THE GAME on Friday evening, he found Ace in the kitchen with Babs. Ace was slouched over the kitchen table with a cup of coffee between his big hands. Babs was leaning against the sink with her arms folded across her chest, her forehead knotted with tension.

Jon looked from one to the other of his summer family with a smile of curiosity. "What's going on?" he asked.

Ace raised his head to look at Jon. "Nothin'. It's okay. How was the game?"

"Yeah. I was surprised not to see you there. We won."

"That's good," Babs said and turned around to fuss over the few dishes in the sink. "Can I get you something to eat?"

"I'm good, thanks, Mrs. Wentzell. Anything I can do here?"

Ace took a sip of coffee. The kitchen clock ticked away the seconds. "How you getting on with Badavas and James at the Thompson place? They're not giving you a hard time?"

"We're good. It's all good."

"That's good," Ace replied. "Glad something is going well."

"What is going on?" Jon asked, looking from one to the other.

"They're accusing Ace of bad workmanship," Babs blurted. "They think that might have had something to do with Mrs. Salsberg's death."

"What?"

"They think Ace might be involved. Think it might be his fault."

Ace held up his hand. "No, no, no. Nothin' like that. I guess they got the report from the doctors, and it said she died from carbon monoxide poisoning. They think it's 'cause of the house."

"They're idiots!" Jon stated. "What did they say to you?"

"They're saying it had something to do with the way things were installed in the building. And since I built that pool house, it must have something to do with me."

"But you finished that house a couple years ago," Jon said.

"Last year. I built it last year."

"So how could it kill somebody now?" Jon sat down at the table across from Ace.

Ace shrugged. "Don't know. Accident of some sort. That's the trouble with construction. Things take a while. Nature's patient. People aren't. People are impatient. Want things to happen right now – right now! And they need someone to blame. So they're pushing it on me."

"It's not right," Babs said.

"Who's 'they'?" Jon asked.

"Well, don't really know. I ran into Prence at Clegg's. He's doing the investigating." Ace dismissed the word 'investigating' with a wobble in his voice and a twist of his hand. "Obviously the Salsberg family is pushing him for quick answers. They're likely to sue me . . . or worse."

"Shit!" Jon mumbled the word. "That's not right. How can they do that? I'm sure it's not your fault. How would they know?"

"It's the medicos. You know. They've got all sorts of gadgets. They cut the body up in little pieces and get down inside and pull stuff out and figure out what went wrong! That's their job. Prence mentioned that they thought it might have been suicide for a while 'cause apparently she had a whole lot of drugs. Don't know if there was something wrong with her. Don't know much of anything."

Doctors, investigations, and rumors of results twisted Jon's thoughts back to his mother's death. Here. On the Cape. Of carbon monoxide poisoning. This place must be hell! Was that faulty construction too? *Was* Ace at fault? Jon didn't want to think that.

Babs poured herself a cup of coffee, pulled out a chair, and joined them at the table.

Jon looked at Ace. The man looked deflated. The skin under his eyes sagged, and his hair flew out in all directions from running his hands through it.

"My mother died of carbon monoxide poisoning," Jon said quietly.

Babs clapped her hand over her mouth. "Oh. That's right!" She thrust herself back in her chair. "I'm so sorry! This must bring back horrible . . . horrible memories."

Jon felt Ace watching him, trying to find words. "There's no excuse for bad construction," Ace said. "It's just ignorance or laziness and that's not an excuse. Blaming the building is like blaming a gun for shooting somebody."

Jon did not want to encourage the molecules of doubt that were now floating in his thoughts, connecting his mother's death to Mrs. Salsberg's.

"Well, we have to get Officer Prence straightened out! You had nothing to do with it. She must have killed herself somehow. Or maybe somebody else did something to her. Maybe somebody wanted her out of the way."

Ace looked at Jon and smiled weakly. "You don't understand, Jon. You don't know these people. They have the money. They have the power. If they want to put the blame on me, they'll do it. Because they can. They can just keep saying it was me. And if they say it enough times, it will become the truth. They're taught to think that way. They know that taking responsibility isn't profitable. And it's all about profitability!"

"That's pretty cynical, dear," Babs said.

"Well, it's true." He stood and walked to the back door and studied the yard. "Jesus, I'm tired of these rich whiners. Get whatever they want whenever they want it and don't care who they step on in the process."

"It'll get better," Babs said. "You know you didn't do anything wrong. You know that. Prence may not be brilliant, but he's a good man. He'll figure it out. You don't have to worry."

"Yeah," Jon said. "Yeah. Maybe we can steer him in the right direction."

Ace looked at Jon. "No. No, you stay out of this and concentrate on your baseball. That's why you're here. Let's let Prence do his job and stay out of his way."

Jon nodded. "But do you think he knows anything about carbon monoxide?"

"Probably not. They told us about it in the Army Medical Corps."

"That was a long time ago, hon," Babs said.

"Yeah. Almost forty years! But not something you forget easily. People died in training as well as in battle. Working on tanks and trucks in enclosed spaces. Breathing in the exhaust fumes. CO makes you do stupid stuff like hang around when you should leave! Makes you feel like you have a hell of a flu."

"But there wasn't a truck or a tank at the Salsbergs," Jon added.

"It doesn't take a tank. Anything that burns can do it. A water heater. A fireplace. A stove. Even candles if you have enough of them. Don't know," Ace said. He started to leave the room. "Better get some sleep. Another day tomorrow. We'll just have to see what happens."

Babs took the cups to the sink and started to wash them. Jon watched her for a moment and then stood. "He has a degree in psychology from Rutgers, you know," she said with her back to Jon. "I think he has a need to analyze people. Thinks he knows what they're thinking before they think it. Can be good sometimes, but it can get in the way." She turned off the water and dried her hands on a dish towel.

"Can the Salsbergs really accuse him of being involved?"

"He's right," Babs replied, "they can do anything they want. Or it seems that way. They're not bad. I don't know who inherits the company now. Who's in charge? Mr. Scoles is married to Mrs. Salsberg's daughter. The other one . . . I forget his name . . . is Mrs. Salsberg's son from her other marriage. There's always more than one marriage and that gets things twisted."

"Reese," Jon said. "Brian Reese."

"Yes. That's it. Reese. Who knows? Maybe they bumped her off to get her money. If they did, of course, they wouldn't want to take the blame, would they?" She snorted. "Money can make people do nasty things. Never had it, but that's what they say."

"Anything I can do?" Jon asked.

"No, dear," Babs said with a smile. "You just keep working on what you have to work on, like Ace said. You're here for the baseball. Don't get tangled in this local stuff. Have you been talking to your father? You can use the phone whenever you like, you know. I'm sure he wants to know how you're doing. Do you write? People don't write much anymore, do they? Used to be the way we stayed in touch. Postcards. Letters. Telegrams. It wasn't always good news when you got a telegram." She looked at him for a moment. "They deliver bad news in person now. Better that way, I guess."

Jon recognized the quiver in her voice and to change the path of her memories he told her he had sent a postcard home, one of those "Wish You Were Here!" ones with the picture of the beach with the sunbathers having fun. Then his sister, Cornelia, the engineer, popped into his mind. She could tell him more about CO. She knew all this scientific stuff. Maybe she could explain what appeared to Jon like an epidemic. He would call her when he knew more. She would be surprised. He didn't call his family often. He certainly didn't call Cornelia. Might be good. Score some points at home and learn more.

Ace shouldn't just roll over. He wasn't careless. He wouldn't make a mistake that could kill someone.

As Jon lay in Dwight Wentzell's bed that night, he wrestled with his own motivations and wondered why life had to be so complicated. He should just not get involved. So why couldn't he? Could a builder be the cause of death and was Ace that kind of a builder? Jon decided that he needed to know more – more about buildings, more about people, more about everything. Ignorance wasn't bliss! It was confusion. It was doubt. Jon did not want to doubt Ace or his skills.

He should be thinking about baseball. He should be concentrating on impressing the scouts, reaching his full potential. What if they offered him a deal? He could take that ticket and ride away from this one-horse town and put the memories in his scrapbook.

Something about lying in Dwight Wentzell's bed in Dwight Wentzell's room caused Ace's worried face to float into his thoughts. "Oh hell. I can't just let some mean, greedy bastard take Ace's life away." And the thought of a heroic, white-hatted avenger surged in Jon's psyche and made him smile.

11
POLICE

Lisa didn't have a quick solution. "I don't know what my father knows!" she exclaimed when Jon asked her about Ace. "Why would my father think Mr. Wentzell had anything to do with Mrs. Salsberg dying? Why? It wouldn't make any sense!"

"That's what I'm saying," Jon replied. "That's just it! It doesn't make any sense. He's not careless. Just the opposite. He's a perfectionist."

They sat in the empty bleachers after the game as the daylight faded.

"I know you think Mr. Wentzell's a nice guy," Lisa said, "but why do you care so much?"

Jon didn't answer immediately. He looked out at the field and wondered what he was doing there, wondered what was important. He inhaled deeply and tried to confront the pall of lethargy that grasped at his bones. He struggled to ignore the inner voice that shouted, "Walk away. Walk away! This is not your fight. Walk away and just let it go." He was simply Ace's summer employee. He was a kid seeking summer fun. He didn't live here. Why should he care? What was it about this place or these people that made him care? Was it his mother? Was it his mother's voice he heard?

"This isn't complicated," Lisa said. "Mrs. Salsberg died. She was old. My father will find out why, and life will go on. It's just day-to-day stuff. It happens."

"Yeah, it does," Jon replied, "but . . . maybe life goes on for only some of us. But everything is connected, Lisa. Everything. Being accused of this could cost Mr. Wentzell his reputation, his business, everything! Who's going to hire him if they think he makes mistakes that kill? False accusations are wrong. They're evil!"

"Well, who's accusing him?"

"I don't know. It's probably that Mr. Scoles."

"Oh. Mrs. Salsberg's son-in-law? He seems like an asshole. Looks like an asshole, too, with that weasel face. But I've never talked to him. Do you think he just gets his jollies blaming people?"

"Maybe he killed her," Jon asked, "and he's just covering up by blaming someone else." He watched a squabble of seagulls that had congregated in the outfield, picking at some of the rubbish the departing crowd had left behind.

"Whoa!" Lisa replied. "Now who's making accusations? False, maybe, or at the very least unfounded!"

"But what if someone did kill her? What if she didn't just die of old age or whatever? Do people just 'drop dead'? Life doesn't just . . . stop, does it? There has to be a reason."

"I guess," Lisa replied.

"I'm pretty sure she didn't die of a broken heart!" Jon laughed.

"Probably not, but, Jon, you can't just throw around stuff like this without something to back it up. And if it was . . . murder . . ." she fumbled to use the word, "how are you going to figure it out? You're just a baseball player. You're not a police officer. We're kids."

"Yeah, that's right! But we're smart, right?" Jon felt himself getting wound up. It was a puzzle – a puzzle he was sure he could solve even without resources. Just piece it logically together. "Okay. But we have to start somewhere, right? Don't you have to start with who has something to gain? Murder needs a reason. There has to be a reason. Even Raskolnikov in *Crime and Punishment* had a reason even if it was a weird one."

"What?"

"No, but the point is that we need to find the reason if we are going to find the killer."

"In books it's always either love or money," Lisa said, "and I'm sure this wasn't love."

"Right. Money. I'm sure Scoles has a lot to gain, right? I mean he probably gets a fatter job and a bigger office and more money! He'd want her out of the way."

"You don't know, Jon," she said.

"No, I don't. But your father should." Jon looked for the seagulls, but they had negotiated the claims to the trash and flown away. "Who else would have a motive?"

"I don't know. Who?"

Jon thought for a moment. "Don't know. Who else needs money?"

"Everybody needs money. That doesn't mean you're going to kill somebody for it!"

"Yeah, but some people need money more than others. Everything is connected. We've got to look for someone with the most problems, someone who is connected to the Salsbergs. So, who has the most problems?"

"Jon, I've got to tell you. This is my first. My first murder."

"You've got to start somewhere," he said.

Lisa looked at him. "That's stupid," she said.

"It's not stupid. If something happens, you need to look for the cause." He stood and stretched. "For sure, Ace didn't kill her. I don't think he needs money. Anyway, he wouldn't do it. No, I think it's someone in her family. It usually is. It's usually someone close to the victim."

"How the hell would you know that?" Lisa asked. "TV cop shows? Besides, I still don't know why you care so much. You still haven't answered my question. Hey . . . Don't walk away from me!"

He shuffled down between the seats, stopped, looked back at her, and shrugged. "Why? I don't know. I just do. I just know that it's the right thing to do."

"So if you think Scoles had something to do with it, why don't you ask him?"

Jon looked to see if she was serious. "You're not serious?"

"Of course not. But I don't see how you're going to do this. You can't just go around randomly accusing people of murder."

"Well, okay. But who else could it be? Who else needs money? You know lots of people in this town. I only know a couple. A bunch of people have been working over at Casa Grande. In and out. Hired help. Family. The murderer could be anybody."

Lisa walked over to him. "I think there's a lot of people in this town who fit the bill of having money problems. A lot of people live paycheck to paycheck."

"So how do we find the murderer?"

"We don't, Jon. We let my father do it. It's his job!"

"Come on. How hard could it be? Do you want some murderer walking around your town scot-free?"

"Oh, come on, Jon. We don't even know that it WAS murder. I haven't seen anyone who looks like a murderer wandering around."

"This is weird," he said. "This is real. It's weird when stuff you read about or see in the movies becomes real. That monster stuff can't become real. Alien stuff can't become real. That's only in someone's head. But this stuff, this life stuff, can be real. Know what I mean?"

"You're weird," she replied. "You think too much."

"All right, but they can't put the blame on Ace. That's not

right. So, let's go talk to your father. Please? Help me find out what he knows."

"He's not going to like that idea," she said, as they stomped down through the stands.

~

THEY FOUND OFFICER PRENCE IN THE TILLEY POLICE station. He looked up at them from the paperwork strewn across his desk. "Hey," he said to Lisa. "What's up?"

Jon looked around the room. There wasn't much to it. He had seen police stations in the movies and on TV shows like *Starsky and Hutch*, but he'd never been in one before. This place wasn't what he imagined a police station to be. It looked more like a cozy, little souvenir shop with mug shots and safety posters instead of postcards and ceramic mermaids. It didn't look like a place where trouble collided with real life.

"Hi, Dad," Lisa said coming around the desk and giving him a peck on the cheek. "How's it going?"

"It's going. How's it going with you? Jon?"

Jon nodded his head and said, "Fine, sir." He watched Officer Prence mentally shift gears from official paperwork to official fatherhood.

"What can I do for you two?" Prence asked.

Lisa looked at Jon. "No. Nothing in particular. You know. Just wanted to see you. How's the thing with Mrs. Salsberg going? We were curious if you've figured anything out," Lisa said.

"The investigation is progressing," Prence replied. "You know I can't talk about it." Prence looked at Jon. "What's your part in this?"

Jon replied, "We heard that Mr. Scoles accused Mr. Wentzell of bad construction. That it's his fault somehow."

"Where did you hear that?" Prence asked.

"Ace . . . Mr. Wentzell, mentioned it."

Prence pushed back his chair and stood up, straightening his gun belt and pulling up his pants. He rocked his head back and forth as he focused on Jon. "You shouldn't get into this," he said. "It's a local issue. Most likely just an accident. These things happen."

"What things?"

Jon felt Prence sizing him up. They looked eye to eye, but Prence had let his body sag, his shoulders slumped, and he stood with all his weight on his left side.

"Things," Prence replied. "Life. People die. It happens. Especially old people."

It was easy to tell that Prence was just saying words with nothing behind them. Jon had enough sense not to start a war with the man, so he retreated. "Anything we can do to help?"

"As long as you're here," Prence replied, "I need your fingerprints."

"Really?"

"Routine. Need to rule people out. I'm getting them from everyone. It's just routine."

"Fingerprints? Why? So, you don't think it was just her time or an accident or something?" Jon asked.

"Can't say. Just need to get people's prints to make sure I have them. Come over here and let's get you into the system."

Jon looked at Lisa. "First time for everything," he said. He wondered what Prence meant by 'the system'. Would these little ink splotches on a piece of cardboard go anywhere besides into a file drawer in Prence's office?

"So, tell me again: what you were doing at the Salsbergs' place that morning? We never had a chance to go through your activities."

"I was working with Mr. Wentzell," Jon said.

"Doing what exactly? Wentzell wasn't there, was he?" Prence squeezed Jon's fingers into the ink one by one and pressed them on the pre-marked card. The fingers of Prence's left hand squeezed into Jon's shoulder, fixing him in place. Prence's right hand pressed each finger onto the cardboard card as though the ink was being emitted from the whorls of Jon's fingerprints. Jon felt himself resisting.

"Relax," Prence demanded. "If Wentzell wasn't there, how could you have been working with him?"

"You know, . . . he pays me to work on the house. I was waiting for him."

With the fingerprinting ordeal over, Jon stepped away from the desk and Officer Prence. Prence handed him a piece of paper towel.

"He was paying you, but you weren't working? You were just hanging around? Seems a bit irresponsible doesn't it?"

"Um. I couldn't start working until . . ."

"Why didn't you both come at the same time? You are living in his house, aren't you?"

"This is stupid," Jon said, turning away, wiping the ink off his fingers.

"Looks sort of like a conspiracy, doesn't it? The two of you, coming and going as you please, inside and outside the house. Anything could have happened, couldn't it? You had the opportunity. In fact, plenty of opportunities. I haven't gotten a handle on your motive yet."

"Dad! Jon didn't kill Mrs. Salsberg! Why would he do that?"

Mark Prence looked at his daughter. He took a deep breath.

"Why would he do that?" she pursued. "It doesn't make any sense."

"No," Prence said finally dropping back into his chair. "I'm just saying it could be anyone . . . or no one. You start talking about it and it gets all tangled up. First thing you know, nothin' is what you think. Chances are good, just an accident . . . if it was anything. Chances are good that she just . . . died! But you know how it is. People want to see the blood. Like on TV."

Jon asked, "Well, in all of the investigating what have you found out? What killed her? Was her company in trouble? What did the M.E. say?"

"Who's the detective here?" Prence asked. "It's an 'ongoing investigation'. You've heard me say that."

"Oh, come on, Dad! I'm not the press. I'm your daughter. You talk about stuff like this all the time at home. It's good to bounce your thoughts off someone, right?" She looked around the small office, waving her hand. "You don't exactly have a staff to help you. Maybe we can."

Prence looked at her and then tilted himself back in his chair and put his feet up on top of his pile of papers. "He's not local." He nodded his head in Jon's direction. "Don't want to jeopardize this investigation, do I? Don't get many murders."

"So, you think she was murdered?" Jon said.

"I didn't say that!"

"You just said 'we don't get many murders.'"

"Jesus! That's what I mean. If I say anything to you, I don't know where it will get to. I can't risk it."

"Is the family still here?" Lisa asked.

"Some here, some there. Hard to keep track. I can't order them not to leave town!"

"So, what did the medical examiner say?" she pushed.

"I can't say."

"Can't or won't?" Jon asked.

"I can't say." Prence looked at Lisa. "You know that."

"What can you say?" Jon asked.

Prence crossed his arms across his chest and glared at Jon.

"This isn't getting us anywhere," Jon said. "But I want to be sure that Mr. Wentzell isn't the scapegoat."

"Look," Prence said, "she died. Mrs. Salsberg is dead. That is a fact." Prence looked at him. "Trouble always comes from the outside. People bring it with them. We get a handful of drunks. Locals. Once in a while. Big troubles come from the outside. Like this. Makes people nervous when stuff like this happens. They start looking at each other. Wondering. Dying doesn't sit well in a small town."

"Can you at least tell us if Scoles is accusing Ace?" Jon asked.

Prence inhaled. "Yeah, and I can sympathize with it! They want to blame somebody for their loss. These things don't hurt as much if you can find a cause, something or someone to blame."

"But you know Mr. Wentzell didn't do anything! This could ruin his whole life, his reputation, everything! He could lose everything."

"Well, we're not at that point yet," Prence replied.

"Who gets all the money? Does Scoles? What do you know about him? Where did he come from?" Jon asked.

"Look, he's part of the family, the Salsberg family. Huh? That's the important thing about Mr. Scoles. He's married to Bryce Scoles, Mr. Salsberg's daughter. Went to Princeton University. He's smart. Got a physics degree or something. He's got it all! He's a chief mucky-muck at the Salsberg empire."

"That's great," Jon said, "but it doesn't tell us anything. Where's he from? How do you know he isn't some sort of international jewel thief, leeching off the family? He stands to gain a lot. Right? Does he get the company now that his mother-in-law is dead? He certainly has motive . . . and opportunity!"

Prence looked at him.

"And what about the other guy? What's his name? Reese? What's his story?"

"He's her son, for god's sake! Why would he kill his mother?"

"I don't know. He said he did it!"

Prence shot a look at Jon. "What did he say? When?"

Jon stuttered, "In the bar . . . I mean the Elks. The other night. He was all broken up."

"Oh, just drunk talk. They call that remorse. Guilt. But killing? That's not possible. Sons don't kill their mothers!"

"He wouldn't do it himself. But he might have hired somebody else to do it. He has money."

Prence jumped up from his desk. "Look," he said, "this is all stupid speculation - just a drunk's slip of the tongue. No point in slinging the blame around in all directions!"

"I just don't want it to land on Mr. Wentzell."

"Why don't you just concentrate on your baseball and other kid stuff. Have fun. Be nice to my daughter. I carry a gun, you know." He smiled.

~

JON WAS NOT SMILING AS THEY LEFT PRENCE'S OFFICE. LISA urged him to cool off. He stomped in the street. He punched a wall and spun around. "Jesus!" he shouted. "*Other kid stuff*!"

"Shshsh!" Lisa hissed.

"I'm sorry. I know he's your father and I'm sure he's very good at what he does. But this isn't right."

Lisa stopped and looked at him. Jon stalked down the street away from her, then turned and walked back. "This isn't right," he repeated. "He's not getting this done. He's just hanging around. Pushing papers. Meanwhile . . ." Jon raised his open hand to the sky as though avenging angels or horsemen were about to rush onto the Main Street of Tilley, Massachusetts.

Lisa put her hands on her hips. "WHAT?" she asked, using that single word as an expletive.

"Your father seems like a very nice man," Jon said.

"But?" Lisa responded. "I'm waiting for the 'but.'"

"No 'but'. It's just that he doesn't seem to be getting anywhere. You know what I mean?"

"What do you mean?"

Jon gathered his thoughts. "When you start out with something like this . . . like a murder or death or . . . something, you start out with a dead body, right? I mean you don't even know what to call it. You just have this dead body. And you really don't know anything else. Everything else is an assumption . . . a guess, right?"

Lisa grunted.

"So, wouldn't the first step be to determine who would want the dead person dead?"

"I'd want to know why he or she was dead."

"All right. Is that what your father would do? And how would he do that?"

There were people around them going about their Saturday morning chores and errands. Lisa grabbed Jon's arm and pushed him away from the police station and around the corner, away from the people. "You're making a scene," she said. They stopped by a stone wall surrounding a parking lot and sat down.

But after a moment Jon jumped up again. "How would they determine why or how she died? Can we assume it wasn't old age? That she didn't just drop dead?"

"We can't assume anything," Lisa replied, "because we don't know anything. Except that she's dead. But I'll humor you and say that somebody killed her. Now what?"

"So, then you have to figure out who. Right? What does he know about this Scoles character besides the fact that he went to Princeton and has some sort of major role at Salsberg Homes? I mean where did the guy come from? What do we know about him?"

"We don't know anything about him," Lisa replied. "Except that you don't like him."

"Well he stands to gain a lot, right? We can assume that, right? Doesn't he seem like . . . I mean if it is a murder. Why would he do it? Why would anyone do it? I mean, it's got to be the money. There's a lot of stuff we don't know."

"Yup," Lisa said. "Of course, there's stuff we don't know. I mean she supposedly had a pretty hard life. There are all sorts of rumors about her past. They say her father was a smuggler, you know, way back. In Florida."

"How old was she?"

"I don't know. How would I know?"

"Maybe we should find out. Like what happened to her first husband? Where did she come from? We don't know anything, and no offense, but I don't think your father does either. Maybe something in her past came back and bit her. Was she doing something illegal? We need to find out. You know?"

"Hey! My father's not just sitting around."

"No, I'm sure he isn't. But what is he doing? What does a policeman do to solve a crime in a small town like Tilley?"

"I'm sure it's the same thing everywhere," Lisa said. "You talk to people. It's not like what they make TV shows about – coming in with guns blazing."

"That's good," Jon replied, "because we don't have any guns. If someone is going to kill someone, they have to have a plan and they have to have a reason. We just have to figure it out. I'm not going to let Ace take the blame for something he didn't do."

"I didn't take you for a crusader. I thought you were just a jock."

"So, what do we know?"

"We know she's dead and she died in her house."

"Yeah, so?"

"That means that if someone was involved, they were in her house."

Jon said, "So let's find out about the people in the house."

"I'm sure we can find some stuff in the library," Lisa suggested. "These are money people, people with connections to society. So, they'd have to be in the newspapers."

"And maybe," Jon murmured, "maybe they've been bad before!"

TILLEY DID NOT HAVE ITS OWN PUBLIC LIBRARY SO JON AND Lisa headed to the Brooks Free Library in Harwich. Jon was impressed by the size of the building.

"Where are they from?" Jon asked. "Where are the Salsbergs from? If we want news about the Salsbergs we have to start from where they live."

"Yup. Someplace near Philadelphia."

"That's helpful, but what town?"

"Don't know," Lisa replied. "Something like Caresses. Something like that."

"Maybe we should start with a map and look at the towns around Philadelphia with names like that," Jon suggested.

So, with the help of the librarian they began digging into maps of the Philadelphia area, but without much success.

"What are you looking for?" the librarian asked.

Jon told her they were trying to find some information about the Salsberg family, the people who had donated money for the Tilley baseball team. "We're writing an article," Lisa said.

"Oh," the librarian said. "Wasn't that the family who recently had someone die?"

"Yes," Jon replied. Librarians must have all sorts of weirdos asking off-the-wall questions, he thought. This doesn't sound at all suspicious, does it? He smiled his ingratiating I'm-a-nice-boy smile.

The librarian showed them how to look up information on the family from newspapers in the Philadelphia area copied onto microfiche. "The town is called Caerwys and they pronounce it 'keerwiss,'" the librarian told them. " It's named after a small town in Wales."

Jon smiled, nodded, and rolled through the pages of the newspapers searching for references to the Salsberg family. There were references to Christopher Salsberg, the development of his company, and his marriage to Faith Reese. Lisa pulled up a chair beside him and leaned over his shoulder.

It was tedious. Not at all like "The Rockford Files" or "Columbo". They looked for stuff about Salsberg's first wife but didn't find anything.

They kept probing, trying to find more information about the family, and they came across the notices of Garrett Scoles marrying Bryce Salsberg. "Now we're getting somewhere," Jon said. The notice of the engagement stated that Bryce Salsberg was marrying Garrett Harold Scoles, a Princeton University engineering graduate from Florence, New Jersey.

"Let's see if we can turn up anything about Scoles's family. How did he get into Princeton? Did he have family connections?"

"Where the hell is Florence, New Jersey?" Lisa asked.

They dug into the maps and found it outside of Trenton.

Jon sat back in his wooden armchair and glared at the ceiling. "So what?" he asked. "So, he came from Florence, New Jersey. What does that mean? Is that some sort of pocket of money place - you know debutantes and polo clubs? Or is it just working-class New Jersey? There are a lot of places like that. He must have done something special to go from Florence to Princeton. Did he get a scholarship or something? What did he get it for? Seems to me something like that would make it into the local papers, wouldn't it?"

"Maybe he's really smart," Lisa suggested.

"You're right," Jon replied. "Let's keep going."

They finally found a local newspaper for Florence, New Jersey, after tedious cranking through page after page, day after day on the microfiche machine. Due to their proximity, every once in a while, Lisa's leg would touch Jon's, and he would find his attention distracted. He would lose track of the nefarious Scoles running through the fuzzy and slightly yellowed pages on the screen. Her touch was warm, and when she saw something that surprised her, she would put her hand on his knee and he would jump at the touch.

And still they persisted. They looked at the reports about the happenings at the schools. They looked on the obituary pages. They looked at the police blotter.

One thing for sure was that the Scoles family was not a community star. Even for the most notable town residents, the newspapers gave barely the thinnest of surface happenings. They didn't get into the emotional conflicts that glued events together. The local paper reported the highlights as the reporters saw them — the historical committee meetings, the parking bans, the Elks Club scholarship winners, and who got arrested. And that's where the nugget lay.

"Look!" Lisa said, pulling Jon over and pointing. "Scoles's father was arrested!"

"Really? For what?"

The story was sketchy. Rudy Scoles was apparently an accountant and was arrested for embezzling money from the company he worked for in Trenton. A picture of a round-faced, balding man with glasses who showed some similarity to Garrett. The article didn't provide detail beyond his name, the company name, and the names of the arresting officers. The story itself was neutral in tone, reporting just another event in the town of Florence for that day.

"We have to find out what happened." Jon said. "Was there a trial? Did he go to jail?"

"This talks about the arrest, but nothing else."

"How old was Scoles at the time?" Jon asked. "Garrett. How old was Garrett?"

"Let's see. This paper is from 1959, and when did we figure out Garrett was born?"

"1950."

"Well, that must have been traumatic for a nine-year-old."

"The way he acts," Jon replied, "he probably didn't care!"

"I don't know," Lisa said, "the guy must have some feelings. This could have been the traumatic event that drove him to nastiness. I don't believe people are born nasty."

"I'm not going to start feeling sympathetic with the guy. Ain't going to happen! Scoles must have done something special to get into Princeton if his father was a crook."

"You're jumping to conclusions, Jon. It doesn't say he was convicted."

"Still. He was arrested."

"How does that reflect on the son? Garrett wasn't arrested. His father was." Lisa emphasized her point by tapping her hand on Jon's knee. "That's in the bible," she said, sending Jon's mind spiraling off in wholly arbitrary directions.

Bible? he wondered.

But they kept on digging, digging through reports of students, the draft, and Vietnam, through reports of runaway dogs, car accidents, scouting events, school plays, and band nights.

They finally found Garrett on the sports pages.

"This could be it. His ticket to glory," Lisa said.

Garrett was a local football hero: captain of his high school team, awarded one of the state's National Football Foundation awards. According to the articles, Rutgers and Princeton competed for his skills. His picture on the front page was a block of granite with facial features, chin thrust out, head tilted back so his eyes squinted and he looked down his nose, unmistakably angry and threatening.

"That's him," Jon observed. "Princeton must have polished him up. Connected him to Bryce Salsberg at a dance somewhere."

Jon leaned away from the microfiche machine and stared up at the ceiling. "You can't find the contents of a person in old newspapers! You can't. Only pieces. Flickers. We're missing most of it."

"Yup," Lisa replied. "Isn't that what life is: memorable moments tied together with daily, boring goo?"

Jon wondered where she came up with these thoughts.

"What if Scoles didn't have anything to do with what happened to Mrs. Salsberg? It's like the old story of the guy looking for his keys under the streetlight because the light is better there than it is down the street where he really lost them!"

Lisa didn't reply.

He stood and stretched. Scanning the room, he noticed a familiar man sitting in one of the easy chairs with his head bowed over a newspaper.

"Hey, Lisa," he said tapping her on the shoulder. "Isn't that the HVAC guy with the funny name? Shalala? Frank Shalala?"

Lisa looked toward the easy chairs. "Yeah," she replied. "I think so."

"I should talk to him."

"Not about Scoles."

"No, not Scoles, but maybe he knows something about some of this. He was at the Salsberg house."

Jon walked over to where Shalala was sitting and said, "Hi, Mr. Shalala, I thought it was you."

Shalala looked up, lowering the paper to his knees. "Hey, kid," he said. "What brings you to the library on a bright summer's Saturday?"

"Oh, not much. Just checking out some stuff."

"How's the baseball? I don't get out to the games much. Busy time of year."

"Yeah. Good, I guess."

Jon smiled. He wanted to find just the right question.

"Something I can do for you?" Shalala asked.

"Yeah. Well, I was wondering, you know they're trying to say that Mr. Wentzell had something to do with what happened to Mrs. Salsberg?"

"Yeah?"

"That doesn't seem right to me. I don't know Mr. Wentzell very well. I mean I just got here, but still, it doesn't seem right, does it?"

Shalala didn't reply.

"Well, they think it might be something in the house that killed her."

"Like what?" Shalala asked.

"I think they've ruled out drugs."

"Rich old ladies do like their drugs," Shalala said. "You wouldn't believe the pharmacies that I see in some of the houses I work on."

"Could it have been carbon monoxide? That's what killed my

mother. Here on Cape Cod. Two years ago in a motel. They blamed a faulty pool heater."

"Sorry about that." He folded up his paper and stood up. "So where are you going with this, kid?"

"Did you install the pool heater, Mr. Shalala?" Jon asked.

Lisa walked up to them. "Hi," she said.

"This is Officer Prence's daughter," Jon said.

"Yeah, I know. Seen you around."

Lisa smiled.

"Who would have installed the pool heater?" Jon asked.

"Pool heater shouldn't be a problem. But they have gotten more sophisticated in recent years. They've built in serpentine heat exchangers that squeeze more of the heat out of the burning gas and added more sophisticated controls. Sometimes I have to read the installation manuals these days!" Shalala laughed. "And I've done a million heaters."

"Could it have been installed wrong?"

The smile disappeared from Shalala's face. "What are you trying to say? Are you accusing me?" Shalala asked.

"Has Officer Prence talked to you?" Jon asked.

"Don't get me involved. He hasn't talked to me and I haven't talked to him. I do my job, okay? Leave it alone, kid. Don't stir the soup unless you know what's going to rise to the top of the pot." He started moving toward the door.

Jon watched him go. "Thanks," he said.

Without turning around, Shalala waved his hand and walked out the door.

Jon looked at Lisa standing beside him. "Did Shalala look guilty to you?"

"I'm sure my father's looking at anyone who could have been involved."

"Does that include me?" Jon asked.

"It's the way real police do these things, Jon."

"Right," Jon replied. He dropped into the easy chair that Shalala had left and looked down at his hands. "Just seems weird, you know. Pool heaters killing people. Strange coincidence."

"Didn't you say your sister was an engineer or something?"

Jon looked up at her. "Yeah! You're right. I should ask her about the CO. She knows all this stuff. Yeah, I should ask her. Maybe we can get some facts."

As they drove back to Tilley, they talked and debated and argued about Garrett Scoles and how he might have accomplished killing his mother-in-law. But what did he know about pool heaters? What did he know about CO or buildings, for that matter? Shalala, on the other hand was a different story. They had to find his motive. "I've got to get a look at that pool heater," Jon said.

12

DUPIN - JULY 9, 1979

Jon told himself to get his head in the game. His mind wandered away from baseball to Lisa to Ace to murder to the bug crawling up his shoe as he stood just off first base. He flicked his toe, and the bug flew off - whatever it was. The Longliners were playing the Harwich Mariners on their diamond at Whitehouse Field. It was the third inning and the Mariners were ahead. Jon felt the Longliners were a made-up team. Not a real team. They weren't playing as a team. Not even thinking as a team. They knew what they were supposed to do. They were supposed to play good baseball and win games. Coach Russell had explained that clearly to them. They weren't motivated. If the players were driven forward by anything, it was simply personal pride; that and getting drafted by a major league team. It felt like they were merely going through the motions of playing a game that they had been playing most of their lives. It was comfortable with just a touch of the spice of *new*.

The environment was comfortable, with the smell of salt in the air, cool breezes off the water, spectators sitting in beach chairs along the edges of the field. It was just too nice. And almost impossible to think of this game as a battle, a conflict between men, a challenge between the pitcher and the batter. It was difficult to rub up the ire. The situation on this field in this environment showed baseball's true heritage as a pastoral game . . . like a movie.

Jon scuffed the dirt with his shoe. He looked around at his team members and watched Dupin go through his motions prior to pitching. There was a mandate not to scratch your crotch because it wasn't polite, and it might end up on film. But it was like telling someone not to think about a pink elephant. Or telling a pitcher not to pitch high and inside. It was all he could think about and the result was preordained.

Dupin walked the Harwich batter with four bad pitches, while forcing Barry Nolan, the Longliner catcher, to scramble around behind the plate to hang on to the ball. Before the next batter took his stance, Nolan jogged out for a meeting with the pitcher and Jon joined them on the mound.

"What the hell are you doing?" Nolan spat. "Do you know where home plate is? If you've lost it, I'm right behind it. I'll point it out to you if you like!"

Jon said, "Ease up, Barry."

Nolan was barely five foot six. He had broad shoulders and resembled a fire plug to Jon. He was from North Carolina and had a soft, southern drawl that made his swearing sound gentlemanly. He cleared his throat and spat to the side of the mound.

"I don't care about whatever the hell is on your mind. It obviously isn't baseball," Nolan said. "I do care about winning baseball games. I do care about my future. So, pay attention and do your job!" He pulled down his mask, pivoted and headed back toward home plate before the umpire could come out and break up their little chat.

Jon shrugged to Dupin and jogged back to first base. "Hey! How ya doin'?" he said to the Harwich runner who didn't take his eyes off Dupin.

"Where ya from?" Jon asked, taking a couple of shuffle steps to his right.

"My momma."

"Really?" Jon said reaching out his glove toward Dupin who was watching both the runner and Nolan, the catcher, trying to remember the signs that indicated what sort of pitch he wanted Dupin to deliver.

"I suppose we all have that in common, don't we?" Jon philosophized.

Dupin spun away from the batter and fired the ball toward Jon who caught it with a SLAP and swept his left hand down toward the feet of the runner who scrambled back to first base. The umpire flung his arms out in both directions indicating a safe return. Jon shrugged and tossed the ball back to Dupin.

The Harwich runner resumed his lead off first base, glancing down at second. Dupin rubbed up the ball, glanced down at his feet, and then resumed his stance. The crowd waited, munched on snacks, and basked in the sun like reptiles on rocks. Dupin pitched again toward Nolan, and again it was in the dirt. The batter stepped back with a grin on his face and waved his bat at Dupin.

Jon could see that Dupin was talking to himself. Jon yelled, "You got this guy, Dupin! You got this guy!"

Except he didn't have him. Dupin threw the next pitch right down the middle and with a mighty TING of the bat, the ball flew over the second baseman's head and dropped onto the grass and bounced out toward the center fielder. The first base runner burned the breeze past second base and came into third standing up as the batter roared straight past first, turned and sauntered back to the base, pulling off his helmet and flinging it toward the bat boy. "And that's how it's done," he said to Jon.

"Yah," Jon replied. "You taught that ball a thing or two!"

Dupin was clearly not on his game. Jon's latest visitor to first base took his lead off the base, legs spread, hands out in both directions. Dupin looked at him, shrugged and threw the ball to the catcher. The pitch was low, but the batter swung at it. The runner took off toward second. Nolan managed to scoop the ball out of the dirt and fire it toward second. But the second baseman was out of position and didn't get back in time. The ball flew over second base and landed in the outfield.

The runner on third sprinted toward home, and seeing what had happened to the ball, the runner from first made a wide turn at second, touching the bag and heading for third, sliding in safely and at least getting his uniform dirty. Jon stood off first base watching all this unfold, instinctively stepping forward. The hometown Harwich crowd was on its feet, spilling drinks and tossing popcorn, cheering the Longliners' error wildly.

"Shit!" Jon spat. It was going to be one of those games. There was very little difference between success and failure besides the score. Over the years, Jon had learned that as the level of skill increased, a few inches to the right or left, a tiny twist of the ball or grip on the bat made the difference between winning and losing. The fundamental skill level of these players was equal. It wasn't the physical variations that made teams win or lose as much as it was the mental variations. And as soon as a player started thinking about their ability to play, about what their girlfriend thought about them in their uniform, about the rumble in their stomach, about all those people in the stands watching, evaluating, judging, criticizing, they were out of the game. Just a single grain of sand in the machine can grind it to a halt.

The Longliners were slumping into a who-gives-a-shit malaise. By the sixth inning they were down by six runs. Icky Bartholomew popped the ball up toward the center fielder and half jogged toward first base on the assumption that the ball would be caught and he would be out. He dropped his bat about halfway to first, the centerfielder caught the ball, and Bartholomew turned and headed back toward the dugout where he was confronted by Nolan.

"What the hell was that!" Nolan yelled at him. "What the hell was that!"

"Huh?" Icky replied, not quite sure what the problem was.

"What the hell was that? When did we stop running it out to first base?"

"He was going to catch it!" Icky replied. "What's your problem? Not enough air behind the plate?"

"That's a T-ball move!" Nolan shouted. "Kindergarten. This is professional!"

"Oh, back off, Nolan. What's got your knickers in a twist?"

In his anger and frustration, a small comment like that was enough to put Nolan over the top. He lunged for Bartholomew's throat, pushing him backward so that he stumbled into the dugout, his cap flying off, stacked bats tumbling. The two of them began to wrestle as Bartholomew tried to push Nolan off. Other team members joined in trying to pull the two combatants off each other. The home plate and first base umpires jogged over.

Coach Russell yelled, "Hey! Knock it off!" He pulled players back, digging his way through the bodies to get to the primary combatants. "Back off! Let go! Act like professionals even if you aren't! Knock it off!"

"What's going on here?" demanded the home plate umpire, taking charge of the situation. "What's going on here?"

The players had managed to pull Bartholomew and Nolan apart. Wrapped in the restraining grasps of their teammates, they stood back staring at each other, breathing heavily.

"Who started this?" Coach Russell demanded.

"He did," the two players blurted out.

"I don't care!" Russell replied. "You're both out of the game! Get away from each other. Sit down and shut up. We'll deal with this later."

"Is your team ready to play ball?" the umpire asked.

The coach nodded and the umpire jogged back toward his position behind home plate and yelled, "Batter up!"

The crowd settled back into their seats, muttering to each other. Jon sat down next to Bartholomew and hissed, "What the hell?"

"Asshole!" Icky replied.

"What?"

"Not you. Him!" He indicated Nolan. "Guy's a prick!"

"What are you thinking about?" Jon asked. "You've got to focus!"

Icky looked at him. "Seriously?" he asked. "Seriously? You telling me to focus? Where the hell is your head at? Strange advice coming from you. Where the hell is this whole team at? We're wasting our time. This is stupid."

Jon looked out across the field. He surveyed the Harwich players staring at the pitcher, waiting for the next moment. He scanned the summer crowd in the aluminum bleachers in their white t-shirts, caps, and floppy hats shading their faces from the warm afternoon sun. The magic of the game wasn't there. It was just too nice.

He released an explosive sigh. "Well, get it together. A lot of things are stupid. You've got to do a lot of stupid things in life. The fact is this. This is what we're here to do. We're here for exactly this. To play baseball. To play baseball as well as we can. And the only way we can do that is to play together. As a team. It doesn't matter whether you think it is stupid or not. Or whether I think it's stupid or not."

Icky looked at him.

Jon said, "Yeah. Sometimes I think it's stupid too. But that doesn't matter. You're good at this. That's why you're here. That's why I'm here. People like to share our success."

"What success?"

Jon smiled. "Yeah, I know. It's not going to happen every time. But there's no reason why these guys are any better than we are. There's talent on this team. Even Nolan. No matter what you're thinking now, he is a good catcher."

Icky looked around as if seeking someone. "Who the hell are you? Knute Rockne? Should I be hearing the swelling of the violins? What kind of shit is this?"

"It's reality, Ick. It's reality. It's what we're working with." But even as he said it, Jon questioned his own dedication to a baseball life.

That wasn't enhanced as the game proceeded. The team made two more errors. The loss of Nolan behind the plate and Bartholomew at short weakened the Longliners' already weak defensive play. Although Coach Russell rotated through several pitchers trying to find someone who would keep the Mariners in line and off the base paths, the game was a shambles. When the pain finally ended for the day, the Longliners had lost by ten runs. The ebullience of the Harwich crowd was like salt in a wound and the Longliners shuffled off the field hanging their heads and dragging their equipment. They would have preferred having the lions devour them in the Coliseum.

They'd lost a game before, but Jon could see that the frustration, anger and fear was piling on their coach. He was glad that he wasn't the one that had to try to push all these disparate egos together into something that would serve as a team. He had to wonder if their season was over, if they had gone over the top of the don't-give-a-shit state of mind. If that was the case, it was going to be a miserable summer and at least some players were going to lose their chance to become stars which would drive further frustration, disgruntlement, and blaming.

As the players headed back to Tilley, Jon sensed that some of his teammates were ready to pack their bags and go home. This wasn't turning out to be what they had expected. The worst of it was that they didn't trust each other. They had begun to expect the worst - the worst outcome for the team, the worst outcome for the game. But they didn't expect to lose one of their own so suddenly.

THE LONGLINERS DIDN'T HAVE A BUS TO TRANSPORT THE TEAM from game to game. They piled into individual cars. They wouldn't return to Tilley all at the same time. And after the day's debacle, none of them felt much like rehashing the trashy game.

Jon and some of the other players slunk off to the Elks Hall to drown their sorrows. Jon hung around a bit waiting for Dupin to return, but there didn't seem to be much point.

The atmosphere in the basement of the Elks Lodge was somber. Enough people had heard about the events of the afternoon to bring the general jovial level of chatter down to a more respectful murmur when the Longliner players walked in. Jon wondered at the power that sports had on the mood of the fans. The bizarre painted faces and bodies at snowy football games, the passions of the tailgaters, the depression that could haunt fans for days after a loss or the elation after a major win - sports was a powerful drug. The team had let the fans down today.

"Good effort," someone at the bar said, slapping Jon on the back.

"Thanks," he responded.

"You guys will get there," someone else added.

"Just give it time."

"Yeah. Give it time. It's early yet."

"It's freakin' halfway through the season!" someone else added less sympathetically.

"Takes time. Takes time. Back off!"

"There's always tomorrow."

Jon and the other players drifted off to a back corner with their beers.

They huddled over the table, leaning over their arms, sheltering their plastic cups, looking into the depths of the liquid to find redemption.

"What the hell happened?" the second baseman asked of no one in particular. "What was that fight all about? What's eating Nolan?"

"Guess he's tired of losing," Jon suggested.

"We're all tired of losing, but you don't have to get into a fight about it! What did that accomplish?"

Jon looked around the room. The fluorescent light glared down from the suspended ceiling. The pale green cinder block walls made him think of schools or government buildings. The

TV up in the corner over the bar was tuned to the Red Sox and Angels game. Mike Torres, the Red Sox pitcher, was struggling to get the Angels out in the first inning. The Red Sox were already down two runs.

"Well, the Sox aren't doing much better than we did!" Jon pointed out.

"And that's supposed to cheer us up how? Zimmer's an idiot as a manager," the left fielder added.

"Coach Russell's not much better," the second baseman said. "I don't get him."

"Wait. What?" the left fielder said.

"What?" asked Jon.

"Just sayin'."

"What are you saying?" Jon asked.

The left fielder shrugged. They dropped back into silence.

A communal groan surged through the bar as Torres gave up another run.

Jon looked over at the TV, trying to tune in what was happening. "At least they're losing as a team."

"Yeah, but they're pros, right?" the second baseman asked. "They get paid to do this."

"Wait. What? What difference does that make? Losing is losing."

Jon saw the bartender turn to answer the phone, then scan the gathered crowd. His gaze settled on the Longliner players. "Hey!" he called. "You guys. Coach wants you back at the field."

The players looked at each other. "Uh oh," someone at the bar chanted. "Trouble!"

The players stood up and shuffled out. "Watch my beer for me, will ya?" the second baseman added as they exited.

"What now?" the left fielder asked.

"Pretty obvious, isn't it?" the second baseman said. "He wants to slap us around for today. Knock some sense into us as my old man likes to say."

In the early evening light at the field the players drifted back together, finding seats in the bleachers, staring out at the field. The mood was somber. Jon found Bartholomew shuffling his feet, off by himself. "Hey," Jon acknowledged.

"Hey," Icky responded.

"What's going on?"

Icky shrugged.

"Where's Dupin?" Jon asked looking around.

Icky shrugged again.

A tingle of horrible recognition shocked Jon's brain, a feeling that he couldn't identify and didn't want to accept.

"Where's Dupin?" he asked again.

Icky shrugged again. "How should I know?"

Jon scanned the team again, figuring he must have missed his friend. The players knew they had behaved and performed badly. They murmured, mumbled, and swallowed their smiles, shuffled their feet and studied the ground. The coach wouldn't have brought them together if it wasn't serious. But how bad could it be? So, they hadn't played well. So they had lost a game. They'd lost other games. So there had been a disagreement. They were under stress. It couldn't be that bad.

Coach Russell appeared, shuffling along the first base path, hands shoved into his pockets with his head down. Even from a distance Jon thought he looked grey -- ashen. He stopped, looked up, raised his hands over his head, and told the players to sit.

When they had settled, he swallowed, looked away, and then snapped his attention back to them. "There's been an accident," he quietly said.

"What?" several players blurted out.

"There's been an accident. A serious accident. On the way back from the game."

"What happened?"

"Well, they're not sure yet how it happened. But apparently on Route 28 . . . you know . . . it's narrow, and they said a car crossed over the line and . . . hit a team car."

The players' silence underlined the disbelief. It couldn't happen to them. "Anybody hurt?" someone asked.

The tingly feeling that Jon had experienced earlier was growing. He could no longer deny it. "Oh, shit," he mumbled.

The coach shuffled his feet but then lifted his head to confront the reality. "Yes," he said. "There were three players in the car - Iandiorio, Thompson, and . . . Harry Dupin."

"Are they going to be okay?" someone asked.

"They took Iandiorio and Thompson to Cape Cod Hospital. From what I hear their injuries were pretty minor."

"What about Dupin?" Jon blurted out.

The coach took a deep breath and said, "He didn't make it."

"What do you mean 'he didn't make it'?" a player asked.

The coach struggled with the words. "He didn't make it. The crash killed him. He was riding shotgun, I guess."

Killed? Jon was having trouble processing the information. Killed? He was just there! He was just pitching. How could he be . . . dead? He was too young. "Are you sure?" he blurted out. Shock and disbelief burbled among the players.

The coach nodded.

"I'm sorry, guys. I don't know any more than that."

Players fired off questions: "There must be more! People just don't . . . die on a clear afternoon in July! Did the guy fall asleep? Was he drunk? What the hell happened?"

"Look, guys, I'm sure more information will be available in the next few days. We'll get details. I'll let you know more as soon as I know it, but for now you might want to call home. Talk to people."

Some of the players got up to leave. Jon didn't want to move. Moving might make it real. He didn't know Dupin all that well, didn't know his family, had barely known him for a few weeks, but he was a friend. They were the same age.

Someone should call Dupin's family. Jon stood up and moved down the bleachers to the field. A small knot of players had gathered around the coach. Jon asked, "Should I call his family?"

"No . . . yeah . . . I mean it's been done" the coach replied. "The police do that sort of thing. Do you know his family?"

"No. Just met him. Here. On the Cape. Just met him. Are they sure . . . the police, I mean?"

The coach nodded and turned away.

Jon found the pay phone by the field parking lot. He stepped into the box, sat on the small, hard seat, and pulled the door closed. The light went on and Jon looked up at the phone. He dialed the operator. "I need to make a collect call." He gave her his home number.

His throat closed for a moment when he heard his father's distant voice. "I have a collect call from Jon Megquire," the operator stated. "Will you accept the charges?"

Although he never doubted that his father would accept his call, a wave of relief swept over Jon as the connection was completed and his father said, "Jon? It's not Sunday?" he chuckled. "You only call on Sundays. Something must be wrong! Bad game? Girl problem?"

"A kid on the team just got killed," Jon said in a rush.

"What?"

"Coming back from the game. Car accident. Pitcher. Harry Dupin. He . . . died."

Jon waited for the second click for his mother to pick up the extension the way she always had, sharing his calls, a click that would never come.

"Are you okay?" his father asked.

"Yeah. I'm fine. I wasn't in the car." Jon relayed what the coach had told them. It should have been more. There should have been more information. There should have been a reason. Old people and sick people died and even distant people, strangers that you don't know. But not friends!

"Oh my god, Jon," his father said. "I'm so sorry. What happens next?"

"What do you mean?"

"What happens next? Will the team keep playing? Are you coming home?"

Jon couldn't answer him. He didn't know what would happen next.

"Do you want me to come up?" his father asked him.

"I don't know," Jon replied. "I mean there isn't anything you can do, right? There isn't anything anyone can do."

A moment passed in silence.

"That's awful," his father said. "How old was he?"

"I don't know. My age, I guess."

More silence.

"I gotta go," Jon said. "Just thought I'd let you know . . . tell you . . . you know."

"If there's anything I can do, let me know." his father added. "Look, talk to me. Tell me what's going on. I can't help if I don't know what's going on."

"I gotta go," Jon said again.

"Sometimes life really sucks."

Another pause.

"I love you, Jon," his father said. "You know that?"

"Yeah. I gotta go."

"Take care of yourself," his father said. "Let me know what's going on."

"I will," Jon replied.

WHAT'S NEXT? HE SAT IN THE TINY BOOTH IN SILENCE AND stared at the phone. What's next? What happens now? Jon couldn't move. Nothing was next for Dupin. He was done. He was out of the game. Just like that, Dupin had no next.

Jon recognized that he couldn't keep sitting in the phone booth. He was compelled to continue and confront the future. The next word. The next thought. The next hour. The next day. What if Dupin's death was imaginary? What if it hadn't really happened? Maybe if he saw the spot of the accident? But what would that prove? Would that make it more real? Dupin's wasn't Jon's first dance with death, but this time it could have been his own. He stepped out of the phone booth and looked up at the stars. And so it goes. One foot in front of the other.

He thought about returning to the Elks Lodge, but the thought depressed him further. They would all be sitting around, mumbling, drinking, smoking, and being stupidly sad. He turned Maybellene into the heart of Tilley and headed back to his summer home with the Wentzells.

Ace and Babs were in the kitchen exactly where he expected them to be. Ace was at the table, his reading glasses perched on his nose, immersed in the paper. Babs, wearing her apron, turned away from the sink, wiping her hands on a dish towel as he came into the room.

"Bad game?" she asked when she saw his face.

He nodded. "Did you hear?"

Babs looked at Ace, who lowered his paper. "Was it that bad?" he asked.

"There was an accident," Jon said.

"Are you okay?" Babs asked.

Jon shook his head. "It wasn't me. Car accident. Coming back from the game. No, it wasn't me."

Ace said, "Thought I heard a lot of sirens. Not that unusual this time of year. People do stupid stuff. Didn't pay much attention."

"Anyone hurt?" Babs asked.

Jon gulped. "Yeah," he said. Then he stumbled through the coach's description.

The three of them looked at each other. "They going to be okay?" Babs asked.

"Two of them," Jon replied.

"What about the third one?" Ace asked.

Jon looked down at his hands. "He died."

Babs gasped and put her hand over her mouth. "Oh my god!" she said.

"I don't know," Jon said. "Dupin. Harry Dupin. Did you know him? He is . . . was . . . a pitcher. Pitched today, in fact. Not one of his best days. Not one of his best days at all."

"Do his parents know?" Babs asked.

Jon shrugged.

"Oh my God!" she repeated.

"Sit down, Jon," Ace directed.

Jon walked toward the table. Babs wrapped her arms around him and pulled him to her. She was warm and soft and smelled of laundry soap and oatmeal cookies. Jon fought the grief welling up inside of him. He swallowed against the lump in his throat and tried to blink away the itchiness in his eyes. Just stupid! Dupin wasn't a close friend. He shouldn't feel this way.

Babs released him and he slumped into his chair at the table.

Ace folded the paper and took off his glasses. "So, he was a pitcher? Was he good?"

"When he was on his game, he was very good. He could make the ball bounce through the air, you know. That's why he was known as *Hoppin*. The ball sort of hopped."

"Where was he from?"

"Texas. Austin. I think he went to Rice."

"Good school," Ace said.

Jon shrugged.

"Did he have a girl?" Ace asked.

Jon brought his focus back to Ace's eyes. He realized that he knew little about Dupin. They had known each other for a few weeks. They had talked about baseball. They had talked about the beer. They hadn't had time to talk beyond the immediate stuff.

"I think I saw him pitch. Did I see him?" Ace asked Babs.

She shrugged.

"Was he really tall? Skinny? Big ears? Bushy eyebrows?"

Jon nodded.

"You're right, he was good."

"He was my friend," Jon admitted.

Ace paused a moment and then he said, "Even though he was only around for a short time, losing a friend makes a hole. You might only know someone for a moment, but it makes a hole when they're gone. I could tell you a dozen stories about people who have been in my life that are gone now. Made a *lot* of holes. Sometimes time fills them in quickly. Sometimes it takes a while. Some holes will live with you forever and never go away.

"But you're better for them being there. It's funny, but the people who are missing help to make you whole. A bit of them will always be with you."

Ace got up from the table and started toward the sink. Babs put her hand over his with a smile, took the cup from him and rinsed it in the sink.

"You'll get through this," Ace said. "You're young. You're strong. You're talented. And you're lucky to be alive. Remember that."

Jon wasn't so sure.

13
SUIT

The next morning Jon stood beside Ace outside the Thompson house and looked up at the roof. There was nothing wrong with the roof. That was done. Issues had appeared when they opened up one of the walls. Jon liked the way Ace called them 'issues'. Not 'problems' or 'defects' but 'issues'.

"Old houses always have issues," Ace said, "mold or rot hidden in walls that were patched and plastered over to avoid actually solving the problem. Cover it up and maybe it will go away."

Today's issue was asbestos, wrapped around pipes that would have to be removed before the project proceeded. Ace told Jon he had worked around asbestos pipe insulation for years. It insulated steam pipes and boilers in old houses and had never been considered much of a problem. Now, however, there were lawsuits and legislation. "You could just rip the stuff out and get on with life!" Ace said. "Not any more. And it's not only this stuff. They keep changing the rules. You have to have permits and paperwork and get trained to breathe! It gets stupidly expensive. Can't believe that just this little bit would mean anything to anyone. Been doing it for years!"

A strange car parked on the street behind them and a man in a suit walked across the grass.

"Asaph Wentzell?" the man in the suit asked.

Ace turned to assess the man. Even with his short construction experience, Jon sensed that a suit on a job site didn't bode well. It expressed some self-important official or salesman. But it wouldn't be a salesman if he was using Ace's Christian name.

"Asaph Wentzell?" the man asked again.

Ace looked at Jon and muttered, "See! Bad thoughts. Hadn't even touched the damn asbestos and they're already on my case!"

Walking over to the suit he said, "Yup. What can I do for you?"

The man handed him a folded packet of papers. "Asaph Wentzell, you've been served."

"That's what a waitress says just before she demands that I 'have a nice day'! What's this?"

The man in the suit didn't respond but simply walked back to his car. Ace fumbled in his pocket for his glasses, perched them on his nose, unfolded the papers, and slogged through the mud of legalese. Jon watched his face, trying to decipher the 'issue' revealed in the papers. But Ace's look was impenetrable.

"What?" Jon asked.

Ace continued to look at the pages.

"What?" Jon asked again.

"Nothin'," Ace replied, as he folded up the papers and stuffed them in his pocket. "Go on back to the plaster." He turned back toward his truck.

Jon was hot and sweaty and thinking about Dupin. Ace had assigned him the task of pulling plaster and pieces of lathe out of the house and getting it in the dumpster. In Jon's jaundiced state of mind, it vexed him to be doing menial, manual labor. He was a college student. He was better than that. But anything, any type of work would have vexed him at that moment. He might have punched someone who wished him to have a nice day and smiled!

Ace had stopped before he got to his truck, turned, and walked back.

"Who was that?" Jon asked as he watched the man in the suit get into his car.

"No one," Ace replied. "No one."

"What'd he want?"

"Nothing."

It was not any of Jon's business, and if Ace didn't want to talk about, he wouldn't. "Dumpster's getting full."

"That's the idea," Ace said.

What's eating him? Jon wondered. He didn't have a friend get killed yesterday. He wasn't hauling crap out of a smelly basement. He didn't have to make decisions about the future direction of his life. He was committed, for Christ's sake! He had found his road! He had his history. He had his job. What the hell was his problem?

Suddenly Ace blurted out, "What do you know about the law, kid?"

"What?"

Ace handed him the papers. "Know anything about the law? You're a college kid. Know anything about the law?"

Jon wiped his hands on his jeans and opened up the pages. "What's this?"

"Aaah! Legal shit! They're trying to blame me." Ace looked back at the house. "At least that's what I think they're trying to do. I'm no lawyer."

Jon scanned through the boilerplate legal language, that pointed the proverbial finger here, there, and everywhere, shedding responsibility from everyone on their side, and loading it on Ace's shoulders.

"Looks like they're suing you." Jon asked, looking up. "For what? That's not fair. Is this for real? Who's doing this? I can't even figure that out."

Ace snatched the papers back.

"Who's doing this? Who's they?"

"Don't know," Ace replied. "Must be that Scoles fellow."

"What do they think you've done? What are they blaming you for?"

"Don't know," Ace replied, stuffing the papers back in his pocket. "I guess they think that something I did . . . or didn't do . . . resulted in Mrs. Salsberg's death!"

"You didn't do that!"

"Doesn't matter. They say I did. They can say anything they like. They have their lawyers say it for them. Keeps it more business-like . . . less personal. 'Don't take this personally,' they say."

"So what are you going to do?" Jon asked. He was watching a proud man be shaken by being forced into the unknown. Ace knew wood and glass and plaster and pipes. He knew saws and hammers and nails and screws. He appreciated the gentle curve of a colonial staircase or the way a wooden gutter guided water off the edge of a roof. But he knew nothing about courts and lawyers. He would have been more comfortable venturing into a haunted forest with gremlins, dragons, and dwarfs than stepping into the swamp of a lawsuit.

"Don't know," Ace replied. "I don't know what I'm supposed to do with this."

"Do you have a lawyer?"

"A lawyer?" Ace asked as though this was a completely foreign question. "I talked to a lawyer once."

"There must be a lawyer in Tilley. Don't you have contracts with clients?"

"Mostly handshakes. Lawyers aren't necessary around here."

Jon looked at him. He didn't know anything about lawyers or lawsuits either. "You're probably going to need a lawyer this time. It doesn't seem as though this is going to resolve itself with a handshake. I can call my father. He might know."

Ace shrugged. "Don't know," he said. "Never been on this road before and don't particularly want to go there."

~

THE LONGLINERS' GAME WITH FALMOUTH THAT AFTERNOON was postponed. Dupin's parents were on their way to Tilley. The team met at the field, and out of habit, they tossed the ball around. They sat on the grass. They kicked the dirt. They talked about what they knew about Dupin. The coach filled them in about what had happened, but it still wasn't particularly clear. An old man had drifted over the line and smashed into the players' car coming the other way. Who was he? Did he fall asleep? Was he drunk? They wanted to know why. They wanted a reason because it didn't make sense. Jon listened as each of them weighed and evaluated and sought answers where none existed.

"I should have given him a ride," one player mumbled kicking the dirt.

"He was just starting to get that curve under control."

"Yeah. He could have been really good."

Graham told them that the other players would be out of the hospital soon.

"Are they going to stick around?"

Graham said he wasn't sure yet. Hadn't had a chance to talk to them about that.

"What's going to happen to the team?"

There was no off-the-shelf answer to that question either.

"We wouldn't just stop, would we?" Barry Nolan, the catcher asked. "I mean we're here. It's too bad and all, but why should we just stop?"

Icky looked at him. Jon could tell that Icky was tempted to berate Nolan for not caring, for not caring about anyone or anything except himself. He surprised Jon when he said, "You're right, Barry. You're right for once. We can't simply stop."

The other players moved into a tighter group. Jon said, "Dupin was a friend. He was a good guy and we'll miss him. But what good would it do for us to just . . . you know . . . stop playing? What would that prove?"

"Yeah!" Nolan added. "Dupin wouldn't have wanted that. Life goes on, right? We can miss him. But life goes on."

"It's a thought, but we could sort of dedicate the season to him," Jon suggested.

The coach stepped back, watching the players, listening.

"Yeah," Icky exclaimed. "Life goes on."

"We have our own lives, our own careers to consider," Nolan said. "This is our big chance, right coach?" He looked at Coach Russell.

The coach looked at the group of young faces. In his hesitation to verbalize what he was thinking, Jon could see in the coach's expressions the threads and pathways of his past - chances missed, paths not taken, moments misread, things that could have gone differently.

"Yeah," the coach finally said, "this is definitely an opportunity not to be missed. I've been trying to tell you that. Dupin was a solid pitcher. Could have had a great career, and it's a shame. A real shame. But it wouldn't be right for the rest of you guys to quit. He wouldn't have wanted that. None of us knew him that well, but he seemed like the kind of guy who really cared about other people."

The players shuffled and mumbled uncomfortably.

"It's up to you," the coach continued. "It's really up to you. You can let this end the season right here. Right now. Or you can get yourselves together and reach out as a team. Feel sad. Go ahead. Feel sad. Remember Dupin in your own way. However you want. But let this pull you together instead of letting it pull you apart. This is definitely a fork in the road. So, take it!"

That brought a few smiles and a chuckle.

"So, what'll it be, guys? Up to you."

Jon looked around at the other players, looking for agreement. It seemed odd that keeping going was the easier path. "So what happens next, coach?" he asked.

"Orleans. Here tomorrow. Let's be ready."

~

THROUGH THE GLASS OF THE SLIDING DOOR AT CASA GRANDE, Garrett Scoles paused for a moment and observed his drunken wife and idiot brother-in-law lounging on the patio in the fading pinks and oranges of the setting sun. He didn't like them plotting. He did not like them chatting in such a head to head manner. Not that Brian could plot. He was not capable of thinking two feet in front of himself. Bryce, on the other hand, was a lovely, velvet schemer. It was one of the things Garrett liked about her. She was perfectly capable of leading Brian by his nose. And despite the fact that she was his wife, Garrett did not trust her. Especially now that Faith was out of the way.

"What are you two up to?" he asked, pushing the slider back and stepping out onto the flagstones.

"What do you care?" Bryce responded.

"We were just enjoying the sunset," Brian said. "You know when the sun gets near the horizon the light has to pass through a lot more atmosphere than when it is higher in the sky. That's what gives it the color and makes it look bigger. It's sort of like a lens - a magnifying lens, what's known as a convex lens. You know, the ones that bow out not the ones that curve in."

"Who gives a shit, Brian," Garrett asked.

Bryce took a swig of her gin and tonic. "Where are the boys?" she asked.

"Oh," Brian replied. "I'm not sure. Off running around somewhere."

"You should take them somewhere," Bryce suggested. "To the beach or something."

"I think they've been at the beach a bunch. Can't let them get too much sun."

"They must be used to that. Living in Florida."

"What? Too much sun? We don't let them spend too much time outside. Audrey read something that said too much sun was worse than too little sun."

"Don't want them to look like little pickaninnies would you?

You know if their skin gets too dark, people might think that they aren't yours."

"They never would, would they?" Brian asked. "At least not Junior with his blond hair."

"Fair hair. Fair skin. Burns more easily." Bryce took another swig. "What's Audrey making for dinner?"

"Why is it always Audrey that's expected to make meals? She's not the help!"

Bryce glared at him. "I hate cooking! And she loves it. Makes her feel useful. We're supposed to be on vacation, aren't we? That's why we're here, isn't it?"

"Yeah, Brian," Garrett said. "Why don't you get yourself a drink? Relax. And while you're at it, get me one as well. And I'm sure Bryce could use a refresher."

Bryce held her glass up and waved it in the air.

Brian heaved himself up out of his deck chair and captured Bryce's glass.

Garrett glided over and dropped into the chair Brian had vacated.

"Great!" Brian said. "Just great." He scraped off to the house.

Garrett looked out at the water and saw the trees turning black as the brilliance of the sun obscured them into silhouettes. "Gotta go to Philly again," he said to his wife. "Gotta make sure those idiots on the Board don't make a mess of things while I'm not right in front of them. They're so old. Their minds are in the past. They can't deal with change. Remember how they were when your father died? It took them years to get their heads screwed back on."

"We all should have stayed when we went down for the funeral."

"For Christ's sake, Bryce, you were the one who wanted us to come back!"

"Well, it seemed wrong to simply leave. I don't like leaving things unfinished, and we weren't finished here. Not for the summer. Not for the house. The house wasn't closed up, remember? It would have been hanging out as an unplanned *coitus interruptus*."

"What?" Garrett asked.

"But now," Bryce continued, "now maybe we should all go home. There's no reason for us to stay here. I, for one, am not relaxing."

"Sheriff wants us here."

"Is he a sheriff? Is that what they call them here?"

"I don't know," Garrett replied. "Sheriff, constable, warden, chief mucky-muck. Who gives a shit? He wants us to stick around."

"So how come you get to leave?"

"I have to take care of business. Can't stop me from doing that."

Bryce waved her empty hand about in the air as though she still held her drink. "You know, Faith's death is awkward. Between you and me, I never saw what my father saw in her, but I was used to her."

"Oh, for Christ's sake, Bryce. Don't get mawkish on me. It doesn't suit you. Fact is, you hated her."

"I didn't hate her!" Bryce retorted. "But her dying was unexpected, and that's awkward. Why did she die? The old battle axe was going to live forever. She provided a sort of synthetic synthesis for passing the time. She was tough, hard, and abrasive as hell. I thought she would outlast us all! She never denied herself anything. So why did she die?"

"How should I know?" Garrett asked. "Maybe she curdled like sour milk. She probably wanted to let us know that she had made a deal with the devil."

The screen door swished open and then they heard smashing glass. Garrett leapt out of his chair, tipping it over. "What the hell!" he exclaimed.

"Clumsy oaf," Bryce mumbled.

"One of the glasses broke. You should have gotten your own

drink," Brian whined. "It's hard to carry three glasses and open a sliding door!"

"Hard to walk and chew gum at the same time too!" Garrett mumbled.

Brian started picking up some of the bigger pieces of glass and looked around for a place to put the shards. "These are the good glasses, aren't they? Why are we using the good glasses? It's just us."

"Should we be using jelly jars? Garrett would probably be using jelly jars." Bryce said. "If that wasn't mine, could you bring it over? That would be pleasant."

Brian brought her glass to her.

"We have to make some decisions," Garrett said. "The world is still turning."

"Faith dying was not planned, was it? Not on our social schedule. Spoiled the vacation, didn't she?" Bryce replied.

"Thoughtless of her," Garrett said.

"Maybe the good sheriff thinks it was one of us who did her in!" Bryce said.

"It wasn't her fault!" Brian started to say.

"We have to talk about the company," Garrett added, handing a large piece of broken glass to Brian. "Obviously Faith wanted me to take over. I'm sure that's what she wanted to talk about. I've got to get back to Philly and meet with the board and make sure they understand that."

"You?" Brian questioned. "You? I'm . . . I was her son. Makes more sense for me to take over."

Garrett snorted. "You don't have the cojones for it! You'd be whining all the time." He put his hand on the other man's shoulder. "I'm not saying you're not doing a great job down there in Florida. No seriously. It's a good place for you. Important part of the company. There's a lot of growth potential there. But the rest of the company is national. You don't want those headaches! You have little kids."

Bryce aimed her gaze at her husband. "And why wouldn't I

take over the company? It was my father's company after all. That's what seems logical to me."

The two men looked at her. The daylight was fading, surrounding objects growing darker. The evening chill was settling in.

"You?" Garrett asked. "Faith didn't like you."

Bryce feigned surprise. "The feeling was mutual. Truth be told, I think she was a bitch! But she was a woman. A businessperson. She knew that companies run by women are more efficient and better run."

Garrett stood looking down at his wife, rattling the ice around in his glass.

"You're not serious?"

"Deadly," she replied.

Garrett swallowed a slug of his gin and tonic. "Pfffft! You haven't worked a day in your life! What the hell do you know about business? Any business? What the hell do you know about developments? About houses, for that matter? What do you know about income statements, balance sheets, return on investments?"

"What do you know about raising children?" Bryce responded.

"You've never raised children either," Garrett said.

"No, but women raise the children. What do you know about what women want? Hmm? Did you know that women make the decisions about buying houses? You probably haven't read about that. You probably think the macho man decides. Women, Garrett my dear, decide what neighborhood the family lives in! They have to stay home to gossip about their cheating husbands! Men don't have the sense to realize that they are being carefully guided by their wives. Women let men think they're in control. Women decide what the house should look like, what color the countertops should be, what plants should be planted in the garden, and who they will buy a house from!" She paused. "And it's not you!"

"Why don't I go and check on Audrey?" Brian suggested.

"Why don't you do that?" Bryce responded. "Ask her how Garrett can help!"

After Brian had slipped through the sliding screen door and back into the house, Garrett asked his wife, "Where are you going with this?"

"I don't know what you mean, dear," Bryce responded with a thin, painted smile.

"You don't want to run the company. Besides, the Board would never approve."

"They approved Faith, didn't they?"

"You're not Faith."

"Thank God!" Bryce replied. "You better thank God for that! Or thank something, whatever it is that you believe in."

Garrett looked off across the water but didn't see anything. The view, the soft evening light, the flickering of house lights reflected on the water, the bobbing of the boats at their moorings had no appeal to him. There was no comfort, no fulfillment in the postcard scene. He could wrestle with directors and bureaucrats, but he could not manipulate his wife. She was his meal ticket. At least for now.

"What do you want?" he asked her finally.

She looked at him. "What I want, sweetie, is what we both want. What we both want. What is best for us. Faith is gone. The road is clear except for our sniveling brother-in-law. The road is clear. We can develop that property in Florida, that boatyard that Faith hung onto so desperately."

"He sold it," Garrett said quietly. "Brian told me he sold the boatyard."

Bryce looked at him. "He what?"

"He sold the boatyard. He didn't want to tell Faith. . .. I don't know if he actually sold it. He committed to sell it or some other horseshit. He didn't have a clear grasp on the details."

"What an idiot! Why did he do that? How could he do that? By what authority?"

Garrett shrugged.

"Is that what killed her?" Bryce asked. "Is that what killed her: her beloved son selling her fucking beloved boatyard?"

"I doubt it," Garrett answered quietly. "Apparently . . . apparently carbon monoxide killed her. Somehow. But . . . I don't know what she saw in that boatyard."

Bryce asked, "How do you know it was carbon whatever? Why didn't you tell me you knew?"

"Didn't seem important."

"It's not," Bryce replied. "But you should have told me. And what does that have to do with a boatyard?"

"Oh, for Christ's sake. You're babbling. You brought it up. I have no idea what she saw in that place."

"Oh, some horseshit about it belonging to her father. Blah, blah, blah, and boo hoo, hooey! Did he tell her?"

"Of course not," Garrett replied. "He doesn't have the balls."

Bryce laughed, a crinkled, dry leaf laugh. "He hasn't got the brains of a dust mite!" She poured more gin down her throat.

They heard the screen door scratch in its track as Brian returned. "Seems to have dinner well under control," he said. "Audrey. Audrey has dinner under control."

"Did you check if the buildings in the boatyard were empty before you sold it?" Bryce blurted.

"What?" Brian asked in surprise.

"Did you check the inside of the buildings?"

"You told her?" Brian asked his brother-in-law.

"I didn't think it was big secret," Garrett replied. "Except from Faith. And she's not around to care."

"You weren't supposed to tell her. I told you about that in confidence. Why should you care?" he asked Bryce.

"I didn't think she wanted to sell her boatyard."

Brian looked stunned. Despite the reds and oranges of the evening light, his face had drained of color.

Bryce turned her face away in exasperation. "You're an idiot, Brian. A fuckin' idiot!"

Brian looked like a fish gasping for air. "I . . . It was a good deal!"

Bryce pursued. "Why did you sell it? Why? Are you gambling again? You didn't lose it in a crap game? Card game? Sports bet? Jesus! You are a vacuous idiot!"

"I . . .," Brian started.

Bryce started to struggle to get up out of her chair. Garrett offered his hand to pull her up, but she waved it away. "I'm living with idiots!" she said. "Idiots! Why does everything have to be so dramatic? Life would be so much simpler if people would simply say what they mean."

The two men stood mute. The patio lights switched on automatically. Garrett had his back to Brian and moved away from him as though to avoid his wife's wrath. "How about those Red Sox?" he mumbled.

"Oh, fuck off, Garrett," Bryce spat. "Won't work this time. Can't change the subject."

"I'm shocked at your language," he replied. "Not very lady-like."

"No ladies here. No need for ladies around pimply-assed wimps like you two."

"You're drunk. Always brings out the best in you."

Bryce hung onto the back of her chair and leaned in toward her husband. "I understand you sued our builder today. Good for you. Throw the man to the sharks so we'll never get this project of Faith's finished. Even after she's dead she's still haunting us. Smooth move, dear heart. You going to finish it yourself?"

"We can't have that man working on our house! He may have killed her! He needs to take responsibility. He needs to pay. He built it wrong and that's what killed her and he's responsible."

"How do you know he built it wrong? How can a house kill a person? It's just a . . . house!" Bryce asked.

"You wouldn't understand."

Bryce glared at her husband. "I wouldn't understand. I'm too stupid, you mean. I'm just a woman. I'm drunk. What the fuck do you mean, I wouldn't understand. Tell me about it! Educate me, oh wise one, you who pulled yourself up from the ghetto! You would know, wouldn't you? From the wrong side of the tracks, after all."

The screen scraped again and Audrey cheerfully said, "Hi! Beautiful evening!"

The three of them looked at her.

"This really is a beautiful place, isn't it? We're so lucky to be able to spend this time together," she continued.

"HAH!" Bryce expelled an explosive laugh and hung onto the chair to keep from falling over.

"Did I interrupt something?" Audrey asked innocently.

"Always," Garrett replied, walking away down the lawn, away from the house.

"I didn't mean to interrupt. Supper is almost ready." She smiled. "Please get the boys."

"Ah," said Brian. "Good."

EARLIER THAT EVENING JON WAS THINKING ABOUT BONGO Boards. A Bongo Board was a simple piece of wood that balanced on a wooden roller. As a kid, Jon had spent a lot of time rolling back and forth as though the balancing board wasn't there at all, as though he was standing on flat, solid, level ground. He could eat standing on it. Watch television. Talk to friends on the phone. Although you could twist it around, it only moved back and forth. It amused him that old people . . . adults . . . were afraid to step on it. They seemed to have lost their sense of balance.

The ground under Jon's feet now was not nearly as stable as that Bongo Board. It felt more like wearing clown shoes in a lake of gelatin. Life had seemed a linear path, with occasional twists and turns, with mostly predictable events.

After the team had separated on the field that afternoon, Jon didn't know where to turn. He hadn't been with the other players long enough to call any of them close friends. Dupin had been about as close as any, and now he was gone. As inspiring as it was to dedicate the season to Dupin, the energy of that team spirit moment had faded.

He didn't feel like dropping into the basement of the Elks Hall and listening to all the babbling chatter. He didn't want to go back to the Wentzells' house. He didn't know what to say to Ace.

For a few moments he sat in Maybellene with his hands on the wheel, staring off at the buildings of the town. Did he have to make a conscious decision about what to do next? Or could he merely sit and let time wash over him? Was it random or was it part of some grand plan? Dupin didn't deserve to die. Ace didn't deserve to be sued. Who or what was making these calls, choosing these rules? He could play along, but he needed to know the rules. And he didn't.

He got out of the car and walked up to the pay phone mounted on the side of the building, lifted the receiver, and dropped coins in the slot, listening to them ping and pong down into the body of the black box. He dialed his home number.

Once the operator had finished clearing the acceptance of charges for the collect call with his father, Jon felt a lump in his throat. "Everything okay?" his father asked. "Don't hear from you for a few weeks and then two calls in two days."

"I know," Jon said. "Ace is getting sued."

"What? Why?"

"Oh, the Salsbergs think he had something to do with the way the house was built and that's what killed Mrs. Salsberg. I don't know. Sounds like bullshit to me."

"Is there any . . . substance, you know, grounds for that?"

"Of course not! Mr. Wentzell's not like that!"

"I'm sure," his father said. "But we all make mistakes. People don't usually sue people on a whim. There's got to be something to it."

"Well, there isn't. There just isn't."

"Okay, Jon. I know, but are you sure? What are they saying that he did?"

"I don't know," Jon replied. "He didn't want to talk about it."

There was moment of silence. "And how are you doing with all this?" his father asked. "It's tough. Lot of tough stuff going on. You doing okay?"

Jon shrugged then mumbled, "I'm okay."

"Anything I can do?"

"He needs a lawyer."

"He doesn't have a lawyer?"

"If he did, I wouldn't be asking, would I?"

"I'm just surprised."

"He's never been sued before!" Jon said. "He's a builder and this is a small town. Not a lot of lawyers here. Thought you might know somebody he could talk to."

His father thought for a moment then he chuckled. "Don't know a lot of lawyers in Tilley, Massachusetts myself! Don't know a lot of lawyers on Cape Cod, in fact."

"Don't need a lot of lawyers," Jon said. "Only need one."

"Lawyers don't come cheap, Jon. Not big-time lawyers. There are some great firms in Boston. It might be better for him to settle this or let his insurance company settle this for him. They might want him to do that."

"What do you mean 'settle this'? Isn't that admitting that he did something wrong?"

"No. Not really. In a way, I guess. Settling merely avoids all the bickering. It doesn't mean anything . . . anything more than money. It doesn't mean right and it doesn't mean wrong. You have to take the emotion out of it. Does that make sense?" his father asked.

"But he didn't do anything wrong, don't you understand? Why should he admit that he did something wrong when he didn't?"

"It's the way the system works, Jon."

"Well, that stinks," Jon replied. "Where's the justice in that? It's not fair."

"Look, Jon, I know you're angry and I know you don't want to hear this, but life isn't always fair."

"Oh, that's such bullshit." Jon paused. "Sorry, dad, but it does make me angry."

"You're dealing with a lot of emotions, son. Let me see what I can come up with, but I think he really needs to talk with his insurance company."

"I don't know what he has for insurance."

"It's not likely to be pretty. Even if he wins in court, he is likely to lose economically."

"Great," Jon replied.

He hung up and drove Maybellene down to Clegg's and found Lisa wiping her hands on her apron. She looked good in a comfortable sort of way. Her long brown hair drifted down over her left eye, and she pushed it back when she saw him. "Hey," she said.

"Hey," he replied. "You shutting up?"

"Just about."

"Doing anything? I mean when you're done?"

"Nothing planned," she replied. "Want some coffee? We could probably throw a burger on."

"That'd be great," Jon replied. He didn't realize how hungry he was.

He watched her work—sweeping, wiping down tables, straightening up chairs, filling the ketchup bottles and the salt shakers. She had a fluid swaying motion as she swung her hips between the tables. Occasionally she pushed her hair back, gathered it back behind her head, and secured it with a rubber band. She noticed him watching her and she stopped and smiled. "You're making me self-conscious," she said.

"Sorry," he replied.

She brought the burger over and set the plate down on the

table and dropped into a chair opposite him. "That's it," she said. "Kitchen's closed."

She watched him eat it; watched the burger juice run down his chin, reached over and dabbed it with a napkin. She had an uncomplicated demeanor that he found comforting. She was also quite pretty, he realized. He watched her eyes behind her glasses until she dropped her gaze to the table. She had high cheek bones and a crinkle at the end of her lips that gave her a bemused look as though something about life was a bit quizzical and entertaining. She had the extended neck of a ballet dancer.

"Stop. Stop examining me," she said and grabbed his empty plate and got up from the table. "I'm not some object. You already had your meat!" She smiled and her whole face lit up brightening the room and his day.

"I . . . wasn't . . . " he mumbled.

"You were," she replied.

He shrugged and grinned.

"Night, Bill," she called out to the cook who was scrubbing down the grill as they left the restaurant. "Where to?"

"Don't know. Didn't have anything in mind."

"Been to First Encounter Beach?"

"Don't think so," he replied.

"I'll show you," she said.

They left Tilley and turned onto the Mid-Cape Highway and headed toward Provincetown. "Got enough gas?" she laughed. "I heard about your little adventure with Mr. Wentzell."

He liked her laugh. "Isn't that the old story about taking a girl out and running out of gas? Not so far-fetched these days."

The evening was warm and the sky was clear and the car was topless. Lisa tilted her head back and watched the stars stream by, punctuated by the dark tree branches. The Mid-Cape Highway shrinks from four lanes down to just two. Jon had heard that it can be deadly as drivers continue to speed along with nothing but their driving skills to keep them apart. Signs advise people to drive with their headlights on even during the day. At the traffic circle in Orleans the road opens up again and seems less ominous as it passes through neighborhoods.

Lisa fumbled through Jon's box of tapes. "This is weird stuff," she commented.

"It's not all great." He reached over to paw through the selections.

"Hey!" she exclaimed as they swerved toward the verge. "You drive. I'll find the music."

"Put on some jazz. Put on Yusef Lateef. You'll like it. He plays the flute."

Lisa found the cassette, looked appraisingly at the black and white image on the cover, and slipped it into the player. The sultry, smoky tones of "The Golden Flute" floated around them. But the subtleties of the notes were buried in the road noise. She turned up the volume. "Nice . . . but not exactly driving music," she said. She popped the cassette out of the dash and slipped in a different one.

Jon looked over at her as a lead guitar started winding up with a pounding beat. "Van Halen!" he said. "Beautiful Girl! Very fitting." He grinned and pounded the beat on the steering wheel. Lisa raised both hands in the air, then gripped the top of the windshield as Jon flowed the little car through the curves. "Isn't this better?" she yelled.

"Yeah," he grinned. "Yeah, good stuff. 'She had her drink in her hand and her toes in the sand . . .'"

"Does that perk you up a bit?" she asked.

The music, the evening, the rhythm of the road swept him away. He felt Maybellene respond to his touch on the wheel, biting into the corners, sliding into the straights. The guitars and the drums and the harmonizing voices flowing into the heart of his brain until he felt it in his soul. A swell of musical joy pushed up in his throat, blinding his negative thoughts.

Lisa guided him to the Samoset Road turnoff. It twisted and wandered through the small neighborhood roads, past houses with their twinkling evening finery, families on the patios, cars in the driveways, people barbecuing in the warm, July evening. All things in their places. Life in the proper order.

They pulled into the beach parking lot and crunched over the gravel, shells, and sand and eased into a spot away from the scattering of the cars. Jon kicked out the cassette, stirred around in his music box, extracted another cassette, and shoved it into the machine. A couple of lead-in guitar notes twanged, and then the slow moving, pulse of Willie Nelson's rendition of *Stardust* filled the little car.

"Wow," Lisa exclaimed. "This is the kind of stuff my parents listen to!"

"Hey. Life doesn't always have to be heavy metal. Look up."

Lisa tilted her head back in her seat and looked up at the heavens as the sky darkened and stars popped out. Jon felt a wave of melancholy ease up the back of his neck. How could life seem so wonderful in one moment and then come crashing back so suddenly? Weren't all these lives connected, running in parallel, sharing the same space? How could it change in an instant? Weren't those stars up there infinite? Wouldn't the waves keep rolling into the beach every day forever? They didn't care about the state of mind of the Arabs who were hoarding the oil or the lawyers who were plaguing Ace or baseball scouts seeking new stars. Or was that all wrong?

He felt the warmth and gentle touch of Lisa's hand settle on the back of his hand and felt a tingle run up his arm to the back of his neck. Suddenly all the lawyers and the Arabs and the scouts disappeared. He wondered momentarily at how hot it was getting.

"You think too much," she said.

She pulled her hand away and jumped out of the car.

Jon cut Willie off in the middle of the *Moonlight in Vermont*, shut the car off, and followed Lisa as she ran toward the beach.

Jon was amazed at how flat First Encounter Beach was at low tide as it extended a long way out in shallow ponds, dips, and tidal flats, stretching off toward the twilight. Lisa paused for a moment to pull off her sandals, hopping on one foot and laughing and then skirting around the patches of water. She stopped on the opposite side of a tidal pool from him. They stood looking at each other for a moment. Then Jon charged forward directly through the water toward her. The depth of the water increased until it reached his thighs. As he labored ahead, his speed slowed considerably. Lisa was laughing hard now, and as she realized that he was succeeding, she quickly turned and scampered away before he could reach her.

He emerged from the water, surged ahead, and caught up to her. Grabbing her, she chirked, emitting a happy high-pitched squeal. He wrapped his arms around her, lifting her from the sand, preventing her from falling backwards into the tidal pond behind her. He felt the warmth of her body on his. He felt the strength of his own arms, and that if he just jumped, he could soar off into the sky and skim the water and then head off toward the moon and the stars. Instead he kissed her. She responded, wrapping her hands around the back of his head and pulling even closer although that seemed impossible.

He twirled her around him, letting her toes momentarily touch the sand then lifting her off again. And then he set her down gently, and she stepped back. They looked at each other again. She looked up at him and said, "You're wet."

"Yah. How'd that happen?"

"There's a lot of water out here," she laughed and stepped up to him, pushing her body against him. She reached up and pulled his head down to hers and kissed him again.

They walked for a while between the pools, along the sand, hand in hand. When they approached the car, he exclaimed, "I can't get back in Maybellene with all this sand on me!"

"Take off your shoes and socks and pants. Wrap them up and put them in the trunk," she suggested with a smile. "I'll wipe the sand off your feet."

When they got to the car, he opened the trunk and then knelt down and untied his running shoes which were thoroughly saturated and encrusted with sand. Then, leaning on Lisa's shoulder, he pulled off his socks. The sand was warm and soft between his toes. He undid the buckle on his belt. The definite bulge in his briefs would be obvious. He hesitated for a moment and then let his pants drop to the beach and stepped out of them.

Lisa picked up his shoes, socks, and pants and dropped them in the trunk and slammed down the lid. "Sit," she ordered.

He opened the driver's door and dropped into the seat, twisting his body so that his feet were outside on the sand. She knelt in front of him, pulled her t-shirt off over her head, and cradled his right foot in her hands and gently stroked the sand off. His head was spinning, and he struggled to sit still while she gently scrubbed the sand away, poking between his toes, rubbing her hand along the bottom of his foot and around the back of his heel, and up his ankle.

He gulped. "You do this often?" he asked.

She stopped and looked up at him. "I'm going to ignore that remark. Other one."

He twisted so that he could set his right foot down on the floor of the car and lifted his left foot into her hands. And she gently dusted his skin again.

He looked down at the smoothness of the skin on her back, the flexibility of her shoulder blades, the boney trail of her spine, wearing only her bra and her shorts, he wondered for a brief moment why bras were sexier than bikini tops. She seemed so matter of fact about all of this, about the fact that he was sitting still, his erection barely hidden by his briefs, about the fact that she was massaging his feet, caressing his toes, and gently dusting the sand off his ankles; only the awkward position he was in kept him from reaching out and pulling her toward him.

She stood up and stepped back, shaking the sand from her shirt and pulling it quickly on over her head. "There," she said. She put her hands on the door, pushing it toward him, forcing him to bring his leg into the car. Then she leaned over and kissed him. "Better?"

"Um . . ." he replied. "Whoa! I mean you expect me to drive now? I've never driven in my underwear before. I mean what happens when we get . . . wherever we might be going next and try to get out of the car? I mean . . . I don't know what I mean!"

"Well, I guess you're just going to have to figure that out, Jon," she replied with a smile, walking around the car, and jumping into the passenger seat. "There are some things in life that you're just going to have to figure out for yourself."

The difficulties of a little car with bucket seats came back to him. He recalled bravado remarks about having more room on the ground, but now she had carefully removed all that sand, they would both get sandy if he jumped out and pulled her to the beach. That's what he should do. That's what they did in the movies. That was what cool guys would do. And that brought familiar faces unbidden into his thoughts, connecting him to friends, teammates, and Dupin.

"Oh," he said.

They both sat and stared out through the windshield. Not panting. Not smoking. Unresolved, wondering and wandering through their own thoughts and emotions about what would happen next. What should happen next?

"Why?" he asked.

She looked at him. "Because you didn't want to get sand in your car."

"That's not what I meant. No. That was stupid. No. I didn't mean that was stupid. That was great. I mean that was amazing. No, I meant . . .."

"You're babbling," she said, holding her breath for a moment. "You know, Jon, sometimes your thinking has bad timing. You need to stop thinking so much and start doing."

Jon thought about that. He thought he had been 'doing'. He was working. He was playing baseball. He was dating. He was trying to figure out what to do with his life. He couldn't remember ever having been accused of inactivity before. And what did she know? She was just a kid. Well, more than a kid!

She was nineteen and sexy as hell. Oh! Maybe that's what she meant! Jesus, he thought, you're denser than a brick! "You're gorgeous," he said out loud with a smile. "No really, you are." But there was no going back now the moment had passed. The spontaneity had evaporated. What could he DO to recover? "Want to sit on the beach?"

The light was dim but he could see the sparkle in her eyes. She pushed her hair back. "Your head is too full. You're not really here."

"Oh, but I am," he protested, and reached out for her. "You have me at your mercy! You've stripped me down to my underwear! I have nowhere to hide."

"I can see that," she replied, leaning away. "But I refuse to be a fond memory or a passing moment. That's not me. I like you, Jon, but I'm not sharing your thoughts with all those other demons you've got in there!"

He sat back. He thought it was unlikely that he would ever think about only one thing at a time. Dupin jumped to the top of his thoughts. Dupin's death was just wrong. Dying could happen suddenly, and that spoke strongly for the idea of seizing the moment. What if a meteor hit their car right now? What if the car exploded? Didn't they do target practice from the Air Force base around here? What if they missed? What if that happened and he had let this moment pass, postponing passion for some unknown future time? And it never happened!

And then there was Faith Salsberg: she died too! Or someone had killed her. And Lisa's father hadn't found the killer yet. Lisa's father. He felt his passion shrink. "I've got to put on my pants," he said and jumped out of the car.

He pulled his pants out of the trunk, shook off the sand, pulled them up, and fastened his belt.

"I'm not doing your feet again," she said as she crossed her arms.

"No, but they shouldn't blame Ace for killing Mrs. Salsberg."

"What?"

"No, seriously. I mean he had nothing to do with it, you know? He's a great builder. He knows what he is doing. He knows houses like I know the back of my hand."

"I don't think you know the back of your hand," she murmured.

"No, seriously. I can't let them do that. He doesn't understand about lawyers and courts and all that stuff."

"So?"

"So, you're right. I have to start doing. I do. You're right."

"Not exactly what I had in mind," she replied.

"Will you help me?"

She looked up at him. He stood beside the car with his hands on the door. His hair was all over the place, but even in the dim twilight she could see the flash in his eyes. And she smiled. "Sure."

14
LAWYERS

When Jon arrived in the Wentzells' kitchen the next morning, Babs was hovering over the stove. She poured him a cup of coffee, he thanked her and dropped into his usual seat at the table across from Ace who was immersed in the sports section of the Times.

"Where to today?" Jon asked, sipping his coffee.

Ace lowered the paper enough so that he could see Jon's face. "Today?" he asked. "Depends on the lawyers, I guess."

"Lawyers?" Jon asked.

"Have to reorganize things. Figure out where I can and where I can't work. Depends on the damn lawyers."

Jon looked over at Babs who shrugged. She recognized her husband's uncharacteristic black mood, but she'd known him long enough to realize there wasn't anything she could do about it.

"I talked to my father yesterday," Jon said brightly.

Ace grunted.

"He is going to see if he can find a lawyer to represent you."

"Don't want no damn lawyer."

"He also asked me about what insurance you had. He's in

insurance, you know. He said you might have insurance for making mistakes and they would help you . . ."

"I didn't make any mistakes!" Ace exploded. "That woman dying was not because of anything I did or didn't do!"

"Ace!" Babs warned.

"I know!" Jon said. "I know. I'm sure you didn't. I wasn't saying that. I wasn't accusing you of anything. I was just asking, you know, if you had some kind of contractors', you know, insurance. If you've been paying for that, well, maybe they would help you fight this. That would save you money. Especially if you've been paying for it all along."

Babs came over to her husband and laid her hand on his shoulder. "We do have insurance, don't we? There was all that stuff Charlie Tinsdale sold us, remember? I don't remember all the details, but he said that it was important to have insurance for the business. You know. Tinsdale Insurance. That little building down near the Green."

Ace grunted again. "Insurance is stupid. If you do your job right, you shouldn't need it."

Jon looked at him. He had heard his father talking about insurance for years. He had tuned most of it out, but some of it had filtered in. He thought about it like having a cold weather fund. His father had explained it like the story of the ant and the grasshopper, with the ant working diligently to save for the cold weather and the grasshopper just bouncing around all summer while the sun was shining. Bedtime stories that insurance salesmen tell.

He looked at Babs. "Maybe you can call . . . Mr. Tinsdale? Tell him about this? Ask him what coverage you might have?"

"Just bull," Ace replied. "Stuff like insurance is just for desk jockeys and paper pushers. Never done a decent moment of work in their lives! They have no clue how to create something beautiful, something real, a thing you can hold in your hands. They just want to create a world of paper and rules. It doesn't exist! Do your job. Do your best. If something happens, take your licks and move on. Don't blame it on someone else. Take your licks. It's these people that squeeze things, trying to get more out of them than is there. Like a teenager popping a pimple!"

They were all silent. Jon could hear Ace breathing heavily. He watched the curtains in the kitchen window float into the room on the morning breeze.

"Let me get you your breakfast," Babs said to Jon.

Ace crushed the New York Times into an unruly pile. He stood up, coughed, and said, "Head over to Thompsons", and he left the room.

After a couple of moments Babs turned to Jon with a plate covered with bacon, eggs, and toast and said, "He's old fashioned or likes to think so. He doesn't like insurance people. Or lawyers. Never did. Can't understand people who don't do things, you know. People who just live off other people's troubles."

"Guess I always thought of it as helping, you know? Someone standing behind you if you get knocked over. Helping you back up. Suppose that's because of my dad."

"I'm sure," Babs smiled.

Jon wolfed down his breakfast. He mumbled through a mouthful, "Thinking of getting a haircut. Is there a barber shop?"

"Of course," Babs replied, wiping her hands on her apron. She carried her mug of coffee over to the table and sat down opposite him. "Of course. There's Fida's. Ace goes there. You've probably passed it and just not noticed. It's got one of those candy cane barber poles out front."

Jon nodded. "I'm sure I've passed it." They were silent for a few moments. Jon looked down at the mug of coffee between his hands, and then tipped it up so that he could see the illustration on the side. "VIVA Las Vegas!" it read with a show girl with a spread of peacock feathers on her head and a grin on her face that was fading as the mug aged. "So, I guess you've been to Vegas?" he asked, looking up at her face.

She was leaning on the table with her coffee held in front of her. He noticed the lines on her face. She had wonderful, weather worn hands that spoke of lives not lived, paths not followed. She reminded him of what Mrs. Santa Claus should look like with some white in her hair, and her arms were round and filled the short sleeves of her day dress. There was a soft gentleness about her that belied her inner strength to fight the battles she had fought and would fight for anyone connected to her. "Oh, no," she answered. "Someday maybe. But that came from a yard sale! Had it for years."

"Nice," he said, rotating the mug so that he could see all sides. He looked into her eyes. "How's Mr. Wentzell doing with all this?"

"Well, you know. I'm sure you could tell, couldn't you? He's never liked the paperwork end of things. He loves wood. He loves tools. He loves making things, building things. But he hates paperwork." She laughed.

"You think he does have insurance? Business insurance of some kind? I mean, he's going to need help with this. Lawyers don't just . . . walk away."

"I'm sure. Yes, I know we talked with Charlie - the insurance man - about this, about something about this anyway. Although it's been awhile."

"I'm sure my father will come up with someone too. Has Mr. Wentzell said anything about what he thinks might have happened? Why would they think that he did anything? They must have a reason. You know. They can't just make this stuff up!"

"People with money can be quite nice, you know? But I think money makes them self-centered. It disconnects them from day to day issues. They plan and scheme about their next dollar. They can be quite nice and sometimes I feel sorry for them because . . . I don't know . . . they don't seem to actually be alive. Their veins are filled with something other than blood. I'm not saying this very well, am I?"

He smiled. "No, no, you are. I just mean if Mr. Wentzell knows what they think he might have done, it might help."

"Well, he tries to do the best he can on every job he does. They do keep changing codes and things. He sometimes grumbles about the materials he has to use and fancy things they make him install. He doesn't like change much. When something works, he wants to just keep doing it the same way. You can't teach an old carpenter new tricks! He is always saying that doing it differently is a risk. I think the Salsbergs wanted some new things in that pool house. He said they'd read some magazines. You know those beautiful home magazines with the pictures of fancy homes from around the world, and they'd wanted him to do some of that. You're going to need to talk to him about it."

"Did he do it?"

"Reluctantly, I'm sure. But he's enough of a salesman in his way to know that he has to give his customers what they want. You know, he'll try to charm them around to his way of thinking. Particularly the ladies! He has a way of making them think that they thought of what he wanted them to think!"

Jon grinned. "I can see that." He wasn't sure that he would be able to get Ace to tell him anything, but nobody would know more about how that building worked. Jon was sure that Ace lived and breathed every building that he created, that he felt the water flowing through the pipes, the air moving through the ducts, how the walls felt when the wind blew against them. The difficulty would be to get him to talk about it.

"I better go," he said.

Jon felt the spirit of Hoppin' Dupin surge up and bring the Longliners together that afternoon and they played as though their own lives depended on it. They hit well. They played together smoothly and in harmony. They backed each other up. Graham barely had to say a thing, but even he seemed swept up in the players' energy and enthusiasm, reminding him why he loved the game.

The Elks basement buzzed with excitement afterward. Even the fluorescent lights seemed to flicker in the excitement. The old timers leaned on the bar and tried to predict where the rest of the season might go. The cigarette smoke hung in the air.

Jon sat at a table in the corner with several of the players including Icky and Barry Nolan. Nolan seemed almost high he was so excited.

"Did you see the way the scouts were looking at us?" he bubbled. "Man! We should play that way all the time! We were smokin'!"

They chugged the beer in their plastic cups. "Yeah," Jon said. "Yeah. That was good." He scanned the crowd of celebrants. Faces turned in their direction with smiles. It did feel good. Winning was a drug. He just wanted to keep doing it. He wanted the high to last longer.

"Hey, how about another?" Icky suggested. "Maybe I can remember another joke. Maybe that was good luck? How do you sink a submarine full of blondes?" Pause. "Knock on the hatch!"

"Oh, Christ! Don't start," Jon said. I'll get the beers."

Jon weaved through the crowd to the bar, acknowledging the good wishes and the pats on the back with a grin and a mumbled "Thanks!" The team's success was contagious. Jon felt the Elks' regulars had been living under a pall. One win was enough to get them back.

When Jon reached the bar, he heard the rasp of a familiar sounding voice, a voice that was out of place. He turned and saw Brian Reese. Jon had heard that some people are born into the wrong bodies. Brian Reese had the luxury of money. He was beer taste in a champagne life.

Jon overheard him praise the Longliners. "Yeah," Reese said, "They've got it now. Cinderella team. They're going to take it all the way!"

"Maybe," the other man said.

"No, seriously. I'd put money on it. I think they've found their groove. I've studied a lot of teams. There is this . . . I don't know . . . what's the word . . . *esprit de corps*. It's a spirit. You can sense it. Maybe you could call it a passion. Know what I mean?"

"Maybe," the other man said.

"Remember the New York Giants in 1951?" Brian continued. "Before they abandoned the city and moved out west. I think it killed them. Took their magic with them. But remember when Bobby Thomson hit that pitch over the left field wall? Man, that changed everything. They went on to the World Series. Beat my guy, Pee Wee. Pee Wee Reese. Best ever. You could feel that come from behind feeling. Named my kid for him."

"Really?" the other man said.

"No. I mean yes. I did name my kid for him. So I should know. The feeling, I mean. Coming from behind. Broke my heart that day. But at least the Giants got pummeled by the Yankees in the end. So yeah, I'd put money on the Longliners going all the way."

"What kind of odds are you giving me?" the other man asked.

Jon turned his head to look at Reese. His face was flushed. He'd clearly had a few too many.

"Friendly bets only," the bartender ordered, pushing Jon's cups of beer across the counter.

Jon walked back to the table juggling the cups, slopping a bit as he bumped into shoulders and backs.

"I just saw Mr. Reese at the bar," Jon said as he dropped back down at the table. "Does that guy just like to hang out here?"

"He's here all the time," Bartholomew said. "Sloppy drunk."

"Yeah. I've seen him here before. He was trying to bet on the team. The Longliners."

"He bets on everything. He'd bet on the length of his dong!" Bartholomew laughed. "I bet he'd bet on who killed his mother!"

"He said he did it," Jon said.

The two other players looked at him. "What?"

"Yeah. He was drunk in here. He was all weepy and mopey and he said that he'd killed her."

Nolan leaned back in his seat and looked up at the ceiling as if seeking inspiration. "Does Officer Prence know this? He was probably blowing off steam. You know how people can get sloppy when they drink too much. They'll confess to anything to have people feel sorry for them. Boo hoo hoo!"

The three of them looked over at Reese through the crowd. He seemed to be lecturing on baseball to anyone who would listen.

"The guy should go home to his wife and family," Bartholomew said.

They simultaneously lifted their cups in mock salute.

"I hear that Dupin's family is coming up," Bartholomew continued.

"They'd have to, wouldn't they?" Nolan replied.

"We should do something," Jon added. "It's not right that this happened. It's not right. And it's certainly not fair."

They dove back into their beers. "You guys ever smoke?" Jon asked.

"Nah," Bartholomew replied. "It stinks. Tough to quit, I hear."

"This place should turn on some fans or something," Jon said. "You can hardly breathe in here."

"I don't have addictions," Nolan stated.

"You're pure as the driven snow!" Bartholomew replied.

"No, seriously. Gambling is an addiction. I mean it's like you can't stop. You think that you're going to be a winner the next time. It's always 'next time' or 'next year' or 'next game'. It's always dangling in front of your nose. What if people are gambling on our games? What if someone on the Longliners wants us to lose? What about that?"

"None of the guys would do that?" Jon said.

"No? No? But hypothetically maybe that's why Dupin died. Maybe he wouldn't go along with it. Huh?" Nolan said.

Jon and Icky looked at him, mouths open. "What? That's crazy. That's really crazy. It was an accident, Barry. Dupin died in an accident. You shouldn't even think those thoughts."

"Crazy things happen," Nolan insisted.

"You've been watching too much TV."

"I'm just sayin'."

"Next thing you're going to say is that Mrs. Salsberg was murdered because her husband donated money to the Longliners and Reese is involved in some kind of conspiracy to win the Cape League championship!" Jon laughed. The deaths were real but Nolan was painting TV land fiction.

"Desperate times call for desperate actions," Nolan said.

"Who's desperate?" Icky asked. "You're being stupid, Nolan. As usual."

"I'm just saying that we don't know anything about any of this. Except what they're telling us. We're in the dark." He looked at Jon. "You're closer to this than any of us."

"What?"

"You're making it with the policeman's daughter."

"I'm not *making* it with her!"

"Well, you could be," Nolan said and grinned. "But whatever. You're close to the source."

"She doesn't tell me anything. She doesn't know anything."

"The thing is I don't know why you care," Nolan said.

"I care because of Mr. Wentzell. They have accused him of being involved somehow, and it's not true. I'm trying to see if he has insurance or a lawyer or something to help him out."

"You know," Bartholomew added, "it would be nice if we could just concentrate on why we are here. Know what I mean? I mean we came here to play baseball—not to mess around with all this other stuff. It's a distraction. I want to concentrate on playing baseball."

"I gotta find out what happened though," Jon said.

"What happened to what?" Bartholomew asked.

"I gotta help clear Mr. Wentzell. It's important."

"So, what do you want to do; help Wentzell? Figure out what happened to Dupin? Straighten out Reese's gambling problem? Turn Coach Russell in for trying to bribe a player and throw a game? You can't do it all, JC!" Nolan leaned back in his chair as though he had made a significant point.

"I'm not asking you to do anything," Jon said. "I'll figure this out."

"Why don't you go ask Reese if he killed his mother?" Nolan said. "Maybe he'll confess to you."

"He already did!" Jon said. "I told you that."

"The guy loves you," Bartholomew said. "Get him to tell you what happened. He's had a few. Maybe you can solve the mystery! Oooh wee oooh!" Bartholomew made the mystery movie sound.

Nolan and Bartholomew laughed. Jon looked over at Reese again. Did he want to listen to the man's bluster? Listen to him babble on about his beloved Brooklyn Dodgers and why they left town? He wasn't even a New Yorker! But maybe he could get something useful out of him. To lift the blame off Ace Jon had to find the details, ask questions, detect stuff. He looked at his two teammates and decided that maybe they had a point. Jon didn't like Reese and didn't want to have this conversation, but if he was going to help Ace, he needed to find out what was going on in that family and his best way in had to be with the idiot at the bar.

JON'S SHOES STUCK TO THE DRIED BEER SPILLED ON THE FLOOR, peeling off, step by step as he worked his way across the room. The heat of the July evening was not helped by the bodies packing the space. The air conditioners jammed through the walls as an afterthought had little impact on the fug. The low ceiling of the basement room, condensed the space and brought the heat and the cigarette smoke down making it impossible to avoid.

As he approached Reese it occurred to Jon that talking to him might screw things up. Reese couldn't really be a killer, but he might have been involved, and talking to him might mess up Officer Prence's investigation.

No. That didn't matter. Jon had to step up.

By the time Jon reached the bar, he still hadn't figured out what he was going to say to Brian Reese. The cops always solved these mysteries on TV. But he wasn't a cop. He couldn't pull out his badge and say, "Just a few questions. Just the facts." He always wondered why police officers yelled at suspects a block away giving them time to run.

But he didn't have to make the opening remarks because when Reese saw him, his face exploded into a wide smile and the man reached out and grabbed him by the shoulder. "Hey!" Reese said. "Here's the man. What a game! What a game! You guys are on fire now. Nothing to stop you. You guys are going to take it all the way!"

Jon smiled in reply. "Don't know about that."

"No! You gotta believe, right? You gotta believe!"

The other men at the bar moved over to let Jon in. There were smiles and slaps on the back and salutes with beer cups.

"So, what's the strategy?" Reese asked forming a serious face. "What's Coach thinking?"

Jon looked at him. "Uhm, keep playing, I guess. Keep winning?"

Reese pounded his hand down on the bar. "Yes! Beautiful. That's what I was saying a few minutes ago. Team's a little thin right now 'til those guys get fully back on their feet. Terrible thing that happened to that pitcher. Dupin. Terrible thing. Once in a million. Terrible."

The other men at the bar looked down into their beers and nodded gravely. "Too young," one of them said.

"Yeah, promising pitcher. Had a great future in front of him."

"Did anyone hear anything more about that?" Jon asked. "Why did it happen? Was the other driver asleep?"

"Hear he had a heart attack," one of the bar leaners said. "Happens. Lot of old people around here. You know they come here to retire. Then they have heart attacks and die!"

"Prence might know," Reese added. "You could ask him. Aren't you friends with his daughter?"

Jon was surprised at the spread of gossip. Jon decided to change the subject and confront Reese directly. "Have you heard any more about Mrs. Salsberg, Mr. Reese? Do they know how she died?"

The men at the bar shifted away. Reese's expression dropped and the color drained out of it. He looked around the room and then up to the ceiling. "She was my mother, you know?"

"Yes," Jon replied.

"She was my mother." The man's eyes began to water. Jon wondered if they were real tears or the smoke in the room or the alcohol in his blood. "She wasn't that easy to get along with," Reese continued. "But she had a big heart. She did want life to go her way. She thought about a lot. She did! She cared about a lot. But she wasn't that easy to get along with."

The crowd at the bar thinned. Public display of feelings made Jon uncomfortable.

Jon didn't want to find out how sweet or sour the woman was or what charities she supported or anything else about her character or her life. He just wanted to find out what or who had killed her. But the man obviously wanted to talk. Maybe Reese didn't have anyone else willing to listen to him and maybe that would lead him to reveal issues that he wouldn't otherwise.

There was an empty table in a dim corner near the entrance. Jon followed as Reese slouched to it where the man dropped into one of the plastic folding chairs like slinging a sack of potatoes. "Sit," he said to Jon. They sat in silence for a few moments. Jon noticed Nolan and Bartholomew were still in their corner, glancing his way periodically.

"So," Jon said finally, "have they told you any more about your mother's death?"

"It's a mess," Reese said. "The whole thing's a clusterfuck! Know what I mean?" He grimaced as he struggled with his words.

Jon nodded. Drunken adults were embarrassing. "How so, Mr. Reese?"

Reese looked at him with watery eyes. "She was my mother, you know. My mother! Do you know about mothers, Megquire?"

Jon nodded.

"So you know what I'm talking about. Not everyone has a mother. Oh, oh, oh. Or, if they do, a powerful, all knowing, rich mother. She never did much of the mothering part . . . really. More of the demanding and directing part. More of that."

The guy is screwed up, Jon thought.

"We weren't all that close, you know? You know you see those mothers in movies who are all wise, occasionally do stupid things to make the story interesting, but are mainly the font of wisdom and kindness and straighten things out in the end. That wasn't my mother. That wasn't my mother. You know I don't think she gave a fuck about being a mother! I think . . . I think I was an accident! Who was my father? I didn't get to know him at all. Not at all. War hero! I only heard stories with black and white pictures of him in his uniform. I was barely two."

He took a chug of his beer. "Why am I telling you all this? What was the question?"

"I was just curious, Mr. Reese, about why you think things are so messed up?"

"Ah!" Reese replied, holding his forefinger wisely in the air. "The clusterfuck!" He looked at Jon as if trying to read or perhaps just see his face. "She didn't like gambling. Didn't. Like. Gambling." He underlined each word by driving his finger into the table. "Some sort of moral rationale. BUT," he paused for emphasis, "BUT her father was a smuggler! Did you know that? A smuggler. Not a nice man apparently, although I never knew him. He took all kinds of chances." He swept his right arm across the room. "Tell me that wasn't gambling? Maybe, just maybe, he didn't bet on horses at the track. Oh, no! He bet on whether or not he could sell homes in a swamp to tourists! That is what he did. His bets didn't wear T-shirts and shorts. His bets wore handmade Brooks Brothers suits so she considered them respectable. They weren't gambling. They were *investments*!" He flopped back in his chair having irrefutably proved his point.

Jon wasn't getting any closer to the truth about the woman's death. Brian Reese was a sad, self-persecuted shell of a human being. Perhaps his mother beat him, and he wanted to get revenge. Perhaps he was simply insane, some kind of split personality. Jon decided that it couldn't hurt to confront the issue head on. He asked, "Can you think of anyone who would have wanted to kill her?"

Reese looked at him as though he had been slapped. His eyes opened wide and he slopped some of his beer on the table. "What?"

Jon repeated the question. "Do you think anyone would have wanted to kill her?"

From somewhere down in the guts of the other man came a rumbling sound that was very faint at first but grew steadily louder. It erupted from his mouth. His head went back until the noise of his laughter seemed to echo off the ceiling. Jon was afraid that Reese was going to roll off his chair. He spluttered words, spittle flying. "Kill her? Who would want to kill her?"

It wasn't the reaction that Jon was expecting. He smiled at the people around them who were staring at Reese's uncontrolled uproar.

Suddenly he stopped and stared at Jon. "Everyone!" he said. "She was a first-class bitch! Upper class. Snobby nosed bitch! Never had a kind word to say about anyone. She was held together with spit, makeup and drugs." Then he started laughing again.

"Ah," Jon said. That narrows it down, he thought.

"I am sure that there were people daily who confronted her who wished she would cease to exist! People whose lives she ruined. Like Mr. Potter in that *Wonderful Life* movie they play at Christmas." He looked up at Jon with watery eyes. He wiped his nose with the back of his hand and looked around.

Jon jumped up, grabbed a couple of cocktail napkins from the bar, and brought them back to the table.

"Nah," Reese said. "She just shriveled up. The devil wanted her back."

Jon didn't reply.

"If I had anything to do with her death it's because I broke her heart." He took another slug of his beer, and sputtered, "Assuming she had a heart!" Then he started laughing again. "No. No. No. More likely if anything was done to her . . . most likely Garrett. Much more likely. He is just like her. Just like her. The only thing he likes in life is . . . himself. No, wait. Himself and money. Two things he likes in life: himself and money . . . and power. Three things. Himself and money and power. Yes: three things."

"Ah," Jon replied. "What would he have done to her?"

Reese shrugged. "Damned if I know. The man has a mind of his own. You'll have to ask him. But . . ." Reese raised a finger into the air, "but he is not likely to tell you."

"Yes, that's probably true. But what happened that day?"

"Which particular day are you referring to?" Reese asked.

"The day she died. The day you found her?"

"I did not find her. No, it wasn't me. I wasn't even there. Who did find her? I'm trying to remember. It's all kind of a blur. Matter of fact, this is all kind of a blur!" he laughed.

Jon waited.

"No. I'm sure I wasn't the one who found her, but I saw her. Maggot Garrett found her. I like that! Maggot Garrett. He found her. She was lying on the floor."

Jon thought about that for moment. "On the floor?" He looked at the other man. "Are you sure? She wasn't in her bed?"

Reese looked at him with a blank glare. "Nope." He shook his head. "On the floor. *Dishabille*. Nightgown akimbo. Hair an uncharacteristic mess."

"There wasn't any blood or anything?"

Reese shuddered. "God no! That would have been awful! You're not saying that she was shot or stabbed or something gory like that? She wouldn't have allowed it! Never. Not on her agenda. No. No gore."

Talking about a dead woman as merely another event of the day was weird – like chatting about shopping or fishing or playing baseball. But it puzzled Jon that she was on the floor instead of in her bed. If she had died in her bed, . . . not that he had experience, but if she hadn't been in her bed wouldn't that suggest that she hadn't died of natural causes? Like dying in her sleep? If she was dressed for the night, that would clearly indicate that she had intended to go to bed and obviously whatever happened to her happened . . . after that. He shook his head, bludgeoned by his own analytical brilliance.

"Did you notice anything else about the room? Had she been in the bed? I mean was it messed up or anything?"

"Oh, my god, kid! My mother was lying there on the floor. Dead. In disarray! I'm not a ghoul! I wouldn't notice if the bed was unmade." Reese paused. "Come to think of it. No. She hadn't displaced her pillows. You know she had these little baby pillows that she liked to arrange under her head. Not quite sure how she kept them all on the bed. But now that you ask, I did notice that they were all in their specific positions. I guess that means that she hadn't been lying on the bed before she . . . ended up on the floor. Is that important, do you think?" He smiled as though he had discovered the true meaning of it all and should be rewarded.

Jon replied, "I have no idea. Might be important. Did you tell that to Officer Prence?"

"I don't believe I did."

Jon didn't know if there was any significance to her not

getting into bed, but it seemed like if she had never gotten into bed, clearly she hadn't died in her sleep. He guessed that people did just collapse from a stroke or a heart attack or something else health related.

"Did she ever . . . you know, sleep on the floor?"

Reese looked as though he had been slapped. "What? Sleep on the floor?"

"Some people lie on the floor because, you know, the bed's too soft and their back hurts or something. I was just wondering if maybe she was lying on the floor because she fell asleep there?"

"I don't think my mother ever got down on the floor for anything except maybe to examine the value of an oriental rug! Sleep on the floor? Not in a million years."

"Sorry. I was trying to put things together."

So how did she get on the floor, Jon wondered? Collapse? Fall? Pushed? "Did it look like she had been fighting with someone? Was anything else messed up in the room? Like lamps knocked over or other signs of a struggle?"

"No!" Reese replied. "She was stone, cold dead on the floor. That's it. Not that I was there when it happened. I didn't see that until later. Then the officials arrived - Officer Prence, the ambulance men, those people. And they took her away." Then Reese's face slumped like soft putty.

"I understand. I understand. It must be hard. Has your family been using the pool house since then?"

"The kids are freaked out by the place! That's where their grandmother died, and Garrett doesn't want people going in there. He says it's a crime scene and he doesn't want it disturbed until all this is resolved."

"Ah. Yes."

"Meanwhile the house is unfinished. There's that big hole in Mother's room because your boss hasn't been back to finish his work."

"Yes. You know Mr. Scoles is suing him?"

Reese grunted. Jon was not sympathetic to the Salsbergs'

displeasure at their unfinished house or what they were going to do about it. He was concerned about the issue that Ace would not get paid for the work he had already done. In fact, the whole thing disgusted him. Anger toward these sniveling, selfish people welled up in the back of his throat, anger whose source he couldn't define. If Ace hadn't been pulled into their personal issues, Jon couldn't have cared less about what had happened to Mrs. Salsberg.

"What would make Mr. Scoles think that Mr. Wentzell had anything to do with what happened to your mother? He wasn't even working on the pool house where she died! What could he have done . . . what could he have possibly done that would do any harm to anyone?"

Reese just shrugged. "I have no control over Garrett. No one does."

Jon wanted to walk away from the man, but this was his opportunity to be a detective. He shouldn't throw it away. Maybe he would uncover that one little nugget of information that would resolve the crime and solve the mystery. Maybe the information that he got from Reese would be useless, blurred by time and muddled by alcohol. But it was likely that it would be the clearest description of the Salsberg family that he would get because it would be unrestrained.

Gritting his teeth, he asked, "So what can you tell me about Mr. Scoles? He seems . . . different. Is he always this way?"

"Different? Absolutely! The man has no class. His family has no pedigree whatsoever! Obviously, he married Bryce for the money. Obvious! I haven't got a clue why she married him. It certainly wasn't for love. Even a blind person could see that there is no love there. I bet their marriage wouldn't last, but I can't remember who I bet. But he went to Princeton. Studied physics or something and wormed his way into the company. I guess he must be smart. He'll tell you that he's smart! Maybe Mr. Salsberg . . . Dad. I still can't call him that. Even though he's dead, but maybe 'Dad' saw something in him." He looked around the room. "Hey, listen I have to go to the Little Boys' Room. You don't own beer! You just rent it! Ha, ha, ha!"

Jesus! Jon thought as Reese bumped his way through the crowd toward the bathroom. The guy's useless. Jon felt weird sitting there by himself at the table. He felt uncomfortable and thinking to himself, "I'm never going to get anything out of this guy", he got up and left before Reese returned.

15

BARBER - JULY 12, 1979

Jon wondered what made a man decide to get a haircut. If it wasn't done from habit, it had to be a conscious decision. Some men are concerned about how they look, how attractive they are to others. Some men need to look neat for their jobs: neatly coiffured hair is part of their uniform whether it be fluffed up like a sheep's back or sheered down in military orderliness. Some men allow their hair to grow in an unruly tangle to show that they really don't care how they appear to others. And there are all the ethnic reasons for hair styles. Some men need to make a statement with their hairstyle as they do with their clothing or their tattoos.

And then there are the men who don't want to spend the money on the barber and treat getting a haircut as a basic, social obligation. Jon was not overly concerned about his looks. He could only see the face that looked back at him in the mirror. When he was home, his mother used to tell him that he was looking 'a bit shabby'. When he went away to school, he had to decide himself. Occasionally, he got in the mood that he wanted to get himself organized and under control; to be mature, to act like an adult, to be responsible.

He was more conscious about his looks here in Tilley. The

adult role came into play. He felt that scouts didn't want to deal with screw-ups or rebels or players who wanted to make statements. He didn't want the length or look of his hair to be the barrier that closed that door. His curly, reddish hair was already enough of a trademark to get him the 'Brillo' nickname. He didn't want to make more of it than that.

When he noticed the back of his hair beginning to curl up over the collar of his shirt, he decided that it was time to fork over the two bucks.

The question then was where to do it. Jon considered a barbershop a continuous commitment. Having some man put his hands in your hair, brush it, comb it, cut it like your mother did when you were an infant, is personal. Having committed oneself to a particular group of barbers or even a particular barber is not something to be taken casually. Jon felt like part of a team . . . a team of customers. All the years that he had been growing up there had been a particular barber shop that was as much a part of home as the ballfield at the high school or the Woolworth's on Main Street. When he left for school, he had to find another barber. And in Tilley he had to change again.

He could have gone to another town for a haircut—like Hyannis or Barnstable. But then he would still have had to choose, and he had no clue and no desire to go from barber shop to barber shop assessing the facility! What could he assess? They all had chairs. They all had mirrors. They all had pictures of sports figures and local notables. Some of the barbers were young. Some of them were old. If they had women barbers, he would have chosen another shop. Barbers were men. That's just the way it should be.

Staying in Tilley simplified the process. Tilley had only one barber shop: Fida's. It had the traditional swirling candy cane symbol by the front door. The front of the shop was a large plate glass window that looked out on Main Street so that the clients and the barbers could watch the world go by and the world could look in and see the clients in the chairs draped with their sheets.

It was tradition—Norman Rockwell or Andy Griffith in Mayberry.

Although Jon had never been in Fido's before, he found the space familiar and comfortable. It had two named barber chairs. Over the mirror in front of each chair was a sign with the barber's name. One that said "BERT" and one that said "AUGIE". Aligned on the narrow shelf in front of each chair was an array of hair care products: Brylcreem and talcum powder, Barbicide® and Burma Shave. There was a glass jar filled with blue liquid and a bunch of combs. Hanging on hooks were electric razors with their cords dangling down to the floor.

Jon hesitated by the door assessing the scene. The two chairs were occupied. The barbers looked up and smiled at him and nodded. A customer waited on the bench reading the day's *Boston Globe* beside a scattering of somewhat worn copies of *Sports Illustrated*.

"Won't be long," the barber under the AUGIE sign said.

The barbers were wearing comfortable shoes and standing on the black, cushioned matts that surrounded the red pleather chairs, strewn with cut hair - blond and grey and brown. Augie was the older of the two barbers. He had a long face, receding hair line, and wire rimmed glasses. His lightweight blue plaid shirt was untucked. A large pedestal fan stood in a corner of the room, lazily sweeping back and forth. The room was long and narrow, with a white linoleum floor. A blank TV screen watched from a corner. The barber under the BERT sign chatted away with his customer, snipping here and there, gathering in the man's hair with his comb. Bert was the younger of the two barbers, sporting a crew cut, wearing a black, short sleeved shirt and jeans.

He held up a mirror behind his customer's head, angling it from one side to the other to let the man experience places on his body that he rarely saw. The customer nodded in acceptance, Bert pulled back the chair cloth and white paper collar from around the man's neck, swept away a few stray hairs with a soft brush, and then pulled away the cloth with a flourish as though revealing a sculpture. The customer hefted himself out of the chair and stiffly staggered over to the old-fashioned cash register while pulling out his wallet. Bert grabbed a small label disk from a drawer and slid it over a spike on the register that allowed them to keep track of the number of haircuts each barber executed during the day—like keeping track of a pool score.

The customer handed him his money, thanked him, and pushed out through the shop's glass door, ringing the spring suspended bell.

Bert pulled a push broom from a corner and swept the hair cuttings from around his chair, shook out the chair cloth, and nodded to the customer sitting beside Jon and Bert began the snipping and chatting all over again.

When Augie's customer had arisen, paid and left the shop, Augie nodded to Jon indicating that his time had come. "Welcome, young man," the barber said. "Welcome. You're a ball player, aren't you? A rising star no doubt. Someday we'll have your picture up on our wall."

Jon acknowledged that he did indeed play baseball for the Longliners. His perusal of the walls of the barber shop had not revealed obvious Longliner pictures. Mostly local sports teams—high school football, hockey, and baseball.

"So, what'll it be?" Augie asked. "Mohawk perhaps? Crew cut? Or just a trim around the edges to keep you looking good for the girls?"

"Just a trim would be good," Jon replied.

The barber set to work, spraying his hair with a mist of water to keep it settled. The scissors snipped like a nervous snapping turtle around the top, the back, and the sides of Jon's head.

"Where you from, son?" Augie asked.

Jon told him he was from New York State. North of New York City. Near the Hudson river.

"Nice part of the world. Spent some time there once upon a

time. Growing apples. It's a great part of the world to grow apples in. Where are you in school?"

"North Carolina," Jon replied.

"Another nice part of the world. Never been there though," Augie said through the rhythm of the snipping. "Why'd you choose Tilley?"

Jon told him that the Longliners had chosen him. His coach had urged him to spend the summer.

"Headed for pro-ball?"

"Don't know. I guess it depends if they want me."

"Got something else in mind for your future? Want to be a carpenter like your boss?"

"Mr. Wentzell is a great guy," Jon said.

"Yes, he is. Yes, he is. Been here longer than I have. My family came from Italy. Name's August Mandelpiano. Nothing to do with music. Everyone calls me Augie. Been cutting hair all my life. That's the thing about hair. It grows back. More or less. And you can't find a more beautiful place than Cape Cod. But Ace has been here longer." He returned to snipping Jon's hair.

Augie continued, "Sometimes . . . sometimes when he comes in . . . sometimes he seems to be overwhelmed by the passion of the wood that he is working with and the world that the walls of a house can create. Like the building is alive or something."

Jon couldn't nod his head without risking the loss of an ear.

"He can get quite poetic. Some people are just lucky, I guess. Like me and hair. Hey, Bert! This guy says he isn't sure he wants to play professional ball. Isn't that a hoot?"

"Wish I had a choice like that to make. Jesus, those guys make a bundle. But I guess they can't all be stars."

"Guess not," Augie replied. Snip. Snip. Clip.

"So how long have the Salsbergs been here?" Jon asked.

Once again, the snipping stalled. Jon felt Augie's warm breath on the side of his face. "We don't talk about them," he said quietly.

Jon turned his head to look at him, to see if he was serious or joking. Augie's face looked extremely serious and dead pan.

"Oh," Jon said.

The snipping and clipping resumed. "How's the team doing?"

"Okay, I guess. You get to the games?"

"Oh, rarely. Some nights are just too hard to resist. Warm and clear. It's poetic, really. American. Kids love it. Tourists love it. What happened to that pitcher?"

Jon's thinking stumbled. He tried to get back on the same track the barber was on. Pitcher? Dupin? He felt his body slump. He'd forgotten about Dupin.

"That was a real shocker, wasn't it?" Augie said. "So sudden. Life is short like that, you know. We have customers come in here one day and be dead the same afternoon. Cancer can do that too. Cancer. Car accidents. I've given haircuts to dead guys, you know. Pretty gruesome. But they've got to look good lying there in the coffin. They can't smile but they can look trim. Not weird anymore. Nothing's weird anymore." He leaned over Jon's ear again. "Mrs. Salsberg was sudden too if you know what I'm saying. Sudden!" He winked.

In the short time he had known him, Jon had reached the conclusion that Augie was not the quiet type. Jon had never thought about it before, but a barber has a trapped audience. You couldn't get away. You were in the chair for the duration. Some barbers took advantage of that. Then there were the stories about characters like Sweeney Todd. Jon unconsciously squirmed in the chair.

"Speaking of dead people," Augie said, "I used to cut the hair of this guy who was a hundred and three! Imagine living that long! I went to his house, you know, 'cause he really didn't get around much. His dancing days were long in the past. I hadn't heard from him for a while so I called him, but there was no answer. Called him a couple of times. Finally, I drove over to his house and there was a For Sale sign in the yard. Now I really wondered. There was a woman that took care of his technical stuff, you know. Paying the bills, but for the life of me I couldn't figure out what I'd done with her number. Tore my desk apart. Found things I'd been looking for for a long time." Augie snorted and snipped.

"There was another guy in the neighborhood that I cut hair for and I asked him what had happened to the old guy, and he told me that they'd put him in a nursing home. So, I went there, found his room, and found him lying there in the bed with his eyes closed. I really didn't want to disturb him, but I couldn't tell if he was alive or dead, you know? But I touched the top of his head and his eyes opened and he looked at me. 'Hey,' I said. 'It's Augie. It's been awhile.'

"'Yeah,' he replied. 'How'd you find me?'

"'I asked,' I told him.

"'They just moved me in here. This is going to be the last stop. I'll be in here until they wheel me out in a box.'

"What can you say to something like that?" Augie looked at Jon.

"And then the guy said, 'You look well. I pray for you every day.'

"'Wow!' I said. 'Thanks. I feel well.'

"'I want you to pray for me too. I talk to God every night, and I ask him to take me away. I've done my thing here. I'm done. My legs don't work. My brain still works, but that's about all. I want to go, but dammit. I keep waking up! I open my eyes in the morning and I'm still here. So, help me out here, will ya? Tell him I want to go.'

"And he looked at me with abject honesty and then closed his eyes. I didn't know what to do. Would have seemed a bit odd to start cutting his hair. Besides it would have been hard since his head was on the pillow." Augie snorted again. "So, what would you have done?"

Jon didn't have an answer. He didn't have a clue how he would feel at a hundred and three sometime in the middle of the next century.

"But then he closed his eyes. And died. I guess he finally completed his call to God."

"Oh," Jon replied.

Augie resumed snipping away. "Anyway. No. The Salsbergs. They only come here in the summer like other money. Let that beautiful house sit most of the time."

Jon didn't reply. Despite the barber's insistence that they 'don't talk about them' Jon was sure that more would come if it was like the last story.

Snip. Snip. Clip. Clip.

"Book smart, I guess. Lots of money. Isn't that right, Bert?"

"Lots of money," Bert replied. "Like to know how they got it. Like to do that myself. I only get the penny stocks. They've got the thousand-dollar ones!"

Jon was trying to sort out what the book smart had to do with the money.

"You're book smart too. Going to be rich like them? Don't forget about us, will you?"

The barber had the tip of his scissors in his ear so Jon didn't move.

"No, we don't see those boys in here very often. Mr. Reese. He likes those 'stylists'," he spat out the word as though it would fester on his tongue. "'Coiffured'. Vanity of vanities. That's what it says in the Bible. Lot of stories about too much vanity."

Jon felt warm breath on his ear again. Garlic swirled around his head. "And if you ask me, I think his brother-in-law, Garrett Scoles, did in his mother-in-law." He pulled his forefinger out of his scissors and held it up to make the point of his statement clear.

Jon managed to say, "What makes you say that?"

The barber stood back and looked over at Bert standing behind the other chair shaking his head.

"We hear stuff. It is pretty amazing what people tell us in these chairs. Pretty amazing what we hear. Some people might say that it's just gossip. But how do you know? What's fact? What's truth? How do you separate the two?"

Jon wasn't sure why you would want to separate facts from truth.

"You know the sheriff comes in here too?" Augie said.

"Not really a sheriff, Aug," Bert said. "May seem like it at times. May seem like the wild west. He's just a police officer."

Augie waved his hand. "Whatever. Officer Prence. He's not a talker, mind you. But like all of us, he can lose his temper now and then. Say things he doesn't mean to say."

"What's he think?" Jon asked.

"Don't ask me. I wouldn't know what he thinks. But I think he's thinking about that other guy. Mrs. Salsberg's son. Now how could a son kill his mother? It's unnatural. But he's a gambler, you know. Maybe he did some gambling he shouldn't have and didn't want Mommy to know about it. Huh? Maybe something like that."

"What did Officer Prence say?" Jon asked.

"Well, between you and me and the lamppost . . . he said something about drugs! Or gas. Some kind of gas." The barber winked.

"Ah." Jon didn't have a clue what Augie's wink meant, however.

"There were too many drugs in her system."

"What did the medical examiner say?"

"Couldn't say. Sheriff doesn't talk much. But he was mad. Guess they were trying to take the case away from him. A jurisdictional dispute as they say on TV. Jurisdictional dispute. And he was pissed that they were saying he couldn't handle it. Too big. Too hot for a little local sheriff. Guess they wanted to bring in the FBI or CIA or some such. And he didn't want any part of it. Don't know. He wouldn't talk about it."

Augie held up the mirror so that Jon could see the back of his head. The barber pulled the little tissue collar out from around his neck and flicked the stray hairs away with his soft brush. He whisked the chair cloth away and bundled it into a rough fold. "There!" he said. "Good for the girls for another week!"

~

ACE HAD ASKED JON TO MEET HIM AT THE OLD Meetinghouse and given him directions. The building was a town landmark that had been falling into disrepair because there was no dedicated ownership. Over the years its purpose had been replaced by new town buildings, new meeting and gathering spaces, that were sparse and modern, glass and brick and purposeful with occasional tips of the hat to tradition with the addition of cupolas and bell towers and the casual column.

Ace told Jon that the Meetinghouse had been in the middle of town and years ago had been considered to be in the way of progress and so, being thrifty New Englanders, rather than tear it down to create something new the building had been moved. There were no telephone wires to worry about in those days. The roads weren't great but they were usable. There weren't motorized cranes, tractors, and backhoes, but there were carts, people, and horses. And the building was solid - as Ace pointed out.

It hadn't been moved far. The town fathers wanted to get it off Main Street because they had some grand ideas about adding gas lights, elm trees, a few statues of famous people, and a Civil War Memorial. Although it was not a small building, it had blended into its new surroundings so that it no longer stuck out with its tall, white columns lining the front porch.

Ace was standing on the front lawn looking up at the aging roof when Jon pulled up and hopped out of Maybellene.

"This is massive!" Jon remarked.

"Used to be the school house back in the eighteen hundreds," Ace replied.

They walked to the porch and up the stone steps. The fluted columns stretched up about eighteen feet. "Doric," Ace said. He pointed to the simple tops. The columns were almost three feet in diameter. "Imagine making things like this? Imagine a forest of trees this big and this straight? They added these after they moved the building."

Jon stared up at the evenly carved flutes.

"They had to have a good eye and a steady hand. They didn't have power tools. Skill. They had skill." Ace looked at him to see if he understood the magnitude of the task. "They had to understand the materials they were working with. They had to appreciate the weight of the roof. I don't think much of the gold paint on the top. That was added in the nineteen fifties when they tried to turn this place into a dancing school."

They pushed through the front door. The air inside that greeted them was cool. "Door's not original either. Some parts of buildings take all the abuse. Nature is always taking it back. It's a constant battle with the earthly creatures: mice, raccoons, ants, and mold as well as the rain, the snow, and the wind. But look at this structure."

The interior plaster and lathe walls were falling away in places. "Horse hair. That's what kept the plaster together. The wet plaster was smeared over the lathe and forced in between the gaps. That's what kept it from falling off. It hardened in the gaps. It must have been a messy job. Especially on ceilings. It's all sheetrock now . . . gypsum, plasterboard. They started doing that in the twenties. Plaster was more expensive, but drywall was considered a cheap alternative. Didn't want to seem cheap. People are amazing. Nice haircut, by the way."

The interior of the building had not been maintained with any love or care. "This place has been ignored for a long time," Ace continued. "Good bones, though. When we get rid of all the ticky-tacky stuff, we'll get down to her heart. Look here."

Ace took him to a corner of the building where all the plaster had peeled away and the structure was visible. Big pieces of rough sawn timber locked into other pieces, carefully notched and pegged. "Beautiful," Ace said with a touch of awe in his voice. "See that! See the way the pieces fit together. It doesn't rely on nails or bolts. You had to apprentice to a master builder for a long time. You had to grow up with wood in your hands.

"Ever watch one of those World Cup soccer games?" he asked suddenly.

"Uhm. I go to games at school."

"No. I mean the World Cup. Sometimes hard to find on TV. People in this country don't have a lot of interest in soccer. But if you get a chance: watch them. Those kids grow up with a soccer ball attached to them. They eat with it. They sleep with it. It's their life. They don't have to look at the ball. They don't have to look at the other players. They just know. When they kick the ball, they know how it will fly through the air, where it will turn, where it will dip. They know this because they just know it. They don't have to study it. They don't have to get a book out about it. A great musician is the same way. Or a chef. Or a painter. Or a carpenter. They know themselves. Their hands. Their fingers. Their eyes. And extending those things with their tools. They know their tools. And they know the materials they are working with. Do you understand what I'm saying?"

Jon nodded.

"A building like this was created to be used. It wasn't built to be put in a museum. The surfaces of the wood aren't smooth: they're rough sawn. They fit together. They get the job done. Beautifully, because of the skill in the hands that created the joints, the structure, which has been standing for over a hundred years. Do you understand?" Ace asked again.

Not waiting for an answer, he continued, "The builder's clients needed a building to shelter the occupants from the weather. He had about as much information as Noah got from God when he built the ark! 'Noah! Build me an Ark. I want it to be three hundred cubits by about fifty cubits. Give or take a cubit!' And cubits were even organic, did you know that? None of this precise stuff. A cubit was the distance from the builder's elbow to his fingertips. And you know, builders don't all have the same length arms!" Ace laughed. "And the parts needed to fit together. They had to stand up through wind, water, and snow. But the builder didn't go to the lumber yard to buy a four by eight sheet of plywood or a two by four stud. They had to make the doors and the windows. Look at this place!" Ace demanded. "It's a work of art that a craftsman would appreciate—appreciate the skill of a fellow craftsman. Can you feel the energy of the students who leaned over their desks in here? Dipping their pens in their ink-wells? Can you hear the laughter? Can you hear the debates from the political meetings as townspeople debated the future of Tilley when the building was used for politics? This is what buildings are all about. This is why I do what I do. I can feel this building's pain from being neglected all these years.

"But don't get me wrong. I know that the builder didn't build this place to last forever. He built it to do a job. And it has! By god it has! Maybe it's time for it to go. Do you understand that too? Wood is an organic material. It's not granite or marble. Maybe it's time for it to return to the earth it came from. What do you think?"

"Me?" Jon asked. "What do you mean?"

"Would you tear this building down? Build something new?"

"Me?" Jon asked again. "Why? How would I know?"

Ace didn't answer. He started to walk around the building, stepping over pieces that had fallen down or been pulled down, the plaster crunching under their feet. The air smelled damp with a slight sweetness of age. The light flickered through the broken windows. Weeds had grown and died in corners. A bird suddenly swooped out of the rafters and fluttered out through a broken gable window. The wood of the stairs creaked under their weight as they made their way down to the basement. Ace pulled a big flashlight out of his back pocket and flicked it on. The air in the basement was even cooler and the dampness almost made Jon shiver.

"Careful where you step," Ace said. "This part of the building was always dark even when they tacked electric lights in here. Kids probably snuck down here for smokes and sex!"

Ace dragged the light from the flashlight over the stones in the foundation walls. "Imagine what they had to do to move this building. The frame was strong enough to stand the stresses while being transported by horses and wagons. They had to dig this foundation out by hand and haul each of these stones and set them in place in such a way that they could accurately set the building back down on top of them. Story goes that these stones —each of which was cut and squared in a quarry somewhere— were used as ballast in ships, their weight being replaced with the goods that were shipped in the other direction.

"So, what do you think? Tear it down? Replace it?"

"Why?"

They walked back up the creaking stairs and stood in the middle of open space. "And just think," Ace continued, "they heated this space with this big open fireplace. Most of the heat flowed up the chimney. Must have used an enormous amount of wood - all cut by hand. They used dried seaweed for insulation in some of these buildings. Seaweed, pine cones, all sorts of creative stuff."

"So why would they tear this down?" Jon asked again.

"Think about it. You're a smart guy. Think about it. It's old. It's done its job." Ace looked at him.

Jon shrugged. "Yeah. True. But it's beautiful in its own way. You said so yourself."

"You have to get rid of the sentimentality, don't you? It's just a building. It's an object. Of course, the Mona Lisa is just an object too. The woman's long dead and gone and so are all the people who knew her. I mean the purpose of a picture is to . . . what? Show someone who to look for at an airport or a bus terminal? Why do we need pictures? A building has a purpose."

Jon looked at the older man. He looked tired. His thinning hair stuck out in all directions. He needed to lose some of the weight that made his suspenders strain to keep his pants in place. It seemed as though his looming stresses had restrained his smile.

"Do they want you to tear it down?" he asked.

Ace sighed. "It's a building. You know there was a time when people just did stuff. They did it because it was their job. They didn't sign their name to it. They didn't want to be celebrated for it. They didn't do it for the fame and certainly not for the fortune. Think of the craftsmen who carved the gargoyles on Notre Dame cathedral! They could have just constructed a box but they had to make it beautiful. They might say that it was for the Glory of God . . . perhaps. Perhaps for something else."

Ace walked over to the brick mass of the fireplace. "Something inside of us makes us want to do more—something that we need to satisfy, something that makes us want fins and chrome on a car or patterns on a sweater or gingerbread trim on a house. We are not satisfied with just a plain, utilitarian box. The box is just the basis . . . the starting point. We have to go farther. That's why we sing songs . . . why we play instruments . . . why we build beautiful buildings . . . why we are always seeking beauty in all we do."

Jon wondered where the hell he was going with all of this.

"I don't understand the ones that don't."

Jon waited.

"I don't understand the ones that don't," Ace repeated, "the ones that just consume. I don't believe that they have souls. The ones who don't want to make things better, the ones who just destroy, the ones who want to hurt, the ones who get pleasure from increasing the suffering of others. It's as though they have a piece missing. They may be rich. They may be powerful enough to manipulate the lives of others. But they have a piece missing. But even so . . . ! Even so they are necessary. It hurts to smile all the time."

Jon wondered why Ace was rambling? Did he have thoughts of pulling out a gun and shooting himself? Was he about to go running out a second-floor window? No, Ace wasn't about to run anywhere. Who was he talking about? Maybe he needed some help. Maybe he needed a vacation. Maybe he needed to move to Arizona where the air wasn't so damp. Then it dawned on him that he was talking about the Salsbergs.

"What's going on, Ace?" he asked.

Ace looked at him in surprise. "What?"

"You've got me . . . uhm . . . totally confused. What's going on? Is this about the Salsbergs? About . . . you know, the lawsuit?"

"No! Of course not. It's about this building. You haven't answered my question: should we tear it down?"

"There isn't anything to what they're claiming about why Mrs. Salsberg died? Is there?"

Ace turned and walked back toward the front door of the old building. "No," he mumbled, "no, but nothing in this life is certain, is it? Makes more sense to tear it down and start over. No place for sentimentality."

Ace did not strike Jon as a sentimental sort of man. He fit the role of a practical, solid, reliable, enigmatic New Englander. Something had short-circuited his brain and all this stuff flowed out. It pushed Jon's resolve to try to get this issue with the Salsbergs eliminated so that he could get the monkeys off Ace's back and out of his brain.

16

SPEAK & SPELL™

Brian Reese sat in the stands flanked by his two sons, watching the Longliners play. Brian tried to explain some of the intricacies of the game, but Brian Jr. was more interested in the kids hanging around the outfield and Pee Wee was annoying, pushing the buttons on his *Speak & Spell*. Brian didn't care to hear the gargly, pseudo-British electronic voice for the millionth time! "Spell *house* . . . H - O - U - S - E . . . you are correct! Now let's spell . . ."

The Longliners were playing well. They seemed to have coalesced as a team. Players reached for balls with an extra effort, ending up in the right place at the right time, anticipating what might happen next. They were playing to win as a team.

And the crowd appreciated it. The spectators were also performing well, cheering and encouraging the players to hit, pitch, catch, and run to the best of their abilities. They were paying attention while the interest swelled with the tensions of a pitcher/batter duel or a stolen base. The crowd jumped to its feet as a hit ball soared into the air toward the center fielder, who raced to get under it and set himself to fire into second base to cut off a runner. And even if the second baseman missed the throw, Jon Megquire was there to back him up.

Brian had enjoyed watching the team develop and play through the actions of Megquire, and he struggled to understand why his sons could not appreciate the beauty of the physical drama in front of them.

"Dad, can I go down with the other kids on the field?" Brian Jr. asked.

"Can't you sit here with me to watch the game?"

"But it's so boring, Dad. They don't do anything."

"Boring? That's just because you don't understand what's going on. This is America's game. You're getting a chance to see some of the future stars up close. Some of these guys are going to be playing in the major leagues in a couple of years. You'll be able to see them on television!"

"Great. I'll watch them then."

"Don't you want me to explain what they are doing? Do you understand why the runner is leading off second base? The pitcher doesn't see him. See? He's just about to steal. The catcher can see him. See? The catcher is sending signals, flipping his fingers between his legs. And look at that! The third base coach is also sending signals to the runner! He's gonna go!"

"I see, Dad. Can I go now?"

And *Speak & Spell* said, "Let's spell dog!" in that muffled, rattily, British accent.

"Can you put that away, Pee Wee?" Brian asked. "Oh, go ahead, Junior. Just stay where I can see you. Want to take your brother with you?"

"He's too little!" Brian Jr. scoffed.

"Hmmm," Brian replied, turning his attention back to the game.

Brian was starting to lose hope that either of his sons had a future in Major League baseball. How do you get kids interested in anything? He thought this would be a good idea—taking the kids out to a ball game on a beautiful Friday afternoon in July on Cape Cod. If his parents had done this for him . . . but then his father had been dead and his mother, when she was alive, had been too tied up in her business. She seemed to work all the time. She had never been at home – with him. Watching any sport required patience which wasn't something that Faith Salsberg could have been accused of. She couldn't sit still.

Faith's driving energy was gone now, but Garrett was always restless too. In fact, Garrett seemed to have less patience than Faith, if that was possible.

What was going to happen to Salsberg Homes? Technically, Brian thought, it should be his. Faith was his mother. It was a blood connection. He'd been part of the company all his life. He'd given up spending time with his mother while she built Buckingham Palms. She'd blended the two companies together when she married Chris Salsberg - just as she had blended their lives and their families. Brian had paid his dues. Sacrificed his childhood. He should be made president. He wondered what Garrett had been saying about him when he went to those company meetings. Brian felt like he should have been there too. He should have been invited to participate, but Garrett said somebody had to stay here to keep the family together.

But, if he was honest, did he want it? Did he want all the pressure and schmoozing and other crap that went along with making decisions and making money? But that wasn't the point. He deserved it. For a moment a cold chill crept up the back of his neck. What if they did make him president? They would expect him to make a lot of decisions. They would expect him to know what he was doing. He might make a mistake, and the second he did - BANG! Garrett would be all over him - pointing fingers, calling him names.

He was losing track of the game. He swore under his breath. Tilley runners were on first and second. He looked out at the scoreboard. Longliners 3. Gatemen 2. Tilley was still ahead. Looked like they might add to their lead. The scoreboard displayed only the inning and the score. It was one of the things that he both loved and hated about these small-town games: the crude scoreboard didn't provide a lot of detail. He couldn't tell what the count was on the batter. He smiled to himself. If Junior was here, he would have explained to him that the 'count' was the number of balls and strikes on the batter. He would have explained how the coaches would have used that information to tell the batter what to look for in the next pitch. He would have told him what the catcher was telling the pitcher. Just a little information like that could shape the game, but the only way you could know the 'count' was to pay attention to the game.

When you were experienced enough, you could use that information to anticipate what happened next. And when it did happen, that was a thrill. The game moved in a way that you anticipated, almost like you were moving game pieces around in your mind.

When pieces didn't move the way you expected, when something happened that you weren't anticipating, it was almost more of a thrill! Even simple moments like a dog running out onto the field. You had to pay attention.

The scoreboard did indicate that the game was in the eighth inning. Brian looked out beyond first base to where the kids were running around just off the field and spotted Junior standing and watching bigger kids toss a football around. They were tossing a football on a baseball field! Brian watched his son watching and sighed.

"Spell C-A-L-F" said the rattily, stuffed mouth, jumbly, metallic voice beside him.

Well, at least it kept Pee Wee amused.

The Wareham pitcher took his stance, looked over at first base, peered down at the catcher, reared back and fired the ball.

"Ball!" yelled the umpire, holding up his fingers to indicate a full count - three balls and two strikes.

"See, the runners will be going now," Brian said to his younger son. "See, it's a full count and there are two out so they'll be running on this pitch because it won't matter if it's a pop fly because if any of them are put out . . . well, the inning will be over. See?"

"Spell B-L-O-O-D!" Brian barely listened. He had a hard time deciphering the muffled beeps and buzzes, but Pee Wee was mesmerized.

Brian leaned forward in his seat. The players on the field tensed up, spreading their legs. Spreading their arms. Glaring in at the pitcher and batter. The sound of the crowd dropped in anticipation. The tension was palpable. The fans and the players knew what should happen next. Only a limited number of actions could occur. Unless something unexpected happened. The batter could walk to first. He could strike out. He could hit the ball. And then everything on the field would move to the prescribed dance. This moment of tension and ultimate result was what made baseball so exciting to Brian. The pitcher had to make a decision how and where to throw the ball. Then he had to do it.

"Dad?" a little voice beside him said. "Dad? I have to go to the bathroom."

Brian was shaken out of his focus. "What?"

"I have to go to the bathroom."

"Oh. Okay. In a minute. We'll go in a minute."

"I have to go now!"

Brian turned to his son and in that moment the pitcher fired the ball. There was a ping of the bat. Brian spun his head to try to find the ball. The crowd jumped to their feet and Brian jumped with them. Pee Wee's *Speak & Spell* clattered to the concrete floor. A moment's reprieve while Pee Wee dropped to his knees to retrieve it. Brian tried to tune into what was happening on the field. The runner from second was rounding third. The runner from first was approaching second!

"I would have bet on a third Strike," Brian said to himself.

"Dad! Now!" Pee Wee had recovered the squawking, electronic box.

"Oh. Okay, okay. We'll go." Brian took his son's sweaty little hand and eased his way in front of the cheering fans. Some of them kindly stepped back and allowed him room to thread the way out to the aisle. Some of them grumpily held their drinks in the air and mumbled, “For Christ’s sake! Now? Really?”

Brian glanced back over his shoulder as he made his way up the steps. He tried to see the scoreboard, but there wasn’t time to focus. “Shit,” he mumbled to himself.

Brian hated being one of those fans who weren’t watching the game. He felt his actions needed explanation. Why he wasn’t in his seat? Why he wasn’t paying attention? He smiled as they hurried toward the men’s room. “Son. My son has to pee. Not me. I’m okay. I could have waited. It’s my son!”

A half dozen or so men populated the men’s room. The floor was wet. Men were standing side by side at the urinals. Brian had to lean over to unfasten Pee Wee’s pants. He didn’t want them to drop down on the floor, but he couldn’t do much about it. There was a stall with a closed door. Brian knocked, pushed the door open, and guided Pee Wee inside.

“Flush when you’re done,” he said. “I’ll be just here.”

He stood in the open doorway not knowing where to look or what to do with his hands. He realized that he was clutching the *Speak & Spell* and had the inclination to push buttons and have gravelly mouthed voice say something. He didn’t want to make eye contact with anyone. He couldn’t just stare at the ceiling. He couldn’t look down as though he was staring at other men’s privates. He turned back toward Pee Wee.

“Done?” he asked.

Pee Wee didn’t answer.

Brian tried again. “How’s it going, Champ?”

“Can’t go, Dad. It hurts!”

“What do you mean you can’t go?”

“All these people. There are all these people around.”

“Want me to close the door?”

“I can’t pee with all these people around. It hurts. I need to. I really need to.”

Brian started thinking of ways to get someone to pee, but the only thing he could come up with was to put Pee Wee’s hand under warm water. That would not work in the stall. He couldn't exactly kick all the men out of the bathroom. "Excuse me. Would you mind leaving? My son can't piss in public!" That would go over about as well as the warm water concept. "Just relax," he said. "Pretend you're all alone. Try to relax and just let it go. Nobody's watching. It's just you and me."

Brian eased himself into the stall behind his son, juggling the *Speak & Spell* and trying not to step on Pee Wee's pants that were lying in a heap around his ankles. "You can do this. Just relax!"

That was like telling a pitcher not to throw a low inside fast ball or "Don't think about the elephant in the room."

For a moment, Brian's thoughts wandered to the activities on the field. It was probably the ninth inning now. Oh, and what about Junior? No one was watching Junior. Audrey would kill him if anything happened to Junior. They had to get back. With diminishing patience, he said, "Come on, Pee Wee. Just let 'er go! I'm getting nauseated in here."

Not the most perfect thing to say to a five-year-old standing in a smelly toilet stall in a men's room. But what was he supposed to do? He couldn't piss for his son. Holding his son's little penis and aiming at the toilet was not going to help either. Clearly it was a problem in Pee Wee's mind, an issue that only Pee Wee could overcome, an issue best addressed with serenity, tranquility, finding inner peace and all that other bullshit that Audrey kept yammering about from her evening classes. But he wasn't about to achieve Nirvana in a men's room stall. Pee Wee was frozen in time. Then someone pounded on the door of the stall which literally scared the piss out of Pee Wee, the urine started flowing, and not all of it in the right direction.

"You guys going to be in there all day!"

"Dad!" Pee Wee whined as though this was all his father's fault.

Brian had attempted to jump back out of the way, but was constrained by the walls of the stall. Pee Wee stepped back and tripped over the pants around his ankles. Brian dropped the

Speak & Spell. He managed to get the door open. He realized as he faced the burly man in the Bermuda Shorts that if one were to assume the worst, and people usually did, that the scene did not look respectable. Brian's pants were wet. Pee Wee's naked legs were wet. The floor was wet.

"Oh!" the man said. "Sorry."

"My son," Brian explained. "My son. Not under control."

"Oh," the man said again, turned away, and banged on the next stall.

"Dad," Pee Wee whimpered. "I'm wet."

"I know," Brian replied. "Let's see if we can get you cleaned up."

Gingerly Brian helped his son to stand. He pulled Pee Wee's pants up and fastened his belt. "What a mess," he said. At the sinks, Brian lifted Pee Wee up so he could get his hands under the water. "Rub them together," Brian instructed. Setting him back on the floor, Brian grabbed a handful of paper towels to rub Pee Wee's face and hands.

"SPEAK!" Pee Wee squalled.

Brian looked at him. No, he thought. Oh, no. Not again.

"SPEAK! SPELL?"

Brian looked around with some relief and saw the toy lying on the floor near the stall and picked it up. Despite the fact that his own pants were wet from his calves down to his Top Siders, he was glad to leave the Men's Room with no more disasters. How do parents do this with multiple children, he wondered, and then he remembered that Junior was out there somewhere. Was the game over?

The game was definitely over. People were heading for the exits. Brian felt oddly disoriented. He held Pee Wee's hand as he pushed his way out toward the field. He felt panic creep up the back of his neck. Would Junior think his father had left without him? Would he have asked for a ride with one of his new friends - if he had been able to make friends? And when he saw Officer Prence walking toward him, his anxiety increased.

"Where's my son?" Brian asked.

"Excuse me?" Prence replied.

"What's happened to my son?"

Prence looked down at Pee Wee and back up at Brian.

"No. No. No. Not Pee Wee! Junior! Where's Junior? What's happened to him? Has something happened to him?"

Prence continued to look confused. "I don't know, Mr. Reese. Did you lose him?"

"I took Pee Wee to the bathroom and the game was still going on and Junior was down on the field. And we had a bit of an accident . . .."

"I can see that, sir." Prence smiled.

"No. No. No. I need to find my son."

Brian pushed forward to get out to the field. Junior was probably kicking the dirt, wondering where his father and brother were. But Brian was sure that he wouldn't wait long. What would happen if Junior were kidnapped? If Junior told the kidnapper who he was . . . oh my god! The ransom demand would be horrible. Brian would look like a horrible father. The police would be all over it. Audrey would skin him alive. And with the stuff going on with Garrett and the company? Oh, my god! Brian pushed harder, dragging Pee Wee who sensed the panic in his father and whimpered.

When they reached the stands, Brian looked frantically down toward the field where Junior had been playing. No one. He looked across the stands. A few people still sat here and there, chatting. Brian looked out toward the score board. Five for Tilley. Two for Wareham. They had won. Hung onto their lead and even scored a couple of extra runs. He had missed the ending of a great game.

"What was your son wearing?" Prence asked.

"What?" Prence was still shadowing him. This was all Prence's fault. He was the authority. He shouldn't have let this happen. Brian glared at him. "How could you let this happen? What did you ask?"

"What was he wearing?"

"Oh. Shirt. Shorts. Sneakers. We just got him a pair of those Adidas athletic shoes. He loves them!"

"What color shirt?"

"Uhm." Brian thought back. He had to get this right. What color had he worn? He never paid attention to things like that. It had never seemed particularly important. He told himself to concentrate, to think back, to picture his son watching the football game on the field. Well, it wasn't really a game. They had been tossing the ball . . .. Was it an appropriate color? Would his grandmother have approved? She probably gave him the clothes. She always gave him clothes. Bought them stuff at Bloomingdales or Saks. "It was a Lacoste white shirt. You know, with the alligator. Khaki pants too. And the Adidas. White socks, I think. He doesn't like socks really. Wants to go around barefoot. You know how kids are."

"Yes, sir. Do you see him out there on the field?"

Brian looked out over the diamond. A handful of kids were taking advantage of the vacant field, running around the bases, pretending to play a game, sliding into home plate, and getting very dirty. But Junior was not among them.

Brian turned to a couple of men sitting in the stands and asked, "Did you see my son? White shirt, khaki pants, Adidas athletic shoes? He went down to the field in the seventh inning. I took my other . . .."

The men shook their heads. "Wish we could help. Lot of kids on the field. We were watching the game, you know."

"Thanks," Brian said.

"Look, he's bound to be here somewhere," Prence encouraged. "You weren't gone too long, were you?"

Brian looked down at Pee Wee who was clutching his *Speak & Spell*. "No. No. No. Not that long."

"Where would he go?" Prence asked. "I mean if he didn't see you in the stands, what would he do? Does he know where you parked? Would he go to the car?

"Yeah! Good idea!" He scooped Pee Wee up and started off toward the parking lot where he'd parked the car almost at a run. Prence hurried after him.

They passed the booster club table where they had been asking for contributions for the team's yearbook. The boosters were pulling off the table cloth, packing up the signs and the cash box.

"Have you seen my son?" Brian asked.

The boosters stopped what they were doing and looked at him in confusion. They looked at Pee Wee in Brian's arms and back to Brian.

"My other son! Wearing a white Lacoste shirt, khaki pants, Adidas athletic shoes? He's nine?"

"Lots of kids around these games," one man said. "Can't say we noticed any one in particular. They often look lost. Sometimes parents send them to these games on their own to get them out of the way, you know?"

"Thanks," Brian said and hurried on.

"He done something, Officer?" another booster mumbled quietly to Prence.

Prence shrugged. "Just lending a hand," he said.

The lot was emptying out. Some of the players were returning to their cars, lugging bags filled with mephitic athletic attire.

Brian stopped, trying to picture where he had parked in this simple, dirt parking lot that held maybe fifty cars. Brian's problem was that his car was a rental and therefor, unfamiliar. Junior's white shirt, blond hair, and nine-year-old whine were quite familiar, however.

"Dad! Where were you? The game's over. I've been waiting forever."

"There!" Brian pointing to Prence. "There he is."

"Ah," Prence acknowledged. "I thought it might be."

"Pee Wee had to go and . . ."

"Uh, listen, Mr. Reese," Prence started, "I'm glad you found your son. I'm glad that's come out well. But listen; I came here to find you. On purpose, you know."

Brian put Pee Wee down. The boy ran over to his brother who tousled his hair. "I had to pee!"

"What?" Brian asked Prence.

"Yeah. I have to ask you some questions."

Brian looked at the officer. "Why? I need to get my boys home."

"Yeah, sure. But I'm afraid this is official. I've got some official questions to ask you about what happened to your mother."

Official questions were never a positive thing in Brian's mind. Although he couldn't think what it might be, avoiding 'official' questions was always the best approach. Official questions meant official issues and official issues never had good outcomes. Although they might be classified as 'just routine', they never were. People didn't ask 'official' questions unless they were linked to . . . problems.

"Can you get someone to take your boys home while you and I head down to the station?"

"What?" Brian asked again. "I don't understand. What can I tell you that I haven't already told you? What can I tell you there that I can't tell you here?" He gestured with his hands, pointing off in a random direction to indicate the local universe.

"There have been some . . . irregularities that we need to square away. Is there someone . . . someone to take your boys?"

"No!"

"I'm afraid it's important. You might not want to have your boys with you. I'm going to have to insist that you come with me."

"What's going on, Dad?" Junior asked. Then he saw Jon coming across the parking lot. Junior let go of his younger brother, smiled at Jon, and said, "Good game, Megquire" as though he were Jon's coach.

Jon acknowledged the compliment with a tentative, "Thanks" a bit put off by the nine-year-old's familiarity. His mind was still on the game - feeling pretty good about his own performance. What would it be like to play in the major leagues, doing this for a living, making product endorsements, having about a million fans looking for his autograph? A rock star! He smiled to himself. He waved at the group by Brian Reese's car and wondered if the man had been drinking. Was that what the discussion was about?

'Hey, Megquire?" Officer Prence asked. "Would you mind running these boys over to their house on Jolo Point while I talk with their father?"

Jon stopped. "What?" He looked at Prence's face to see if he was kidding. "What's going on?"

"I need to talk with Mr. Reese down at the station. Just routine stuff. We need to clear up some things."

"Are you arresting him?" Jon asked.

"What?" Junior asked the policeman. He had pulled his eyes away from a girl in a halter top walking across the parking lot.

"Wait! What?" Reese asked. "You're arresting me?"

"No, no," Prence smiled. "No. Just questions. Routine questions."

Jon looked back and forth between the policeman and Brian Reese trying to extract the meaning of what was going on. "I don't understand," he said. "If you're not arresting him . . .?"

"Look," Prence said, assuming his official stance, "look! This is police business. Can you give the boys a ride or not?"

"Sure," Jon said. "Sure, I can do that, but they're going to have to share a seat."

"Oh, damn!" Prence replied. "That's right. You have that little car."

"They're small enough. They can share the seat."

"Cool!" Junior said. "That's a really cool car!"

"That's not safe," his father said. "I can't let them do that. It's not safe!"

"We'll be okay, dad," Junior assured him. "It's not that far. We'll be okay."

Jon could see that Prence did not want to make a scene. "I'll get them home," Jon said.

"Damn it, Jon!" Prence spat. "Just drive safely."

"Of course, officer. Glad to. Let's go guys."

Jon herded the two boys over to Maybellene. Junior stood back and admired her. Jon opened the trunk and dropped his gear in, then he came around to the passenger door. "You're Brian, right?"

"Yeah. But they call me Junior because my father's name is Brian too. Junior's okay, I guess."

"What's your name?" he asked Pee Wee.

"He's Pee Wee," Junior informed Jon. "My father likes baseball . . . a lot. So, he named him after the Pee Wee Reese. Shortstop for the Dodgers a long time ago. Granny wasn't very happy about it. She didn't think it was proper to name him something like that. She said it was *inappropriate*. She said that a lot."

"Yeah. I know who Pee Wee Reese is. But that isn't his real name. It's a nickname. But nobody remembers his real name."

"Do you know him?" Junior asked.

Jon laughed. "No. He's retired. Doesn't play anymore. I did have his baseball card though."

"Do *you* have a card?"

Jon laughed again. "No. Not yet!"

"Who you going to play for? Do you get to pick the team? Anywhere? How much are they going to pay you?"

"Don't know any of that stuff," Jon said with a smile. "I don't even know if I want to play professionally."

"Why not? Who wouldn't want to? You could be on television!"

Jon looked down at the boy, at his infectious grin, at his blond hair, blue eyes, and little Adidas athletic shoes and thought about his own past, thought about how he was when he was nine. It seemed like forever ago. Had he imagined himself as a professional baseball player? He couldn't remember. "It's complicated," he said, and he felt like such an adult saying it. At the same time the end of the fluffy tail of pride slipped out of his brain. "Do you want to play baseball?"

"Don't know. Don't know if they'll let me. But now that Granny's dead . . .. You know. Things might be different."

"How so?"

Junior shrugged.

Pee Wee said, "I can spell! Lots of words!" He held up his *Speak & Spell*.

"I see," Jon replied. "Let's see if we can get you guys home."

"It's not home," Junior said. "It's Tilley. It's where we go in the summer. Home is in Fort Lauderdale. That's in Florida. You don't need to take us there."

Jon opened Maybellene's passenger door. "Climb in," he said to Junior, "and scooch over and make room for your brother." Jon lifted Pee Wee into the car.

"He can sit on my lap. He's not heavy. Pee Wee, put your toy thing on the floor. You're banging my knees!"

"Good?" Jon asked.

Jon got into the driver's seat and started the car.

"Cool!" said Brian. "Make the wheels spin!"

"Yeah!" added Pee Wee.

Jon pulsed the accelerator. Maybellene did not have an impressive roar. The car didn't rock on its suspension as the rpm of the engine varied. But it could kick up some rocks and dust as Jon whipped it out of the dirt parking lot while the two boys grinned and hung on.

"Yeah!" shouted Junior. "Do that some more!" He reached out to hold onto the door handle and let go of his brother who flopped over toward the middle of the car.

Jon slowed and pushed Pee Wee upright. The boy looked a bit pale.

"Do it some more," Junior urged.

"We've got to get you home safe," Jon said, smiling. That felt like another adult phrase. Belatedly it occurred to Jon that it was odd that Prence would let him take both boys in one seat. He must have needed to talk with Mr. Reese about something pretty serious. Was this even legal? He slowed the car even more.

"So did Officer Prence say why he needed to talk to your father?"

Junior didn't answer right away.

Jon looked over at him.

"No," Junior replied finally. "He was lost for a while. I mean I was down on the field with the other kids. Then the game ended, and he wasn't where he was when I left him in the stands. So, I came out to the car. But that wasn't our car. Our car is white. It's a Mercedes. I thought maybe he found a different car. We don't have it up here with us. We rent a car for the summer. And the policeman was with him."

"Oh," Jon said.

The *Speak & Spell* bubbled. Somehow Pee Wee had recovered it from the floor and started it.

"You like that thing?" Jon asked.

"Uh huh," Pee Wee nodded.

"Drives us all crazy," Junior said maturely. "You can't shut it off!"

Jon wove Maybellene through the summer traffic. The beautiful evening weather brought everyone out. They didn't stay on the sidewalks but wandered out into the street; gossiping, reading guidebooks, pointing at buildings, laughing, drinking from plastic cups. The crowds converted the street into a continuous party and tied up traffic. Restaurants had dragged out tables and umbrellas, taking up the sidewalk, forcing more people to walk in the street.

A group of girls pointed to Jon and the boys in the car and laughed. Jon waved at them.

"Do you have a girlfriend?" Junior asked.

Jon's mind had been hip-hopping from baseball to crowds to Ace to Officer Prence to Hoppin Dupin. "What?" he asked, coming back to the here and now and thought of Lisa.

"Athletes always have beautiful girlfriends."

Jon laughed. "Hey! It's not all glamor, you know. You only get to see the tip of the iceberg. The fun part. Athletes have to work really hard to get to the fun part. Do you have a girl friend?"

"Nah! They're so immature! And they mess things up."

Jon stopped Maybellene suddenly as a couple gazing into each other's eyes stepped out in front of the car. Pee Wee slid toward the dashboard as Junior reached forward to brace himself.

"You should have blown the horn!" Junior demanded.

Jon eased the car slowly forward. "Doesn't help. People are in their own little worlds when they're on vacation. Don't see anyone else on the face of the earth. I think they leave their minds behind."

"Are you on vacation?" Pee Wee asked.

Jon laughed. "Good question, Pee Wee. No. I'm not on vacation. I'm working."

"Oh. Are you working now?"

"I'm driving you home now."

"Is that working?"

Jon thought about that for a minute. Where was the line between working and not working? Some people worked at taking a vacation from working. Maybe it was doing something different. He decided to change the subject. "Was your Granny on vacation?"

The two boys were quiet. Junior looked out the side of the car.

Pee Wee looked up at Jon and said, "Granny's gone home. She smelled."

"Oh," Jon replied.

"I don't think Uncle Garrett liked Granny very much," Junior said suddenly.

Jon took his eyes off the road and flicked a look over at the boy to see his expression. "What makes you say that?" he asked.

"They yelled a lot."

"People do that in families."

"You can say that again," Junior nodded wisely.

"But just because they yelled doesn't mean that they didn't like each other. That's just the way some people communicate."

"What's *communy* mean?" Pee Wee asked.

"Talk. Communicate means talk."

"Oh," Pee Wee said.

"He said that the heating system in the Lanai wasn't working properly."

At the end of Main Street, the driving was easier, but Jon had lost the path of Junior's thinking. "What?" he asked.

"He said he would fix it. He said that you couldn't trust contractors to know what they were doing."

"Who?"

"Uncle Garrett."

"What does that have to do with your Granny?"

Junior sighed loudly in exasperation. "Granny had to stay in the Lanai because they were working on her room. They argued about her room. They argued about everything."

"Oh." Jon thought for a minute. "What was wrong with the heating system? It's summer. Do you need heat now?"

Junior shrugged and looked out the window again. Pee Wee pulled on the *Speak & Spell* again which burbled out another word.

Jon drove through the stone pillars that marked the entrance to Jolo Point and wound his way along the drive by the water and turned up into the driveway to Casa Grande.

Jon hesitated and then he asked, "Can you show me the Lanai? That's what you call it, right?"

"Of course," Junior replied, unceremoniously dumping Pee Wee off his lap. "Wee!" he demanded, "Go tell mom we're home and that Daddy's in jail and we're going to look at the Lanai."

Pee Wee scampered off into the house. Jon smiled to himself and thought, that'll be interesting. Junior led him through the foyer of the house, across the white and black marbled floor, to the sliding doors that led out to the pool. The blue of the pool water rippled as a light breeze blew across the water. A single leaf dared to scud across the surface like a small boat. Jon looked down across the lawn at the waters of Vineyard Sound. Everything seemed perfectly in place as though some photographer had put the trees, the grass, the clouds, and the waves just so and demanded that they stay that way. And nature patiently didn't object.

The Lanai was a comparatively small, white, single story building facing the pool. It had a covered breezeway or porch with a bar and barbecue grill along one end. The head of an outdoor shower stuck out of one wall like a snake. Sliding glass doors fronted on the pool and opened to the interior living room with weathered grey wood barnyard walls and polished concrete floor that seemed to have frozen the surface of the pool locking it in forever. A large fieldstone fireplace angled across one end.

Furniture consisted of overstuffed sofas and chairs that spun and ottomans that slid around on wheels. There was a large, round dining table surrounded by ten comfortable chairs. All the fabrics matched and murmured subtle, sporty elegance. Maps and antique prints of important American Indians graced the walls. Jon wondered if the interior designer had considered these to be local flavor, regardless of their tribe.

The kitchen area was open to the living room, with a high counter that would hide any cooking clutter than might occur.

Large sliding glass windows looked out on the lawns at the back of the house and down to the water of the Bay.

Junior flopped onto one of the ottomans on his stomach and drove it around the room. He stopped, looked at Jon, and asked, "So? This is it."

"I see," Jon replied. "Where was your grandmother?"

"There," Junior pointed toward a door.

"May I?" Jon asked, walking in that direction.

Junior twitched his shoulders while he remained prone on the ottoman which Jon considered to be acquiescence to his request.

He opened the door and peered into the empty bedroom. He tried to imagine it as the scene of a murder. What was he looking for? What should he be looking for? He didn't even know if Mrs. Salsberg's death was a crime! There wouldn't be anything obvious – a bloody dagger or a bottle with a skull and crossbones on the label that everyone missed. What would Ace see? This was an empty room!

His ruminations were cut short by the sound of a woman's demanding voice behind him say, "Excuse me! What's going on here?"

Jon turned to face Junior and Pee Wee's mother.

"Junior was just showing me around the Lanai," Jon explained. "I brought them home."

"I'm grateful for that," Audrey said, "however, that doesn't give you license to wander around the house! Who are you? What are you doing in here?"

"Nothing. I . . . .. Jon. I'm Jon Megquire. I play with the Longliners. I . . . .."

"What do you mean my husband's in jail? What does that mean?"

Jon pulled the bedroom door closed behind him and stepped back into the living room. Junior had arisen from the ottoman and was standing behind his mother. "I didn't say he was in jail," Jon said.

"Well, what did you say? What did you tell Pee Wee?"

Jon recounted what happened after the ball game that ended up in his driving the boys back to Casa Grande. Audrey wanted to know why Brian hadn't called her, which, of course, Jon couldn't answer. Although it seemed a bit late, Jon couldn't help adding, "I'm sorry about your loss."

"What?" Audrey asked.

"The loss of your mother-in-law."

"Oh. Yes. Thank you. We were all so surprised. It was so sudden. I guess death can be that way. Sometimes people get these long illnesses with plenty of warning, and sometimes it's: one minute you're here and the next minute you're gone."

"She was staying here? In this house?"

"Yes. Her room is being worked on."

"I know," Jon laughed. "I'm one of the people working on it."

Audrey looked at him more carefully. "I thought you looked familiar. I couldn't place where I'd seen you before. I don't share my husband's love of baseball so I never go to the games. Are you good?"

Jon asked, "Was she in good health . . . Mrs. Salsberg? Was Mrs. Salsberg in good health?"

"Yes. She was a warhorse, you know. I thought she was going to live forever. Tough. Tough as nails. She pushed herself hard. Maybe that's what killed her. Do the police know?"

"I don't know," Jon replied with a smile. He hesitated for a moment before he asked, "I am curious about why you're suing Mr. Wentzell. He's a wonderful man."

Audrey stepped back and crossed her arms. "Wentzell? Who's Wentzell? Oh, yes, the builder. Suing? Why? Oh, that's Garrett. He blames everybody for everything."

"Is there anything about this house that would . . . make it dangerous? Anything that Mr. Wentzell did wrong or could have done differently?"

"I don't have a clue. You'll have to talk to Garrett about that. Smells sometimes. House smells sometimes, but that's the Cape. It's damp here. I mean the ocean is right there." She pointed at the Sound through the windows.

Jon sniffed. "Do you think it's smelling now?"

Audrey sniffed. "Not now. No. Sometimes. Smell's gone now. Listen, thank you for bringing the boys home. Did the officer say why he wanted to talk to Brian?"

"Oh, I'm sorry. I'll get out of your way," Jon said. "No, he didn't say. He, Officer Prence, just wanted Mr. Reese to come down to the station with him."

"That's really strange. Isn't that really strange? I can't imagine what that was all about. Why couldn't he let Brian bring the boys home?"

Jon eased himself toward the doors. "Nice to meet you," he said. "Thanks for showing me the Lanai, Junior." And with a desultory wave he slipped out.

17

DISCOVERY

Bureaucracy kills, Garrett ruminated. Everybody has to have an opinion! And people's feelings get hurt if you don't carefully consider their opinion, praise the brilliance of their thinking, and then punch them in the face! No. Can't do that last part! Even if that was what you want to do. Like choosing a car, it was quite simple: should I buy the red one or the green one? Red one. Buy it and move on. This was equally simple: who should be the new president of Salsberg homes? Faith, the previous president, was dead. Sudden vacancy. Tut tut. What a shame. Who was the obvious choice to replace her? Ah, yes! Garrett Scoles! Marvelous! Congratulations, Mr. Scoles. So now let's develop that property in Villanova!

It was just that simple.

He was tired of waiting. He hated waiting. He didn't understand how people found it relaxing to lie on a beach for hours, burning their skin. He didn't understand how so many people were capable of doing . . . nothing! And this was 'family time'. Somehow there was supposed to be a bonding, to bring the family together, to provide them with fond memories that they could reminisce about when they were in the nursing home when they were ninety, waiting to die! Fighting back a debilitative disease like cancer or arthritis, sitting around the TV, drooling, or being forced into one of those stupid, adult exercise classes. He laughed to himself thinking about doing some sort of stupid dance in a room full of stupid, old farts. Wouldn't happen! Just wouldn't happen.

At least the otiose police had finally come to the conclusion that Faith had died of carbon monoxide poisoning. How long had that taken? More than a freakin' month! He could have told them immediately. Just look at her color. Test her blood. What the hell were they doing in that crime lab? Good thing no one was in a hurry here. They weren't going to cure her. She was dead. But a month?

At least the carbon monoxide conclusion complemented his lawsuit with the stupid builder. That was entertaining too -- making the old-fart 'craftsman' battle with the instruments of the law, respond to discovery to dig out all his papers and records and demonstrate his sloppiness and disorganization. It was unfortunate that the lawsuit would require an investment up front, but Garrett had no doubt that it would pay off in the long run. And it would be clear: Faith's death was the result of ineptitude—sloppy workmanship and that couldn't be tolerated.

At the same time . . . at the same time (he rubbed and twisted his mental hands together enjoying the futility of their actions) the lawyers would have the police run around, chasing their tails, staying far away from the actual perpetrator of Faith's unfortunate demise.

He creaked back in his cushioned wicker lounge chair looking out over the lawn. The fact was, it wasn't so bad here. Not when he was on his own and could think, contemplate, construct a vision of the future in his mind. He sloshed the ice cubes around in his glass, lit a cigarette, and blew a cloud of smoke up toward the sky.

He restrained himself from jumping up to grab paper to draw out the future of Salsberg Homes. Discipline, he thought to himself. Discipline. Work it out mentally first. Probably better not to have everything written down anyway. If you write it down and some nosy ass finds it, you'll have to explain it. No better to not write anything down. Evidence.

He took another careful sip of his drink as though he was paying for every drop. Sell off Buckingham Palms. That was the right thing to do. Sell it off, take the cash and send old brother-in-law Brian out to pasture! God knows what sort of deal he had made for that stupid boatyard.

No. No. No. Back up! He sat up in his chair. First the board had to make him president, and although that should be a simple, straightforward decision, the board was not predictable. They were a bunch of old men who liked to mumble and cogitate and discuss . . . discuss to death! Who else was there?

If he had been talking out loud, it would have become silent at that point. Who else was there? Old brother-in-law Brian. The police could have . . . could have at least accused him of drugging the old broad. It had almost made him dance his happy dance when Prence hauled Reese down to the station! Jesus, that was great. Reese almost wet his pants he was so scared. And Audrey nearly lost her mind thinking that her husband could possibly transgress to the point where he killed his own fucking mother! God that was funny. People will believe anything! Of course, it wasn't true. The bitch didn't die from all the pills that she took every day. She couldn't have done the decent thing and just . . . died. Nope. She had to be encouraged.

He smiled to himself. And it was so easy! So very easy. And so very clever. Using the house as a weapon! Who would ever have thought that you could actually use a house as a murder weapon? In that stupid kids' game, *Clue*, there was the candlestick and the rope and axe and gun and all those other things. But the house wasn't one of them! He laughed quietly to himself. Just use a little negative pressure and pull the carbon monoxide back into the house. Nature could be so helpful. The simple basic, second law of Thermodynamics - hot moves to cold, wet moves to dry, and high pressure moves to low pressure! Simple. Turn on the clothes dryer, suck the air out of the house and down the flue and . . . nighty night.

He paused his thoughts and turned to the right as though he had a companion with whom he was discussing the situation. Maybe, he thought, maybe he should just use it again. Get rid of Brian and then truly who would there be? No one. Absolutely no one.

He stood up, put his hand in his pocket, and fiddled with his keys. Nice jingly sound. Always good to have something in your pocket. The board might decide the right way. The board meeting was just a couple of days away anyway. He probably should wait. If they decided the right way and made him President, the problem would be solved and he wouldn't have to do anything. If they decided the wrong way, well there was always the Lanai! It was hard to wait. Garrett itched to have Brian gone.

JON RETURNED TO THE WENTZELLS' KITCHEN WITH A victorious grin, buoyed by a Longliners win over the Falmouth Commodores, where he was met by Ace slamming a pile of legal papers down on the kitchen table. "I hate paperwork. Hate it! And they want me to put it all together. I don't even know where it all is!"

Babs sat at the table, as she looked at her husband with some sympathy. He was generally a very calm person, but pushed to the edge of his ignorance, the fringe of things that he didn't want to understand, frustration drove him to anger. He didn't understand it. He didn't want to understand it. He couldn't control it.

"Discovery! That's what they call this you know. Discovery! As though they were going to uncover and reveal something that is useful. Look at this!" he demanded, slamming the back of his hand on the pile of papers. "They want records for every time I pissed in the last six years! I don't keep records like that! Waste of goddamned time. What do they really want, eh? What do they really want? If they told me that, maybe I could help them out. Maybe."

"It's not that bad," Babs said with a supportive smile.

"Hah!"

"Lawyers! Goddamned lawyers!"

"What's happened?"

Ace pushed the legal papers at him.

Jon took off his cap, dropped into the chair opposite Babs at the table, and started trying to decipher the legalese that would reveal the source of Ace's anger. It appeared that Garrett Scoles' lawyer had demanded documents that would uncover Ace's culpable building practices. They wanted to know how Ace had selected the materials he had used, documentation of time and place and cost of all his selections in the construction of the Salsbergs' pool house. They wanted his definition of best practices, how he had determined them, and how he had complied with them. They wanted pictures of everything he had done from the beginning of the project. They wanted all of his business records for the last five years.

"How can they do that? What right do they have to ask for all this shit?" Ace fumed. "I think I should just trash it! Throw it all in the trash. They can go through my garbage if they want to. I'll throw some banana peels in there, coffee grounds, other stinky, sticky garbage. I don't have records like that!"

"Have you talked to a lawyer yet?" Jon asked.

Ace looked at him. "No. Never needed a lawyer before."

An awareness of the unknowns exploded in Jon's brain. He could see that Ace's gentle balance of daily routines and flow of life had disconnected. Problems with buildings and customers he could confront and resolve. A legal problem was foreign to him. He couldn't defeat it because he didn't know what 'it' was. He didn't know where it began and how it could end. There was no logic to it. For the first time in Jon's life he was watching someone step into the dark room of infinite unknowns and uncontrollable fears, a room that had no known definitions –

seemingly no walls, ceiling, or floor. For Ace there was no cause that resulted in this effect. No reason. No why. No logic. He hadn't done anything wrong, anything that he could blame or chastise himself for. Even the death of his son, Dwight, in Khe San made more sense than this. Dwight had gone to war and war results in people dying. That was the unfortunate point of war.

Jon's mother had died too. Her death had been pointless and totally out of his control. But her death had compelled Jon to move forward to find and confront the boundaries of that room of unknowns. This lawsuit was just paperwork - annoying and frustrating perhaps. The result was anger - not breath stopping, gut wrenching pain. This would end. Dwight's death never would.

Jon said, "It's going to be okay, Mr. Wentzell. These people are just being stupid. It's going to be okay. My father will be here tomorrow. I'll talk to him."

"I'm looking forward to meeting him," Babs said with a soft smile. She stood up and took her cup over to the sink, rinsed it and put it on the drainboard. She turned Ace around to face her and looked up at him. "It's okay, Ace. It's okay. We'll fix this. We've faced worse." She put her hands on either side of his face and pulled his head down and kissed him. "It's going to be okay."

❧ 18 ☙

FAMILY - JULY 15, 1979

Jon wasn't sure where to go next. Lying in his bed on Sunday morning, he stared up at the ceiling and watched the light ripple in waves. Working with Ace had guided Jon's vision to see through the old plaster to the joists to the structure of the attic above. For a moment, he wondered what Dwight, the Wentzells' son, might have been thinking, lying in this same bed on the morning before he headed off to the army.

The Wentzells had suffered enough heartache. They didn't deserve senseless legal troubles. Why did Scoles have to be such an asshole? What did he gain from blaming things on Ace? Money? The Wentzells didn't have any money. Maybe it was something else entirely.

Turning Scoles' joy of malevolence another way, perhaps he had killed his mother-in-law and this was the cover-up. The guy was a son-of-a-bitch but was he that evil? Did people actually kill people who got in their way? Weren't there more business-like ways than murder? If he had killed her, how had he done it?

The light filtering through the trees outside his windows winked and blinked. Another beautiful summer day on Cape Cod—completely disconnected from death and dying.

It suddenly struck Jon that this would be a tough trip for his father, returning to where his wife died, amplifying bad memories. It was nice that he was coming, but Jon wasn't sure why he was. His father had seen him play baseball before. This was almost pro-ball, though. Maybe it would be – next time. But this wasn't like visiting summer camp.

Jon rubbed his hand on the stubble on his chin. No. He wasn't a kid. What would his father think of Lisa? His mother would have thought that she was too young. Cornelia, his sister, would disapprove. She thought Jon was an immature jock. But it would be good to see her. Ask her about the carbon monoxide stuff. She was a brain. She would probably be able to figure out how Scoles had killed his mother-in-law in a second. If he had. Maybe she would tell him how that would have been impossible. Still he was reluctant to admit to himself that he would be glad to see her.

Jon heaved himself out of bed to start his Sunday.

WITH MAYBELLENE'S TOP DOWN, JON PULLED INTO CLEGG'S parking lot and raised both his arms in the air in greeting to his father and sister, who were waiting for him. After a round of hugs and comments about how everyone looked and how Jon's father was feeling, they pushed through the screen door into Clegg's and stood there. The place was packed. The summer swarm of people had infested the Cape.

Cornelia asked, "Why aren't all these people on the beach?"

"I guess they gotta eat," his father replied.

Others were waiting for tables and there was no order to the chaos.

"I'm going to wait outside," Cornelia said. "This is too crazy for me." She pushed back out through the door.

"It's not like this during the week," Jon said. "I haven't been here on a Sunday before."

Feeling awkward, Jon and his father watched the crowd shift and flow, and eventually a table opened up in a corner. Jon stepped outside to tell Cornelia.

"You've gotten bigger," she said.

"Don't know," he replied with a grin.

"No, I mean you look bigger. Not the little brother."

"Thanks . . . I guess."

She put a hand on his arm and stopped him as he turned to go back in. "Are you going to be a professional baseball player?"

"What?"

"No, seriously. I never thought about you . . . about this baseball stuff . . . as being 'professional' before."

"Don't know, Corny. I've been asked. I've been approached by a scout from the Angels."

"Seriously? I guess people really do this for a living, don't they? What do you think Andy will think of the idea?" Cornelia had decided that it was time to stop referring to their father in childhood terms. He was no longer Daddy. He was 'Andy'. Jon wondered if it was some sort of trendy fashion thing to relinquish respect and level out the relationship. But she was his older sister and her authority set the pace, and although he was still struggling with the naming, he accepted it.

"I can't believe he let you buy that car!" she added.

"Don't know. Yeah. The car's great. I call her Maybellene!"

"You know, you need to grow up, Jonny."

"Talking about growing up, I can't believe that NASA hired you," Jon said. "Congratulations. Are you going to be an astronaut? Walk around in space!"

"We'll see."

"So, if I tell people you're a space cadet, I'll be right. Right?"

She punched him in the arm. "Don't know exactly what they'll have me doing, but they told me to take some time off before I started."

"Cool," Jon replied and he held the screen door of Clegg's open for her.

"How's work?" his father asked after Jon and Cornelia had joined him.

"Oh, work's good. Learning a lot about houses."

"Good. That's good."

Jon tried to fathom his father's face, wondering where his thoughts and memories of his mother and the Cape were now. Although Jon knew that this wasn't the best time or place, he blurted out, "How are you feeling, Dad?" He watched his father's eyes.

"What?" his father asked. "Oh, I'm fine now. The old noggin's completely recovered. I just wasn't paying attention."

"No," Jon said. "No, I mean that's great. No, I meant about . . . you know . . . about being here. About mom. You didn't have to come."

"Of course, I did. Of course, I did. For your mom if for nothing else. She would have loved to see you play ball. She wasn't a major baseball fan or anything, but she was really proud of you."

"Yeah," Jon said. "A scout for the Angels has been talking to me." As he said it, Jon realized that wasn't the right response. He had left his father hanging in the closet of his memories, and mentally turned away and then the waitress appeared to take their order.

After the waitress was gone his father leaned over the table toward him and asked, "She's not your new girlfriend, is she? The one you told us about?"

Jon glanced over his shoulder as if to check who his father was asking about and said, "No!" with a laugh.

"Is this place always this busy?" his father asked looking around the room.

"It is summer," Jon replied. "The number of people in the town doubles or triples or something . . . I forget the statistics . . . but it's a lot . . . in the summer. At least that's what they tell me. Kind of quiet in the winter."

"I came here . . . to the Cape . . . as a kid," his father said.

"Did I tell you that? I don't remember anything about it. I guess I was just a baby. There are pictures somewhere. I just remember the pictures. The beach."

Jon considered his father's expression and finally returned to his father's memories. "But this must be hard for you - being here? Being back here? After . . . you know . . ."

"No," Andy said with a smile. "Got to get back up on the horse, you know. Whatever that old expression is. No, I'm good. Let's eat."

Jon looked at his sister.

While they were eating Jon said, "Dad, I need to talk with you about Mr. Wentzell. He really needs some legal help."

Jon described the discovery request that the lawyers had made and Ace's frustration.

"So, what happened?" his father asked.

Jon told them about going to Casa Grande the morning they found Mrs. Salsberg's body.

"Why would they think that Mr. Wentzell had anything to do with it?" his father asked.

Jon shrugged. "I don't see how they can think he had anything to do with it. He did build the pool house. That's all! I think that Mr. Scoles . . . that's Mrs. Salsberg's son-in-law . . . is just a bastard. In fact, I think he might have killed her!"

"You can't jump to assumptions like that," Andy said.

"What was the cause of death?" Cornelia asked.

"It took a while for the police to figure that out. I think they thought it was drugs at first, and I thought they had arrested Mr. Reese . . . that's Mrs. Salsberg's son from her first marriage."

"I thought you came up here to play baseball," Cornelia laughed. "Jesus. How did you get tangled up in all this mess?"

Jon gave her a brotherly smile. "I am here to play baseball."

"So how did she die?"

"Now they say it's carbon monoxide poisoning."

"Who's 'they'?" his father asked.

"The police. Well, actually there is only one police person in Tilley: Officer Prence. It's actually Lisa's father."

"Lisa! The girl you're dating?" his father asked.

"Yes. Well, we're not exactly dating. I mean we've gone out a couple of times."

"Jon and Lisa sitting in a tree . . .," his sister began.

"Have the police . . . has Officer Prence . . . arrested Mr. Wentzell or accused him of being involved?" Jon's father pursued.

"No, No. Nothing like that."

"So why does he need a lawyer? You said something about discovery?"

"No. No . . . no, I mean yes. It's just the lawsuit. He hasn't been accused of being a criminal or anything. It's just Scoles. He's suing him for building a bad house. How can he do that?"

"Well, you can sue anyone for anything these days," his father said, shaking his head.

"Was she in the house when she died?" his sister asked.

"She was in the pool house—not the big house."

"But that was where she died, right? Your Mr. Wentzell built it? Did he follow the building code?"

"Of course, he did! I mean he's good . . . very good at what he does!"

"Is there a building inspector in the town?" Cornelia challenged. "Is there a heating system in the pool house? Something that could generate carbon monoxide?"

Jon looked at her. "I suppose. Don't all houses have heating systems?"

"Maybe not," his sister replied. "Do you need heat in a pool house?"

Jon's father asked, "What are you driving at, Corny?"

"Well, for CO poisoning you need some kind of combustion. In a house, the most common source is a heating system of some kind. And if Mr. Wentzell put it in wrong . . . I'm not saying he did . . . but if he did, it might spill carbon monoxide into the house under the right conditions and if there was enough of it, it can kill someone pretty fast . . . in minutes."

"Wait a second," Jon said. "Just wait. If Officer Prence thinks Mr. Wentzell killed her because he screwed up, why doesn't he just arrest him? I mean if Mr. Scoles thinks Mr. Wentzell is a murderer, why wouldn't he just have him arrested? Why sue him? Jesus! He really does need a lawyer."

His father laid a hand on his arm. "Let's take this a step at a time. The police must not consider Mr. Wentzell a murderer . . . that's such a terrible word . . . at this point if they haven't arrested him, right? They'd have to accuse him and arrest him. But they haven't. So right now . . . from what you're telling us . . . the biggest concern is this lawsuit, right?"

"I guess."

"So, what we need to do is prove that he wasn't careless."

Jon asked his sister, "Why would the heat be on? I mean it's summer. It's been in the eighties!"

"It's a pool house, right? Is there a pool heater? Is there air conditioning?"

"What?"

"Look," she said, "if the pool heater is in the house and the air conditioning was turned on and it wasn't installed properly . . . or someone messed with it . . . the air handler could have made the pressure in the house negative and caused the fumes from the pool heater to come down the chimney. Instead of going up the chimney the way it's supposed to."

"What do you mean 'make the pressure in the house negative'? What pressure?"

"Like when you deflate something. You suck all the air out of it and it collapses. Right? High pressure moves toward lower pressure. A range hood fan sucks the smoke and fumes out of the house, effectively lowering the pressure in the house. That air has to come back in from somewhere. If the house was built well enough so that there aren't a lot of holes and cracks in it, the air might be pulled back down the chimney."

Jon looked at her. "How do you know stuff like that?"

She shrugged. "It's just physics. It's obvious . . . if you know what you're looking for."

"Could somebody do that on purpose?"

She thought for a moment. "I suppose," she replied. "But they'd have to know something about thermodynamics. It would be rather clever," she continued. "It would be rather clever because you can't smell CO. You can't see it. It's invisible. You don't even know it's there until it's too late. Clever."

"Jesus," Jon said. "You're weird." He thought for a moment. "Would the police be able to figure that out?"

"Probably not. No, that's not fair. They might if they're smart."

"How could you do it? Figure it out, I mean."

"Well, you'd have to get in there, obviously."

"Obviously," Jon said.

"You'd have to find whatever generated the CO and you'd have to see if it was vented properly."

"Whoa! Don't go giving your brother ideas," Jon's father said. "Let's let the police do their job. I'm sure I can help to find a lawyer. Lawyers can talk to lawyers!"

They finished eating and Jon's father waved the waitress over to ask for the check. "Speaking of lawyers," he said as he was pulling out his wallet, "there's something that I wanted to talk with you about, Jon. I need your opinion on something."

"Sure," Jon said as they walked out to the cars.

Cornelia separated herself, heading out toward the street.

Jon looked at her and then his father and said, "Must be something serious if you're talking about lawyers. Something wrong?"

"No, no. Nothing wrong. I just need your opinion. Your professional opinion."

"Wow," Jon said. "I'm not professional in much of anything. You want a baseball opinion?"

"I do," Andy said, stopping in his tracks, forcing Jon to stop with him.

Jon studied his father's face to see if he was kidding. "You want a baseball opinion? Are you making bets on professional sports?"

Andy laughed. And then looked serious. "It's complicated," he said, "but there's big money in sports."

Jon was getting increasingly confused. What did his father have to do with professional sports?

"The thing is that teams are getting corporate sponsors now and well . . . Patera Healthcare . . . my company, is thinking about getting into it. Sponsoring a team and a stadium. MLB, Major League Baseball, is considering expansion including a Florida team. They like the South Florida market. Lot of retirees in Florida and health care goes well with retirees. Fort Lauderdale."

"Wow," Jon replied.

"What would you think about a professional Florida team? Might be a job there for you. Something to think about."

"Wow," Jon said again. "Lot of spring training games there now."

"Shows that there's a market. Something to think about."

"Interesting, dad." Jon just couldn't blurt out the 'Andy' moniker.

"Hey," Cornelia said, "Why don't you give me a ride in this British bolt bucket? Let's go see where you're living!"

Andy drove behind Jon through the town to the Wentzells' house on Bartlett Street where Babs invited them into the kitchen and offered them coffee and sandwiches if they were hungry.

Jon's father thanked the Wentzells for taking such good care of Jon. Babs laughed and wiped her hands on her apron and pushed a stray hair off her face and said he was no trouble, no trouble at all. He was such a nice young man with such a bright future.

After some casual strangers-first-meeting discussions about the weather and the town and other odds and ends, Andy took Ace aside and said, "Jon tells me you're having a bit of legal trouble."

Ace grunted and claimed that it wasn't anything. Just lawyers and fools puffing out their chests and strutting around being stupid. It would all go away.

"I'm sure," Andy said. "But let me see what I can do about connecting you with a decent lawyer of your own. You don't want to take on this sort of thing alone."

Ace thanked him and said it wasn't necessary. He could take care of it. Then he changed the subject. "How about those Red Sox?"

They went on to discuss the baseball season. They agreed that rooting for the Yankees was better even if you did live in Red Sox country. Andy congratulated Ace for sticking by the New York team despite the pressure of being surrounded by Red Sox fans. Both of them admitted that they hadn't been to an actual major league game in years. They chatted about how hard it must be for players to have passionate affiliations for any team since they could be traded and bounced around from one team to another. They could be anywhere in the country.

"The Angels!" Andy exclaimed, smiling at Jon. "Jon says he's been approached by the Angels. Los Angeles! What are the odds of that happening?"

Ace admitted that he didn't have a clue.

JON LEFT HIS FATHER AND SISTER AND HEADED OVER TO THE Tilley field to get himself ready for the game. He had developed a routine to push the distractions aside, to focus his mind. A baseball game has a rigid overall format - three strikes, four balls, three outs, nine innings. But within that format unpredictable events happen - batters hit the ball to different places, players throw or catch or drop the ball in different, unpredictable ways. Like life itself. Rigid format - birth and death. No matter how rich or how poor, no matter how famous or unknown every life begins and ends. And a whole bunch of stuff happens in the middle.

Preparing for a game means preparing for the unpredictable. Jon would begin by imagining a simple game—three batters up, three batters down, inning after inning. Except one batter swings the bat and hits the ball out of the park. Jon mentally travelled out of the real ball field he was standing on. The dirt and the grass and his father and Cornelia and Lisa and Ace disappeared. He imagined himself protecting first base, moving his body left and right, fielding a ground ball, a throw from third, reaching for a high throw from short. He imagined standing at the plate, watching a ball fly past, slapping into the catcher's mitt, the shout from the umpire, calling out the ball or the strike. He tried to lock himself into the vision of success, the cheering and the excitement of winning. Not so much winning as being one with the game itself and maintaining that vision for nine innings without thinking about his family or Lisa watching or Ace's problems or carbon monoxide or a million-dollar contract with the Angels or an undefined job with this father's company or Hoppin' Dupin's death. He had to find that quiet place in his mind like a private room or a sound-proof booth that he could step into. Other player activities flowed in around him.

His focus was disrupted when his father and Cornelia arrived. He wondered when Lisa might show up. He wondered why she was such a distraction. Would Brian Reese show up? What was the coach saying?

Icky Bartholomew asked, "What's the difference between boogers and broccoli?"

"What?" Jon asked.

"What's the difference between boogers and broccoli? Kids won't eat broccoli!"

"For Christ's sake, Icky."

"What do you call a guy who never farts in public?"

"Come on!"

"No. A private tooter!" and he laughed heartily while the other players groaned.

"Where do you get these things?"

"A better question is why do you repeat them?"

"It's part of my sparkling personality," Icky replied with a grin. "Which would you rather have: feet for hands or hands for feet?"

"That's a really stupid question, Ick. How old are you anyway?"

"No, really. I'm serious," Icky said. "You have to decide. You're standing on the edge of a cliff next to a rope bridge and the gnome guarding the bridge asks you that question and you can't cross unless you answer it correctly, how would you answer?"

Jon stared at Icky. "I like things the way they are. That's a really stupid question," he said. "I don't want to change."

"Then the gnome will throw you off the cliff!"

Coach Russell tried to get them to settle. He tried to get them to focus on the importance of winning that day's game, the impact it would have on the outcome of the season. As though winning was the meaning of the day. "And I would like to announce that Megquire will be playing in the All-Star Game in Fenway! Congratulations, Jon."

The other players patted him on the back and congratulated him as he contemplated playing in Fenway Park - another distracting vision that he would need to control.

And when the game was over and the Longliners did win and Jon could drop the stress of envisioning the success, he reset his thinking to introducing Lisa. His adrenaline was still high and he was grinning broadly when he saw her standing at the end of the stands, trying to look casual. She was wearing a black t-shirt with the Red Sox logo, khaki shorts that showed off her tanned legs, and tennis shoes without socks.

She pushed her hair back off her forehead and tucked it behind her right ear. "Good game," she said.

"How much did you see?"

"Enough."

He jerked his head back in mock surprise. "One of these days you'll have to sit through a whole game. All the pieces of the game work together."

"Yeah, but no offense: it can be pretty boring."

"That's because you're only seeing bits of it."

"Oh! Is that the problem?" she smiled.

Andy and Cornelia were walking toward them. Jon introduced them to Lisa. "Jon's told us so much about you."

Lisa held out her hand. "That's me," she said. "He's told me a lot about you too."

"He played well today. Did you see the game?" Jon's father asked.

"I had to work for much of it."

Andy smiled. Cornelia looked away. "I don't know what men see in these games," she added. "I can't believe that grown men pay other grown men money to whack a ball around with a stick and then run around going nowhere! Now if they started running off in a straight line and just kept going and the other team had to catch up to them . . . that might be an interesting challenge!"

"Don't listen to her," Jon said. "She's a scientist. What do they know? They think about things that don't even exist. They think math is fun!"

"Do you want to go somewhere to get some ice cream or something?" Andy suggested, trying to move the conversation along.

Jon proposed that he go shower, and they all agreed that would be a splendid idea.

After changing and climbing into Maybellene, Jon and Lisa led the way to Starks for ice cream.

"Busy place," Andy commented. Jon led his father to place their order. They were waiting in the pick-up line when Jon heard a voice call out, "Hey, Baseball!" He turned and scanned the crowd for the source and finally spotted Jimmy from the Nova at the drive-in.

"Hey," he replied.

"This your brother?" Jimmy asked with a grin, his buddies popping up around him.

"My father," Jon replied.

"Oh! Hey guys. It's Baseball and his daddy. Did daddy buy you that fancy little car, Baseball? Hey, daddy. Want to buy me one too? It would only be fair! After all, me and Baseball are buddies. Aren't we, Baseball?"

"Friend of yours?" Jon's father asked.

"No," Jon replied.

"Are you telling daddy that we're not buddies, Baseball?"

"Why don't you go away, Jimmy?"

"See! You even remember my name. Is Lisa here with you?"

"I won't buy you a car, Jimmy, but I can buy you some ice cream," Andy suggested in a coaxing parent voice. "Would you like that, Jimmy? Would you like an ice cream?"

Jimmy looked around at his friends who were waiting for him to make the next move.

Finally, he said, "Fuck off, old man! I think I should just take that little car your little baby boy is driving. I don't think he's old enough for it anyway."

"Listen, son . . .," Andy began.

"So now I'm your son! Do I get a car now, daddy?"

"Listen, son," Andy began again, "and I use that term metaphorically. Do you know what that means, Jimmy? Do you know what a metaphor is?"

"Fuck off!"

"You have a choice here, and I think you should choose wisely. You can either accept the ice cream or you can walk away before you find yourself in a place where you don't want to be. It's a little win or a big loss. Your choice. This is a busy place and a pleasant evening. Don't make trouble where there isn't any. Your choice."

"Are you threatening me, old man?" Jimmy fluffed himself up.

Andy looked at him but didn't say a word.

After a moment or two Jimmy couldn't take the silence any longer. "Are you? What are you going to do, old man?"

Andy still didn't say a word. For Jon the crowd noise seemed to have quieted almost completely. Jon could hear the clink and clank of the kitchen utensils through the open windows of the ice cream stand.

Finally, very quietly, Andy asked, "Strawberry or Chocolate?"

Jimmy spat on the ground, spun on his heel and repeated, "Fuck off, old man!" and stomped away.

"One Twenty-Six!" someone yelled from the pick-up window.

"That's us," Jon said.

19
A MATTER OF LEADERSHIP

Garrett was thrilled that it was not going to be another intolerably beautiful day on Jolo Point. There was fog, and it threatened to drizzle. He didn't understand people who liked to just hang around doing nothing. He looked forward to returning to Pennsylvania that afternoon to do battle with the board of Salsberg Homes, to metaphorically slap the 'old boys' of the board around, and formalize his right to succession. He would bring his attorney to clarify that once and for all, he was the manifest ruler of the company.

He had worked at Salsberg Homes long enough to have found the critical path through the paperwork, to understand the Venn diagrams of relationships, and whose arm could be twisted to bend his way. It was always that way, wasn't it? Although there are piles of money here and there, it is people that control the piles and defend them and regulate them. And those people have personalities and relationships with other people who have motivations and lusts and jealousies that twist and tangle with others forming the deep, dark forest of the business.

Clearly, Garrett thought, *clearly,* he didn't want the blob of the board to even think that someone else could guide the company in Faith's stead. He didn't want them to think about Bryce as the blood connection to a Salsberg dynasty. She hadn't worked a day in her life. She couldn't fumble through a Profit and Loss Statement and she would find a way to unbalance the immutable balance of a Balance Sheet. He didn't want to even appear to be working <u>for</u> her.

Garrett could deal with Bryce. He had successfully neutralized her by marrying her. He allowed her to imagine she lived in a life of her own creation by keeping his mouth shut at the appropriate times, salted with the occasional, "Yes, dear."

Then there was the bouncing, baby Brian. Perhaps he was the more dangerous hot heir. Garrett, in a moment of doubt, realized that he might have misjudged Brian's position. Brian was undoubtedly an ineffectual idiot, but would the board think of him that way? He was blessed with the unquestionable white male bias. Plus, he was connected by blood to Faith. Plus, the board might consider that Brian's position as President of Buckingham Palms superseded Garrett's role as Chief Operating Officer. But that was not the way Garrett interpreted the corporate by-laws.

He tapped a fresh Pall Mall against his thumbnail to pack the tobacco down, placed the cigarette between his lips, flicked open his Zippo, lit the cigarette, and inhaled deeply before blowing out a cloud of smoke that surrounded his head. He was not really concerned about Brian. He blew out another cloud of smoke. Brian was just a bump in his road. A pimple on the ass of time. Something to deal with if the situation warranted it.

He opened the Business Section of the Sunday *New York Times*. At least the paper got delivered to the house. He did wish that Bryce would hire some help. He could have used some breakfast. Nothing fancy. But it would have been nice. He'd made his own coffee in one of those Mr. Coffee coffeemakers promoted by Joe DiMaggio. And it wasn't all that bad if he did say so himself. But he wasn't about to start making breakfast. He would have to wait for Audrey to haul her lazy body out of bed.

He lowered the paper to his lap. Maybe he could go out and get some donuts. There was a thought. What kind? He was fond of the glazed ones, or cinnamon, perhaps. No. It was too much of an effort. They should have a cook. Wouldn't it be nice to be able to ring and have some round and bubbly biddy . . . no upright and efficient cook . . . bring out a couple of freshly baked, hot cinnamon rolls? Simply because she knew that he wanted them? Perhaps it should be a male cook. In uniform.

When he controlled Salsberg, he would get rid of this stupid house so that they didn't have to waste all this time sitting around! If they needed to get away, they should be someplace with a country club where they could connect. They could . . . go on a cruise! He shuddered at the thought. Well, maybe there were some cruises that would be useful. And at least there would be people to make breakfast! He didn't mind working. Working was good, but you should be able to pay people to do stuff that you didn't want to do. You should get paid to work at the skills you were good at. Some people enjoy cooking and cleaning and doing laundry and if you had money, you had an obligation to pay people to do those things for you. It helped the economy move along. And it left time for people with important skills, like his, to do the important and more complex tasks.

For a moment his thinking shifted back to his childhood. He was ashamed of the menial jobs that his parents labored with every day. Rudy, his father accounting for every penny for the rich people he worked for, struggling to find a way to turn the numbers in his favor. But although he worked with them every day, the numbers were not his friends. Cash ran off in the other direction when it saw him coming. Rudy repeatedly tried to create these little deals, little projects that would turn their life around. But it never worked. The Scoles were locked in the concrete of their status, and it would never change because despite the struggle they didn't want it to change. And if one of his father's deals had worked, they were only 'little' deals, only big enough to keep them in the same place.

His mother, Clara, could not stand even the thought of unpredictability. She wouldn't buy a lottery ticket because she was afraid of the consequences of a winning number.

Both his parents were afraid of his success. They had come reluctantly to his wedding. They had never seen this house - and never would. He exhaled another cloud of smoke and looked out through the fog to the water - fishing boats chugging out to sea, gulls wheeling and diving. It was clear to him that his parents were ashamed of him, but he didn't know why. Aren't parents supposed to be proud of you when you are a success in life? And he was a success. Look at this! Look at this! And when he was fully in control of Salsberg Homes he could have all the staff he wanted. He would give little people opportunities. He wasn't in the least afraid to step forward, to open any door in the room, to face an even more successful future. Fuck his parents' petty fears!

Only one person had stood in his way, and moving that minor impediment was so very easy. He smiled and thought that perhaps this house wasn't all that useless after all.

He opened up the sports section. Now here were people who knew how to make money. Not the athletes. They were just bone headed jocks. Always were and always would be. They were merely money-making machines. The people who surrounded them got the ride. And they rode along with multiple money machines, and they were not permanently hitched to any one star. They could jump off when the outlook looked grim. He had to admire them.

His money ride was not as flexible. Although when he controlled the company, he could move it in other directions. He could buy up suppliers, spin off unprofitable elements - like Buckingham Palms. The possibilities made him squirm in his chair. Maybe he should shock his wife and wake her with his naked body! For a moment he smiled to himself again and then remembered he was thinking about Bryce who was about as cold and unresponsive in sex as she was in life. But she had served her purpose. He could deal with that later. For now, he found the physical pleasure he needed with people who were skilled in that trade. Clear and simple. All the pieces were there in life. You simply had to put them together in the logical order.

Lost in the wonderland of his personal thoughts, he made an unconscious, guilty twitch when he heard Bryce behind him ask, "Are you going home today?"

"Don't sneak up on me!" he demanded. "Shit. You could have given me a heart attack!"

"I wasn't sneaking. I don't 'sneak' and certainly not in my own house."

"Have to. Have to make sure the board doesn't do something stupid." He lowered the paper to his lap and looked up at the ceiling as though appealing to the heavens.

"I'm not sure I trust this little dinky airline that flies out of here," Bryce replied. "Those old planes . . . what are they DC3's? I thought they went away after the second world war! And after that crash into the woods last month . . .. I'm not sure they should still be flying."

"They're the most reliable planes in the air." He stood up and looked at his wife. She wasn't bad looking. With the help of her hairdresser she struggled to keep her hair blond but it always looked prickly to him, like it was glued in place. Her figure was starting to sag, moving the curves to places that were less attractive than they had been when he had met her. There was still a demanding intensity in her eyes. "What's for breakfast?"

She gave him the look without words that said, "I haven't the slightest idea."

"Where's Audrey?"

"Haven't seen her. I'm thinking of eliminating breakfast from my day. It's kind of a stupid meal anyway. Anything in the paper that I should know about?"

"No. There may be a major league baseball team in Florida. Oh, and I'm thinking about investing with some character called Bernie Madoff. Seems to be making quite a bit of money for his investors. What do you know about these computers? They are saying that someday everybody will have their own computer. I think it's a fad. Gadgets for tinkerers. No one will want to have one of those monsters at home! Know anything about it?"

"Oh," she said. "It's not a nice day for a walk."

"No. You don't know anything about Madoff or computers, nor do you care. You don't read the papers except for the social shit and who has the best hat at the flower show. You need to pay closer attention to what is going on in the world. 1984 is not that far away, you know. Did you ever read that?"

"What?"

"1984. It's a book. George Orwell wrote it. Did you ever read it?"

"Stop being such an ass, Garrett, and get me some coffee."

"Yes, dear," he replied obsequiously, dropping the paper on the floor beside his chair and heading off toward the kitchen.

"You didn't answer my question: 'Are you going home today?'" she shouted after him.

"Actually, my dear, I did answer your question. Yes; I am going home today. Listening is an art all Christians should learn."

"What do Christians have to do with anything?"

In the kitchen, he leaned on the counter, looked up at the ceiling, and muttered under his breath, "Patience. Give me patience."

"I'm not sure what you mean," she called to him from the living room. "You're just full of flumdiddle this morning."

"Full of what?"

"I don't know. Flumdiddle."

"Did you make that up?"

"No," she insisted. "I read it somewhere. It's a perfectly good word.'

"She reads?" he muttered to himself while he carried a small mug of coffee out to her.

"This looks like just black coffee," she said as she held it up to her nose and crinkled up her face. "You know I don't drink it black. For god's sake, Garrett! How long have we been married?"

"If you don't know . . . ," he muttered to himself.

"Milk and sugar like civilized people."

"Perhaps, mistress should fix it herself!" he suggested, slurring his words, imitating Lon Chaney while thinking to himself, "Watch your step, honey. Don't push me too far. You don't know what I am capable of. I don't 'suffer fools gladly'." He dropped back into his chair.

Hair uncombed and without makeup, Audrey shuffled into the room in her terrycloth slippers, looked out the windows and proclaimed, "Ooof! What an awful day!"

Garrett looked up from his paper to determine if she was talking about the same foggy day he saw outside. "How about some breakfast?"

"What are we going to do today? We can't go to the beach or anything."

"I have to go home this afternoon," Garrett said.

"Did you make coffee?" Audrey asked Bryce.

"Garrett did," Bryce said.

Audrey wrinkled her nose while glancing over at Garrett. "Maybe we could all go out to breakfast. We haven't done that in a while."

"Where's Brian?" Garrett asked.

"The boys are watching TV."

"No, I meant your husband."

"In the shower."

"It would be best if we had breakfast here," Garrett said. "Restaurants get so damned crowded. It would have been okay earlier, but now . . ." He threw up his hands in mock despair. "I'll have to leave soon. There's paperwork to be dealt with. Issues to be resolved."

"Should Brian go with you?" Audrey asked.

"Not necessary," Garrett replied.

"Will the board decide on how Salsberg will . . . you know . . . move . . . I mean be run or whatever?"

"Nothing to worry about," Garrett soothed. "Nothing to worry about. I'll take care of it. It will all be fine." He smiled.

Audrey looked at him, trying to read his face. "Still . . . ," she said.

"I'll help with breakfast," Garrett said. "What kind of toast does everyone eat?"

Even though it was a large kitchen, this was an uncoordinated scrum. Garrett observed Audrey's poor leadership while the three of them moved around grabbing plates, opening and closing the refrigerator door, putting pans on the stove, breaking eggs, burning toast, pouring juice. It became even more complicated when Brian and the two boys joined them. Finally, they settled around the large kitchen table.

"What are we going to do today?" Brian Jr. asked. "We're not going to the zoo again, are we? That place is so boring."

Pee Wee put his *Speak & Spell* on the table beside his place and heaved himself up into his chair.

"Do you have to drag that thing around with you everywhere?" his brother complained. "That voice drives me crazy!"

They munched and slurped and clinked their plates. The air smelt of toast and coffee with a touch of sea dampness.

"Is it supposed to be like this all day?" Audrey asked no one in particular.

"I have to go home anyway," Garrett said.

Brian replied, "I heard. Audrey told me."

Garrett looked at him. "Nothing for you to worry about."

"I should be there. If you're going to be talking to the board, I should be there."

"We both don't have to be there. No. No. No. You stay here with your family. Relax. Enjoy the Cape. Even days like this can be pleasant, can't they?" Garrett smiled at his wife and forced a soft chuckle.

Brian got up, walked over to the window over the sink, and

looked out at the fog. "Seriously," he said, "where do you think this is going to go, Garrett? Mother ran the company with an iron fist. People were fearful of crossing her and losing their jobs. And where is the market going anyway?"

"At least you won't have to talk to her about her beloved boatyard!"

"That seems to be minor now . . . now that she's dead."

Audrey said, "Why don't you boys go watch TV? Scoot along now."

"What we have to do now, Bri, is work together." Garrett almost choked on the unfamiliar familiarity of his brother-in-law's name. "Okay? We just can't let those idiots on the board run the company into the ground. They don't have a clue what it's all about. Not like you and I do. If we both go, it will seem like we're ganging up on them. Let me take care of this. They just have to anoint one of us president. It's that simple. Right? Does it really matter which? Maybe it should be you. Maybe it should, you know."

Brian looked at his brother-in-law who was leaning back in his chair with his hand wrapped around his coffee mug, smiling. "I can't believe my mother didn't leave instructions. That wasn't like her. She should have said what she wanted to happen to the company."

Garrett looked around the room. "It's our company, isn't it?"

Audrey stepped over beside her husband.

Garrett stood up.

"I don't know if this is such a good idea," Brian said. "No offense, Garrett, but I sometimes get the sense that . . . you know . . . you think you deserve the whole operation. It was *my* mother who ran the business."

"How can you say that?"

"Well, she did," Brian laughed nervously. "She did."

"I know that! But she was my mother too." Garrett looked at Bryce.

"I know. Sort of. But not really . . . your mother. I just think we should both be there."

"And what? What would that accomplish? Do you know any of the people on the board? What are you going to do - stand around and whine about 'It's my turn to run the company! She was my mother! It's my turn!' Jesus, Brian. Grow up, will you? We're adults here. Let me take care of this. We can work out the details later. You have to trust that I have all our best interests at heart. Right?" He looked from his wife to Audrey and back to Brian.

"I don't know."

Garrett massaged the silence in the room, using it like a staring contest.

"Be honest," Brian said to his brother-in-law. "Be honest. You think you would do a better job running the company than I would. Don't you?"

"Oh, come on, Brian! Is that what this is about?"

"I've been part of this family a lot longer than you have. I grew up with Buckingham Palms! I know what I'm doing. I do know the people on the board."

"Buckingham Palms maybe, but certainly not all the rest."

"I'm older than you."

"Oh, bullshit!"

"What? I'm not older than you? Am I wrong about that too?"

"He is older than you," Audrey added.

"That's not the point! Age only merits rank in high school or summer camp!"

"Oh. I get it. So, I should be subordinate to you. You want to be able to boss me around. Right? It was my mother . . . my mother who ran the company. You can say that she was your mother, but she wasn't. It was just because you married Bryce. And Bryce . . . no offense Bryce . . . doesn't know anything about running the company!"

Bryce looked like she'd swallowed a mouthful of rotten brie. The voices echoed off the hard, tile surfaces of the kitchen.

"So, what do you want to do, Brian? You want to do rock, paper, scissors for the company? Is that what you want? How about a duel in the fog . . . sixty paces with pistols? Do you know what a pistol is, Brian? Do you know what a duel is?"

"You weren't born into this. No, I mean it," Brian held up his hand to hold back unwanted criticism of this line of reasoning. "You weren't born into this. It wasn't your fault, but your family . . . and I hope you will forgive me for saying this . . . are just not the right sort of people. I know you went to Princeton. You told us that a million times. But you don't know how to talk with our kind of people."

"What the fuck does that mean?" Garrett yelled.

"That's the sort of thing I was referring to. Vulgarity. Scatological humor," Brian said quietly.

"Well, now," Garrett said. "Let's get this all out on the table. Let's do that, shall we? Shall we pull apart the family tree and see who has the right lineage to run a company? Shall we do that?"

Audrey interjected, "This is getting stupid. Name calling is not going to resolve anything. Shouldn't we leave this for the board of directors?"

"It comes down to ownership. Not lineage," Bryce said. She paused. "I should be running the company."

The two men looked at her. The kitchen clock ticked. The refrigerator compressor cycled on.

"We'll just have to wait and see what the board thinks," Garrett said.

Brian said, "I need to be there. I'm going with you."

"Oh, that will be fun. Look, if you want to talk to the board, go ahead. You're free to do that, but they didn't invite you to talk to them."

Brian looked surprised. "Did they invite you?"

"Of course," Garrett lied. "They're seeking my input."

"What about mine?"

"That's between you and the board. Maybe they've already

made up their minds. I don't know why they asked me and not you. Maybe it has to do with trust."

"I'm going to call them," Brian said.

"You do that! You do that. Go right ahead."

"I'm going to see what the boys are doing," Audrey said.

"Who's going to clean up?" Bryce asked.

"You," Garrett said to his wife. "I'm going to call the airline." He would clarify all of their futures in the coming days.

20

NEAR DEATH

Jon had a choice. He had to either break into the Lanai at Casa Grande in order to clear Ace or do nothing. He was convinced that the answer to what had really happened to Faith Salsberg was there. He had to check out the science his sister had told him. He had to prove that it wasn't Ace's fault, that someone or something had converted that house into a deadly trap. He had to determine once and for all if the house could have been used as a weapon to kill Faith Salsberg.

Lisa's father was not looking for that. He might be a good police officer, but he solved problems by the book. If Mrs. Salsberg had been killed with a gun, he would have been looking for a gun - simple effect and cause. Even poisoning or strangulation would have been simpler. Cornelia had told him that carbon monoxide is colorless and odorless. You can't see it or taste it or smell it. It is invisible. What a great weapon. You just had to get your victim in the right place at the right time. The only way that Jon could prove Ace innocent was to search the scene of the crime with his eyes open and with an understanding of the physics.

For a moment he considered the alternative: doing nothing.

But he was past that. He had received the subpoena from his soul, motivating him to risk breaking and entering to relieve Ace's alleged guilt. Everything in his life led him to knowing that this was the right thing to do despite the fact that the law said it was wrong.

He didn't play his best game that Thursday afternoon. He had been thinking about the house all week after his conversation with his sister. His father's advice about leaving it to the police, that Ace's problems could be resolved by a good legal defense, whispered in his mind. Committing a crime to solve a crime was a tangle of the end justifies the means. Sometimes the law could prevent doing right. The result of it all going wrong, of his getting caught breaking into the house, and the impact on his future barely tickled his consciousness. And despite his intellectual understanding of the risk, the sense of adventure pushed a bubble of excitement up into his chest, hardening his resolve and supplanting reason with excitement.

If he'd been thinking more clearly, he wouldn't have told Lisa what he was about to do.

"I've got to find out," he told her after the game.

"Why don't you just tell my father what you're thinking. Let him deal with it."

"I can't let Ace take the blame for something he had nothing to do with! Nothing against your father, but . . ."

"But what? Do you think he wouldn't understand? And why do you care so much? I don't understand . . . you. Why would you risk everything?"

"It's not that," Jon objected. He saw the spark of anger in her eyes, and a flicker of the risk to his future of what he was proposing twinkled in the back of his mind, but he pushed it aside. "You're right. I don't know what I'm looking for. I don't know what I might find. You can't 'find' carbon monoxide." He stepped back and looked at her. "Why do I care? I don't know why I care. Oh, I don't know, maybe it's justice. Fairness. What would you do if your father was accused of killing somebody? Would you just . . . do nothing?"

"Of course not, but Mr. Wentzell isn't your father," she replied.

"You don't understand," he said.

"That's just the point. Why you shouldn't go in there. Breaking into a house is serious. If you get caught, you'll be screwed. And what do you expect me to do now that you've told me you're going to do it?"

"I hope you won't do anything! You wouldn't do that to me, would you?"

They looked at each other, and then she turned away. She took a couple of steps and then came back to him. "Do you even know how to break into a house? What's your plan? Smash through a window? Force a lock? Do you have tools?"

"Ace does."

"Oh, that's great! Use the tools of the guy you're trying to protect so if you get caught, he gets blamed too. Good plan, Jon."

Why did she have to be so practical about this, he thought? Smearing over the idea with a layer of gooey practicality just got in the way. These things had a way of working out. He was resolved. It was something he had to do. "I'll figure it out," he said. "I've been in that house before. There's probably an unlocked window or something. How hard can it be?"

"There are a lot of people in jail who could tell you otherwise. And you're going to do this tonight?"

He nodded.

After several days of struggle Garrett had returned from meeting with the Salsberg Homes board of directors even more frustrated. The otiose farts couldn't make up their minds. It was no wonder that the world was such a mess! Nothing could get done. They were always taking things *under consideration*. Or they wanted to do another study or more research or check with the lawyers or some damn thing. And while they were considering or researching or checking with higher authorities the clock was ticking and opportunities were drizzling down the drain.

He had made his case. He had suffered through dinners, asking them about their wives and their children and their grandchildren despite the fact that he couldn't have cared less. He had to say nice things about Brian that he didn't mean, but he had to sound sincere while making them recognize how completely unsuitable the man was to take over the reins of the organization. He had to subtly point out to them how poorly the Florida organization, Buckingham Palms, had done under Brian's guidance, damning it with faint praise.

And what he thought was the coup de grace, Brian's sale of the boatyard which he reluctantly revealed, fell flat! Not only did they not seem to care, they informed him that there was more to the story than he knew, that Brian hadn't shared with him. Apparently Major League Baseball was considering putting a franchise in Florida and building a stadium on the site! It wasn't confirmed yet and might be years off, but the members of the board were impressed by his bold move. And they knew about it before he did! The bastard had let him walk into it like a blind man stepping in front of a bus! There was a chance that they might select Brian over him! He wasn't being paranoid. It was a real possibility. And it was out of his control. Or was it?

The thing about traveling is that it gives you time to think. Sitting under the wing of the Air New England Twin Otter, Garrett felt like he was being whisked back off to exile. The world was alive. Decisions were being made. Money was being made. Power was being transferred. He was stuck in a hole, unable to move. Pulled out of line. Benched. It was frustrating. The thought of working for Brian made him want to puke.

He glared out the window as the Connecticut shoreline slid

slowly by underneath him. All those houses! All those properties. Changing hands. There were large tracks of undeveloped land that he could see below him. Those could be turned into cash. What a waste!

Brian wouldn't see that. He had no vision. Oh, what about this baseball thing? No, that wasn't vision. No, that was pure, shit-faced luck! He couldn't see a wall if he walked into it. People like Garrett had to make their own luck. They had to work at it. Struggle with it. People like Brian had it handed to them. Born with money. Surrounded by money and connections, they just had to put their hand out and more cash, more opportunity was dropped into it.

Faith would have been pissed that Brian had sold the boatyard but only because she hadn't done it first. That was one thing about Faith, one thing he had to give her credit for: she was a fighter. Completely unlike her son. She had been a bitch, and he wasn't sorry that he had helped her shuffle on to the great beyond, but she was a fighter. He gave her that. Brian was an idiot.

Brian had to go. It would be so very easy.

WHEN GARRETT HAD ARRIVED BACK AT CASA GRANDE earlier that afternoon, anger and frustration were bumping up against the seawalls in his mind like a high tide before a hurricane. It was all he could do to be calm and chatty and provide just enough information about his meetings with the board to satisfy the little minds that surrounded him. He gave himself a mental pat on the back as he told them that the meetings went well, that the board had been stunned by Faith's untimely demise. They hadn't had a contingency plan. They thought Faith would go on forever. They were going to need some time to consider who was to take the lead. These were difficult times for construction. "Difficult times!" he mocked the board, burbling into his chin like an old man from a Charles Dickens tale. He even laughed. He even made his family smile.

They chatted about the weather, about what the kids had done that afternoon - swimming in the pool, going to the beach (again), shopping at the mall. The tedium made him want to scream, but he applauded himself as he sat calmly, nodding his head occasionally, with a rictus of a smile plastered across his lips while he wondered internally if he could accomplish a second kill with one building.

He would have to set it up the same way as he had done before. He would have to come up with a good way of leaving Brian alone in the Lanai long enough for the carbon monoxide to do its job. And wouldn't that be lovely! It would prove that the building was defective. That builder . . . what was his name? Wentzell. Oh my god! He was a dangerous builder, a killer builder. He created buildings that killed people. God. He should not only lose his building credentials and lots of money. He should be in jail. The blame would fall clearly and categorically on Wentzell. The house was the weapon! The builder who had created it was a dangerous killer!

Garrett's smile softened a little as he reveled in the joy of a job well executed. And then . . . then there would be no Brian, and the path would be clear to the top of the company. The doddering fools would have no choice. It would be a slap in the face . . . wake them up, move them along. "Move along little doggies," he sang to himself.

It would be easy to get Brian into the Lanai. He would simply propose a manly discussion of company business maybe with brandy and cigars. Certainly, without the women. It was 'man' talk. Not something to be discussed in front of the gentler sex. But how to get him to stay there long enough . . . alone?

And then Brian, out of the earshot of their wives, shocked him by conspiratorially proposing that they watch "Project UFO: Sighting 4018" on TV! Brian had already seen it, but UFO stuff was fascinating, he promoted to Garrett. The women would want to watch The Waltons or Mork & Mindy or some other drivel on the TV in the house, but the two of them could hunker down in the Lanai and watch this mentally unstable woman try to prove that she really had seen UFOs . . . that she wasn't just making it up.

Garrett feigned reluctance. Too much enthusiasm with his brother-law's stupid idea might have given the game away, but inside he was clapping his hands together and jumping up and down for joy. Might have been better had it been a baseball game, but the choices were limited. There were no games on that evening. Killers can't be choosers, he chuckled to himself.

He had slipped out before the family gathered for supper to make sure that the Lanai was properly set up. He checked that all the windows were closed and locked and that the boys had thrown their damp towels in the clothes dryer but hadn't turned it on. When he saw that stupid red plastic toy of Pee Wee's on the bed in the back bedroom, he was tempted to throw it in the dryer as well. The constant mechanical whine of the electronic voice in the thing was driving him crazy. Perhaps he would claim that as his defense if he were caught. "Echo" it coughed. "Angel" it whined. Why couldn't kids learn that stuff in school? Why did they need some robotic voice to get them to push buttons and talk to themselves? He was very tempted to silence it permanently, but that would have been noticed. The boy was obviously addicted to it so he left it on the bed.

The flue to the pool heater was still disconnected. The police were so stupid. Especially Officer Prence . . . "Gee Officer Prence. I didn't know that needed to be connected!" The old lady had died of carbon monoxide poisoning and Prence hadn't even noticed the disconnected flue! What an idiot! When this was done, he'd have to be sure to remember to reconnect it. The Lanai had worked well, but this would have to be the last time. He couldn't push his luck. He was too smart for that.

The family had gathered and eaten pizza. He was concerned that all the debating about how many pizzas and what to put on them was taking too long. Should they be plain cheese pizzas? Should there be anchovies? Was pepperoni good for the boys? And what about mushrooms and green peppers and extra cheese?

And once the order was placed, they had to sit around and wait which was interminable. The ticking of the grandfather clock in the hallway pounded into Garrett's head. The boys got to watch TV while they waited. And the adults drank.

Garrett practically ran to the door when the delivery boy arrived. He was careful not to overtip him in his excitement.

"Pizza's cold."

"It's not bad though. Not as good as what we get back home, really."

"They don't put many mushrooms on any more. Seems like they're cutting back."

"Boys! Turn that off and come and eat your supper."

"But, mom!"

"Now!"

"Who wanted the anchovies? I hate anchovies. They're so salty!"

"Anything on the news today? It's so isolated here. It's like the world just stops when we're here, you know?"

"It doesn't."

"I mean you don't hear anything about murders or massacres or plane crashes or revolutions. I suppose that's good in a way."

"That's probably why people come to places like this. To get away from all that stuff."

And on and on. Garrett squirmed in his chair, put down his pizza, and got up and made himself another drink. There were more important things in the world than the quality of the pizza or the lack of communication in a small dot on the surface of the planet like Tilley, Massachusetts.

And finally, the meal was over. "Brian," he said companionably, "let's head over and watch your show and let the ladies have this TV."

Brian looked at him. God, Garrett thought to himself, it's like putting an old, lame dog to sleep! Out of his misery.

"Got to put the boys to bed," Brian replied.

"Why don't you let Audrey do that?" Garrett smiled at his sister-in-law.

"My turn," Brian replied and looked at his brother-in-law with a I-have-kids-and-you-don't look that fell uselessly away. Garrett had absolutely no desire to have kids of his own. Even a dog would have been an annoyance.

"Well, show starts in ten minutes," Garrett stated with a smile.

"I'm surprised you're interested," Brian replied. "Not like you to be interested in a TV show."

"Oh, you did a good job of selling me!"

Jesus, the guy is annoying! Garrett thought. He's prolonging this just to annoy me! He can't even cooperate when he doesn't know he needs to cooperate. Actually, the thought of sitting side-by-side on a sofa watching a stupid TV program about UFOs turned his stomach. How could people waste their time watching such unsubstantiated drivel? Brainless people were willing to believe anything from UFOs to invisible gods and places like heaven or hell. They did not have an inkling that such ideas were conjured by kings and priests and politicians and television executives to manipulate them into behaving as brainwashed automatons. People fought and died in wars for ideas and manifestations that did not exist.

But he would make the sacrifice. He would sit quietly with his brother-in-law and make chatty comments, and try not to be too obvious about how stupid he thought the show. At least for a while. Just enough time for Brian to be drawn into the narrative and want to know what happened next. "Was that light in the sky from some mystery planet . . . or was it trick photography? Stay tuned!" Sucker!

It was a surprisingly warm night. Keeping the windows closed and turning on the AC in the Lanai was not going to be regarded as odd behavior. People wanted to believe that if you lived by the water, you didn't need central air conditioning. But Garrett saw no reason to be uncomfortable. And, he lectured to himself, when you are using central air conditioning it was the same as using central heat; you kept all the doors and windows closed. And then . . . he smiled at his own brilliance . . . when exhaust fans were turned on it sucked the air out of the house it pulled nasty things like . . . oh, I don't know . . . exhaust fumes down the chimney. Which just might be . . . oh, I don't know . . . deadly?

He slid the screen door closed behind him and stepped out on the patio. There was no central AC in Casa Grande. The house was too old and Faith didn't want to spoil its heritage . . . except for individual window air conditioners which were worse, Garrett thought.

Oh, what an evening! He was thinking aesthetically in the artistry of the setting sun. The warm air almost caressed him. He heard the rhythmic nattering of women's voices behind him. He stood for a moment by the edge of the pool looking down into the rippling, dark water. Water must be cold, he thought with a smile. Have to turn the pool heater on, won't I? Someone might want a late-night swim!

Then he looked up at the reds and oranges and pinks of the evening sun and sucked in his breath. It could . . . it just could make you think that there was something else, someone else somewhere, he thought. The sudden, overwhelming joy of a new beginning and resolution of an old problem made his scrotum tighten like a fist. "Wow!" he said very, very quietly. "Wow, wow, wow!"

And then he strode purposely on to the Lanai, slid open the big glass door, and stepped into the cool, dry air and shivered slightly. He worried for a moment if it would be too cool for Brian, that he might want to shut off the AC, but Garrett knew that it wasn't that cold. It was just the sudden difference in temperature and humidity that was startling.

He walked across the polished concrete floor of the living room and into the kitchen area, opened a cabinet, pulled out a glass, and poured himself a healthy measure of Ballantine's Blended Whiskey. After swallowing a fortifying gulp, he set the glass down and made one more check of the house, turned on the television, and tuned it to NBC.

He looked at his watch -- his *every day* watch, the old Timex that his father had given him on his eighteenth birthday. Although Garrett didn't think of himself as sentimental in any way, for some reason this old cruddy, cheapo, watch kept him focused. He even remembered his father's face when he flung him the watch in its unadorned plastic package when he got home from work as though he had suddenly remembered his son's birthday and stopped at the drugstore and plucked it off the rack. "Takes a lickin' and keeps on tickin'!" "Happy birthday," his father had said. "Hope you like it." and turned away without another word leaving Garrett standing there.

Timing was important. He didn't want to turn the clothes dryer on too early because it might stop too soon. He didn't want to fire up the pool heater too early either because he really didn't want to be in the building when carbon monoxide and nitrogen oxides and the other nasty stuff started flowing into the living room. He looked at his watch again. Should he be sitting on the sofa when Brian came in? Should he greet him at the door? No, that would look weird.

He lit a cigarette and poured another shot of whiskey into his glass and sat on the sofa and tried to take in the prattle on the TV screen. The picture wasn't all that great. Faith didn't want an unsightly television antenna stuck on the roof of either house. She barely consented to having a television in the house at all. No television and no telephone. That was her ideal. Cape Cod was a place to get away from all that worldly noise. It was a retreat. She had reluctantly given in to the telephone. It would be useful to be connected if there was an emergency. It had taken even longer to get the television installed principally for her grandchildren. She would not proclaim that the TV was there by sticking a wire tree on the roof. The antenna was in the attic and the picture was sketchy.

Brian was taking forever. He probably read stories to his kids like a 78-rpm record run at thirty-three and a third: "w. u . n . s . . u . p . o . n . . a . . t . i . m . e . . ." Tick, tock, Brian. Kids need their sleep. And so do you. How could ten minutes move so slowly?

It was after eight when Brian finally slid open the door.

"You missed the beginning," Garrett informed him.

"Brian Jr. thinks he's too old to go to bed at the same time as his brother. I think he'd stay up all night . . . or try to . . . if we'd let him." He slid the slider closed with a thump. "Chilly in here," he looked around as if to seek the source of the chill.

"You'll get used to it. It's just the shock of the difference between inside and outside temperatures. Drink?" Garrett asked, jumping up from the sofa.

"Sure," Brian replied angling over.

Garrett pulled another glass out of the cabinet in the kitchen.

"So how did it really go with the board? Seemed like you didn't want to talk about it at dinner?" Brian asked.

"Oh, you know. The board is a bunch of old farts. Can't make up their minds."

"But did they say which of us they want to run the company?"

"You know, Brian, they didn't. I couldn't even get them to confirm that it would be one of us."

Brian turned away from the TV to look at him. "What?"

"No. It's true. They might bring someone in from the outside."

"No! Why would they do that?"

"Because they're idiots. They don't understand the business. They're stuck in the past." Garrett poured more Scotch into his glass and walked back toward the TV carrying both glasses. He handed one to Brian.

"I can't believe that. I don't know why mother didn't simply say who she wanted. You know. To the board."

"Don't know, Brian. She was your mother. Why did she do any of the things she did, God rest her soul. Maybe she wasn't expecting to die! But don't worry about it. I have it under control. They'll come around. Just enjoy your show."

He started to sit down and then jumped back up. He set his drink on the glass side table with a 'Clink'. "Wait," he said, "I need to turn the dryer on. I forgot we put the boys' towels in there after they swam this afternoon."

The dryer was in a closet by the kitchen with louvered doors to hide the utilitarian device. He twisted the timer, pushed the button, and heard the drum begin rotating and the towels thump as they dropped again and again. The switch for the pool heater was on the wall and Garrett flipped it on and heard the 'whump' of the burner start. He left the closet doors open and came back to the sofa.

He tried to focus on the air force characters in the story on the screen to appear that he was at least marginally interested in the television program, seeking to increase Brian's engagement.

"Hard to believe that anyone would believe that this woman saw real things flying through her sky," he said.

"But look at those pictures she took! How could you not believe her?"

"Besides the fact that she had a history of mental illness?"

"But wait," Brian said. "She has more evidence. It's hard not to believe her. You'll see. It's very compelling."

"You've seen this before?"

"Yeah. It's a repeat. But it's good."

Garrett looked at his brother-in-law with disgust. Not only could this imbecile like programs like this. He could watch them more than once. He was truly a waste of space. He stood up.

"I've got to go back to the house for a minute. Let me know what happens."

He slid the slider open and felt the gentle flow of warm evening air being sucked into the building, stepped out and thumped the big door satisfactorily closed behind him. So much easier and cleaner than pulling the trigger of a gun, he thought to himself and strode off toward Casa Grande.

~

PEE WEE COULDN'T EXPLAIN WHY HE LOVED HIS *SPEAK & Spell*. He had his reasons. He clutched the bright red box and responded to the synthesized voice, and it praised him or encouraged him when he pushed the right keys. And blue/green words appeared on the screen. *Speak & Spell* was reliable and responsive. It was his friend.

But he was only five and demands on his time abounded. There was his brother, Bri, and when Bri wanted to do something, it had to be done! It wasn't always fair. Bri never wanted to do the things Pee Wee wanted to do, but he was older which Bri was always telling him. "But someday," Pee Wee told himself, "I'll be the oldest. Then we'll see."

Then there was the pool. The pool at night was fun but scary. The lights under the water shimmered way down there. The first time that Brian had dared him to swim down, under the water, and touch the surface of the glass dome that protected the light, the water was cool but the light was surprisingly warm. And those jets! The water jets that pushed a strong stream of water out into the pool. You could put your tummy up to them and they would tickle your skin. He forgot all about *Speak & Spell* when he was in the pool. You couldn't take it in the water with you. The pool lights were made to get wet. *Speak & Spell* wasn't supposed to get wet. His brother had made sure he understood that when he threatened to throw *Speak & Spell* in the pool. Even the thought of that now made Pee Wee want to cry.

And now *Speak & Spell* was missing! He knew it was time for bed. He knew that he would be in trouble if he wasn't ready when his mother told him it was time, but he couldn't sleep without knowing where *Speak & Spell* was. He knew that he wouldn't be able to sleep if something had happened to it. When his parents couldn't find things, they always wondered if someone had broken in and stolen them no matter what the random object might have been. So maybe someone had broken in and stolen *Speak & Spell*. His parents seemed to be angry about something that was going on. There were strangers in and out of the house. Maybe it had something to do with Granny leaving for good. Maybe she took *Speak & Spell* with her! No. That couldn't have been true. He'd had *Speak & Spell* with him today and Granny had left a long time ago.

He could see *Speak & Spell* in his hands. He could feel the smoothness of the plastic, the round, cool curves at the top and the bottom, and hear the metallic voice as he pushed the buttons.

When he saw other kids playing with other *Speak & Spells* on TV they were happy too! They laughed with each other. They played games together. Bri didn't like *Speak & Spell*. He thought it was stupid. He told Pee Wee that it was only for babies. He already knew how to spell and didn't need some stupid machine that didn't even sound real telling him how. He had learned how in school. Real people -- teachers -- had taught him how.

Maybe Bri had hidden *Speak & Spell*! Maybe he had thrown it in the pool! He had to look. Even if it was in the pool, he had to know. He wouldn't be able to sleep if he didn't know.

He was in his pjs. The ones with the sports balls all over them - footballs, baseballs, soccer balls. He slipped out of his room, down the hall, and hesitated by the sliding glass door to the patio and pool. The door was heavy, but it wasn't closed! Just the screen door, and it was so much lighter. Sometimes it moved wrong and got stuck and made screeching noises, but if he was careful, maybe it would be okay.

He looked back into the house to see if anyone was watching him. Outside, it was still so light! He always thought it unfair that they had to go to bed when it was still daylight out! They should at least be able to wait until night really came. Why should they have to go to bed when it wasn't even nighttime? He could hear voices, but he couldn't tell where they were coming from.

Uncle Garrett had come back this afternoon. He didn't seem too happy, but then he never seemed too happy. It was like he was mad all the time. He was scary. And when he was mad that made him even scarier. Pee Wee didn't want to run into Uncle Garrett. He would probably say something mean.

Pee Wee reached up and put his fingers in the little handle on the screen door and pulled. At first it wouldn't move and then it jumped as he pulled harder. He let go and stood quietly with his back to the screen, putting the fingers of his left hand in his mouth, waiting for someone to come running out to find out what was going on.

But nothing happened.

Pee Wee took a deep breath and reached up to the handle again. The door was partly open now, and for a moment he wondered if he could squeeze through just that opening, but decided against it. Slowly he pulled the screen open just a bit further. It seemed to scratch painfully loudly. But still nobody came.

He stepped through the opening and felt the warmth of the flagstones on the patio surface on his bare feet. He stood still for a moment listening. He swallowed hard. He wasn't sure that he wanted to see *Speak & Spell* at the bottom of the pool. If that's where it was, what was he going to do about it anyway? He couldn't jump in and swim down and save it. Would he be able to see it anyway? The lights weren't on. Uncle Garrett was always yelling about turning lights off that weren't needed, and nobody was swimming right now so there wasn't any need for the lights to be on in the pool. But he had to know if it was there.

He tip-toed over to the edge of the pool, stopped, and looked around. He could hear adult, male voices now - his father and Uncle Garrett. In the Lanai. Why were they in there? Didn't matter. He peered into the dark water of the pool. It looked deeper than it did during the day. Threatening. It wasn't fun. The surface of the water rippled gently. An inflated ring bobbed at the end. That was Bri's fault. He had been playing with that. It wasn't put away. It should have been put away.

Pee Wee eased closer to the edge and tried to see down to the bottom. It was really hard to see anything. And was he going to have to walk all the way around the edge of the pool and look at the whole bottom? If the lights had been on, it would have been so easy. Just for a second he thought about trying to find the light switch and turning on the lights, but then everyone would know he was here.

Why would Bri have thrown *Speak & Spell* in the pool? That would just be mean. But if it wasn't in the pool, where was it? Pee Wee tried to concentrate. His mother was always telling him to think for a moment. To stop and think: where was he the last time he had it? Think about what he had been doing. And he always tried hard to do that. It was easy to lose things. It was frustratingly hard to think back through time.

He couldn't do it! He couldn't think! He just wanted to go back to bed. He wanted *Speak & Spell* and to go back to bed and close his eyes. And suddenly it was clear to him: he had been playing with *Speak & Spell* in the Lanai after they went swimming! That's where it was. He could almost see it lying on the bed in the back bedroom. Yes! Why hadn't he thought of that before? It was so obvious!

But his father and Uncle Garrett were in there, maybe he could sneak in through the back door, the kitchen door without them seeing him. He might not be able to see them and they wouldn't be able to see him because the counter tops were so tall.

He tip-toed around to the path at the back of the Lanai,

walking on the warm stones, holding his arms out as though he were walking a tight-rope. He stood by the back door and listened. The exhaust vent for the clothes dryer was by the back door and hot air was spewing out of it. He could hear the adult voices inside, loud enough to be heard over the sound of the vented air. He wondered if they had been swimming, but that would have been really strange. Uncle Garrett didn't like swimming.

He reached up and turned the knob on the door and carefully pushed it open just a bit. He could hear the voices more clearly, and they seemed to be out in the living room which was good. The back bedroom had a door to the kitchen, so he could slip in and they wouldn't know he was there. He just had to do it quietly, like they did on TV. He pushed the door open enough to almost jump into the kitchen and then pushed the door closed behind him. It thumped. The voices stopped.

Pee Wee stood very still, trying hard not to breathe. Trying hard not to make a sound. The kitchen was lit by the spill-over light from the living room making dark shadows. It was like one of the scary parts in the movies that Bri liked to watch, when someone would fall out of a closet or jump out of a secret opening in a wall. Pee Wee hated those parts, but he couldn't help watching and now . . . now he was in one! He didn't really think that a mummy or ghost would suddenly appear, but maybe Uncle Garrett would pop out from around the corner of the counter, fangs dripping with blood, face glowing green. Pee Wee tried to force himself to stop thinking about those things. He was suddenly afraid that he might wet his pants and that would be really, really bad!

Nothing happened though.

The back-bedroom door was open and he slipped in, and there on the bed was *Speak & Spell*! Just where he had imagined it would be. He hopped up on the bed and clutched the bright red plastic box to his chest. He really, really, really wanted to push the button and make sure that it was alright, but he knew that would be a very bad idea, just because *Speak 'n Spell*'s comforting, metallic voice would be really, really loud and the results would be bad. So, he decided to wait until his father and Uncle Garrett left, and then he could go back to his own bed. In the meantime, this bed was pretty comfortable. He'd taken naps there before. He decided to just lie down and wait.

21

CHASE - JULY 26, 1979

Jon recognized that parking Maybellene in Casa Grande's driveway would broadcast his presence. In fact, it would be difficult to park her anywhere on Jolo Point. But if he didn't drive there, it would be a long walk, and if anyone saw him just walking along that, in itself, would look suspicious. No one took long walks at night on Jolo Point who didn't live there and didn't need to go out to walk the poodle in the moonlight!

He decided that he would appear less suspicious if he ran. After all he was an athlete just exercising on a warm evening. What was a mile or two for an athlete in training? And at eight o'clock the sun was just setting anyway.

He had been thinking about Lisa's question about how he was actually going to get into the house. Breaking the law was unfamiliar. He'd never had to. He always had the key. Sure, he drank before he was eighteen. He drove faster than the speed limit. He had parked in a no-parking zone for a short time. He had smoked dope, once, with some friends, but he didn't like feeling out of control. It made him feel oddly wimpy to have not done more nefarious and evil things in his life. He didn't think of himself as JC – the occasional moniker for Jonathan Creesy

Megquire, as *holier than thou*. The need to commit a crime had never arisen. He never sat down in the middle of the street at a demonstration. He wondered if it made him less of a man to have lived by the rules. You could steal a base in baseball, but if you broke other rules, you could get ejected or your team would forfeit. He couldn't imagine ripping up one of the bases and walking off the field with it in the middle of a game. There wouldn't be much point. Everybody played by the rules or the game wouldn't work.

Jon's only experience of breaking the law or breaking into a building came from the movies and TV. That should have been a good thing especially when he was dating the daughter of a police officer. He lacked that cool, swashbuckling, dangerous character that he imagined characterized a thief. As a criminal he was, in fact, a rank amateur.

Jon understood that there are a limited number of ways to get into a house. Using the door is the most obvious. And then there are the windows. Unlike the fairy tales, he wasn't going to fit down the chimney, or crash through a wall or erupt from the ground. Someone had told him that you could open a door with a credit card if you slipped it in just right. You could do the same for flipping the lock on a window. You stuck it in the crack and pushed the lock around. He did have a BankAmericard that he'd used for buying gas. He was hoping that a door would be unlocked. Jolo Point was not a high crime area. The pool house did have a back door that was out of sight of the main house. The view of the water was limited from that side so the landscaping was designed to hide unsightly mechanical equipment like the air-conditioning condenser which made that side ideal for his purpose.

But there were the wide sweeping manicured lawns that he would have to cross, and he hadn't been able to spend a lot of time walking around the grounds. He'd never been a guest.

Jogging through the streets of Tilley wasn't a problem. He saw a few people sitting outside watching the day dwindle down to darkness. When he reached the stone markers of Jolo Point, his anticipation heightened when he saw a car slowly coming toward him. The driver looked him over as he passed. Jon smiled and held up his hand in a casual, royal wave. *Professional athlete in training. Lucky I acknowledged you. Move along. Don't gawk.* The car didn't stop.

Jon slowed as he approached the drive up the hill to Casa Grande. He continued to jog beyond the house to the trees that separated one mansion from the next. He stopped, looked up and down the road, and then jumped off into the scrub and started up the hill, hidden from the house, slipping from tree to tree. He imagined eyes peering down at him from the upper stories and felt both obvious and silly.

The police should have done this. He should not have to break the rules to catch a killer. And what was he looking for anyway? Would he know when he saw it? Or was he just being a fool? If he was caught, it could ruin his career and doom his future. He heard his father's voice admonishing him in his head.

Then he thought about what was happening to Ace. An honorable man's life could be entirely destroyed by a false, spurious accusation. Jon was convinced that Mrs. Salsberg's death had not been an unfortunate accident, an accident that had been caused by sloppy construction. Ace was too experienced to make that kind of mistake. Houses talked to him. Boards sang to him. The house would have told him if something was wrong. He would have known if he had done something that could be dangerous. Ace was slow to adopt changes in building technology because changes created dissonance like a violinist playing a note differently in a symphony orchestra. A conductor could hear that note and correct it. Ace could sense changes in the harmony of a building. It was in his blood. Jon was sure that Officer Mark Prence didn't know that.

He stood for a moment looking at the house and the Lanai up the hill through the trees. No. He should do this at night - or at least when it was darker. What had possessed him to attempt to break into a house, to break the law in daylight? The orange glow from the setting sun blazed off the west facing windows. It was easy to see that they were all closed. The air conditioning must be running. That would mean that there were probably people in the house. It was stupid to do it now.

But they wouldn't hear him coming. He'd come this far. He had to keep going. He had to clear Ace.

He stepped carefully through the brush, the crackling of the leaves beneath his feet sounding to him like a herd of elephants. He remembered reading in The Last of the Mohicans the way the Indians ran silently through the woods, and he wondered if they really could do that, or if it was just something that James Fenimore Cooper imagined and transmogrified with his words. There was no way to place your foot so that something in the underbrush didn't crunch, crack, or shuffle.

When he was a few yards from the back door, he stopped and listened. Far away was the swish of the waves on the beach. But where he was in the back of the house it was dead calm so there was no rustling of the leaves. Even the gulls were quiet. The air conditioning condenser was humming away and from the dryer vent he heard the thump, thump, thump of the dryer running, and from inside the house heard the repetitive drone of the voices from a television. Well, that cinched it. People were in the house watching TV. How was he going to break in and poke around to find something that he didn't even know existed? It made no sense. Why would he attempt to open that door? He ran the conversation through his head, "Excuse me, I'm just here to find a murder weapon. Go ahead and keep watching what you're watching. Don't let me bother you." That wouldn't go so well.

Abruptly his sister's voice echoed in his mind. If the house was closed up and a combustion appliance was running and something like a clothes dryer was pushing air out of the house, the carbon monoxide could be pulled down the chimney and kill the occupants. The clothes dryer was running. They wouldn't have the heat on. The AC was running so the windows were closed. What else could be running?

He backed away from the house looking for a chimney. When he found it, he didn't see anything coming out of it. So, nothing was burning. No. If nothing was coming out of the chimney, maybe the combustion gases were going into the house! His heart started beating a bit harder. That suspicion was a good reason to enter the house! Maybe the killer was at it again! The evidence of a disaster in the making was thin, but it was possible.

There was a window in the back. He looked around for something to stand on and found an old cinder block. He dragged it over so he could peer in the window. He put his hands up to either side of his face to shield out the fading evening light reflections and put his nose up to the glass. In the darkness inside he could see the outline of appliances - a water heater, an air handler, and the lights glowing on a squat little box that he recognized as a pool heater. Clearly the pool heater was running.

His reluctance for entering the house disappeared and he jogged back to the back door, took a deep breath, pushed the door open, and was greeted by the noxious odor of combustion gasses. He almost immediately began to feel dizzy. He stepped into the kitchen. He looked across the counter into the living room beyond and saw the TV continuing to babble on about life without regard to the drama in the room. He held his hand over his nose and mouth, turned, and looked into the back bedroom. One of the beds had been disturbed but there was no one there. He came back into the kitchen and saw the top of a head sticking up above the back of the sofa.

"Excuse me," he said. "Excuse me?" The head didn't move so he walked closer. His dizziness increased. He lost any concern for intruding or breaking the law. He walked up to the end of the sofa where he saw Pee Wee with his head on his father's lap and Brian leaning over to one side.

"Who are you?" Brian asked, slurring his words.

"I'm Jon. We have to get out of here. The house is full of combustion fumes."

"Combustion what?"

Jon moved over to the big sliding glass doors and heaved one open, sucking in the fresh air.

He hustled back to the sofa, picked up Pee Wee, carried him outside the house, and laid him down on the patio. He quickly made sure that he was breathing and then returned to Brian to help him outside as well.

"What happened?" Brian asked. "Why was Pee Wee there?"

"I think it was carbon monoxide," Jon said. "I think carbon monoxide was getting sucked into the house."

"Why?"

"I don't know. We need to call an ambulance. Do you know the emergency number?"

"How's Pee Wee? Is he all right?"

"He's breathing. I think we got him out in time. Do you know the number?"

"What number?" Brian asked.

Jon was reluctant to go back into the pool house so he ran across the patio and knocked on the glass slider to Casa Grande and then pulled it open. Audrey came out of the kitchen wiping her hands on a dish towel.

"Yes?" she asked. "What are you doing here?"

"There's been an accident, Mrs. Reese. We need to call for an ambulance."

"What?"

"An accident. Your son needs an ambulance."

"Where? What happened?" She dropped the towel and ran for the door.

Garrett strutted into the room. He looked defiantly at Jon. "What did you do?"

"I didn't do anything. Would you please call for an ambulance or the police or let me do it?"

Garrett continued to look at Jon. "The boys are in bed. You're lying!"

"Mr. Scoles, Pee Wee is lying out on the patio barely breathing. I carried him out of the pool house. The house is full of combustion gases. We need to get an ambulance here now!" Jon looked around for a telephone. Why was this man being so recalcitrant?

"What was Pee Wee doing there?"

Jon felt like he was moving in a gelatinous world of goo. There was a phone on the sideboard. Ignoring Garrett, he stepped over to it, picked up the handset, dialed 0, and impatiently listened to the clicking and buzzing.

Garrett stepped up to him. Jon could smell whiskey on his breath. Garrett ripped the handset away from Jon's ear. "What the hell do you think you're doing?" He slammed the handset back into its cradle. "What the hell do you think you're doing," he repeated.

Jon stepped back. Stunned. "I'm calling an ambulance."

"Where's Brian? What about Brian?" Garrett demanded. "Is he dead?"

Jon looked at him. "You mean, Mr. Reese?"

"Is he dead?"

Jon took a deep breath. The man wasn't acting rationally. An ambulance was needed or Pee Wee might die, and this man was useless -- worse than useless -- he was in the way. Jon pushed Garrett aside, grabbed the phone, and dialed again. For a moment Jon wondered if Garrett was going to hit him. But he just stood there. When the operator answered, Jon asked her to send an ambulance and a police car to Casa Grande on Jolo Point. Immediately. There had been an accident.

Jon hung up the phone and stepped back toward the sliding doors.

Garrett mumbled, "I didn't do anything. Pee Wee wasn't supposed to be there. What was Pee Wee doing there?" Then he looked up at Jon. "What the hell were you doing there? You're trespassing! I'm going to have you arrested. You're all sweaty. What the hell are you doing here? You shouldn't be here!"

Jon backed out through the door.

Audrey was cradling Pee Wee's head and clutching him to her breast and crying. Pee Wee's face was pink. Brian was sitting with his back up against the wall of the pool house, shaking his head.

"Is he okay?" Jon asked, indicating Pee Wee.

Audrey looked up at him with tears running down her cheeks. "He's breathing. I guess that's good."

Bryce appeared on the patio, slapping the patio stones with her slippers, carrying a drink. "What happened?" she asked, looking at her husband.

The distant whine of a siren disturbed the quiet of the evening.

Jon ran to answer the pounding on the front door and came back with the EMTs. He outlined what had happened as they ran back through the house to the pool.

Mark Prence arrived, gave a sideways look at Jon, and then asked Garrett what had happened.

Jon stood back to listen to Garrett justify his own actions as he described sitting down with Brian to watch TV in the pool house, leaving because he had some business details to take care of, and the next thing he knew Jon was bursting into the house shouting about needing an ambulance!

"What about the boy? Why was the boy there?"

"What boy?" Garrett asked. "Oh, you mean Pee Wee. How the hell should I know? He wasn't supposed to be there."

The EMTs headed back to the ambulance, carrying Pee Wee and helping Brian. Prence stopped Brian for a moment. "Could you tell me what happened?"

"I was watching TV with Garrett. He left and then Pee Wee appeared."

"What do you mean?"

"I mean Pee Wee was suddenly there. I guess he left his

spelling toy there this afternoon. He likes that damn thing. Plays with it all the time. It has this scratchy voice that gets annoying but he really likes it. I guess it's good for him."

"So what happened?" Prence encouraged.

"Don't know. He appeared. He should have been in bed, but you know how kids are with televisions. He sort of curled up beside me. I was involved with the show. I figured I would take him back to bed when the show was over. I guess we dozed off. The next thing I knew we were out here. Is Pee Wee going to be alright?"

The EMTs encouraged Brian to keep walking with them to the ambulance. Audrey demanded that she go with them.

"What did this?" Prence asked

Jon said, "The place . . . the pool house . . . it's full of carbon monoxide."

"Why?"

"I don't know. Something must be wrong."

"That seems obvious," Prence replied. "You mean right now? The fire department should be here."

"I told you it was a defective building!" Garrett shouted. "It is that builder. And this kid works for that builder, doesn't he? What was he doing here anyway?"

"What *were* you doing here?" Prence asked.

Jon couldn't shrug off the question. He couldn't say that he was passing by and just thought he would stop in for a chat. That question was one of those inflection points that come along in life, a point where a life changes direction. His presence certainly had a positive result, but Jon's motivation for his presence was harder to explain or to excuse. If he had chosen not to invade the Salsberg's property or not to step into the pool house but turned away and gone back to the Wentzells, it would have meant the almost certain death of Brian and his son. He had come there to determine what had happened to Faith Salsberg, to prove that it wasn't Ace Wentzell's fault, that there was a murderer here and that that murderer was Garrett Scoles. How could Jon explain a motivation that wasn't connected to the result of his actions?

Jon looked at Officer Prence and asked, "Could we talk in private?"

Raising his voice, Garrett protested. "I want to press charges! Handcuff him, Officer!"

"I've got this, Mr. Scoles," Prence said. "I've got this." He grabbed Jon's arm and guided him away. "Tell me what you were doing here. Seems like a pretty dumb move."

"Mrs. Salsberg's death was not an accident," Jon said quietly. "It was murder. And I'm sure the murderer used this house . . ." he pointed to the pool house . . . "as the weapon. You know Ace! He wouldn't build a bad building."

Prence looked glum. "Didn't I ask you to stay out of this? Didn't I?"

"Yes. You did. Of course. And I would have except that I didn't want any more bad stuff to happen to Mr. Wentzell."

"And what? You didn't think I could do my job?"

"That wasn't it. But look. It was a good thing that I was here, right? Those people would have died!"

Prence studied him. "So, I'll ask you again: what were you doing here?"

Jon explained how he had decided he had to get into the pool house and try to figure out what had happened. He explained his conversation with his sister about how carbon monoxide might have been drawn back into the house.

"Where's your car?" Prence asked.

"I ran. Got to stay in shape," he smiled.

"And then you just . . . what . . . broke in?"

"Something weird was going on. No smoke was coming out of the chimney. All the windows were closed. The clothes dryer was running."

"Doesn't sound very weird to me. Why *would* there be smoke coming out of the chimney in July? It's hot!"

"Because the pool heater was running!"

"How did you know that? It's inside the house!"

"The lights were on, the indicator lights. I saw them through the window around the back."

Over Jon's shoulder, Prence noticed Garrett moving toward the pool house. "Hey!" he called. "Stay away from there. It's a crime scene. And it's dangerous."

"Are you telling me to stay away from my own house?"

"I am," Prence said. "Fire department has to clear the scene before anyone goes in."

Garrett glared at him. "I'm just going to open the windows," and he started moving toward the building again.

"No! You're not going in there." Prence strode back toward Garrett.

"It's my fucking house!" Garrett exclaimed. "You can't keep me out. I have a right to go in!"

Prence stood in front of him almost stepping on his toes. "What is your problem?"

Garrett was breathing heavily.

Prence could smell the alcohol on the man's breath. "What is your problem?" he repeated. "Is there something in there that you don't want me to see? Did you do this?"

Garrett stepped back. "Do what? I didn't do anything. I wasn't even there! It was that kid. I asked you before: what is that kid doing here? He doesn't belong here. Arrest him. He's trespassing! Arrest him for trespassing. Arrest him for attempted murder!"

At that point Brian Jr. emerged from the main house rubbing his eyes. "What's going on? Where's Pee Wee? Why are all these people here? Is the house on fire?"

"There was an accident," Bryce said. "Pee Wee's been taken to the hospital."

"Is he okay?"

"He's going to be fine. Trust me. Your mom went with him."

They heard the fire trucks pull up into the driveway and a

couple of burly fireman burst out of the main house in full gear. "What's the problem, Mark?" the chief asked.

"CO in the pool house," Prence answered pointing over his shoulder. "Had a couple of victims. I think they're okay."

The firemen pulled on their masks and penetrated the pool house. Out on the patio Jon could hear the windows being opened, and after a few minutes the firemen reemerged.

"Pool heater," the Chief said. "Chimney was disconnected."

"Why?" Prence asked. "Did it fall off?"

The fire chief replied, "Can't say. We'll have to investigate."

For just a moment Garrett kept his mouth clamped shut. Then he said, "I told you! I told you! Poor workmanship! Wentzell. The builder. The builder is liable! The place is falling apart. It has been there for less than a year! A year! And it's falling apart. It's dangerous. It could have been deadly. Somebody could have been killed. I could have been killed. I was just in there. Oh my god! I could have been killed!"

The fire chief, Officer Prence, Jon, Garrett's wife, Bryce, all looked at him, waiting for an explanation of the outburst.

"You weren't in there when I . . . uh . . . entered," Jon said.

"That's another thing: why were you in there?" Garrett replied.

"You weren't in there and nobody died. But they could have. Did you disconnect the flue?" Jon asked.

"Now wait a minute," Prence said. "Are you accusing Mr. Scoles of deliberately causing this? Why would he do that?"

Garrett glared at him.

"He's done it before."

"What?" Bryce asked. "What the hell do you mean?"

"He killed Mrs. Salsberg the same way."

"That's ridiculous! That's slanderous! That's totally false," Garrett blasted.

Officer Prence held up his hands. "Now wait a minute. Let's not go flinging around accusations. We need to get to the bottom of this. Chief, is it safe to go in?"

"I wouldn't. Let it air out. We'll get the investigators in there."

Jon could sense Prence's indecision. The Salsbergs were a powerful family with major influence in the town. If Prence got this wrong, he would be stepping on the wrong toes. Jon was very sure that Scoles was guilty, that he was standing with a killer, that the man had to be punished, that he had almost killed his nephew and his brother-in-law. That was why Scoles had tried it again! He'd moved his mother-in-law out of the way and he had to get rid of his brother-in-law as well.

"The man's a killer!" Jon blurted out, not able to contain himself. "It is as obvious as if he had shot Mrs. Salsberg. He just used a house instead of a gun."

Scoles laughed. "The kid's hallucinating."

"All right," Prence said finally, "We're taking this down to the station."

"What?" Garrett shouted. "We're not going anywhere. You can't do that!"

Prence looked at him. "Do you have a better suggestion? Perhaps we could all sit in your living room, have some cold drinks, and chat about it?"

"I don't like your tone, Officer," Bryce responded.

"I'm calling my lawyer," Garrett said, turning back toward the main house.

"Do you have something to hide, Mr. Scoles?"

Garrett stopped.

"Yeah," Jon said, "what have you got to hide? You had motive to kill your mother-in-law — taking over the company, getting your hands on all the family money. You had means: you studied physics at Princeton. And you certainly had opportunity. What have you got to hide? Seems like Mr. Reese might have been in your way. Easy enough to disconnect the flue pipe, crank up the pool heater, and turn on the clothes dryer to suck the carbon monoxide down the flue. And once you did it once, you could do it again. Simple. I'll bet they'll find your fingerprints on the flue pipe! You might not have known that your nephew was in there! That was probably an accident."

"Oh, my god!" Garrett exploded. "Fiction. All fiction! That's ludicrous. Why would I do that? This kid is trespassing! Arrest him! He's had it out for me. He threw a baseball at me, for Christ's sake." He headed back toward the main house. "I'm calling my lawyer."

"Stop!" Prence shouted. "Just stop where you are. We're going to get to the bottom of this. We're going to take this to the station. You can call your lawyer from there!"

"I'll take Junior back to bed," Bryce said.

Garrett hesitated and looked back at them. "I don't think so," he said calmly and then he started running, pushing past Bryce, as he threw open the screen door, sprinted off across the living room toward the entry hall.

"What the hell?" exclaimed Prence. He froze for a moment, trying to sort out the situation. "Come on!" he said to Jon.

By the time they emerged from the front door they saw Garrett's Mercedes 450sl spin around the end of the driveway and roar off down the Jolo Point Road, spewing gravel behind it.

"The man's nuts!" Prence exclaimed.

"I'd guess you'd have to be to kill people," Jon replied.

"Get in the front. Let's go."

They jumped into the police cruiser and Prence maneuvered in the driveway, turning the car around and launching off after the rapidly disappearing Mercedes.

Prence grabbed the microphone on his radio, pressed the button, identified himself, and described the situation. "In pursuit of a blue Mercedes sports car. A suspect in a murder! On the run!"

The response was one of disbelief. "Really. In Tilley? It's July. It's Cape Cod! Where's he going to run to?"

"He's not a local," Prence almost shouted. "Not from around here!" Prence wrestled with the wheel of the cruiser.

Jon hung onto the door. "Where's he going?"

"Damned if I know!"

~

GARRETT COULD NOT EXPLAIN WHY HE HAD RUN OUT AND jumped in the car. There was no logical explanation. It was like a fugitive running to the top of a building. "Shit! Shit! Shit! This is stupid! Stupid! Stupid! Stupid!" Some instinct out of his past, some memory of his father trying to avoid confrontation drove him to act irrationally.

The Mercedes did not feel like a small car. It was solid and powerful and responsive, leaping forward to his light touch on the accelerator. The surge of adrenaline pushed him. He roared out of the end of Jolo Point Road and swerved left as he would have toward the airport. He had only moments of open road before an old Buick pulled out of a side street and cut him off. Garrett punched the horn and accelerated around the old man in the hat driving.

The warmth of the evening was amplified by high humidity and Garrett was sweating bullets as he wrestled with the wheel. Tourists and locals were out for an evening stroll. Garrett, in his anger and frustration, forced himself to not think of them as targets. His aggressive and erratic weaving through the crowd made people stop and stare at him.

He looked in his rear-view mirror and notice a flash of red police lights in the distance behind him. A small void in the crowd ahead allowed him to push the accelerator and leap ahead. But only for a moment before he had to wrench the wheel to the left to avoid a teenager on a skate board who emerged from nowhere.

He had to get out of these crowds. He had to get away from all these annoying, cloying people. He had to get away. He pulled the wheel to the right, the heavy car screeching its tires as he rocketed down narrow St. Anne's Street. Not knowing the area was a handicap. He didn't know the streets and roads and alleys.

He should have planned it better. He should have planned his escape route. But he shouldn't have needed an escape route! It had all been going so smoothly, until that meddling kid showed up. He didn't mean to put Pee Wee's life in jeopardy. He hadn't meant to hurt anyone, just move them calmly and peacefully out of the way so that life could move on the way it was meant to move on. "God! Why do they always have to make such a big fuss about these things?"

He thought, it had been time for Faith to go. Yes. She had done her part, lived her life. Why would they have to wait until she became senile or sick or ended up in the hospital wasting everyone's time and money. Elderly people in other cultures were encouraged to wander out in the woods and die. But not in our civilized world. "Oh, no," he said to the windshield. Oh, no. In this civilized world we let people -- encourage people -- to go on forever. To sit around in the hallways of 'retirement' homes and wait to die. To sit on their front porches and count the Winnebagos! Before they became senile and useless, we should encourage them to wander out in the woods and die! We wouldn't have to spend all that money on funerals or go all weepy-waily. Nobody likes funerals anyway! Nobody! He was just doing his part.

Of course, mourning Faith hadn't worked! They'd still had to have the goddamned funeral. They still had to sit around and talk about how wonderful the damn woman was.

Now was not the time for these protracted thoughts. He spun the car around a Volkswagen Beetle that was ticking along ahead of him. He heaved the car to the left and ducked down Capt' Charlie's Lane.

People didn't know how to drive. He was not out for an evening cruise. There were too many people. Too many cars. The roads were too narrow and not well lit. They had too many potholes. He swerved around a car attempting to back out of a driveway, punching his horn in frustration. "Idiot!" He wanted to find some open road where he could roar off, but, on the other hand, these narrow roads and crowds might give him a chance to lose any pursuers. He could use his brain. Something they didn't have. He smiled to himself. He could disappear. He'd just let things cool off, get in touch with an army of lawyers, clear it all up, and settle into running the company as he should have from the beginning. He wanted it that way and so that's the way it would be.

He just had to escape this momentary, minor inconvenience.

JON HUNG ON AS PRENCE PUSHED THE POLICE PLYMOUTH FURY to the limit before slamming on the brakes and sliding around the corner out of Jolo Point Road in pursuit of the much smaller Mercedes. Prence was not an adventurous driver and the Mercedes brakes lights were fading away as they watched it swerve through traffic.

"You're going to lose him," Jon said.

"He's crazy!"

"He's a killer! Don't let him get away."

"Where's he going to go?"

"Jesus, I don't know!" Jon replied. "This is your town. I'm just visiting."

Summer people were coming out to enjoy the evening, strolling along the sidewalks, sitting on the benches. Heads turned as the screaming siren of the police car roared into view.

Up ahead he saw Garrett heave his car onto St. Anne's Street.

"He's turning," Jon said.

"I see it!"

"Where does that go?"

"Everywhere! It's not a dead end. Toward the high school? I don't know where he's going any more than you do!" Prence was breathing heavily. He accelerated around the corner. Jon was pushed into the back of his seat. He tried to think about why Garrett would run like this. It didn't make any sense. He seemed like the kind of person who would let his lawyers solve his problems for him. He would bully his way through. But then bullies are generally cowards. Maybe he thought that if they didn't arrest him, he could get away with it.

Jon peered forward through the gathering darkness, trying to pick out the 450sl's taillights. "Up there. He's turning left."

"You sure?" Prence asked.

"No! What's there?"

"More roads. Nothing. Where's he going?"

"Can't you call ahead? Get them to put up a road block or something?"

"Where? What road? How do we block him off if we don't know where he's going?"

Jon tried to imagine where Garrett might run to. The Cape was a tangled web of small neighborhood streets with a handful of more major roads traversing the peninsula from south to north and Routes 28, 6, and 6A running east and west. If Scoles had any sense at all, he would avoid the more congested roads like Route 28 which was populated by dozens of visitor friendly attractions like miniature golf courses, restaurants, T-shirt and souvenir shops, and motels. Maybe he would duck down into one of the darkened neighborhoods and wait, hoping the pursuit would just pass him by.

"Have we lost him?" Jon asked. "Did you get his license number? Can't you just have all the cops looking for a dark blue Mercedes 450sL? There can't be many of those?"

"You'd be surprised," Prence replied. "Lot of money around here."

A Ford wagon pulled out of a side street despite the fact that the Fury's *Kojak* light was swirling and flashing. Prence blared the horn which only seemed to surprise the driver of the wagon and cause him to slow down. Prence swerved around him and accelerated. At the last moment he decided to slide into Capt' Charlie's Lane.

"Is this where you saw him turn?"

"Maybe," Jon replied. "Could he be headed for the highway?"

"Well this isn't how I would go."

The Lane was less busy and easier to see any taillights ahead. But there was nothing to indicate the fugitive was ahead of them. Just normal traffic. Then the Lane ended at a 'T' where they had to stop: left or right? North or South?

"Cockle Creek Road," Prence said.

"Where does it go? Did we pass him?"

"No. No there wasn't any place for him to turn back. He must have gotten to here."

"Which way would he go?"

"You gotta stop asking me that! How the hell should I know. I'm not a shrink!"

"He may be a killer, but he's not stupid," Jon said. "He's got to realize that if he keeps making left turns, he's just going to end up back where he started, right? If he wants to get out of here, he's got to turn right."

"Yeah. Maybe. But around here you can get twisted up. Roads run all over the place. Developers keep adding new ones to open up properties. For all he knows, this could just be in the middle of a development!"

"Is it?"

"No, but he doesn't know that." Prence looked to the left, shrugged and spun the wheel to the right. "Good as anything I guess."

He punched the accelerator and the car leapt ahead.

GARRETT COULDN'T SEE ANY FLASHING LIGHT BEHIND HIM anymore, but that only made him more frenzied. He argued with himself that it meant that he had lost his pursuers, but another voice asked him where they were. At least when he could see them, he knew how far behind they were. This way his situation was unknown. It was like hiding in a dark warehouse, hoping that the pursuer would pass him by, holding his breath, trying not to make a sound, trying not to scream or have the baby cry or whatever the situation was. The reality of the situation was hard for him to grasp. Running from a deadly pursuit was not something he was familiar with.

Not that this was deadly. The police weren't likely to shoot him! This was the United States. He was a wealthy, white man in a Mercedes sports car. Why would they shoot him? He relaxed for a moment and slowed down as he approached the end of Capt' Charlie's Lane. He looked left and right, let one car speed past, and then turned left.

It would have been helpful to know where he was. There might be a map of Cape Cod in the glove compartment, but there was no time to stop and refer to a map. He just needed to get away. He admitted to himself that he'd made a mistake. He should have picked a better time to get rid of his brother-in-law. He'd been impatient. In the future he would have to learn to be more patient. He hated waiting. He shouldn't have been so impatient.

It was so damn hot! He should have put the top down. Oh, that would have been good! Wouldn't it? If he'd told the cop to wait, while he put the top down on his car so he could have been more comfortable! He snorted out a couple of laughs at the thought.

AC. He could turn on the AC. No! He should pay attention to his driving; to the road. He couldn't take his eyes off the road ahead to access the AC controls. That would be stupid. He could end up in a ditch or worse. He shouldn't be thinking about being uncomfortable. He should be planning. Thinking ahead. Playing chess. This could be fun. The car was handling beautifully. He should leave that crappy police Plymouth in the dust! It was a pig! A pig driving a pig! He snorted again.

On a whim he swung the car to the right down a road that had one of those Indian names. Something like Pemagonquitt. They must have had a lot of Indians around here. This one was pretty dark. No street lights. Houses tucked up behind their lawns. Aww! All those peaceful Cape Cod summer evenings. Something to put into the scrapbooks. Pictures to send home to the family. "Wish you were here!" No, you don't. You wish they could die. I can help you with that, he thought.

Enough of these god damned little lanes, he thought. Out loud he said, "This is getting tiresome." And as though Tinkerbell had just granted him his wish, he swerved around a right-hand corner and came to the end of the Pema-whatever Street and emerged onto a more substantial, main road.

The Mercedes throbbed at idle, loyally waiting to dash off at his command. And he was in command. He was in control. He willed himself to calm his breathing. He'd come a long way. Now . . . now it was time to move forward with resolve and care. He knew just enough about the geography of the Cape to know that if he headed north, he would run into the Mid-Cape Highway and once he got there, he could simply head west and drive off symbolically into the sunset although in reality the sun had already set for the day. No need to stress. He would take this one step at a time and quietly disappear for a while. In fact, he thought, now would be the time to put the top down. It would make the car look different. They were so stupid they would probably not recognize the car!

JON PEERED AHEAD, HOPING HE HAD GUESSED RIGHT. THE overhanging trees shaded the twilight, making it tunnel-dark. Some light spilled out of the houses, but they were set back from the road and didn't help to illuminate the way ahead. Over the roar of the big Fury's engine he could hear families and friends celebrating the summer evening. A row of cars parked up a driveway. The smell of burgers on the grill. It seemed to be another world - like years ago since he had been doing the same thing back at home with his friends. This would not be a summer he would quickly forget!

"Did Lisa tell you to do this?" Prence asked.

Jon was shaken out of his reverie. "What?"

"Did Lisa . . . no, let me put it this way. Did Lisa encourage you to chase after a murderer?"

"No, sir!" Jon replied. "No. She tried to talk me out of it."

"I didn't think there was anyone more stubborn than she is!"

Jon hung onto the door as Prence wrestled the Plymouth around another corner. The road must have followed the course of the eponymous creek; twisting back and forth.

"Where does this come out?" Jon asked.

"You'll see," was Prence's terse reply. "You shouldn't have gotten messed up in this. You have a career to think about. You don't live here. This is none of your business."

"If I hadn't," Jon replied, "there would be two more dead people."

"Humph!" Prence grunted punching the accelerator on a short straight stretch. Then he slammed on the brakes as the street ended and they found themselves facing a wider, straighter, north-south avenue.

"Oh," Jon exclaimed as he recognized the strip malls and the lumber yards and the banks. "I know where this is!"

"Great," Prence replied. "Where's Scoles?" He looked left and right. "No point in freaking out the locals." He reached over and shut off the *Kojak* light and the siren, and they sat there.

"Look," Jon said, "if he's ahead of us there's no point in our sitting here. Maybe he's not even in this area! Can't you call ahead . . . talk to some of your buddies in other police forces, find out what's going on?"

"Yup," Prence replied. "I could do that. But then again . . .." He nodded his head, indicated a small dark blue convertible headed leisurely in their direction up the street.

"No!"

"Yup." Prence flipped the light and siren back on and roared out after the Mercedes. "Glad he's enjoying the evening with his top down and all! What an arrogant asshole!" He reached over, grabbed the microphone, and alerted the other police departments that the fugitive was heading north, looked like toward the Mid-Cape Highway.

~

OH, WHAT A GORGEOUS EVENING! GARRETT THOUGHT WITH an ironic grin on his lips. Warm, summer twilight. An evening for vacationers. An evening for lovers. An evening for . . . getting away with murder! He was untouchable! The air was filled with frying food scented by the sea perfumed by salt water taffy and Castrol® in engine exhaust! He had come such a long way from that backwater town in New Jersey. What would his parents think of him now, driving this Mercedes, about to become president of a major development company on the Main Line in Pennsylvania with his prestigious degree from Princeton! He was a star! There was just one, little problem . . . one fly in the ointment . . . one pimple on the ass . . . one zippity in the doo dah. But the lawyers can take care of that. Lawyers can always take care of that from tax fraud to murder! They are magicians . . . as long as you can pay for them. Just like mommy: they can make it all better!

It was at that moment that he passed the end of Cockle Creek Road and saw Officer Prence's car, saw the flashing red light illuminate, and his scrotum tightened, and he pushed the accelerator to the floor. All eight cylinders grabbed the wheels and launched the car forward. "ASSHOLE!" Garrett yelled as he rocketed off. "Where the hell did you come from?"

The reality of the traffic and the pursuit caused him to lose touch with his enchanted evening. He blared the horn as he came to a busy intersection, festooned with the reds and greens and yellows of traffic signals. Cars turning, cars stopped, cars waiting. He swerved around them and between them and managed to avoid them with just a few scuffs, scrapes and swears.

On the other side of the intersection he roared ahead and saw the entry signs to the Mid-Cape Highway. He hesitated for a moment, considering whether it made more sense to stay off the highway, losing his pursuer on the back roads as he had before, but committed himself at the last moment to the speedier, limited access road. It was a Thursday, after all, how much traffic could there be?

Garrett pushed the 450 up and around the entrance ramp and onto the highway. For a few glorious moments there was no one ahead of him and he accelerated to seventy. Coming over a rise he saw the taillights of a station wagon -- white with fake wood paneling and packed with family. In moments Garrett reached them as the family appeared to debate at what seemed like twenty miles an hour. Mile after mile they crawled along. Not able to stand the lethargic pace, Garrett blared the Mercedes' horn. He saw the driver glance up into his mirror, flip him off, argue with the other occupants of the car, and slow further.

Garrett glanced in his own mirror and saw the throbbing red flashes of the police car. "SHIT!" he yelled into the wind. He looked ahead. This was not the time to be concerned about abiding by the rules of the road. Seeing a gap in the oncoming traffic, he swerved the car over the double yellow lines and into the eastbound lane, squeezing back into the westbound lane while the driver of the station wagon hammered his horn in anger and frustration.

"Got him!" Garrett said in triumph, speeding ahead, over another hill and around another curve and up to the back of another pokey driver. Constant traffic roared by in the opposite direction. Garrett weaved the 450, kissing the centerline and back to the edge of the road. He flashed his headlights as his frustration grew. He glanced in his mirror and saw that the station wagon had pulled over, succumbing to the flashing red light of the police car.

Garrett had no choice. He swerved the Mercedes into the breakdown lane and bouncing over dirt and trash, accelerated around the car in front of him. More blaring horns and screeching tires and he was back into the lane.

If he could get to the divided part of the highway where it opened up into four lanes, he could speed away. How far away was that? Why didn't these somnolent, idiotic drivers get out of the way? People like this clog up the roads like slugs of greasy hair in drain pipes. They impede progress. They ruin lives. They are self-absorbed. Thoughtless. They think about no one but themselves. Other people have work to do, meetings to attend, sales to make. There should be someplace where they could send all the tourists so that they could just poke around at a snail's pace and stay out of the way of real people!

Despite the wind and the direction of the sound, Garrett sensed the whining of the police siren. There was no time to think. This was no time for rational thought. This was all instinct and gut reaction. This was Garrett's apocalypse.

A small gap in the oncoming traffic allowed him to surge into the left lane, leap ahead, and cut back in front of an old pickup.

A couple of moments of creeping along with the frustrated pickup looming over his tail.

A surge to the right through a rest area at sixty miles an hour and back up onto the highway and a bit of open road, feeling a moment of elation, a taste of freedom. He wiped the sweat from his forehead.

Over another rise, and a sign for an exit appeared. In a kind of perverted glee, he swerved the car to the left, cut across oncoming traffic blaring their horns and screeching their brakes and entered the on-ramp in the wrong direction.

"Follow that, you stupid cop!" Garrett shouted. Joyously the ramp was empty. No cars or trucks or vehicles of any kind to avoid. But as he flew around the corner, he saw a lot of flashing red lights reflecting off the trees, and with a mental crash he realized that his run was done.

~

Restrained as they were by obeying the law, Prence and Jon had been slowed by the traffic on Route 164 before reaching the Mid-Cape Highway. Jon was surprised at how many people just ignored the siren and the flashing light of an emergency vehicle. Some drivers practically wrecked their cars in a desperate attempt to get out of the way. But others paid no attention at all, totally absorbed in their own lives and their own problems.

"The guy's a maniac!" Jon said. "What does he think he's going to accomplish?"

Prence kept his eyes on the traffic ahead, squeezing by cars in nonexistent lanes, trying to keep the disappearing Mercedes in sight.

"Where's he going to go? In this traffic? He's a maniac. I thought he was smarter than this!"

"He's taking the Mid-Cape!" Prence stated as he watched Garrett swerve onto the on-ramp. "Jesus! He's going to end up killing somebody."

"He already has!" Jon said.

Prence grabbed the microphone on his radio and called in the status. "Set up blocks on the next couple of exits! He's not going to get far. Not in this traffic."

The Mid-Cape highway is hilly, rural, and as circuitous and winding as an old river, which makes it quite lovely for a quiet, sylvan, summer drive but frustrating and blinding for an aggressive driver trying to get somewhere. Which is why it is frequently called 'Suicide Alley'.

As they entered the highway, Jon couldn't see Garrett up ahead, blocked by a hill and a turn in the road. Cars on the opposite side of the two-lane road, noticing the flashing light, pulled over onto the verge despite the fact that the immediate road ahead of the police car was clear. Jon hung on as Prence pushed the Plymouth until they saw the Mercedes ahead. Jon held his breath as he watched it cut into the left lane and then pulled back ahead of the station wagon.

"Shit! That was close."

Moments later they had closed with the station wagon, whose driver waved at them in his rear-view mirror and then pulled off to the right, waving them ahead through his open window.

They watched as Garrett danced back and forth across the lane, pulling back into oncoming traffic, swerving to the right into a rest area, kicking up clouds of dust as he pushed and bounced and kicked his car ahead.

As they approached the cars ahead not all the drivers had recovered from the surprise of having a speeding car surge up behind them and then pass them on the right. One driver was so shocked that he slammed on his brakes just in front of them, almost coming to a full stop in the middle of the westbound lane, causing Prence to have to take evasive action and pull into the middle of the road to squeeze past on the left.

Then they saw the Mercedes fly across the oncoming traffic and into the on-ramp on the opposite side.

"Shit!" Prence yelled. "I hope they set up a roadblock!" He pulled into the right-hand exit ramp, following it down the hill, and under the highway to be greeted by a festival of flashing lights, police cars, and police with guns drawn. Jon saw that the Mercedes had come to a complete stop and Garrett sat there with his head down looking at his knees.

22

DIAMOND'S EDGE

When Officer Prence dropped Jon off at the Wentzells', Jon came into the kitchen and found normalcy: Ace reading his paper and Babs jotting numbers in the account books. "Did you have a nice evening?" she asked looking up. "Your car was still here."

For a few moments Jon was unable to unravel the events that had just transpired. They came out in little fistfuls of information, not all in a logical sequence.

"Garrett Scoles has been arrested."

Ace put down his paper.

"We had to chase him."

"He tried to kill his brother-in-law. Brian. Brian Reese."

"In the pool house."

"Nearly killed his nephew as well."

"I ran. There. For the exercise. That's why the car's here."

"Lot of cops. Probably a half dozen. Or more!"

"Ever been in a car chase? Prence is not the best driver!"

As Jon unraveled his tale and reached the end of Scoles and the police chase and murder, he was shaking like a plate of gelatin in an earthquake. Babs listened with her hand over her mouth. Jon paced the kitchen as he talked, bouncing around from window to wall.

Ace said, "Sit down, Jon. Take a deep breath." He pulled out a chair and Jon dropped into it. Ace rummaged in a high cabinet and pulled out a dusty bottle of Chivas Regal. He glanced at Babs who quietly shook her head. He set a couple of small glasses on the table and poured the golden-brown liquid into them and pushed one over in front of Jon who looked up at him.

Ace capped the bottle and set it down on the counter and resumed his seat. "Are you okay?" he asked.

"Oh," Jon replied. "Yeah. They got him. He killed his mother-in-law. I knew. I just had to prove it."

Jon explained how Garrett had used the pool house to murder Faith Salsberg, disconnecting the flue, turning on the pool heater, accelerating the spillage of combustion gases into the house with the clothes dryer. "It doesn't take long when the carbon monoxide concentrations are high enough. That's what my sister told me. Scoles knew that too."

"That's awful!" Babs said. "Just imagine!"

"There wasn't anything wrong with the house?" Ace asked.

"The only thing they could blame you for would be building it too well! Making it too air tight!"

"Didn't know," Ace replied. "I guess I should have thought about it more. Learned more."

"You can't know everything," Babs said.

"You can try. Maybe I should go back to school about this." Jon said.

Ace grunted. Some of the tension had drained out of his face.

By the following Sunday enough time had passed to smooth out some of the rough edges of the attempted murder. Jon was beginning to be able to push the whole Salsberg saga to the back of his mind to focus on the All-Star Game and what might come after. Time to think about what he wanted to do with the rest of his life. The summer and the baseball season were winding down and for the first time in his life nothing in his future was inevitable.

He'd driven over to the field early in the morning to try to loosen up – to get his head in the right place. Icky showed up and they tossed the ball back and forth, throwing increasingly harder.

Icky called out to him, "Hey, Jon, you know what a manager is? A manager is someone who thinks that nine women ought to be able to produce a kid in one month!"

"Just throw the ball, Icky."

"No seriously. You know they only call it premarital sex if you're intending to get married."

"Where do you get this stuff? Does your head ever settle down on one subject?"

"Just trying to keep you loose. Remember that you play better when you're not thinking. You're not good at not thinking. A pro! Remember that Humpty Dumpty had a great fall because he'd had such a lousy summer!"

"I haven't had a lousy summer. Not at all," Jon said. The ball slapped hard into his mitt. "Complicated, maybe, but not hard." He grunted a little as he flung the ball back. "How about you?"

"No, it's been good." Icky massaged the ball before setting himself to throwing it back. "No, it's been good," he repeated. "Except for Dupin."

"Yeah, except for Dupin," Jon replied. "That was a bummer."

For a while they didn't talk, thinking about their friend, thinking about their own futures. "Hey, you think Coach Russell is going to lose his job after this season?" Icky asked.

"I hadn't heard about that. Why? Why would he lose his job? It's been a pretty successful season. We've done okay."

"Yeah, but there are bound to be changes, right? I mean where's the money going to come from? Will the Salsbergs keep on putting money in?"

"Mr. Reese is more of a ball fan than Scoles ever was. If he takes over the company business that's better for the Longliners."

SLAP. The ball slapped into Jon's mitt. GRUNT. SLAP. GRUNT. The rhythm of the game emphasized their words.

"Any major league prospects for you, Ick?"

"Not this year, but I'm a Junior. 'Nother year. I'll be wiser. More experienced."

SLAP. GRUNT.

"Think you're getting an offer from the Angels? That'd be cool. Are you still going to talk to us? Get us tickets?"

"Don't know. They haven't asked. I mean I don't know if I'm going to play pro ball even if they do make me an offer."

Icky held the ball in his glove and put his hands on his hips. "What? Seriously? Still? You gotta be kidding?"

"No, I don't know, Ick. How do I know that professional baseball is my life?"

"Oh my god!" Icky threw the ball back with added strength. "Really? This is a chance of a lifetime. Guys would give their left nut for this sort of opportunity and you're considering turning it down? It's like the Irishman at his first baseball game. When he was told that the batter didn't have to run because he had four balls, the Irishman yelled, 'Walk with pride! Walk with pride!'"

"Look, you idiot, if you knew that what you were about to do was the most important thing that would ever happen in your life . . . like you could do this but nothing else . . . bang! You're done. Would you do it or would you wait and see what else might happen?"

"You mean if someone told me I could have one orgasm would I want to blow it in a wet dream?"

"Uhm. Not exactly. But something like that."

"How do you know that anything else IS going to come along that's better? I mean it's not like you can put this opportunity in a bank. Like something you could take out later when you're ready. You can't go back, Jon. Life goes by and then it's done. You can't go back and say, 'Okay, now that I've been through it, I think I'll do that instead of that!' Time is weird. I mean if a cow laughed, would milk come out of her nose?"

"Well, they haven't made me a formal offer anyway," Jon replied. "Until they do, I don't have to think about it. I can take this one day at a time."

WHEN HE GOT TO FENWAY PARK AND WALKED OUT ONTO THE field, his breathing took a little hitch, a gasp, a pile of overwhelming unreality. Great players had stepped onto this grass and this dirt, looked up at these stands, stands full of seats, seats full of fans yelling and screaming and applauding ball players and rock stars. These sorts of connections with all that history was addicting. Even if he did not desiderate becoming a professional baseball player, he couldn't help but be sucked into the aura that surrounded that moment along with the other players around him.

"Oh, my god!" someone said.

"The Green Monster! Look at that!"

"Didn't Ruth play here before he got dragged off to the Yankees?"

"Him and Yaz and Martinez and Ted Williams."

"Yeah!" someone emitted in awe.

"And now there's us! Let's get this show started!"

Jon had played baseball on a lot of fields in high school and college, but there was a definite difference stepping out onto a professional diamond like Fenway Park. It wasn't the game of pitch and catch. It didn't seem like a game. The grass was serious - perfectly mowed and trimmed and groomed. The infield was serious - its reddish dirt raked in perfectly straight lines. The white lines were serious. The bases were serious - not the canvas bags or flat, plastic things that you could throw across the room. The dugouts were serious. The stands were serious. The lights soared high into the sky like steeples on a cathedral. Jon could understand why players took the sport seriously on a field like this. But if it was serious and professional, would it be fun? Even the autographing session seemed more serious, like leaving his mark for someone to collect and brag about in the future.

Oddly, Jon found this more like a pick-up game – playing with players he had been competing against during league games. In a sense it reduced the pressure of winning and losing. But at this level, the competitive juices flowed through the veins, blended with their personal pride and drive for success. There was still the desire to beat the pants off any opponent. And since this was the All Stars of all the Cape Cod Baseball League competing against the All Stars of the Atlantic Collegiate Baseball League, there was League pride to defend, a feeling of *all being together in this*.

As the team warmed up, Jon scanned the stands for his father who had arrived in Tilley the night before. During supper his father had said, "All-star? Imagine that. Fenway Park! Amazing. Remember those T-ball games? Wish your mother could have been here."

They went on to reminisce and rehash the past which led naturally through the present to the future. "What's next?" his father asked.

Jon didn't want to talk about it. "What do you mean?"

"I mean I'm glad you had the summer playing ball, and I'm really glad you lived through this murder thing – you took some foolish risks – but the summer's almost over." His father looked at him expectantly.

Jon wanted to express petulant responses to the unspoken question such as, "You don't understand" or "I know what I want" or "Can we talk about this later" but he didn't say any of those things; he just looked at his father sitting expectantly in the surrounding noise of the restaurant. Even though Jon knew that his father could not give him the answer, even though he knew that his father's answers for his own life could not be Jon's answers, he wished the perfect solution would drop from the heavens onto the table in front of him.

"Would you consider an offer to play pro ball?" his father asked, trying to help.

"Don't know. That hasn't happened yet."

"Would you consider joining the army?"

"What?"

"The military could be a great place to start."

Jon looked at his father as though he had lost his mind.

"When did you decide you wanted to work with health insurance?" Jon asked.

"I didn't exactly choose. The job just kind of happened. You know. Seemed like an offer I couldn't refuse." His father laughed at the *Godfather* reference.

When they got to dessert, Jon's father said, "By the way, you remember that Florida baseball project I mentioned to you when your sister and I came up here? Expansion team. It's odd, but there apparently is a connection with the Salsberg family you've been working with for the land for a stadium. I could probably get you a position in management there if you want to keep your baseball connections . . . and don't get a pro offer."

"I don't know, Dad," Jon said. "That would be pretty weird."

Now Jon saw his father, sitting in the stands at Fenway behind home plate, the future still unresolved.

THE GAME WAS CLOSE, ENDING WITH A SIX TO FIVE WIN FOR the Cape Cod Baseball League. The team played well with fire in their bellies. Jon played well getting two hits and a run batted in, and making clutch plays at first. It was one of those days when baseball came easy to him, feeling the flow of the game and pulse of his teammates. After the last out, they celebrated around home plate as though they had won the world series. When you get to the top of the mountain, there is nothing left but to go back down, and then look for the next mountain.

Tim Boynton, the scout for the Angels approached him as he was heading back to the locker room.

"Good game," he said. "You're developing well."

"Thanks, Mr. Boynton. Felt good."

Boynton looked at him and fiddled with the change in his pocket. "What about your future?"

"Dunno." Jon replied.

"I think there's a spot for you with the Angels if you want it."

"Thanks, Mr. Boynton. I just don't know yet."

The scout looked him in the eye. "Here's the thing, Jon. Wanting it is everything. If you don't want it, you'll play like you don't want it. You have to want it. You'll be standing there surrounded by other players who want it so desperately they can taste it and you'll be like a limp dishrag in the middle of a bunch of prom dresses! If you don't want it, we'll find someone who does." He started walking away.

"Wait," Jon exclaimed. "Wait. I didn't say I didn't want it." Boynton stopped and turned back. "I didn't say I didn't want it."

"What's the problem, then? I'm not sure I believe that you have baseball in your soul. If the girl of your dreams said, 'Take me! I'm yours!' would you hesitate and say, 'Well, I'm not sure'. What about that car of yours? Did you want it?"

Jon smiled. "Are you telling me that all pro baseball players are totally committed to the game?"

"No. It's not one thing. It's a complex elixir of tangible emotional risk and reward. It's the money. It's the fame. And it's the game, a game they're good at. They're willing to take the chances and make the choices and sacrifice their bodies and their time to the gods of fame and fortune. Are you?"

"I have to talk it over with my family."

"No, you don't," Boynton replied. He paused to emphasize the point. "You're not a kid, Jon. This is your decision. This is your life."

"What would they pay?"

Boynton stepped back to him. "You're first base, right? You're not going push Rod Carew out of the way. I mean he gets the big bucks, right? Bumping up against that big seven figure line." He shook his head and laughed. "You got to start with the other budding stars. I can get you nineteen. Not bad for a kid."

A starting salary of nineteen thousand dollars a year sounded pretty good.

"Oh, and by the way, you would get to play baseball in the major leagues with teammates like Carew and Nolan Ryan and Joe Rudi and Frank Tanana! Not too shabby work mates! Not a bad starting position for a kid."

Jon smiled.

"Of course, you would still have to go through the tryouts and minor league play. Got to get used to playing with the big boys. They use wooden bats so you'd have to get used to that. When was the last time you swung a good piece of ash at a ball?" He laughed. "God, I love that line. Piece of ash!"

As the other players jogged past the two of them on their way to the locker room, they patted Jon on his back and called out, "Good Game! Good Game!"

Fans and fame, Fenway Park and Frank Tanana inflated his mind and pumped up his soul. The Angels wanted him! And if the Angels wanted him, were there other opportunities? Did he need an agent?

"I'll get back to you, Mr. Boynton," Jon said.

THE GAME WAS OVER. GROUNDS CREWS WERE CLEANING UP. Jon met his father on Yawkey Way outside the Park. "You played well, Jon. It was amazing to watch you. Different world. How did it feel? You're like a professional now. You have no idea how amazing it is to see your child grow up like that. Go out into the world. Things were not so great in the T-ball days!"

They laughed, remembering the little kids in tee shirts that were too long for them, dragging bats across the dirt, not knowing which direction to run after they knocked the ball off the tee and it started dribbling out into the field. And now they were strong enough and coordinated enough to whack the ball hard enough to clear the forty-foot-high Green Monster three hundred and fifteen feet away! Growing through all the steps to have the opportunity to attempt that feat.

"Not many people get this chance, do they?" his father added. "Want to grab a beer?" He looked around at all the bars and restaurants. "Maybe we could sit and have a beer or grab a burger or something. Talk?"

They entered the *Who's On First* bar. "Great routine," his father said, recalling Abbott and Costello.

Jon was fired up. "I just talked to the scout for the Angels. You know that guy I told you about? Mr. Boynton? Yeah? Didn't I tell you?" Jon had to shout to make himself heard over the noise in the bar. "He made me an offer. It would be something to be playing with people like Nolan Ryan and Rod Carew."

His father smiled. "It would. You would be one of them. A dream come true."

"Nah," Jon smiled back. "They're in another world."

"Are you going to do it?" his father asked. "How much?"

"Nineteen thousand to start."

"Didn't I hear that they just offered one of their players a million dollars?"

"Nolan Ryan."

"A million dollars a year?"

"A year," Jon confirmed with a smile.

"And they offered you nineteen thousand? Seems like quite a difference."

"That's what I mean," Jon said. "It's another universe."

"But this is what you've been working for all these years."

They sipped their beers and looked around at the crowd of

baseball fans. Jon's father shook his head. "Whether you recognize it or not, Jon, you're not a kid anymore."

Jon grinned. "I know."

"But if you want to stop playing games and get a real job . . . ."

"Dad . . . seriously, dad."

"No, I'm just saying this project in Florida might just be what you're looking for. You'd still be connected to baseball but you wouldn't be risking . . . you know, getting hurt or something." Then he laughed, trying to make light of it.

"Thanks," Jon said. "But I don't see myself sitting behind a desk in Florida."

"Just a thought."

"You know. Maybe building houses. Maybe I could build houses or fix houses. You know I always liked making forts out of the boxes at Christmas. And there's some pretty exciting stuff going on with solar heating and new technologies."

"I guess I'd forgotten the boxes. Well, whatever you decide is good with me. I hope you know that."

Outside the bar and after a parting hug, Jon's father said, "I'm proud of you, son. And your mother would be too!"

LIFE BACK IN TILLEY WAS DIFFERENT. IT FELT DIFFERENT. THE magical myth of a pro offer swirled around Jon. On the field the players looked at him differently, Coach Russell treated him differently. He found it harder to focus on fundamentals of the game. The more he struggled to get back to where his thoughts had been before the All-Star Game at Fenway, the encounter with Scoles, and the looming end of the season, the more tangled his thoughts became.

The Longliners had had a good run after their rocky start, but they were fading and it wasn't likely they would make it into the playoffs. Some of the players were thinking about wrapping things up early and getting back home. The play was sloppy.

There was less enthusiasm. The summer fun in the salty air of Cape Cod was evaporating. Life was getting increasingly serious.

Returning to the Wentzells' kitchen one evening after a game, Jon almost felt nauseous. Babs took one look at him and told him to sit down, and she would make him some tea. "I know you don't usually drink tea but it will settle your stomach. You look like you're carrying the world on your shoulders. You should be thrilled! All these, what I call, chocolate choices! No matter which one you pick, it's going to be good."

"Why is it so hard?" he asked. "I mean, you're right. This should be good."

"Major decisions are always hard. They should be. That's why they're major decisions. How long will the Angels wait?"

"Not long," Jon replied. "If I don't take it, they'll find someone else who will. And besides, if I don't take it, they'll think I don't care - that I don't want it."

"Let me tell you something," Babs said, putting his mug of tea in front of him and settling herself down into the chair across the table. "Ace didn't tell you this because it's painful for him. Dwight had the opportunity to play professional baseball. He got an offer from the Yankees just before he got drafted into the Army. Ace was elated. He envisioned his son playing with the great baseball players, playing in the World Series, playing right in Yankee Stadium. That's why we've always taken in summer players. He loves to watch them grow up, develop, always hoping that they will succeed. I think he sees himself out there with Babe Ruth and the others. I don't know all their names, but I think he sees himself.

"When a child dies, so much goes with them. So very much, and you find yourself trying to find ways to fill the hole they left behind. But of course, it can never be filled. It's just always there.

"Dwight didn't have a choice like you do. He couldn't choose between Vietnam and professional baseball. He was drafted. His country needed him and so he went.

"I shouldn't be telling you this." She got up from the table.

"You've got to do what's right for you. Not what's right for anybody else. It's fine and noble to think about how your decision will affect other people." She stopped, turned and looked Jon straight in the eyes. "Ace would never have told you about Dwight, and don't you go talking to him about what I told you. If the decision's not right for you, it won't be right for anyone else either, no matter what they say."

Jon heard Ace's truck door slam. Babs busied herself at the sink.

"Hey," Ace said as he stepped through the kitchen door. "Season over?"

"One more game," Jon said.

Ace gave Babs a peck on the back of her neck. "What now? California?"

"Not sure."

Ace sat down at the table with a thump that Jon felt through the floor. And then primarily addressing Babs he said, "I got the contract today for that new house up on the old Mayfair farm."

"That's great," Babs replied.

"Yeah. Some crazy architectural thing. Don't know what these architects are thinking. Nice couple though. Kind of out of my normal stuff, you know. Make me try some things."

Jon was surprised. He had thought of Ace as an old house advocate, working with old wood and elaborate craftsmanship.

"Could use some help. Hard to find good help these days."

Jon was not always aware of subtle hints, but this seemed clear even to him that Ace was offering him a job, asking him to stay in Tilley. "I didn't know that you liked modern . . . I mean new buildings."

"Sure," Ace grinned. "That Lanai of the Salsbergs is a new building, isn't it? Some state-of-the-art stuff there."

"Sounds great, Ace. But I have to move on."

"Oh, I know," Ace replied. "I wasn't suggesting you give up the pro ball offer. No, no. You shouldn't do that. I was just telling Babs about the new project. But if you want, you could think about it. If you haven't made any permanent decisions yet. Might be fun. There's a lot to learn. Can't pay you a million dollars a year. You'll never make a million dollars a year building around here."

"You're babbling, Ace," Babs said, putting her hand on his shoulder. "Jon's not a kid any more. He has to make up his own mind."

"I know," Ace replied. "He has to go to the greenest grass. Do what's right for him. I know."

"WHAT ARE YOU GOING TO DO NEXT?" LISA ASKED.

"I don't know," Jon replied, more harshly than he intended. "I don't know. How do you ever know what the right decision is before it's happened?"

They were sitting in the bleachers after the last game of the season.

Lisa looked at him, but he avoided her eyes. He would have to go. He would have to make some decisions. He couldn't sit here forever.

"Ace just got a contract for a new house," he blurted out.

"Oh?"

"Yeah. Some sort of energy efficient, solar house. Young couple . . . with money, I guess."

Lisa was pretty, Jon thought, and smart. She had a kind of sparkle that appealed to him. She was starting at UMass Dartmouth in a few weeks. He wondered why he was inventorying her.

"Are you going to commute to UMass? That would be a haul. Are you going to get a car?" Questions poured out, covering the passage of parting moments.

"Do you want to be a professional baseball player?" Lisa asked.

"I mean, who are the California Angels anyway? They're not the Yankees or even the Red Sox! Would I get stuck there?"

Jon looked down at his feet. He looked out toward the outfield fences. Salsberg field was a friendly little baseball diamond. So different than the Green Monster and seats for thousands at Fenway. Did he want to be a professional baseball player? Did he have the drive, the passion, the dedication to play this game every day of his working life until something happened to sideline him?

"It's not forever, you know," she said.

Jon looked at her. "Of course it is. You can't be a part time professional. Either you are or you're not."

"I thought all you guys loved this stuff, loved it a whole lot more than you loved other people. I thought this was your life."

"Not me," he said.

"Well, then. There's your answer."

He looked at her. "What?"

"Well," she replied, "you just told me you can't do this part time. And now you said you don't think this is your life. You can't have it both ways. 'Either you are or you're not'." She threw it back at him.

"It's not that simple. Should I give up everything else to do this? Should I give up this opportunity most people would give . . . everything to have?"

"Most men. Most men would give everything."

He looked at her. "Of course. Most men. Women don't play professional baseball. Not in the majors anyway."

"I know. What about me?"

"Of course. I mean you probably could play baseball . . . if you wanted to."

"No, I meant what about me. Would you give me up to play professional baseball?"

"What? Um. I didn't think . . . I mean. I don't know. I can't think about that right now. I mean I like you and all, but . . . I mean I'm going to have to go home and all . . .."

"Never mind," she replied standing up and striding down over the top of the benches to the field. "You do what's right for you. Get that right and then think about me."

"Wait!" he said, hopping over the benches down beside her. He pulled her around to face him and then held her at arm's length with a hand on each shoulder.

"You're right. You're right. I should probably do this. I should probably go. I have to try this . . . don't I."

"Did they actually make you an offer?" Lisa asked.

"Not yet."

"Did Mr. Wentzell make you an offer to stay and keep working for him?"

"What?"

"I tell you what," she said, "I'll make you an offer. I think you should go home, get your shit together, make up your mind, and then come back. Because that's what I know you want to do anyway. You just don't know it. You're not some stud muffin, professional baseball player who's dreamed about Yankee Stadium and Fenway Park all his life."

Jon felt like he was looking at his life through a kaleidoscope with all the pieces shifting and turning and falling into place as he watched.

"And I'll tell you something else, Mr. Megquire, I love you. So now close your mouth and take me home."

Lisa stalked off to Maybelline waiting in the parking lot. Jon would have taken her home, but Maybelline voiced her opinion by refusing to start.

ACKNOWLEDGMENTS

Days pass. Each person has a prescribed passage. You think I'd know by now. Things start. Life gets in the way. Things stop. Things start again. Since 2014 on a flight from Chicago to Seattle from notes on the plane, typing on the laptop, trying to look important. After a bunch of travel, teaching, meeting characters, and other issues, I *finished* this in 2016 and sent the manuscript out to kind and responsive victims—David Goehring, Rana Belshe, Tamasin Sterner, and Mike Moore. With their extraordinary input, I realized it was not finished. I am so grateful for that gentle kick in the pants.

And then Elizabeth George came along with her book *Write Away* to give me a new perspective, and I discovered *Scrivener* as writing software and *Scapple* for diagramming how the pieces all connect.

Restarted in 2017. I started looking for an editor and established connections with Dara Syrkin. And then I decided I needed to update *Residential Ventilation Handbook* and write the *Residential QCI Handbook* to help weatherization teams get through their certification exam. Oh, and then I got back to *this* book with Dara's perceptive input.

This time the ball kept rolling, and I reached this point

where I am ready for it to go out into the world. There were just a few interruptions in politics, pandemic, quarantining, and economic collapse. So I sent it out again, seeking the technical help of Jason Wolfson for airplanes and police cars, David Goehring (again) for professional publishing input, Cathy Holmes for plot untangling, Becky Charles for early plot input, and Mary Grauerholz for pinpoint editing. And I can't say enough good things about Barbara Kraus who read above, beyond, and between the lines and commas. Thanks too to Brandi Doane McCann for the great work on the covers.

Then, of course, there is my dear wife, Kate, who was willing to read it multiple times as I edited it. The book is so much better for her insights, thoughts, and ideas.

This book is a collection of moments without which it wouldn't exist. I hope Ellen Hedlund will forgive me for using the name of her friend and James Reber for borrowing a name extracted from his wonderful dinner tales.

Thank you all for weaving in and out of my head and through the pages of this book for the past six years. And so we all keep traveling together through the passages of time. I'm still trying to figure out what I want to do when I grow up!

Falmouth, June, 2020

REFERENCES

Music References

Chicken Dance — Werner Thomas (1950's)
The Logical Song — Supertramp
Muskrat Love — Captain & Tennille
My Sharona — The Knack
YMCA — The Village People
Maybelline — Chuck Berry
Reunited — Peaches & Herb
America the Beautiful — Katherine Lee Bates
This Land is Your Land — Woody Guthrie
Stars and Stripes Forever — John Philip Souza
Bad Girls — Donna Summers
Old Cape Cod — Patti Page
The Golden Flute — Yusef Lateef
Beautiful Girl — Van Halen
Stardust — Willie Nelson
Moonlight in Vermont — Willie Nelson

Literary References

Catcher in the Rye — J.D. Salinger, 1951

Gone with the Wind — Margaret Mitchell. 1939

Murder Imperfect — Neal Sanders, 2009

The Last Best League — Jim Collins DaCapo Press 10th Anniversary Edition, 2014

ALSO BY PAUL H. RAYMER

The Residential Ventilation Handbook

Recalculating Truth (A Novel)

The Residential QCI Handbook

CPSIA information can be obtained
at www.ICGtesting.com
Printed in the USA
FSHW021036010820
72115FS